Small Souls

by

Louis Couperus

The Echo Library 2010

Published by

The Echo Library

Echo Library
Unit 22
Horcott Industrial Estate
Horcott Rd
Fairford
Glos. GL7 4BX

www.echo-library.com

Please report serious faults in the text to complaints@echo-library.com

ISBN 978-1-40689-634-3

SMALL SOULS

By

LOUIS COUPERUS

Author of "The Footsteps of Fate," etc.

TRANSLATED BY

ALEXANDER TEIXEIRA DE MATTOS

NEW YORK

DODD, MEAD AND COMPANY

1914

TRANSLATOR'S NOTE

This story is translated from the Dutch of Louis Couperus, the foremost novelist in a country which has lately had the good sense to join the Berne Convention. Friends who have seen my version in manuscript suggest to me that certain details of the action and dialogue strike an exotic note to English ears and may therefore need some interpretation. But I could not bring myself to burden a work of fiction with an array of foot-notes nor to believe that it is really necessary to explain to readers of Couperus' fellow-countryman, "Maarten Maartens," that Dutch men and women of the upper classes still call their parents "Papa" and "Mamma," as the English did in the sixties, and still drink tea after dinner, as the English did in the forties; that, in Holland, persons of quality are not addressed by their titles in conversation; that it is not quite correct, or that it is at least a departure from the aristocratic tradition, for a lady of family *not* to wash up her own breakfast-china at the table; that the Dutch speak of Java as India and sometimes marry native wives, who, *nihilo obstante*, are "received" by the "family" at home.

I have done my best, by a complicated and perhaps only partly successful system of italics, hyphens and dots, to render the various eccentricities of speech of Cateau van Lowe, Adolphine van Saetzema and Aunt Ruyvenaer. The few Malay words employed by the last-named, by Otto van Naghel's wife and by her native nurse are explained in notes as and when they occur.

Small Souls is the first of a series of four novels describing the fortunes of the Van Lowe family and known in Holland by the generic title of *The Books of the Small Souls*. The remainder will be translated and published if and as the antecedent volumes find favour with English and American readers. They are called: *The Later Life, The Twilight of the Souls and Dr. Adriaan.*

ALEXANDER TEIXEIRA DE MATTOS.

CHELSEA,

4 *December*, 1913.

CHAPTER I

It was pouring with rain; and Dorine van Lowe was tired out when, by way of a last visit, she dropped in on Karel and Cateau just before dinner. But Dorine was pleased with herself. She had gone out immediately after lunch and had trotted and trammed all over the Hague; she had done much, if not everything; and her tired face looked very glad and her bright black eyes sparkled.

"Have meneer and mevrouw gone in to dinner yet, Sientje?" she asked, nervous and breathless, in a sudden fright lest she should be too late.

"No, miss, but it's just on six," said Sientje, severely.

Dorine van Lowe whisked through the hall and rushed upstairs, forgetting to put her wet umbrella in the stand. She clutched it in one hand, together with her skirt, which she forgot to let fall; in her arm she held a parcel pressed close to her, under her cape; in the other hand she carried her muff and her old black satin reticule; with the same hand, making a superhuman effort, she felt for her pocket-handkerchief and managed to blow her nose without dropping anything but four or five tram-tickets, which flew around her on every side.

Old Sientje followed her with her glance, severely. Then she went to the kitchen, fetched a cloth, silently wiped up a trail of rain and drops along the hall and staircase and carefully picked the tram-tickets off the stair-carpet.

Dorine walked into her brother's study. Karel van Lowe was sitting placidly by a good fire, reading; his smooth-shaven face shone pink and young. He wore his thick, glossy hair neatly combed and brushed into a fine tuft; he dyed his moustache black; and, like Dorine, he had the black eyes of the Van Lowes. His broad figure looked comfortable and well-fed in his spruce clothes; his waistcoat lay in thick creases over his stomach; and his watch-chain rose and fell with his regular breathing. He seemed calm and healthy, full of calculating prudence and quiet selfishness. He gently put aside the magazine which he was reading, as though he felt that he was in for it, that he would have to listen to his sister for a quarter of an hour at least; but he made up his mind to interrupt her pretty often. So he rubbed his large, fat, pink hands and looked at Dorine impassively; and his glance seemed to convey:

"Go on, I'm listening, I can't help myself...."

Dorine stood near his writing-table, which was in the middle of the prim room, while he remained sitting by the fire.

"I've been to all of them!" Dorine began triumphantly.

"To Bertha?"

"To Bertha."

"To Gerrit?"

"To Gerrit."

"To Adolphine?"

"And to Ernst and Paul: I've been to all of them!" said Dorine, triumphantly. "And they've all promised to come."

"Dorine, would you mind putting your umbrella outside? It's so wet."

Dorine put her umbrella in the passage outside the door and she now also let fall her skirt, the hem of which showed an edge of wet mud at which her brother kept staring as though hypnotized.

"And what did Bertha say?" he asked, pretending to be interested, but giving all his attention to the wet hem.

"Well, Bertha was very nice! I must say, Bertha was very nice!" said Dorine; and the tears, always so ready with her, came into her dark eyes. "She was very busy with the girls, drawing up the lists of invitations for Emilie's wedding; and to-morrow they have one of their official dinners. But she said at once that, if Mamma wished it, we must all of us obey her wish and go to Mamma's to-night to meet Constance. And Van Naghel, who came in for a moment, said so too. Bertha never agreed with Mamma, about encouraging Constance to come back to Holland; but, now that things had gone as far as they had, she said she would look upon Constance as a sister again, quite as a sister."

"And what did Van Naghel say?" asked Karel van Lowe.

Karel was not really interested in what his brother-in-law, Van Naghel van Voorde, the colonial secretary, had said, but he had a methodical mind and, now that he knew Bertha's opinion, he also wanted to know her husband's opinion and the opinion of all the other brothers and sisters. Meanwhile, he continued to look at the wet hem of Dorine's skirt and longed to ask her not to touch his paper-knife and paper-weight, which she kept playing with half-nervously; but he said nothing, calculating within himself that, presently, when Dorine was gone, he would have a moment, before dinner, to put everything straight.

"Well, I gathered from what Van Naghel said that he hoped Constance would show the greatest tact and not be too pushing at first, but that, as their brother-in-law, he would welcome Van der Welcke and Constance very cordially."

Karel nodded placidly, to show that he understood what lay at the back of Van Naghel's words and that he quite agreed.

"And what did Van Saetzema and Adolphine say?"

"Well, of course, I had more trouble with Adolphine than with any of the others!" cried Dorine, triumphantly waving the paper-knife, while Karel anxiously followed the movements of her hand. "First, she didn't want to come and said that Mamma had no morals and all that sort of thing. I answered that I respected her views; that, of course, every one was free to think as he pleased; but that she must not forget that Mamma was an old woman, a very old woman, and that we ought to try and make her happy in her old age. Then I said that Constance was Mamma's child as much as any of us; and that it was only natural for Mamma to want us all to take Constance back as a sister, as it had all happened so very long ago and she had been married to Van der Welcke for fifteen years and their boy is thirteen...."

"Dorine, please, would you mind leaving the paper-weight alone? Else all those letters are sure to get mixed.... And what did Adolphine say to that?"

"Well, at first, Adolphine wouldn't hear of going, said she was afraid of Constance' bad influence on the girls, said she couldn't possibly take them. In fact, she talked like a fool. But, when I told her that Van Naghel and Bertha were coming and that not a word had been said about their girls—that they were coming too—then Adolphine said that she would come after all and bring her girls. And Gerrit and Ernst"—Dorine opened Karel's stamp-box, but shut it again at once, terrified when she saw the stamps neatly arranged in the compartments, according to their values—"I saw Gerrit and Ernst too; and Adeline spoke very nicely; and Paul...."

A gong sounded.

"That's dinner," said Karel. "I suppose you won't stay, Dorine? I don't think there's much: Cateau and I always dine so simply...."

"Oh, I eat very little; I should like to stay, if I may; then we can all go on to Mamma's afterwards...."

Karel van Lowe gave one more look at the muddy hem; he remembered that the dining-room had been cleaned that day; and he could restrain himself no longer:

"Dorine," he said, in despair, "in that case, won't you let Marie brush you down first?"

Then, at last, Dorine realized that she was not fit to be seen, after trotting and tramming the whole afternoon in the rain. She looked in the glass: when she had taken off her wet cape, she would be less presentable than ever. And so she dolefully changed her mind:

"You're right, Karel, I don't look nice; and my boots are wet: I think I had better go home and change for the evening. So good-bye for the present, Karel."

"Good-bye, Dorine."

The gong sounded again. Dorine clutched her reticule, hunted all round the room for her umbrella, until she remembered that it was outside, and hurried away, while Karel repaired the disorder on his writing-table and put the paper-weight and paper-knife straight.

In the hall, Dorine met her round-faced sister-in-law staring at her with startled eyes like an owl's. Cateau asked, in a slow, whining voice that emphasized every third or fourth word:

"Oh, Do-rine ... are you re-ally ... staying to din-ner?"

"No, thanks, Cateau; it's very kind of you, but I must change my things. They're all coming this evening, to Mamma's."

"Oh, are they all ... com-ing?"

"Yes.... And I am so glad.... Well, don't let me keep you. Karel will tell you all about it. So good-bye, till later...."

She hurried away; Sientje let her out, severely.

Karel and Cateau sat down to dinner. They had no children; they were now living in the Hague, after many years spent in a pretty village in Utrecht, where Karel had been burgomaster. They had a large and handsome house in the Oranjestraat; they kept three servants; they kept a carriage. They loved good fare and took their meals by themselves, just the two of them; they never entertained: there were no small dinners, for relations, nor dinner-parties, for friends. They lived according to the rules of opulent respectability. Everything in their large house, with its heavy, comfortable furniture, was solid and respectable, in no wise luxurious. They both looked healthy and opulent and Dutch and respectable. Cateau was a heavy woman of forty, with a pair of startled round eyes in a round face, and she always wore a neat, smooth, well-fitting dress, brown, black or blue. They lived by the clock: in the morning, Karel took a walk, always the same walk, through the Woods; after lunch, Cateau did her shopping; once a week, they paid a round of visits together; and that was the only time when they went out together. They were always at home in the evening, except on Sundays, when they went to Mamma van Lowe's. Notwithstanding their comfortable life, their three servants and their carriage, they were thrifty. They considered it a sin and a shame to spend money on a theatre, an exhibition, or a book. Every spring and autumn, they bought what they needed for their house and wardrobe, so as to have everything good and nice; but that was all. Their one vice was their table. They lived exceedingly well, but kept the fact from the family and always said that they lived so very simply that they could never ask an unexpected visitor to stay. And, as they never invited anybody, the secret of their dainty table did not leak out. They had a first-rate cook and Cateau kept a tight rein upon her, telling her that meneer was so particular. But they both feasted, daily. And, at their meals, they would exchange a glance of intelligence, as though relishing some voluptuous moment of mutual gratification, because everything was so good. Softly smacking their lips, they drank a good glass of good red wine. And then, at dessert, Karel's face beamed fiery red and Cateau blinked her eyes, as though tickled to her marrow. Then they went into the sitting-room and sat down at the round table, with their hands folded in their laps, to digest in silence. Karel, for appearance' sake, would undo the parcel from the circulating library. Now and again, they looked at each other, reflecting complacently that Anna had cooked that dinner beautifully. But, as they considered that this enjoyment was sinful and, above all, un-Dutch, they never spoke of their enjoyment and enjoyed in silence.

This evening, they reckoned out that they had quite an hour left in which to digest their dinner by the big stove; and, as they did not like Mamma's tea, they had a cup of tea at home. At eight o'clock, Sientje came to say that the brougham was at the door. So as not to let the brougham wait longer than necessary in the rain and spoil, they got up at once, put on cloak and great-coat and started. They did not so much mind if the horse got wet, for the horse was jobbed; but the brougham was their own.

CHAPTER II

Dorine van Lowe lived by herself in a boarding-house, though old Mrs. van Lowe had a large house in the Alexanderstraat. Their friends all thought this odd; and Dorine was a little perplexed at having constantly to explain that she would have liked nothing better than to live with Mamma and keep house for Mamma and look after Mamma and spoil Mamma. But, as a girl of twenty-two, she had left home to become a nurse; and, when she found that she had mistaken her vocation, Mamma had refused to let her come back. But surely, Mamma, who was so fond of gathering all her children round her, the friends would say. Yes, that was so, said Dorine: Mamma doted on her brood; and yet she preferred to be alone in her big house, she preferred to do her housekeeping herself and did not care to have any one staying with her or fussing about her.... No, it was better that Dorine should stop in her boarding-house. Mamma was still so active, saw to everything, knew about everything. Dorine would have been of no use to her at home.... Besides, Mamma herself wouldn't hear of it, and used to say, laughingly, but quite in earnest:

"Those who go away can stay away...."

And the Van Lowes' friends thought it odd, for the old lady was known for just that motherly quality of hers, for loving to keep all her children round her, in a close family-circle, at the Hague or in the immediate neighbourhood. And she did not look at all a difficult old lady, with her gentle, refined old face of a waxy pallor and her smooth grey hair; not at all a managing old dame who could not possibly live in the same house with her unmarried daughter. And so Dorine was always a little perplexed at having to explain, especially as she herself thought it odd of Mamma. But Mamma was what she was; and it couldn't be helped....

Dorine felt less tired after she had had some dinner and changed her clothes; and she put on her goloshes and went on to Mamma's at once. The rawness of the March evening bore down on the deserted Javastraat with a shudder of dripping fog. It had rained all day; and now the heavy grey sky was blotted from sight in a mist that clung in masses of woolly dampness to the roofs and tree-tops; the wind whistled from the north-west and skimmed over the rippling puddles; the trees dripped as heavily as though it were still raining; and the pale-yellow light in the clouded street-lamps shimmered down upon the street. Hardly any one was out of doors so early after dinner; a man, carrying a parcel, left a shop and shuffled close to the houses, with wide, hurrying legs.

Dorine tripped across the puddles in her goloshes, hugging herself in her old-fashioned, long fur cloak. And she talked to herself and muttered out loud. She grumbled at the rain, grumbled at all the trouble which Mamma had given her that day, sending her to all the brothers and sisters, for Constance' sake.... And you'd see, Constance wouldn't even be grateful to her, Constance would think it only natural....

Every one always thought it only natural, that Dorine should run about for the family; and no one was ever really grateful.... Every one was selfish, Mamma included.... Well, she would try it herself one day, being selfish ... and sit all day long by her fire, as Karel always did ... and live only for herself, for her own pleasure ... and leave them all to their fate.... Just imagine, supposing, to-morrow, she were to say to Bertha and Adolphine, whose girls were soon to be married, that she had no time to go on everybody's errands.... It was always Dorine: Dorine could do it all; Dorine didn't mind the rain; Dorine had to be in the Veenestraat anyhow.... Running about, running about, running about, without stopping, all out of sheer, silly good-nature; and who thanked her for it? Nobody! Not Mamma, nor Bertha, nor Adolphine.... It was all taken as a matter of course! Well, she would like to see their faces to-morrow, if she said, "I've no time, you know;" or "I'm staying at home to-day;" or, "I'm feeling rather tired." Dorine feeling tired! What next!

Still grumbling, she rang the bell at Mamma's, in the Alexanderstraat; she took off her things in the hall. And now she emerged from her long cloak, a lean and wiry little woman of thirty-five, with a thin and sallow face, her breast shrunk within a painfully tight, dark-silk blouse; her dull, mud-coloured hair drawn tightly from her forehead into a knot at the back; very thin, with no hips, with not a single rounded line and with those dark eyes of the Van Lowes, which in her were bright and intelligent, but with an odd sort of silent reproach and secret discontent at the back of them, as though brooding under her glance. Withal she had retained something very young and girlish, something innocent and gay and lively. While pulling off her gloves, she spoke pleasantly to the servant, made a playful remark about the wet weather. She felt her hair, to see if it was smooth and drawn back properly, and tripped up the stairs with a swinging gait, her shoulders bobbing up and down, her legs wide apart. There was now something quite young and unconstrained in that gay liveliness of hers.

She found Mamma upstairs, in the double drawing-room, where Klaartje was lighting the gas:

"They're all coming, Mamma!" Dorine blurted out.

Then, starting when she saw the servant, she whispered:

"I've been to all of them; first to Karel, then to Bertha, then to Adolphine; no, first to Gerrit...."

She became muddled, laughed, made Mamma sit down beside her and told her what all the brothers and sisters had said. The old woman's face beamed with satisfaction. She kissed Dorine:

"You're a dear girl, Dorinetje," she said, with the motherly voice which she used when speaking to any of her children—even to Bertha, who was fifty—and which she had never learnt to give up. "You're a dear girl to have taken so much trouble. And it's very nice of all the others to come to-night, for I know it means a great effort to some of them to forgive and forget and to take back Constance as a sister. And I appreciate it all the more...."

Mrs. van Lowe said this in a tone of approval, but a little autocratically, as though she granted her children a right to their own opinion but yet thought it only natural that they should obey their mother's wish. And she and Dorine watched the servants putting out the card-tables: one in the big drawing-room, one in the second drawing-room and one in the boudoir. It was the sacred Sunday, the evening of the "family-group," as the grandchildren naughtily called it among themselves. Every Sunday, Mamma collected as many Van Lowes, Ruyvenaers, Van Naghels and Saetzemas as she could, minding the name less than whether they were relations, even though they were only relations of relations. It was all brother and sister, uncle and aunt, cousin and cousin. Years ago, the Van Lowes—Papa, the retired governor-general, and Mamma—had instituted that Sunday gathering of the members of the family who happened to be at the Hague; and they had all, as far as possible, kept themselves free on Sunday evenings to come to the "family-group." This very regularity bore witness to the close bonds connecting the several families, Uncle Ruyvenaer could not remember missing a single Sunday evening, except when he ran over to Java, on a six months' return-ticket, to see how the sugar-factory was going on.

The Ruyvenaers were first, as usual, arriving very early and at once filling the rooms. Uncle, with a shiver, abused the Dutch climate: he was tall and stout, wearisome with his noisy attempts at humour, full of a superficial good-nature and an affectation of kind-heartedness. He was always blundering out things that fell like a sledge-hammer. He at once filled the whole room with his blustering joviality, his ponderous efforts to make himself agreeable. His sister, Mrs. van Lowe, so gentle, so distinguished, was always afraid that he would break something. Auntie was a rich *nonna*,[1] who had brought the sugar-factory as her dowry: she too was heavy and fat, like a Hindu idol, and covered with big diamonds; still, there was something kind and friendly about her: looking at her, you had a vision of a spicy rice-table[2] and toothsome *kwee-kwee*,[3] a promise of material comfort, of a lavish supply of good things to eat and drink. And, with it all, she was not unsympathetic, with her soft, dark eyes. They brought with them their three daughters and two sons: the two elder girls of Dorine's age, gay and boisterous, regular natives; a son of twenty-eight, who was also in the sugar-business, when in Java; a third daughter, a couple of years younger; and the youngest son, a little brown fellow, fifteen years old, very short and thin, who seemed to have come much later, by accident. All the Van Lowes—though Mamma was born in India and Papa had made his way there until he reached the highest office of all—were ultra-Dutch and always laughed a little at the Ruyvenaers, while cheerfully resigning themselves to the Indian strain, which shocked them a bit, made them a trifle uncomfortable in the presence of their purely Dutch friends and connections. Still, the old lady, whose family-affection was very strong, declared that

---

[1] A half-caste.

[2] The lunch or tiffin of the Dutch East Indies, consisting of rice with a great variety of spiced meats and vegetables.

[3] Cakes.

they were in their right place there, even though Uncle Ruyvenaer was only her half-brother and Auntie very Indian; for Mamma van Lowe carried her family-pride to the point of maintaining that all that formed part of the family was good. To be related to the Van Lowes seemed, in a sense, to ennoble, to exalt, to improve the very stock. And so she always looked severe when her children—Gerrit, Adolphine and Paul—laughed at Aunt Ruyvenaer and the Indian nieces, who were good children, always cheerful, always amiable, bright and pleasant.

Uncle was very noisy, strode up and down the rooms, with straddling legs, to warm himself:

"So we shall see Constance here to-night? Well, it's a long time since we did. Let me see: how long is it? How long is it, Marie? Twenty years? Yes, it must be twenty years! At least, I haven't seen her since she married De Staffelaer! Lord, what a sweet child she was! What a sweet, pretty child! Twenty years ago: why, it's an age! She must have grown old! Yes, of course she must: she *must* have grown old! How old is she? It's easy to reckon: she must be forty-two, eh? And Van der Welcke is a nice fellow, what? Very decent of him, I'm bound to say, very decent...."

Mamma van Lowe turned very white; Dorine gave an angry look; Toetie Ruyvenaer pulled Papa's sleeve:

"*Allah*,[4] that Papa!" she whispered, good-naturedly, to her sister Dotje. "No tact...."

"Ye-es," Aunt Ruyvenaer began in a fat, slow voice, "was it so long ago? *Kassian*!"[5] she added, sympathetically. "Poor Constance! I'm so glad I'm going to see her!"

"Papa!" said Poppie Ruyvenaer, the youngest.

"What is it?"

"How can you?"

"What?"

"You're upsetting Aunt Marie: don't you see?"

"But, good Lord...!"

"Oh, do stop about Constance."

"What have I said?..."

"If you don't stop, you'll make Aunt Marie cry. Don't you understand?..."

"Oh, mustn't I talk about Constance? There's always something in our family one mustn't talk about.... It's beyond me!"

And Uncle began to stride up and down the rooms again, rubbing his hands, which were still cold.

---

[4] Lord!

[5] Poor dear!

Two very old aunts entered. They were the Miss Ruyvenaers, very old ladies, turned eighty and looking more than that, unmarried sisters of Uncle and of Mrs. van Lowe. Their names were Dorine and Christine; but the younger generations called them Auntie Rine and Auntie Tine:

"So nice of you," said Mrs. van Lowe. "So nice...."

"What?" asked Auntie Rine.

"So nice of you, Dorine!" screamed Mrs. van Lowe in her ear.

"Marie says," screamed Auntie Tine, "it's so nice of you ... to come to-night.... Dorine is so deaf, Marie.... Really, she's getting unbearable...."

Auntie Tine was the young one, the tetchy one, the bitter one; Auntie Rine was the older one, the good-natured, deaf one. Outwardly, the two old ladies resembled each other and looked like old prints in their antiquated dresses; they wore black lace caps on the grey hair that framed their faces, which were wrinkled like a walnut.

The old ladies went and sat far apart; and it was strange to see them sitting at either end of the drawing-room, quietly, watching attentively, not saying much....

Now the others came, gradually. The first to arrive were the Van Saetzemas: Adolphine, her husband, Floortje, Caroline, Marietje and three noisy boys, all younger than their sisters; next came Gerrit and his wife Adeline: their children were still in the nursery; next, Karel and Cateau, still digesting their good dinner and their good wine; Ernst entered, gloomy, timid, queer and shy, as usual; Paul followed: he was the youngest son, thirty-five, good-looking, fair-haired and excessively well-dressed; last came the Van Naghels, Bertha and her husband, the colonial secretary, with their children: the three elder girls, Louise, Emilie, with Van Raven, her future husband, and Marianne; young Karel; and another Marietje: the two undergraduates were away, this time, at Leiden. There was a general humming and buzzing: the uncles, aunts, nephews and nieces exchanged greetings; many of them had not seen one another all the week; but they made it a rule to meet at Mamma's Sundays. And this evening there was great excitement among them all, though they restrained it for Mamma's sake: a mutual whispering and asking of opinions, because Constance was returning to the Hague, to her family, after twenty years' absence.

Adolphine overwhelmed her eldest sister, Bertha van Naghel van Voorde, with a torrent of whispered words:

"It's Mamma's wish," said Bertha, laconically, blinking her eyes.

"But what do you think? What does Van Naghel think? You surely can't think it pleasant...."

"Constance is our sister...."

"Our sister, our sister! If my sister misconducts herself...."

"Adolphine, Constance has been married to Van der Welcke for fourteen years; and there comes a time when one overlooks...."

"But what are you going to do? Will you have her at your house?"

"Yes, of course."

Adolphine had it at the tip of her jealous tongue to say, "And I suppose you'll ask her to your big dinners," but she restrained herself.

The younger nephews and nieces were also busily talking:

"Isn't she here yet?"

"No, she's coming later."

"Is she old?"

"She's between Uncle Gerrit and Aunt Adolphine...."

"How nervous Grandmamma is!"

"Oh, she doesn't strike me so!..."

"Why is she so late?"

"To make a triumphal entry...."

"Oh, triumphal!" said Floortje, Adolphine's daughter. "That would be the finishing touch!"

"There she is!"

"Yes, I hear some one on the stairs."

"Granny's gone outside to meet her."

"And Aunt Dorine, too."

"I'm awfully curious to...."

"Yes, but we mustn't stare like that," said Marianne van Naghel to the boys.

"Why shouldn't I, if I want to?" asked Piet Saetzema.

"Because it's ill-bred," said Marianne, angrily.

"Oh, indeed? It's you that's ill-bred."

"And you're a boor!" cried Marianne, losing her temper.

"Marianne!" said her sister Emilie, soothingly.

"It's those horrid boys of Aunt Adolphine's!" muttered Marianne, in her indignation.

"Then don't take any notice of them."

"Here comes Aunt Constance...."

Mrs. van Lowe had gone to meet her daughter in the passage; she embraced her there. The door was open; the brothers, sisters, nephews, nieces looked out and at once began to talk busily to one another, in artificial tones. Then Mamma came in, leading Constance by the hand. On her face was a smile of quiet content, but she was trembling with nervousness. She remained standing for a moment, looking through the crowded room. Constance van der Welcke, holding her mother's hand, also stopped. She was still a pretty woman, very pale, with hair beginning to go grey around her young and charming face, in which the dark eyes loomed big with anxiety; she still had the figure of a young woman; and she wore a black-satin gown.... There was a wait of a few seconds at the door, a pause just perceptible, yet poignant, as though a stubborn situation were being forced into the easier groove of polite manners and kind words, because of this sister's home-coming. But then Bertha came up and smiled, and found the kind word and the polite manner. She kissed her younger sister, said something charming. Mrs. van Lowe beamed. The other sisters and brothers followed, the nephews, the nieces. At last, one by one, they had all welcomed her. Constance had kissed them, or shaken hands; and she was deathly pale; and her black eyes trembled, misty with tears. Her voice broke, her hands shook, she felt a sinking at her knees. A passion of weeping was rising to her eyes; and she found it almost impossible to control herself. She kept hold of her mother's hand, like a child, sat down by her, tried to smile and to behave normally. Her words almost choked her; her breath throttled her. Her black eyes started from their sockets, quivering, in her deathly-pale face, and she shivered as though in a fever. She tried to do her best, to talk as though she had only been away a year. But it was no use. She had not set foot in those rooms since the day, twenty years ago, when she married De Staffelaer, the Dutch envoy at Rome.... Since then, so much had happened in Rome, oh, so much! Her life had happened, her life of mistake upon mistake. How could she talk the usual commonplaces now? She saw herself here, twenty years ago, coming back from church, in her white bridal dress; she saw her father, now dead; she saw De Staffelaer; she saw herself, after she had changed into her travelling-dress, saying good-bye, going away with De Staffelaer.... Since then ... since then, she had never been back! Since then, her father had died! Since then, she had only twice seen her dear mother, for a moment, at Brussels. Oh, since then!... Since then, all her brothers and sisters had become strangers to her; and she herself had been a stranger, never in Holland, always abroad, always an alien.... Now ... now she was back! Was it possible? Was it a dream?...

Her brother-in-law, Van Naghel, the cabinet-minister, came up to her:

"We are very glad to see you at the Hague, Constance."

"Thank you, Van Naghel."

"And shall we soon be making Van der Welcke's acquaintance?"

There was something in his words as though he were forcing the situation, for Mamma van Lowe's sake.

"He has some business to settle in Brussels. He will be here in a week."

It was very difficult to keep up the conversation; and he was silent.

"So one of your girl's is engaged?" she asked, tactfully diverting the talk from herself.

"Yes, Emilie, the second. Emilie!"

He beckoned to his daughter. Emilie came up, bringing Van Raven with her:

"May I introduce Mr. van Raven, Aunt Constance?"

"Van Raven." And she gave him her hand. "My best wishes for your happiness, Emilie."

"Thank you, Aunt."

"And there's another wedding in prospect," said Mamma. "Floortje and Dijkerhof...."

And she beckoned to Floortje, who introduced Dijkerhof.

Meanwhile, the members of the family tried to behave as usual. They talked together, as though in ordinary conversation. Uncle Ruyvenaer arranged the parties at the card-tables:

"Karel, Toetie, Louise, Gerrit.... Bertha, Cateau, Van Saetzema, Ernst...."

His voice marshalled the troops. The younger generation were put to play round games at a long table in the conservatory.

Constance gave a soft laugh:

"What a lot of us there are, Mamma, at your Sundays!"

What a lot of *us*: the word had a special charm for her.

Meanwhile, Uncle Ruyvenaer was teasing his two old sisters:

"Come Rientje and Tientje.... Don't you want to play bridge?"

"What?"

"Herman wants to know if you're going to play bridge?" screamed Auntie Tine in Auntie Rine's ear.

"Bridge?"

"Yes, if you want to play bridge? She *is* so deaf, Herman!..."

"They won't remember me," said Constance, speaking of the old aunts. "They must have forgotten me in these twenty years. How old they have grown, Mamma!... How old we have all grown! Bertha is grey. I am going grey myself. ... And all those little nieces, all those young nephews whom I have never seen.... Do they always come, on Sundays?"

"Yes, child, every Sunday. There's a great kindness and affection among them all. I always think that so delightful."

"We are a large family. I am glad to be here, but they are still like strangers to me. How many of us are there here, Mamma?"

"Oh, quite thirty! Let me see...." Mamma van Lowe counted on her fingers. "Uncle and Aunt Ruyvenaer, with Toetie and Dot and Poppie and Piet and young Herman: that makes seven; then, Van Naghel and Bertha, with the four girls and Karel: that's seven more; fourteen...."

Constance listened to her mother's addition, and smiled.... Twenty years, twenty years ago! She felt as though she could have burst out sobbing; but she controlled herself, smiled, stroked Mamma's hand:

"Mamma, dear Mamma.... I am so glad to be back among you all!"

"Dear child!"

"They have all received me so nicely. So simply."

"Why, of course, Connie. You're their sister."

Constance was silent.... Dorine, with two of the young nieces, poured out the tea, brought it round:

"Have a cup, Constance? Milk? Sugar?"

How familiar and pleasant it sounded, just as though she were really one of them, as though she always had been one of them: "Have a cup, Constance?" ... As if it wasn't the first cup of tea she had had there for years and years!... Dear Dorine! Constance remembered her as a girl of seventeen, shy, not yet out, but even then caring, always caring, for others. She was not pretty, she was even plain, ungraceful, clumsy, badly-dressed....

"Yes, Dorine, I should like a cup.... Come here, Dorine. Sit down and talk to me: the girls can see to the tea."

She drew Dorine to the sofa beside her and nestled between her mother and her sister:

"Tell me, Dorine, do you still look after everybody so well? Do you still pour the tea?"

Her voice had a broken sound, full of a melancholy that permeated her simple, bantering words. Dorine made some vague reply.

"When I went away," said Constance, "you were not seventeen. You were always cutting bread-and-butter for Bertha's children. Otto and Louise were seven and five then; Emilie was a baby. Now she's engaged...."

She smiled, but her eyes were full of tears, her breast heaved.

"My dear child," said the old lady.

"It's a long time ago, Connie," said Dorine.

It was twenty years since any one had called her Connie.

"So you're thirty-six now, Dorine?"

"Yes, Connie, thirty-six," said Dorine, uncomfortable, as usual, when anybody spoke of her; and she felt her smooth, flat hair, to see if it was drawn well back.

"You've changed very little, Dorine."

"Do you think so, Connie?"

"I am very glad of it.... Will you like me a little, Dorine?"

"Why, of course, Connie."

"My dear child," said the old lady, much moved.

They were all three silent for a while. Constance felt so much, was so full of the past years, that she could not have uttered another word.

"Why didn't you bring Addie?" asked Mamma.

"I thought he might be too young."

"The two Marietjes always come; and so do Adolphine's boys. We never sit up late, because of the children."

"Then I'll bring him next time, Mamma."

Dorine stole a glance at her sister and reflected that Constance was still pretty, for a woman of forty-two. What a young and pretty figure, thought Dorine; but then it was a smart dress; and Constance was sure to wear very expensive stays. Regular features: she was like Mamma; a clear-cut profile; dark eyes, now dimmed with melancholy; very pretty, white hands, with rings; and her hair especially interested Dorine: it was turning into a uniform steel-grey and it curled.

"Connie, does your hair curl of itself?"

"Of course not, Dorine; I wave it."

"What a labour!"

Constance gave a careless laugh.

"Constance always had nice hair," said Mamma, proudly.

"Oh, no, Mamma dear! I have horrid, straight hair."

They were silent again; and all three of them felt that they were not speaking of what lay at their hearts.

"Constance, what lovely rings you have!"

"Ah, Dorine, I remember you used to admire me in the old days; when I went to a ball, you used to stand and gaze at me. But there is nothing left to admire, Dorine: I'm an old stick, now...."

"My dear!" said Mamma, indignantly.

"You needn't mind, Mamma: you're always young, a young grandmamma...."

And she pressed Mamma's hand, with a touching fervour.

CHAPTER III

"Dorine," asked Constance, "where is Papa's portrait?"

"In the boudoir."

"Oh, so Mamma has moved it! I want to see it."

She went with Dorine through the drawing-room, past the card-tables.... She noticed that the conversation at once stopped at the table where Adolphine and Uncle Ruyvenaer were playing and that her sister raised her voice and said:

"Did I deal?... Diamonds!"

"They were talking about me," thought Constance.

She went into the boudoir with Dorine: there was a card-table, with cards and markers, but there was no one in the room. Decanters and glasses, sandwiches and cakes had been put out in readiness for later.

"Papa," said Constance, softly.

She looked up at the big portrait. It was not a work of art; it was painted in the regulation, wooden style of thirty or forty years before; and it struck Constance as an ugly daub, dark and flat, in spite of all the gold on the governor-general's uniform, all the stars of the orders. The portrait represented a tall and commanding man, with a hard face and dark, stony eyes.

"I ... I used to think that portrait much finer," said Constance. "Was Papa so hard?..."

Her eyes were riveted on her father's face.... She had certainly been his favourite daughter. Her marriage to De Staffelaer, his friend, a man much older than herself, had pleased him, because it flattered his ambition.... But then, then he fell ill; he died soon after, soon after the thing that happened: that and her marriage to Van der Welcke.... Oh God, was it she who had killed him?

She drew Dorine to her:

"Tell me, Dorine.... Was Papa ill for long?"

"Yes, Connie, very long."

They were silent. They thought of their father, of his ambition, of his longing for the greatness which he achieved; of his wish to see his children also great, high-placed and powerful....

"I say, Dorine, how strange it is ... that not one of Papa's sons ..."

"What do you mean, Connie?"

"Nothing.... I don't know...."

Papa had always helped Van Naghel.... Her thoughts ran on:

"Dorine, is Karel still a burgomaster?"

"Oh, no, Connie! Karel and Cateau have been living at the Hague for years."

"And Gerrit is ... a captain?"

"Yes, in the hussars."

"I am quite out of everything.... And Ernst ... does nothing?..."

"Ernst has always been rather strange, you know; he really fights shy of people. He collects things, all sorts of things: china, books, old maps...."

"And Paul?"

"No, Paul does nothing."

"But how strange!"

"What?"

"That they have none of them done anything to distinguish themselves: none of Papa's sons...."

"But, Connie, they're all quite nice!" cried Dorine, indignantly. "Well, yes, Ernst is rather queer; and of course it's not right that Paul should do nothing...."

"I oughtn't to have said it, Dorine.... But Papa would have liked to see his children distinguished...."

Dorine felt annoyed, and at the same time, confused: distinguished, distinguished.... And her thoughts muttered within her mind, while Constance stood looking at the portrait: distinguished, distinguished.... Constance did well to talk of being distinguished!... True, she had made a great marriage: De Staffelaer, the minister at Rome, an old diplomatist, a friend of Papa's.... True, she had been distinguished, no doubt; and it had turned out nicely, her distinguished marriage. Distinguished indeed!... Could Constance really be vain still ... perhaps because she was now Baroness van der Welcke? A fine thing, that scandal with Van der Welcke!... Distinguished, distinguished ... well, no, they were none of them distinguished. But then everybody couldn't be Viceroy of the East Indies.... Constance had always had that sort of vanity; but Constance talking or thinking unkindly of her brothers, whom she hadn't seen for years, that Dorine could *not* stand, no, *that* she couldn't: they were the brothers, they were the family, they were the Van Lowes; and she couldn't stand it.... She had always stood up for Constance, for Constance was a sister, was herself a Van Lowe; but Constance must not start giving herself airs and looking down upon them with her "distinguished," her "distinguished." ... Very well, the brothers were not distinguished, but there was nothing else to be said against them, never had been; and against Constance there was!... And Dorine's voice suddenly sounded very cold, as she asked:

"Shall we go back to the drawing-room?"

Constance, however, absorbed in thought, did not notice the cold voice and took Dorine's arm. But, when she again passed Adolphine's table, she heard her call quickly, in a startled tone:

"No trumps!"

"Ss! Ss! Ss!" Uncle Ruyvenaer, who was losing, hissed between his teeth. "What a card-holder!... Constance, won't you cut in after this rubber?"

Constance was sure that they were still talking about her:

"No, thanks, Uncle; I really don't feel like playing to-night...."

Her voice sounded faint, in spite of herself.... She stopped for a moment, but, when nobody else spoke, she moved on aimlessly, leaning on Dorine's arm.... She felt contented and yet strange, in those rooms, in which she saw herself as she was on that last day, the day of her marriage with De Staffelaer; she could see herself at the wedding-breakfast and afterwards, when the time came to say good-bye.... Since then, her own people had become strangers to her.

Like a little child, she went in search of her mother, who was talking to Aunt Ruyvenaer, sat down in a chair by her and took her hand....

"Well, Constance, it is nice, to have you back again!" said Auntie, energetically, laying a firm, Indian stress on her words. "So nice for Mamma too, *kassian!* Where are you staying now?"

"At the Hotel des Indes, for the present, Auntie.... As soon as Van der Welcke arrives from Brussels, we shall look out for a house."

"I am so curious to meet your husband."

Constance gave a vague laugh....

"Do you often go to India, Auntie?"

"Yes, child, almost every year: Uncle likes going ... because of the business, Daranginongan, the sugar. And then home again, on our return-tickets. Oh, it's so easy, with the French mail.... No trouble at all.... And Alima, my maid ... she knows everything ... knows Paris, the custom-office, does everything, helps Uncle with the tickets.... You should see her: dressed just like a lady, stays and all, splendid; you'd laugh till you cried!... How long did you live in Brussels?"

"We were eight years in Brussels."

"Small, Brussels, I think, compared with Paris. What made you go to Brussels? Tell me."

"Well, Auntie," laughed Constance, "we had to live somewhere! We used to travel a great deal besides. We were often on the Riviera. But suddenly I got terribly homesick for Holland, for Mamma, for all of you. Then I talked about it to Van der Welcke, about moving to the Hague; and he too was longing to get back to his country. And there was Adriaan, my boy: he's thirteen now; and we wanted him to have a Dutch education...."

"Does your son talk Dutch?"

"Of course he does, Auntie."

"What is he going to be?"

Constance hesitated:

"He'll probably enter the diplomatic service," she said, in a low voice, thinking involuntarily of her years in Rome, of De Staffelaer, of all that had separated her from her people.

"Really?" asked Mamma, greatly interested.

"Yes, Van der Welcke would like it...."

She was still holding her mother's hand; and Mrs. van Lowe sat very erect, looking pleased to have Constance back.

"Marie," said Auntie. "Do you know what I think so funny of you? You're mad on your children, mad on them. But, when you see your daughter after all these years, you let her sleep at the Hotel des Indes! Why is that? Tell me."

"I saw Constance once or twice in Brussels," Mrs. van Lowe protested.

Constance laughed:

"But, Auntie, Mamma's like that, she has her own ways! And Adriaan, Addie, would be too much for her ... though he's a very quiet boy."

Mamma said nothing, smiled peacefully. Yes, she was like that, she had her own ways.

"I was saying to Uncle to-day," Auntie continued, "if it didn't look too funny, I'd ask Constance myself to stay with us. 'There's that Marie,' I said. 'She's got a big house and leaves her child at the Hotel des Indes!' It's beyond me, Marie.... Constance, you must come and eat rice with me and bring your husband and your boy. Do you like *nassi?*"[6]

"Yes, Auntie. We shall be delighted."

Constance and Auntie stood up; Constance walked towards the conservatory. The young nephews and nieces were sitting at their round game, but had stopped playing. And Constance shrank from going farther and talking to them, for they hurriedly took up their cards again and went on playing.

And she turned away and thought:

"They were talking about me...."

The servants came in with the trays:

"Who'll have a sandwich? Uncle, shall I mix you a drink?" asked Dorine, moving restlessly about the rooms.

---

[6] Rice.

CHAPTER IV

Yes, she had longed for them all, for her home and for Holland! Oh, the passionate longing of those last years, ever and ever more passionate! Oh, how lonely she had been, and how she had pined for Holland, for the Hague, for her relations! During all those years, she had been an outcast from her home, an exile, as it were, during all those long, hungry years. Twenty years she had spent abroad! For five of them she had been married to De Staffelaer, the five years in Rome, and then ... oh, the one mistake of her life! Ah, how she had pined since that mistake, incessantly!... And, after the child was born, she had pined incessantly.... Yes, for thirteen years she had pined! During all that time, she had seen her mother twice, for a couple of days, because travelling was such an effort for Mamma, because she herself dared not go to the Hague, which was so near, so near!

Her brothers, her sisters, her whole family had denied her all that time, had never been able to forgive the scandal which she had caused, the blot which she had cast on their name....

She was a girl of twenty-one when she married De Staffelaer. He was an intimate friend of Papa's: they had been at the University together and belonged to the same club. Now De Staffelaer was Netherlands minister at Rome: a good-looking, hale old man; fairly well-suited to his post: not a political genius, like Papa, she thought; but still full of qualities, as Papa had always said. She was Papa's favourite; and he had thought it so pleasant, was proud that De Staffelaer had just fallen in love with her, like a young man, and been unable to keep away from the Alexanderstraat when he came to Holland, to the Hague, once a year, on leave. She remembered Papa's smile when he talked to her about De Staffelaer, hinting at what might happen.... They had then been living for five years at the Hague, after Papa had been governor-general for five years.... She remembered the viceregal period—three years of her girlhood from twelve to seventeen—remembered the grandeur of it all: the palaces at Batavia and Buitenzorg; their country-house at Tjipanas; the balls at which she danced, young as she was; the races; the aides-de-camp; the great gold *pajong;*[7] all the tropical grandeur and semi-royalty of a great colonial governorship.... After that, at the Hague, a quieter time, but still their crowded receptions, their great dinners to Indian and home celebrities; Bertha back from India, with Van Naghel; she herself presented at Court.... She loved that life and, from the time when she was quite a young girl, had known nothing but glamour around her.... Papa, too, breathed in that element of grandeur: a man of great political capacity, as she thought, never realizing that Papa had merely risen through tact; through mediocrity; through a certain opportune vagueness in his political creed, which was curved and shaded with every half-curve and half-shade that the needs of the moment might dictate; through good-breeding, through the eloquence of his meaningless, easy-flowing sentences, full of the high-sounding commonplaces of

---

[7] Umbrella or parasol.

the day; through his suavity and suppleness, his smiling amiability, all the personal charm of him. She had always seen her father important; she saw him so still. And she herself, at that time, longed for importance, for every sort of worldly vanity: she had it in her blood. As a young girl, she loved brilliancy, titles; loved spacious, well-lighted rooms, fine carriages; loved to see men in stars and ribbons, ladies in court-dress; loved to curtsey very low before the King and Queen: the little Princess Wilhelmina was then still a baby.... Thanks to De Staffelaer, their receptions were sometimes attended by members of the *corps diplomatique* and of that particular set at the Hague which fastens on to the diplomatists: the little band of people who, at the Hague, are stared and gaped at wherever they go, who talk loudly at the opera, swaggering in all the arrogance of their smartness and conceit, looking down upon all and everything that does not form part of their own little set and encouraged in their blatant self-assertion by the Hague public, with its flattering tribute of open-mouthed curiosity. She did not see all this, especially as a young girl: she thought it grand if a Spanish marquis or a German count, a member of one of the legations, showed himself for ten minutes at her parents' receptions; and, if Mrs. This or the Freule[8] That, of "the set," came for only five minutes, Constance would brag about it, with an assumption of indifference, for the next three months. Vanity was born in her blood and had been nourished at Batavia and Buitenzorg, where she was made much of as the young daughter of the governor-general. Now, at the Hague, full-fledged, she struggled, above all, to be invited to the drawing-rooms of "the set." It was very difficult, though Bertha and she had been presented at Court, though her parents still had ever so many connections. She was constantly encountering coldness on the part of "the set," coupled with great incivility, which she had to swallow; but she had some of Papa's tact and she went on struggling: she left cards on Mrs. This to all eternity, with a snobbishness for which she came to blush later; she bowed and talked pleasantly, to all eternity, to the Freule That, receiving nothing in return but a snub. She had found that the Hague was not the same as Batavia; that, though you had been the highest personage at Batavia, you were not so easily admitted into that very high circle of the Hague, "the set." ...

Now, she laughed softly at all this, after that first family-evening, sitting in her room at the hotel, while her boy slept.... Yes, Papa had always smiled because De Staffelaer was so much in love with her; and she herself had thought it delicious to be wooed by this diplomatist, with his ribbons and stars, by this smiling, courtly man of sixty, who did not look a day more than fifty. And, when he asked Papa for her hand, she accepted him, very glad and happy, a little flushed and triumphant, rather inclined to preen herself in the delectable atmosphere of congratulation; she was now, thanks to De Staffelaer, decidedly a member of "the set" and, at the same time, did not need "the set" so very much, now that she was going to Rome, to spend her life in circles such as that of the Quirinal and the "white" Roman world.... She had attained her aim.

---

[8] The title borne by noblemen's unmarried daughters.

She had a charming husband, not young, but none the less passionately in love with her and vain, in his turn, of his young and pretty wife. She had a title. She had money enough, even though De Staffelaer's affairs were somewhat involved. She found the Court balls at Rome more splendid than the routs at the Hague; she was introduced to all sorts of great names. The Italian aristocracy, it is true, was even more exclusive than that of the Hague; but she moved in a brilliant circle of diplomatists and foreigners. Only, she was struck by the fact that, abroad, the members of the *corps diplomatique* were not stared at so much as in the opera at the Hague or on the terrace at Scheveningen. It almost annoyed her: she would have liked to be stared at in her turn. But, in the society of a big capital like Rome, the wife of the Netherlands minister, even though she was young and pretty and well-dressed, was not so important a person as the Marquesa This, of the Spanish Legation, or Mrs. This or the Freule That, of "the set," was at the Hague. People did not stare at her, in Rome; and this was almost a disappointment.... Besides, her increasing and often wounded vanity left a certain void within her, a sense of boredom. De Staffelaer, ever courtly, pleasant and in love, with the apprehensive love of an old man for the young wife whom he is afraid lest he should soon cease to attract, ended by irritating her and upsetting her nerves....

But this, at the time, was nothing more—nor anything more serious—than boredom and vague discontent.... Since then, life had set its mark on Constance. Often now, as a woman of forty-two, she felt a dull melancholy in pondering on her life; she let her life, one woman's life, glide past her gaze once more; she began with her childish years in India; saw once more the splendour and grandeur of Buitenzorg; criticized her own vanity during her girlhood at the Hague; saw her marriage as the great mistake of her life; saw, as the second, irrevocable mistake of her life, all that had happened with Van der Welcke.... Her life had been warped beyond remedy. She had gone from vanity to wantonness, to reckless play-acting with that life, big with fate, which she had first seen only as a dazzling reflection, a reflection of mirrors, candles, satin, jewels, titles and orders: the setting of the play; a little flirtation, a little jesting—not even always witty—with smart men of the world, refined and elegant in their dress-clothes, who assumed airs of mysterious importance about the great affairs of kings and countries, affairs which were settled by just two or three supermen in Berlin, London or St. Petersburg, while most of the others, the exquisites, gave weighty decisions on a matter of ceremony, a visit, a card with or without the corner turned down, a little matter of etiquette, trivialities around which their whole existence and that of their wives revolved. She, too, had given weighty decisions in all these matters: a three weeks' mourning for this royal highness; an eight days' mourning—very light, with a touch of white—for that royal highness; and her life was so full of all this ado about nothing that she had hardly had time to reflect. In Rome, as the wife of the Netherlands minister, with some pretensions to lead the cosmopolitan circle which here and there touched upon that of the exclusive Roman aristocracy, she was so busy with her hairdresser and her tailor, with shopping in the morning, half-a-dozen visits and a charity *matinee* in the afternoon, a Court ball at night, followed by a little supper: so busy that it affected her health and often left her tired and pale. But she had grudged none of it, so long as she saw her name mentioned with the others in the newspapers. And, when, in the midst of all this empty glamour, in the midst of all this empty bustle, she met Van der Welcke, the new young secretary of the Netherlands Legation, and, of course, saw him nearly every day, she had allowed him to make love to her, just because a couple of her friends declared that he was making love to her and because a serious flirtation, a passion, formed part of the game, as it were. And then, in very elegant language, she had complained to Van der Welcke of the void in her life and said all sorts of fine things about soul-hunger and life-weariness, without knowing anything about soul-hunger or life-weariness and remembering that she had to go to her dressmaker, that afternoon, and to two receptions and that she had her own reception in the evening. Then she parroted bits out of a French novel, acted a scene or two after the same model, thinking it time to bring a little literature into her life. He, a good-looking fellow—short and well-knit, sturdy without being clumsy, with a pair of boyish blue eyes, a shapely, round head with lightly-curling, short, brown hair, like a head of Hermes, and still exceedingly young—thought that it would look well for him to make a little love to his chief's wife, without going any farther, of course.... But it was impossible for them to play with fire unscathed, in an atmosphere like that of Rome. They saw so many French novels acted around them that, quite involuntarily, they began to feel not only like a modern hero and heroine of fiction or a pair of fashionable actors, but what they were: a young man and a young woman; she the wife of a man old enough to be her father. What had started with a compliment and a laugh—because of what her friends had told her—led to a warmer pressure of the hand, not once but many times, the abandonment of a waltz, a kiss and the rest.... They both glided towards sin gradually, as though inevitably. She was at first greatly surprised at herself and annoyed and, for the first time in her life, felt the danger of playing with life ... especially when she, who had never loved, fell in love with the man who had acted with her in this drawing-room comedy and turned it to earnest. In her soul, choked with vanity and false glamour, one genuine emotion now sprang up: she fell in love with Van der Welcke. She did not love him for any quality of soul or heart or temperament, but she loved him all the same, loved him as a young woman loves a young man, with all the blind impulse of her womanhood. Her feeling for him was primitive and simple, but it was whole-souled and true. Until now, she had cared for nothing but Mrs. This or Freule That, of "the set;" the ceremonial splendour of the Court; dinners, dresses, decorations; and all sorts of important matters concerning visits and visiting-cards. Now, she cared for a human being, a man, not for the sake of a wedding-ceremony, or stars and ribbons, or visits of congratulation, but simply so that she might hold him in her arms. She felt something real blossoming within her; and the feeling was so strange to her that it made her anxious and unhappy. Their love was anxious, their love became unhappy, as though it had a foreboding of all their hidden fate. They both heard it, the heavy footfall of their fate. It was as though, at their meetings, in their most passionate embraces, they listened outside to the rustle of one spying on them ... and to that heavy footfall of their fate. And, from the French novel, with its seasoned intrigue that seemed to suit them so well, their love turned into the real tragedy of their lives. She had envious enemies, jealous because she had given a finer dinner than they, jealous of a handsomer dress. De Staffelaer was first warned by anonymous letters. Then a footman whom he had occasion to rebuke flung it in his face that mevrouw was carrying on with meneer the secretary.... He traced their place of assignation. He found Van der Welcke there, while Constance had just time to escape down a back staircase. Amid this damning confusion, Van der Welcke's denial was tantamount to a confession....

Of course, the scandal was spread abroad at once, in Holland as well as in Rome. A divorce followed. Constance was condemned by her family and cast out, left as it were homeless.... She always fancied that the scandal had been Papa's death: a year later, he pined away, died, slowly, from the effects of a stroke, broken-hearted over the stain which his favourite daughter had cast upon all the blameless decorum of the aristocrat and statesman that he was. She was left as it were homeless, with a small allowance from De Staffelaer, which she refused as soon as she was able to do without it....

Then she saw Van der Welcke come to her, to Florence, where she had, so to speak, taken sanctuary. But he did not come to her of his own accord; he came sent, forced to go, by his father. For his father would not suffer him to go his own way and leave this woman to her misery. As she had given herself to him, his father ordered him, in his turn, to give up all to her: his name and his career.

Henri van der Welcke had been brought up, from childhood, to yield unquestioning obedience to his parents. His father and mother were both descended from those strict, religious, doughty, aristocratic Dutch families to which the Hague "set" is a thorn in the flesh; and they had judged the matter thus, with rigid and scrupulous justice, as a duty before God and man. And their heir, at this, the supreme moment of his life, once more showed himself a dutiful son. He obeyed his parents' command. He resigned his post, broke off his young career. He went to Constance, telling her that his parents had sent him; but, in their mutual misery, they still seemed to find some love for each other in what remained of their first passion. She was too desperate to indulge in long reflection or to decline the way of escape which he offered her. As they could not be married at once by Dutch law, they were married in London as soon as it was possible. Constance wrote to Henri's parents to express her gratitude; but they did not answer her letter. They refused to know her, refused to see her. They had sacrificed their son to her, because they thought it their duty before God; and they had made this heavy sacrifice, because they were religious people, honest, righteous people; but their hearts were bitter against Constance: they would never forgive her the sacrifice which their honesty, their righteousness had required of them, the parents....

Henri and Constance had lived in England, travelled in Italy and ended by settling down in Brussels. Their son was born; the years passed. Slowly, in Brussels, they made acquaintances, made friends; and, in the course of years, those acquaintances and friends dispersed. Twice, amid heavy emotion, they had seen Mamma van Lowe in Brussels for a couple of days at a time: the other members of the family never. The lonely years dragged on. They both came to look upon their lives as one great mistake. Constance' vanity, moreover, resented the dull existence which they led; Henri, who was four years younger than his wife, was for ever regretting that he had sacrificed his future to this woman at his parents' behest. They were fettered to each other in the narrow prison of marriage. Passion dead, the despairing illusion of love killed, they had never been able to accommodate themselves to each other; and without mutual accommodation there is no happiness in marriage. Whatever they said or thought or did led to discord. Their lives were never in step, but stumbled and shambled and shuffled along. Every word spoken by the one was an offence to the other: they could not endure each other's going and coming. Latterly, they could not speak but their speech caused a quarrel. Between them stood the child, still the child of their love. But the Child did not unite them, was a cause of jealousy to both. They grudged each other their offspring. He could not bear to see his son in her arms; she could not bear to see her boy on his knee. He turned pale when she kissed the boy; she cried with envy when he took him for a walk. Yet they did not think of a separation, deeming the thought ridiculous, not so much for the world as, above all, for themselves. They would continue to bear their fetters together, until their death, in hatred.

The intolerable nature of their existence was enough to give Constance a feeling of home-sickness for Holland. The last few years in Brussels, now that their acquaintances were scattered, had been so lonely, so melancholy, so forlorn, so bitter, so full of dislike, hatred, envy of Henri, that she yearned for consolation, for some sort of love that would come to her with open arms and understand and pity her. There were days when she did not utter a word, after a scene with Henri, until Adriaan threw his arms about her, while she burst out sobbing on his childish breast. The boy, in other respects a sturdy lad, had his nerves so much shaken by this open conflict between his parents that he often fell ill.

Then both Henri and Constance, greatly alarmed, would suggest parting from Adriaan, for the boy's own good, so that he might not be a witness to their inevitable disputes. But they were both too weak. In their intolerable life Adriaan was the only alleviation. And neither of them had ever been able to resolve upon this parting; both merely promised themselves to exercise restraint in future, so that the boy might not suffer....

Gradually, Constance had talked more and more about Holland, confessed that she was yearning for all those whom she had left behind. She longed for them all: her mother, her brothers, her sisters. She yearned for affection, for family-affection, for the fostering warmth and love and sympathy of a large circle of relations, who would show her the kindness which she had known of old, at Buitenzorg, at the Hague. And Van der Welcke also began to feel that strange nostalgia which urges a man towards the land of his birth, of his own tongue, of his kindred. Weary of living abroad, he fell in with Constance' view, really because of a chance word from Addie, who also often had the word Holland on his lips; the father was now thinking of his child's future.... But they must first learn how the family would receive them. Van der Welcke wrote to his parents, Constance to Mamma van Lowe. They wrote with all the humility of exiles; once more asked for forgiveness, after those fourteen years; said that they were longing to see their country again, their parents, brothers, sisters, to enjoy the sweet happiness of living where they would be at home. Both had felt the old inviolable bonds drawing them towards Holland, as though there were something which they needed before they could grow old and be a father and mother to their son.... Henri's parents had not yet written, did not at once reply to his question whether they could not forgive him now that those long, long years were past, whether they would not receive his wife, who, after all, was their daughter-in-law, who, after all, was the mother of his son, their grandchild. But Mamma van Lowe had sent Constance a sweet and loving letter, a letter which Constance had kissed, which had made her sob with happiness. Mamma had written that her child was to come to her, that all was forgiven, all forgotten, that the brothers and sisters would receive her with open arms. And she had expressed her own delight, as the old mother, who found it so difficult to get about, who disliked travelling, though it was but a two or three hours' journey to Brussels, and hated being so far from her child, for Constance was her child, in spite of all. Then Constance could restrain herself no longer and, without waiting for the letter from Henri's father and mother, had gone on ahead with Adriaan. Henri remained behind to settle a few matters of business: he was to follow in a week.

And Holland, yonder, so near and yet so long unattainable, was to them as a land of promise, a land of peace, of happiness long-deferred, where they would find, for themselves and for their son, all that of which they had been starved for years and years: parents and relations, old friends and acquaintances and, as the very essence of it all, that fragrant Dutch atmosphere, so indescribable and yet, as they now realized, craved for by their parched and famished souls. Both, as with one thought, had suddenly, for all the discord of their lives, known as a certainty, both for themselves and their son, that, to grow old and be a father and mother to their boy, they must return to their country, to which they were attached by those strange, mysterious and long-unsuspected bonds which may be denied for years, but which end by reasserting themselves, irrefragably, for ever and all time....

CHAPTER V

It was Sunday afternoon.

"We must re-ally, Ka-rel, pay a coup-le of vis-its, this af-ter-noon," drawled Cateau van Lowe.

Karel assented: it was visiting-day.

"Where?" he asked.

She named one or two acquaintances:

"And then we must al-so go to Aunt and Un-cle Ruyvenaer; it's their turn.... And then, Ka-rel, to your sis-ter, to Con-stance...."

"Hadn't we better wait till Van der Welcke's there? Otherwise we shall have to go again."

"I don't think it looks friend-ly ... to wait till Van der Wel-cke comes.... Mamma *did* set us the exam-ple, Ka-rel, you know."

"Then wouldn't it be better, Cateau, for you to go alone first: then I can call on Van der Welcke later. Or do you think I ought to wait until Van der Welcke has been to see me?"

"We won't cal-culate it quite so close-ly as all *that*," said Cateau, generously. "It looks as if we were not friend-ly.... It would be bet-ter if you came with me *to-day*, Karel."

So they decided both to call on Constance that afternoon; and they were on the point of starting when the bell rang and Adolphine van Saetzema entered:

"What a nui-sance," thought Cateau. "Now the carriage will ab-solute-ly have to wait."

It was raining; and this meant that the brougham would get wet. The horse was jobbed; the coachman did not count: he was only a man.

"Ah, Adolph-ine! This *is* nice of you...."

"I see your carriage is at the door.... Are you going out?"

"Yes, pres-ently, to pay a visit ... or two...."

"So am I. But don't let me keep you. I am going to Constance this afternoon."

"So are we."

"Oh, are you? I would really rather have waited till she had called on me."

"Oh," said Cateau, "it looks as if we weren't friend-ly, to cal-culate it so close-ly, don't you think, Adolph-ine? But do sit down, Adolph-ine."

Adolphine sat down, for she was paying Karel and Cateau a visit; and, if she had not sat down, the visit would not have been paid, would not have counted as a visit. Perhaps that was also the reason why Karel and Cateau urged Adolphine to sit down: otherwise, she would have been obliged to come back another day.

They all sat down: the brother, the sister, the sister-in-law. Outside, the rain was pouring in torrents; and already the brougham was glistening with the wet: Cateau's saucer-eyes watched every drop through the curtains. The usual drawing-room talk began:

"What terrible wea-ther, isn't it, Adolph-ine?"

"Terrible."

Adolphine was thin, angular, envious, badly-dressed. Beside the prosperous, opulent respectability of Karel and Cateau, sleek with good living, heavy with comfort, radiating money and ease—Karel in his thick frieze great-coat, Cateau in a rich silk dress and a rich fur-trimmed jacket, with a rich toque crowning her round, pink-and-white, full-moon face—Adolphine looked shabby, peevish and pretentious. The stuff of her clothes could not compare with Cateau's, which were eloquent of money, good, substantial money; and yet Adolphine had certain pretentions to fashion and elegance. A thin, straggling boa wound its length around her neck. Her fringe, out of curl because of the wet, hung in rats'-tails from under a shabby little hat, draped in a limp veil. It was as though Adolphine felt this, for she said, enviously:

"I didn't trouble to put on anything decent, in this beastly rain."

Cateau looked meaningly at the carriage outside:

"So you're going to Con-stance' al-so?..."

"Yes. But when will Van der Welcke be here? Saetzema is waiting to pay his visit until Van der Welcke comes...."

"You see?" said Karel to Cateau.

"Oh?" asked Cateau, drawling her words more than ever. "Is Saet-zema wait-ing until Van der Wel-cke comes?... Oh, I told Karel to come with me because, per-haps, it wouldn't look friend-ly.... What do you think of Con-stance, Adolphine? Karel thinks his sis-ter so al-tered, so al-tered...."

"Yes, she's altered. She has grown old, very old," said Adolphine, who, herself four years younger than Constance, looked decidedly older.

"Oh, I don't know!" said Karel, trying to defend his sister. "You would never say she was forty-two...."

"Oh, is she forty-*two*?" drawled Cateau.

"I'll tell you what I think," said Adolphine. "I don't think Constance looks a bit distinguished."

When Adolphine was envious and jealous—and that was generally—she said the exact opposite of what she thought in her heart.

"Not a bit distinguished!" she repeated, with conviction. "There is something in the way she does her hair, in those rings of hers—I don't know—something not quite respectable...."

"Yes, something foreign," said Karel, feebly, by way of an excuse.

"I think," said Cateau, "Con-stance has something about her that's not quite prop-er...."

"Oh," said Adolphine, "but propriety isn't her strong point!"

"Never was," grinned Karel, in his turn.

"If she had only stayed in Brussels!" snapped Adolphine.

"Ah!" said Cateau, opening big owl's eyes. "Do *you* think so *too*?"

"Yes. And you?"

"So do *we*, re-ally," drawled Cateau, more cheerfully, forgetting the brougham waiting in the wet.

"Yes," said Adolphine, with conviction. "What are we to do with a sister like that?"

"Whom you can't let any one meet," growled Karel under his breath.

"Oh, dear!" whined Cateau to Adolphine. "Do *you* think so *too*?"

"And," said Adolphine, "mark my words, you'll see, she's full of pretensions. You know the sort of thing," with an envious wave of the hand. "Society ... pushing herself ... perhaps even going to Court."

"*No!*" drawled Cateau. "Sure-ly for *that*, even Constance would have too much *tact*."

"I'm not so sure!" growled Karel.

Unlike Bertha and Constance, Adolphine had not been presented at Court, because, after Constance' marriage Papa and Mamma van Lowe, feeling old and tired, had taken to living more quietly. She could never forgive them for it.

"*No!*" droned Cateau. "But then you are such a regular, good, *Dutch* wife and mo-ther, Adolph-ine. That's what I al-ways say to Ka-rel."

Adolphine looked flattered.

"Yes, but," said Karel, by way of excuse, "you mustn't look to Constance for what she has never been. She went straight to Rome after her first marriage."

"Those Court circles are always fast," Adolphine declared.

"And then, in *Rome*," cried Cateau, clasping her fat hands, "*such* things hap-pen!"

Adolphine rose: her visit was paid. She had a great deal more to talk about, among others the way in which Bertha had, so to speak, forced her daughter Emilie into her engagement with Van Raven; but it was growing late: she took her leave. Karel and Cateau went straight to the brougham:

"Oh, de-ar!" said Cateau, in a startled voice. "How wet the carriage has got!"

They drove to pay their visits. First, they drove to the Ruyvenaers: Karel rang; fortunately, Uncle and Aunt were out. Cards for Uncle and Aunt. Next—Cateau consulted her list—to Mrs. van Friesesteijn, an old friend of Mrs. van Lowe's. At home. A cantankerous, shrivelled little old lady, always alert for news:

"Glad to see you, Cateau. Sit down, Van Lowe. So, Constance is back, I hear."

"Ye-es," drawled Cateau, "it's ve-ry unpleas-ant for *us*."

"And how is Constance?"

"Oh, she's all right," said Karel, casually.

"You see, me-vrouw," droned Cateau, "she's Karel's sis-ter, *isn't* she?"

"So you're all receiving her?"

"Yes, because of Mamma, you know."

"And Bertha too?"

"Ye-e-es, Berth-a, too."

"And will she go to Court again, do you think?"

"Well, Adolph-ine said that she'd be *sure* to go to *Court* again."

"I think that's wrong of Constance," said the old lady, sharply, inquisitively, eager for a bit of scandal. "And Bertha's Emilie is soon to be married."

"Ye-es. And Adolph-ine's Floor-tje too."

"I hear Emilie is to have a splendid trousseau," said the old lady. "Floortje's will be much less grand, I suppose?"

"Not so *fine*," drawled Cateau. "But still ve-ry *nice*. What terrible wea-ther, me-vrouw!... Come, Ka-rel, we must be go-ing on...."

In the brougham again. Next visit to Mr. and Mrs. IJkstra, cousins of Cateau, who was born an IJkstra:

"How d'ye do, Pie-ie-iet? How d'ye do, An-na?"

"How d'ye do, Cateau? How d'ye do, Karel? So Constance is back?"

"Yes. What *do* you thi-i-i-ink of it? And they *all* say ev-erywhere, that she is go-ing to Court."

"Oh!"

"Nonsense!"

"Yes, Adolph-ine said so ... and so did Mrs. van Frie-sesteijn."

"How mad of Mrs. van der Welcke, with that past of hers!"

"Perhaps it's her husband who wants to go."

"Oh, no doubt it's her husband."

"And how does she look?"

"Oh, so-so! Of course, she's Ka-rel's sis-ter, but I think her not so ve-ry distin-guished."

"Oh, well, I think her rather smart!" growled Karel, a little crossly.

"Oh, Ka-rel!... Well, *smart*, if you like, but not what I call good ta-aste."

"Rather foreign, I suppose?" asked Anna IJkstra.

"Ye-es. And so many *rings:* that's what I don't like. And her *hair:* all curled and waved, puffed *right* out, you know. So ridic-ulous ... because she's ve-ry grey, you know...."

"Oh, really!"

"Yes. What terrible wea-ther, An-na.... We ought to be go-ing on, Ka-rel."

"Where?" growled Karel.

"To the Van Ra-vens."

"Oh, no!" muttered Karel. "It's raining so.... And I have to get out all the time and ring the bell."

"But haven't you a footman?" asked Anna, pretending not to know.

"I say, what next!" muttered Karel. "A footman, indeed!"

"But, Ka-rel, in that case, let us just go on to Constance."

"Oh, are you going to Mrs. van der Welcke's?"

"Yes, we must re-ally pay her a vis-it, to-day...."

"Well, come along then!" growled Karel, who was irritable without knowing why.

And they drove to the Hotel des Indes. The porter left them in the hall for a moment, then showed them up.

"How nice of you to come!" said Constance. She was genuinely pleased. "And in this awful weather! But, as you see, you have to come up to my bedroom. I have no sitting-room; and the drawing-room is such a bore. Really, it's very nice of you to come," she repeated, "and in this rain, too! Adriaan!"

"Yes, Mamma!"

"Here are Uncle Karel and Aunt Cateau."

She beckoned to the boy to come from his room. She was smiling with happiness, glad to see the faces of her brother and her sister-in-law, longing for the sympathy of family-affection, though she had not known Cateau in the old days.

"Ah, is that your *boy*, Con-stance?... Well, he *is* a big boy!"

"How d'ye do, Aunt? How d'ye do, Uncle?" said the lad, a little coldly and haughtily.

"Is he like his father?" asked Karel.

"Yes," said Constance, grudgingly.

Karel and Cateau looked at Adriaan. The boy stood bolt upright before them, a strikingly handsome lad: he certainly resembled his father; he had Van der Welcke's regular features, his round head, his short, soft, curly hair. At thirteen, an age when other boys are overgrown, gawky and clumsy in their ways, he was not tall, but well-proportioned and rather broadly built, with a pair of square shoulders in his blue serge jacket, with something about his gestures and movements that denoted a certain manliness and self-possession, uncommon in so young a boy. He tried to be polite, but could not conceal a certain mistrust of this unknown uncle and aunt. His small mouth was firmly closed; his eyes stared fixedly, dark-blue, serious and cold.

Constance made her sister-in-law and brother sit down:

"Forgive all this muddle," she said with a laugh. "I was taking advantage of the rainy day to arrange my trunks a bit."

Cateau gave a sharp glance round: there were dresses hanging over the chairs and from the pegs; a couple of hats lay on a table.

"Oh, Con-stance!" said Cateau; and she felt a little impertinent at saying, "Constance," just like that—she had married Karel after Constance' marriage to De Staffelaer and this was only the second time that she had seen her sister-in-law—and had it on her lips to say, "Mevrouw," instead. "Oh, Con-stance, *what a lot* of clothes you have!"

"Do you think so? Things get so spoilt in one's trunks."

"*I* haven't as many dress-es as that, *have* I, Ka-rel? But *what* I have is re-ally good. But yours are good, *too*, Con-stance. I like re-ally good clothes.... Only, such a lot of *lace* would fid-get me.... Bertha dresses well, too.... But Adolph-ine.... Oh, what a *sight* she al-ways looks!"

"Does she?" asked Constance. "But she has to consider the cost of things, hasn't she?"

"I have only two dress-es every year; but those are re-ally good."

"And will Van der Welcke be here soon?" asked Karel.

"On Tuesday. Then we shall look round for a house. I do think it so delightful to be back at the Hague, among all of you. I see Mamma every day. Yesterday, I was at Bertha's: a busy household, isn't it? I came plump into the middle of all sorts of rehearsals, for the wedding. And I was at Gerrit's: Adeline is a dear; and oh, how I laughed, how I laughed! What a lot of children! I can't tell them one from the other yet. But how charming and delightful, that fair-haired little woman, with that fair-haired little troop; and she's expecting another baby this summer! And Dorine is nice too.... Oh, you don't know, you don't know how glad I am to see you all! We are a big family and life at the Hague is so busy.... Look at Bertha.... And Gerrit and Adeline too are busy with their little troop.... But I do hope to take my place among you all again. It is so long since I saw you all! Ah, I didn't want to force things! Mamma did come to see me twice in Brussels. But my brothers and sisters ... No, it wasn't kind of you! But I daresay it had to be! Things were as they were! You couldn't very well respect me, you had to disown me, it couldn't be helped!... I suffered tortures, all those years! I never had any one to talk to, except him, my little son! It wasn't right of Mamma, was it, Addie, to be always talking to you? But I couldn't speak out to Henri, to Van der Welcke. Oh, we are very good friends, quite good friends!... I can't tell you how, all of a sudden, I longed for the Hague, for my family, for the people I used to know, for all of you, for everything! I always wrote to Mamma regularly; and Mamma gave me all the news, sent me the photographs of my little nephews and nieces. And yet my brain's whirling, now that I am seeing you all. There are such a lot of us: I don't think there can be many families as big as ours. Bertha's alone is a big household.... Fancy Bertha a grandmother!... It's dreadful, how old we're growing! I am forty-two! Oh, I couldn't have gone on living in Brussels! We had no one left there: our friends were scattered, gone away. Van der Welcke, too, was beginning to long for Holland, for Addie's sake as well as his own. Addie speaks very good Dutch, though: I always made him keep it up. He has a bit of a Flemish accent, perhaps: what do you think, Addie?... We had a Flemish servant.... Oh, what a lot I have to tell you!"

she laughed, happily. "Nothing interesting, you know, but I feel as if I must tell you everything, talk and talk and talk to you, to all of you, my brothers, my sisters!" She suddenly got up. "Karel, do you remember, in India, how we used to play in the river, behind the Palace; how we walked on those great stone boulders, you and I and Gerrit? We three always played together. Yes, Bertha had been married a year or two, while we were still children. Is Bertha fifty yet? She's quite grey! I'm going grey myself!... Dear Bertha!... And Louis and Gertrude, who died at Buitenzorg.... Do you remember, Karel? It was we three who were always together. You used to carry me over the water on your back. How naughty we were! I was quite thirteen or fourteen, at that time.... And things are so funny, in India: next year, I was in long frocks and going to the balls.... I thought it delightful, all that grandeur: the aides-de-camp; the national anthem wherever we went: I used to imagine that they played it for me, the viceroy's little daughter!... Yes, Van Naghel was at the bar then, at Semarang; Bertha didn't come in for any of it.... Oh, it's past now, my vanity! That shows you how a person changes. You are changed, too, Karel: you have become so sedate, so dignified. What a pity you are no longer a burgomaster: you're cut out for it, Karel!"

She tried to speak lightly, suddenly feeling that she was talking too much about herself, letting herself go, while Karel and Cateau sat staring at her. And yet she cared for them: was not Karel her brother, who had always been bracketed with Gerrit in her childhood memories, and was not Cateau his wife, though she had not a sympathetic face, with those great round eyes of hers? Were they not members of the family, for which she had longed so? She tried to speak playfully, after her all-too-spontaneous outpouring; but she suddenly felt that this was out of tune too. She felt that, after all, she had not seen her brother for twenty years, not since the day of her marriage to De Staffelaer, and that they had become as utter strangers to each other. She felt that she did not know Cateau at all. And so, though Karel and Cateau were her brother and sister, they were also strangers. But that was just what she did not want: she wanted to win them all, the whole family; to feel that they were all warm-hearted and indulgent towards her.... And she spoke of Mamma, of the Sunday evenings, of Mamma's mania for the family, which she herself now felt so strongly, intensified as it had been in those lonely, joyless Brussels years. She asked their advice about taking a house at the Hague.

"The best thing you can do is to consult an estate-agent," said Karel. "There's one close by; he'll know about all the houses to let."

"It will be difficult to find the right thing," said Constance. "We had a pretty flat at Brussels; and I really prefer a flat to a house. But there aren't any in Holland."

"Oh, Con-stance!" said Cateau, round-eyed. "Don't you find a flat ve-ry stuff-y?"

"Not at all; and I love to have everything on one floor. I don't care for maids running up and down the stairs."

"Yes, but the place *must* be kept *clean*."

"Well, it was.... Only, in a flat, abroad, the bell doesn't keep ringing as it does at one's front-door in Holland. The cook goes to market in the morning...."

"And does she just buy ev-erything?"

"She buys enough for a couple of days: vegetables and eggs and whatever she wants."

"Do you leave that to the *cook*?"

"Oh, yes! Imagine if I didn't!" laughed Constance. "She simply couldn't understand it! I used only to give her a few instructions."

"Well, I *must* say that I don't think that at *all* a prop-er way of house-keeping!... Do *you*, Kar-el?"

"It's the way of the country," growled Karel, under his breath. "Were you thinking of looking for a house in one of the new districts, Duinoord, for instance?"

"I'd rather not be so far from all of you."

"Dear Con-stance!" laughed Cateau, with her round face. "But we *all* live more or less *far* from one ano-ther!"

There was a knock at the door: the porter showed Adolphine in.

"Ah, Adolphine! How nice of you to come, all the more as we are to meet at Mamma's this evening. You're a good sister." And she kissed Adolphine. "This is my boy. I brought him to see you the other day, but you were out."

"How d'ye do, Aunt?" said Addie, stiffly.

"Forgive the muddle, Adolphine. I was just unpacking my trunks."

"We ought re-ally to be go-ing on, Ka-rel."

"Are you going so soon?"

"Yes, it's rain-ing so; and the brougham is getting so we-et."

"Constance," said Karel. "Did you say that Van der Welcke would be here on Tuesday?"

"I expect so."

"Well, then, give him my kind regards and ... and would you give him my card? Then that'll be all right."

He took a visiting-card from his pocket-book and laid it on a corner of the console-table. Constance looked at him in momentary perplexity. She could not speak for a second or two, did not understand. She herself had been brought up and had lived according to very punctilious rules of card-leaving; but yet she failed to understand how one brother-in-law could leave a card on another brother-in-law, before that other was in town and during a visit paid in his sister's bedroom, amid all the muddle of her unpacked trunks. But she had been so long away from Holland and the Hague; she did not wish it to appear that she did not understand; and, as a woman of the world, she did not, above all, wish it to appear that she thought Karel's performance with the card not only stiff, but intensely vulgar.

She said, with a gentle smile.

"Thank you, Karel. Van de Welcke will appreciate your call greatly."

Her voice sounded friendly and natural; and neither Karel nor Cateau had any idea that Constance had controlled herself as she had sometimes had to control herself in Rome, in a diplomatic *salon* full of intrigue and polished envy.

In the brougham, Cateau said:

"You did that very clev-erly, Ka-rel, with that card...."

"Yes, I thought it the best way," said Karel, in a burgomasterly manner.

CHAPTER VI

Adolphine looked enviously around her. What a lot Constance must spend on her clothes; and it was not as if they were well off either, for all they had to live on was an allowance from Papa and Mamma van der Welcke, the money which Constance had inherited from her father and the little that Van der Welcke could scrape together at Brussels, as a wine- and insurance-agent. Nothing to speak of, all told: that Adolphine knew for a fact. She admired in particular a magnificent fur bolero and wondered what two kinds of fur it was made of; but she said nothing: she never praised anything in another, not his raiment, nor his intellect, nor his virtues. Even if she had had anything to gain by it, she could never have brought herself to say:

"Constance, what a pretty bolero that is!"

But, pale with envy, she kept looking at the fur as it hung over a chair; and the sight of it caused her almost physical pain, because it was not hers and she did not know how one like it ever could be hers.

Constance was rather tired. First, she had been unpacking trunks with Addie; then Karel and Cateau had come and she had talked copiously in the pleasure and excitement of seeing them. But that visiting-card of Karel's had depressed her; and now she talked listlessly:

"So your girl is going to be married soon, Adolphine?"

"In May."

"I haven't seen either of them since Sunday. A couple of days ago, I found their cards and Dijkerhof's. How quickly a week passes! I didn't find any of you at home either."

"We are so busy shopping all day long, for the trousseau."

"Is Dijkerhof a nice fellow?"

"Yes; and they are a very good family."

As it happened, the Dijkerhofs were not in quite the same set as the Van Lowes; and Mamma van Lowe was not over-enthusiastic about the engagement.

Constance was silent: she was tired, she had a headache and she thought that Adolphine had better keep the conversation going. But Adolphine was too much distracted by the bolero to be in form. She cast about for a subject. And yet there were plenty, for she was dying of curiosity to know all sorts of things: for instance, what Constance thought of Bertha and Cateau. If only that wretched bolero were not there! At last, she began:

"So you're looking for a house?"

Constance answered at random; and, because of her headache, her expression became stiff and haughty and her lips were tightly compressed. Adolphine thought her arrogant and reflected that Constance had always been stuck-up, after her marriage to De Staffelaer and all the smart society in Rome. Adolphine suspected Constance of looking down upon her; and Constance merely had a headache.

"And shall you call on many people?"

No, Constance thought not.

"Won't you go to Court?"

No, Constance hadn't given it a thought.

"Is your boy going to the high-school?"

No, he was to pass his examination for the grammar-school: Van der Welcke wanted him to go to one of the universities, later.

"What photographs are those?"

"Friends of ours, in Brussels."

"Had you many friends there?"

"Not so many, latterly."

Suddenly Constance' eyes met Adolphine's. And Constance did not see Adolphine's hateful hostility: Constance saw only her sister, four years younger than herself, but worn out by a tiresome, difficult life, a life full of money-bothers, full of trouble with spoilt, disagreeable children, receiving no assistance from her husband, Van Saetzema, who was chief clerk at the Ministry of Justice; Constance saw her sister, thin, yellow, eaten up with worry and bitterness, in her almost shabby and yet pretentious clothes. And, notwithstanding her raging headache, she was filled with pity, because Adolphine was her sister. She rose and went to Adolphine:

"Phine," she said, frankly, "don't be angry if I am not very talkative, but I have such a headache. And I really do think it nice of you to look me up. Come often. Let us see a lot of each other. I only came to the Hague because of you all. I wanted you so badly. I have dragged through so many dreary years. I have no one in my life, except my boy. And he is still so young; and I tell him too much as it is. I have been very unhappy, Adolphine, Phine. Be nice to me, be a little fond of your Constance. She did not always behave as she should, she did not always behave as she should. But forgive her, forgive her the past," she whispered, more softly, so that Addie should not hear. "Forgive her that past which is always there, which has never become the past for good and all. Forgive her ... and love her a little!"

She burst into nervous sobs and, impulsively, knelt down by her sister and laid her head on her breast and felt how poor and thin Adolphine was in her arms. A damp smell of rain was steaming from her muddy dress.

"Dear Constance!" said Adolphine, really touched. "Certainly, I care for you. And that past was so long ago: we have all of us forgotten about it."

But Constance sobbed and sobbed.

"Mamma!" said Addie.

She drew him to her also, held her sister and her boy in a close embrace.

"Come, Constance...."

"Mamma, don't cry.... You always have such a headache, Mummy, after crying like that."

She controlled herself, stood up; and Adolphine found a few kind words. Adolphine was certainly touched, but she was cross about that bolero and, besides, she found Addie better-looking, more taking, almost, than any of her own three ugly, lubberly boys. However, she kissed Constance and arranged for Constance to come and take tea with her next evening. When Constance was a little calmer and had laughed a little through her tears, Adolphine took her leave with a warm kiss:

"And I'll just leave Van Saetzema's card, shall I, Constance, here, by Karel's, for Van der Welcke? Then he'll get it when he arrives...."

She put down the card and, suddenly unable to restrain herself, went, as though in passing, to the bolero, looked at it and said, in a voice that bore no resemblance to the envious thoughts that still smouldered in her heart:

"But, Constance!... Do you still wear those short little jackets?"

"Oh, they've been the fashion so long!" answered Constance, still thinking of the visiting-cards.

"Well, I don't know: they'd be too short for me, at my age, I think!"

Seeing that she was younger than Constance, the remark was not only unkind, but dishonest; and Adolphine, now satisfied, went away.

Constance stared at the two visiting-cards and suddenly burst out sobbing again.

Addie took her in his arms. He was already nearly as tall as she was:

"Mamma," he said, gently, with his resolute lad's voice, "don't cry so; and go and lie down a little. You have to go to Grandmamma's to-night; and you'll be too tired if you don't rest first."

And he helped her to take off some of her things and settled her pillows for her.

She lay on the bed, sobbing convulsively, without really remembering why.

The boy sat down by the window, near the console-table, and took up his book, a story of the Boer war. A movement of his arm sent the two cards over. He just glanced down at them, at those two pieces of paste-board formalism, let them lie on the carpet and went on reading....

CHAPTER VII

That evening, Constance played bridge, though her head was still very bad. At Mamma van Lowe's request, she had brought Addie with her; and he had joined his boy- and girl-cousins in their round games. Constance was playing with Bertha, Gerrit and Uncle Ruyvenaer.

"Constance," said Bertha, "you mustn't think me unkind for only coming once to see you—and when you were out too—but I am so busy. I have sent you your invitation to-day for the wedding-functions. You'll come, of course, won't you?"

Bertha was the eldest daughter, Mrs. van Naghel van Voorde; her husband was secretary for the colonies; in their house, Constance had at once felt something of her father's house, in the old days: a big family; a circle which took a faint colonial tinge from the presence of the great Indian officials home from Java. Van Naghel had made his career through the protection of his father-in-law, the late viceroy; and their set also just grazed the edge of the diplomatic world and, of course, included a number of the chief officials of the home government as well. Although Constance had been only once, as yet, to their house, in the midst of the bustle of rehearsals for the wedding-theatricals, she at once felt something congenial there, something that was familiar to her, something of her former home: an atmosphere of distinction, of importance, which she had not known for many years past, but to which she yet felt herself drawn through the innate, instinctive vanity which she imagined was dead in her.

Constance was happy, though she still had a headache. Uncle Ruyvenaer was fussy but gay, because he was winning, with Gerrit for his partner. Bertha and Constance, their thoughts both far from the cards, went on talking, played badly. Bertha was almost entirely grey, greyer even than Mamma van Lowe. She had a rather ceremonious face and resembled her father: she had his hard, stiff features, his hard, dark eyes, his thin lips. Her eyes were always blinking, as though she had a difficulty in seeing. And in her manner of talking there was something abstracted, as though she were always thinking of something else. She was well-dressed, simply, in good taste.

"I think it so nice that your house is a sort of replica of our old house, when we were children," said Constance.

"Yes," said Bertha. "What are trumps?"

"You went diamonds yourself," said Gerrit, the cavalry-captain, tall, broad-chested and fair. "Attend to your game, Sis."

"And you have a very busy home, I suppose, Bertha?"

"Yes," said Bertha, "very busy."

And she played the wrong card.

"I have known all that bustle myself," said Constance. "It was like that in Rome, terribly busy: four or five things every day which you couldn't possibly avoid...."

Bertha smiled vaguely; and Constance suddenly felt that she mustn't talk about Rome. She winced: she could not mention De Staffelaer's name, must ignore all that period of importance.... It suddenly upset her nerves, for she had not reflected that, even among her brothers and sisters, she would have to be careful, to exercise tact. She had come to them just because she wanted to be able to let herself go, to be frank and natural; but she felt strongly that Bertha disapproved of her for venturing to refer to Rome. She would have liked to talk about Rome, partly from vanity, to remind her sister, the wife of a minister, who was "in the movement," that she too had known greatness and lived in the midst of it. But she felt that she must be humble, that she was nothing more than Mrs. van der Welcke, the sister who had made a false step in life, who had married her "lover" and who, years after, had been taken into favour by the charity of the family. This was clearly expressed in Bertha's hard, ceremonious Van Lowe face, with the blinking eyes, even though Bertha spoke not a word.

Constance was silent, went on playing; Uncle Ruyvenaer was noisy, cracked his jokes:

"The queen falls," he said, in his fat voice. "One more unfortunate!" he shouted, clamorously.

And, playing his ace, with a wide sweep of his hand he gathered in the trick. Constance went pale; and Bertha blinked her eyes till they closed entirely. But Bertha was too much used to Uncle's astounding vulgarities to be much disturbed by them and she answered her partner's call correctly.

Constance kept her presence of mind, played her cards. She could have burst into one of her nervous fits of sobbing, but she restrained herself, knowing that Uncle was tactless, noisy and common, but that he would never hurt her wilfully. And she was grateful to Gerrit when he came to her assistance:

"What a nice lad that boy of yours is, Constance."

"My Addie? Yes."

"A bit dignified for his years, but otherwise a fine little chap."

"He's always very good to me. We both dote on him."

"You must let him come to us often. Our house is one big nursery; and he'll keep young among that troop of mine."

"Very well, Gerrit, gladly. It's very kind of you."

"What is he going to be?"

"Van der Welcke wants him to go to the university first and then into the diplomatic service."

"Is that his line?"

"I don't know.... He's a little too stiff, perhaps.... But he's so young still."

"Send him to lunch with us on Wednesday; and then he can go for a walk with my crowd."

"Very well, I'll tell him."

"Yes," said Bertha, more cordially, as though waking from a dream. "He's a charming boy, only a little stiff."

"He's still rather strange here."

"He is very polite," said Bertha, "but distant. He has very nice manners, but, when he says, 'How d'ye do, Aunt?' it sounds as if he were talking to a stranger."

"Oh, Bertha, he is meeting such a lot of new uncles and aunts all at once!"

"He is a very nice boy. A handsome little fellow. Is he like his father?"

"Yes," said Constance, grudgingly.

She felt again that the past had cropped up once more. She felt that Bertha was thinking that Van der Welcke was a very good-looking man—she had seen his portrait at Mamma's—and that was why Constance had fallen in love with him.

But Gerrit laughed:

"Why do you say that in such a funny way, Sissy?"

"Did I?"

"One would think that you did not approve of your son's taking after his father!"

Constance was grateful: Gerrit was so easy, so natural; and she laughed:

"What nonsense!"

"Do you think I can't hear? 'Is he like his father?' 'Ye-e-es!' ..."

Of a sudden, she became very sincere, with Gerrit:

"Did I speak like that? Yes, it's silly of me, but I am a little jealous of Van der Welcke, where Addie is concerned. Silly of me, isn't it?"

Bertha looked severe, blinked her eyes. Uncle gathered in trick after trick:

"Game and rubber to us. We'll carry on the stakes, shall we?"

The sandwiches and drinks went round.

"Gerrit," said Constance, as she moved her chair beside his, "you're happy, aren't you, in your house, with your little wife and your children?"

Gerrit looked surprised:

"Why do you ask?"

"I had the impression."

"But why do you ask?"

"Well, aren't you?..."

"Yes, of course, of course. Of course I am, of course I am. Adeline!"

He beckoned to his wife, a plump, fair-haired little doll, a dear, sweet little woman of twenty-eight: she had seven children already, because Gerrit, who had married rather late in life, said that he must make up for lost time and get a whole troop together.

"Constance wants to know if we're happy."

"Silly Constance! Why, of course we are!" said Adeline.

"You have a dear little troop of children."

"Your boy is a darling, too."

They smiled, happy in their offspring. Gerrit, restless, moved his big limbs almost violently:

"Children, that's the one thing in life!" he shouted. "We don't mean to leave off till we have a dozen, do we, Line?"

"Gerrit, you're quite mad!"

"Oh, but I say, Constance, why leave that lad of yours all by himself? It's not good for a child."

"No, Gerrit, it's best as it is. It would not make us any happier to have a lot of children."

"I say, you were indiscreet enough to ask if we were happy; now it's my turn. I don't believe that you and your husband get on so very well together."

"Oh, well, we understand each other! Perhaps not even that! But Addie keeps us together. We both dote on him. Van der Welcke dotes on his boy. So do I. So do I. He is everything, both to him ... and to me...." Her eyes filled with tears. "We are nothing now ... to each other!" She was sitting between Gerrit and Adeline. "I did so *want* all of you!" she continued, taking each of them by the hand. "Be nice to me, will you? I am simply pining for affection. My child is all to me, but he is still so young; and I tell him too much as it is.... Heavens, what a life I have had these last few years! No, you were not kind! Why did you never, never once come to me, in Brussels?"

"But, Constance dear," said Gerrit, "if we had only known that you would have liked us to! Remember, you never sent us a line. You only wrote to Mamma; and she did go to see you once or twice. Own up: we had become strangers."

"Let us be friends again, then! Be nice to me! Your dear little wife ... I don't know her.... But you are my sister, too, Adeline, are you not? Be a little fond of me."

"Yes, of course, Constance. And let us see a lot of each other."

"Tell me, Gerrit; what is Bertha like now?"

"Bertha is very nice. Bertha is an exemplary mother, an excellent wife. Bertha has a busy life. They do a great deal of good, they live for their children, they see heaps of people. They are in the upper ten, or, rather, the upper two or three of the Hague. We are not, you know. And we never go to their big dinners; we are not in their set at all."

"I don't even go to Bertha's at-homes," said Adeline.

"And yet we are very good friends. And Bertha is very nice; and, when Adeline is expecting a baby, which is the usual state of affairs with us, Bertha is just like a mother. But she and her husband live in their own circle, which is very big and busy and important and smart and all the rest of it."

"So Adolphine and Van Saetzema...?"

"Oh, you needn't ask: they don't go to their dinners, at-homes, balls, etcetera, either. And that makes Adolphine furious. But we don't care in the least."

"And Aunt and Uncle Ruyvenaer?"

"They go to the at-home days," laughed Adeline, "but not to the dinners. And they have their own little Indian clique, which is very lively, but of course a thing quite by itself."

"Yes," reflected Constance. "A big family like ours necessarily has all sorts of sections...."

"And that is why Mamma is so devoted to her 'family-group,' in which all the different elements meet."

"Sometimes we don't see one another for weeks and months at a time, except on those Sunday evenings...."

"And tell me: Karel and Cateau...."

"Ka-rel and Ca-teau," said Gerrit, mimicking Cateau, "live ve-ry com-fortably and have ve-ry nice little din-ners all by their lit-tle selves, *don't* they, Adel-ine?"

They laughed.

"I was always fond of Karel," said Constance. "Of Karel and you, Gerrit.... Do you remember, in the river, behind the Palace at Buitenzorg...."

He looked at her long, seeking their childish past in her eyes:

"Yes, you were a pretty child then. You used to act all sorts of fairy-tales with us, among those great, spreading leaves: stories of a princess and fairies and knights and I don't know what. You were a darling of a child: such a dainty, pale little elf, in your white cotton *baadjet*[9]; and your brothers were in love with you.... But two years later, when I was a boy of sixteen and you fifteen, you suddenly became a stuck-up girl, in a long ball-dress, and you refused to dance with any one except old staff-officers and the secretary-general...."

"And what am I now?" she asked, smiling, with her soul full of sadness.

"The lost sister ... found again."

"Yes, the lost sister, indeed!"

"Come, Sissy, not so gloomy!"

"My life has been hard to bear."

"But you have your boy, your child. Children are everything."

"My life has been nothing but mistake upon mistake. And I am so afraid that I shan't bring up my boy properly."

"Then leave that to your husband!" said Gerrit, man-like.

"Oh, really?" said Adeline. "Is she to leave that to her husband?"

"Yes, Adeline. Just as we do. I the boys, you the girls."

"Oh, really?"

"But, Gerrit, if I leave Addie to Van der Welcke, I shall have nothing left, nothing."

---

[9] A diminutive of kabaai, a native jacket with sleeves.

"Then be bolder and have no fear."

"Oh, life is sometimes so difficult!... So, Adeline, Gerrit, you will care a little for your lost sister who has been found again?"

Adeline kissed Constance.

Mamma van Lowe approached, radiant, as always, at the "family-group" which she had brought together.

"Mamma, I am so glad, so happy, to be among you all!" murmured Constance.

The maids entered with the coats and wraps.

CHAPTER VIII

Two days later, Addie went to meet his father at the station.

"Daddy, Daddy!" he shouted, as Van der Welcke stepped from the train.

They embraced; Van der Welcke was much moved, because it was fifteen years since he had been in Holland. Addie helped Papa with his luggage, like a man; and they drove away in a cab.

"My boy, it's ten days since I saw you!"

"What kept you so long, Daddy?"

"Everything's settled now."

"And are we going to hunt for a house?"

"Yes."

He looked at his child with a laugh of delight, threw his arm over Addie's shoulder, drew him to him, full of a strange, oppressive sadness and content, because he was back, in Holland.

They pulled up at the hotel. Constance was waiting for them in her room.

"How are you, Constance?"

"How are you, Henri?"

"I've done everything."

"That's good. Your room is through here."

"Capital."

He rang, ordered coffee.

Her face at once became stiff and drawn. Addie poured out the coffee:

"Here you are, Dad."

"Thank you, my boy. And how do you like your Dutch country, my lad? How do you like all the little cousins?"

"Oh, I haven't seen much of them yet, but I'm going to Uncle Gerrit and Aunt Adeline's on Thursday."

"How many children have they?"

"Seven."

"By Jove! Is Mamma well, Constance?"

"Yes, very well."

"I've ... I've had a letter from Papa," he stammered. "They want us to come and see them soon at Driebergen...."

He was at last bringing her the long-expected reconciliation. She looked at him without a word.

"Here's the letter!" he said, handing it to her.

She read the letter. It was couched in the groping words of an old and old-fashioned man, who wrote seldom; an attempt at forgiving, at forgetting, at welcoming: laboured, but not insincere. The letter ended by saying that Henri's parents hoped soon to see him and Constance and Addie at Driebergen.

Her heart beat:

"So they are condescending to take me into favour!" she thought, bitterly. "Why only now? Why only now? My boy is thirteen; and they have never asked to see their only grandson. They are hard people! Why only now? I don't like them...."

But all she said was:

"It is very kind of your parents."

She had learnt that in Rome, to say one thing and mean another.

"And when do you want to go to Driebergen?" she asked.

"To-morrow."

"We were to have gone to tea, after dinner, at the Van Saetzemas': Adolphine and her husband."

"I am longing to see my father and mother."

"Very well; offend my family for the sake of yours and write and refuse the Van Saetzemas."

"There is no question of offending anybody. I am longing to see my parents; and we must show them that we appreciate their letter."

"Appreciate?" she asked, bitterly. "What am I to appreciate? That it took them thirteen years to say they would like to see their grandchild?"

"Your family weren't pining to see you either, all those years."

"That's not true. Mamma came to see us at Brussels."

He laughed, scornfully:

"In thirteen years, twice, for two days each time!"

She stamped her foot:

"Mamma is an old woman; she never travels."

"My parents also are old; and they have had a hard struggle with their principles and convictions."

"So I am to be grateful to them?"

He looked at her fixedly:

"Grateful?" he echoed. "You've never been that. Not to them nor to me...."

She clenched her fists:

"Again!" she screamed. "Always again and again! Nothing but reproaches for ruining your career, for ... for...."

She sobbed aloud.

"Mamma!" said Addie.

The boy was between them. He was everything to both of them. He never understood the cause of those quarrels, the ground of those reproaches: and, until now, he had never reflected how strange it was that his father's relations and his mother's were always so far away, so inaccessible. But he did not ask, even if he did not understand; and yet, though he did not understand this particular thing, he was no longer a child. He was a little man by now; and his heart was all the heavier because he did not know and did not understand. But he shouldered his burden like a hero.

She kissed the boy:

"Ah!" she wept. "You like him better than me, Addie: go to him, go to him!"

"Mamma," he said, "I love you both the same. Don't cry, Mamma; don't be so quick, so impatient...."

Van der Welcke drank his coffee.

She clasped the child to her, kissed him fiercely:

"I'm going out, Addie. You're very good, but I'm going out: I want air."

"Shall I go with you?"

"No, stay with Papa...."

She could not bear to see them together at this first moment of his return; after the past ten days, she must harden herself again to seeing him caress the child; and now, now she was running away, so that she might not see it. She put on her hat; kissed Addie once more, to show that she was not angry with him, was never angry with him; and went out.

"Papa," said Addie.

Van der Welcke looked gloomy, apprehensive.

"Why do you say those things to her, Papa?"

"My boy!" He drew a deep breath, embraced his son. "Addie," he said, "you've grown bigger than ever. How broad you're getting! You're quite a big chap, Addie; almost too big for your father to kiss and take on his knee."

"No, Daddy; I'm your own boy."

He sat down on Van der Welcke's knees, flung his arms about his father's neck, laid his soft, childish face against his father's close-shaven cheek.

"My little chap!"

Van der Welcke pressed the boy to him, felt calmer now, with that soft cheek against his.

"What do you start quarrelling at once for?"

"It's Mamma."

"And you answer her. Mamma's nerves are all on edge. Then don't answer her."

"What are Mamma's people like?"

"I think they're rather nice. Granny is very kind; and so are Aunt Bertha and Uncle Gerrit and Aunt Adeline. Mamma is very glad to see them all again. Are you glad to be in Holland and to be seeing Grandpapa and Grandmamma soon?"

"Yes, my boy."

"Then let us arrange when we shall go to Driebergen. Not to-morrow, for then you and Mamma are going to Uncle and Aunt van Saetzema's. Thursday, I promised to go to Uncle Gerrit's; but I can see the children any day. So let us go down on Thursday. And then to-morrow you can begin to look for a house."

"Very well, my boy, that will do."

"Shall I tell Mamma it's settled?"

"Yes." He clasped the child to him. "My Addie, my boy, my darling, my darling!"

"Silly old Father!"

He remained on Van der Welcke's knee, cheek to cheek. Outside, in the Voorhout, the rain pelted on the bare March trees; and grey mists loomed out of the distance, pale and shapeless, while the damp evening fell....

CHAPTER IX

That evening, after dinner, Van der Welcke, Constance and Addie went to Mrs. van Lowe's, where they found Dorine, who wanted to meet her brother-in-law.

"I was thinking of you to-day," she said. "I had a lot of errands to do, for Bertha; and so, as I was going through the town, I thought to myself, 'I'll go on to Duinoord and see if there are many houses to let.' I'm simply worn out!"

"But Dorine, how sweet of you!" said Constance.

Van der Welcke too was surprised:

"That's really extremely kind of you, my new sister!"

"Here is a list I made, with the rent, in most cases."

"Only, Dorine, Duinoord is so far from Mamma."

"Yes; but, Connie," said Mamma, "you can't get anything in this neighbourhood for eight hundred guilders."

"What's the use of living at the Hague," said Constance, impatiently, "and being an hour away from you? I want to live near you."

"Well, we shall see," Van der Welcke ventured to put in.

"See, see, see!" said Constance, angrily. "I want to have my own house quickly. The hotel is expensive; and I dislike it. By the time the furniture has come from Brussels, by the time we are settled...."

"Oh, well, Mummy," said Addie, decisively, "Rome wasn't built in a day, you know."

She smiled at once. Every word spoken by her child was a balm, an anodyne. The old grandmother smiled. Dorine smiled.

"Addie," said Mamma van Lowe, "you must do your best to help Papa and Mamma with the house."

"Yes, Granny. It won't be plain sailing...."

The child was more at his ease than on the Sunday evening. Granny was very kind; so was Aunt Dorine, to trot about like that, after those houses.

"Aunt Dorine, do you always run errands?"

Everybody laughed: it was a mania of Dorine's to traverse the Hague daily from end to end; she was a very willing creature and she was particularly busy just now for Bertha and Adolphine, because of the two weddings.

Ernst and Paul entered.

"We heard that Van der Welcke was at Mamma's," said Paul, "and we've come to be introduced."

"These at least are not visits *in optima forma*," thought Constance to herself.

Ernst resembled Bertha and blinked his eyes; but, in addition, he was odd, shy, always timid, even in the family-circle. There was something bashful about him, as though he wanted to run away as soon as he could. But he made an effort and suddenly asked Constance:

"Are you fond of china?"

"Delft, do you mean?"

"Yes. Are you fond of vases? I love vases. I have all sorts of vases. Have you ever thought of a vase: the shape, the symbol of a vase? No, you don't know what I mean. Will you come and see me one day, in my rooms? Will you come and lunch: you and your husband? Then I'll show you my vases."

Constance smiled:

"I should love to, Ernst. Have you so many rare vases?"

"Yes," he said in a proud whisper. "I have some very rare ones. I am always afraid they will be stolen. They are my children."

And he laughed; and she laughed too, while shrinking a little from him and from coming to those rooms filled with vases that were children. She did not know what more to say to Ernst; and she now told Mamma, softly, that old Mr. and Mrs. van der Welcke, her father- and mother-in-law, had asked them to Driebergen.

Mrs. van Lowe beamed and whispered:

"Child, I am so glad! I am so glad they have done that. It's been running in my head all this time, what attitude they would take up to you. After all, Adriaan is their grandson as well as mine."

"For thirteen years ..." Constance began, bitterly.

"Child, child, don't bear malice, don't bear malice. Make no more reproaches. All will come right, my child. I am so glad. They are different from us, dear, not so broad-minded, very orthodox and strict in their principles. And, when, at the time, they insisted that Van der Welcke should marry you, that was a great sacrifice on their part, child: it shattered their son's career."

"Why?" exclaimed Constance, in a whisper, but vehemently. "It shattered his career? Why? Why need he have left the service?"

"Dear, it was so difficult for him to remain, after the scandal."

Constance gave a scornful laugh:

"In that circle, where there is nothing but scandal which they hush up!"

"Hush, child: don't be so violent, don't be so irritable. I am so glad, Connie! I could kiss those old people. I will call on them too, when you have been ... to embrace them...."

Mamma was in tears. Constance pressed her hands to her breast: she was suffocating.

"Very well, Mamma," she said, softly and calmly. "I will be grateful, all my life long, to Papa and Mamma van der Welcke, to Henri, to you, to all of you!..."

"Child, don't be bitter. Try to be a little happy now, among us all. We will all try to be nice to you and to make you forget the past...."

"Mamma!..."

She embraced the old woman:

"Mamma, don't cry! I am happy, I really am, to be back, back among all of you!"

CHAPTER X

Two days later, Van der Welcke, Constance and Addie were in the train on their way to Driebergen. The boy, to whom Holland was a new country, was interested in the vague, dim, low-lying expanses bounded, on the mist-blurred horizons, by straggling rows of trees, with here and there a village-steeple; the wind-mills flung out their sails like despairing arms to the great jaundiced clouds, whose gloomy masses, driven by a rainy wind, scurried across the lowering skies. The boy asked question after question, sitting with his hand in his father's; and, to avoid the sight of that caress, Constance gazed out of the opposite window, in silence.

They had been to the Van Saetzemas the evening before; and, though Constance felt irritated at first, she ended with a passion of pity. Good heavens, how was it possible that Adolphine had become so common! Whom on earth did she get it from! Mamma, so refined and distinguished! Papa, her poor father, such an aristocrat, a gentleman of the old school!... And yet, perhaps, from the Ruyvenaers. You would never have taken Uncle for a brother of Mamma's. Was it from the Ruyvenaers, perhaps? Great heavens, how common Adolphine was!... Her husband was a boor; her house pretentious and slovenly; her girls, the two elder, pretentious, priggish, envious; Marie, the youngest girl, a sort of Cinderella, but a sweet, shy, down-trodden, quiet child.... But then there were the three boys, so repulsive, so slovenly, so rude.... What a crew, what a crew!... They had gone to take tea there quietly; but it turned out to be a sort of little evening-party: a regular rabble, as Van der Welcke, who was furious, had said. Two men in dress-coats and white ties; the others running through the entire scale of masculine attire: frock-coats, dinner-jackets, tweeds. Adolphine seemed always to send out ambiguous invitations; and people never knew what they should wear nor whom they would meet.... Floortje in a dirty, white, low-necked dress, if you please; Caroline and Marietje in walking-dress; Van Saetzema himself looking like a fat farmer, carrying on in his noisy way with Uncle Ruyvenaer: it was all so vulgar!... Aunt Ruyvenaer was always good-natured; and the girls, though very Indian-looking, were pleasant and natural and simple; but, for the rest, the evening, with all sorts of strangers, was a snare, especially for Van der Welcke, whom, as a brother-in-law, they might surely have welcomed in a more intimate and heartier fashion the first time they saw him, after refusing, for years, to recognize him as a member of the family! And, once back in the hotel, she had had a violent scene with her husband: he abusing that rabble of a family of hers, she, defending her family, against her own conviction, until Addie woke, got out of bed and begged them to be quiet, or he wouldn't be able to sleep.... The darling, how prettily he had said it, in that dear little decided way of his, like a regular little man: oh, where would they be without him! She sometimes thought, if he died, if they ever had to lose him, she would do away with herself! He was not their child: he was their treasure, their life. And she gave a glance at him; but, when she saw him sitting hand in hand with his father, while Van der Welcke tried to make out the distant village-steeples after all those years, she turned round again, quickly, with a jealous pang at her heart.... Oh, she felt sorry for Adolphine! She saw in Adolphine a struggle to be "in the swim," a desperate struggle, because Van Saetzema had nothing but a fine-sounding name: in everything else, he was an insignificant person, who had great difficulty in obtaining his promotion, after long years of waiting; married to Adolphine, no one knowing why she had taken him or he her; first trying to set up as an advocate and attorney at the Hague; later, receiving a billet in the Ministry of Justice, but never liked by Papa and never helped on by him, as Van Naghel had been; never thought much of by his superiors; now pushed into all sorts of little jobs and committees by Adolphine; trying to botch up some kind of political creed, in order to stand as a candidate for the Municipal Council, because Adolphine, always jealous and envious of Bertha's importance, wanted to see her own husband coming more and more to the front and had so little chance of realizing that ideal.... Yes, Adolphine must be inwardly furious when she thought of Bertha's household: her husband colonial secretary, after making money at the bar at Semarang; their house a replica of the dignified, stately paternal home of the old days: the same big dinners, the same good society, just verging on the diplomatic set. And so Adolphine gave those impossible "little evenings:" all sorts of persons dragged in anyhow; diversified elements that knew nothing of one another, never saw one another, were astonished to meet one another in those cramped drawing-rooms, full of faded specimens of amateur needle-work and dusty Makart bouquets; a rubber, a jingling duet by the girls, next the tables pushed aside and suddenly, by way of a dance, a mad romp, which sent a cloud of dust flying from the carpet: everything, everything in the same execrable taste, uninviting and, especially, common, with the thick sandwiches and the sluttish maid-servant, who shrugged her shoulders impertinently if the girls asked her to do a thing! Oh, Constance felt sorry for Adolphine, who was, after all, her sister; and she became aware, after years, as though it had been slumbering, of a warm family-affection for all her brothers and sisters and their children. Did she inherit it from her mother? A warm family-affection. She would have loved to have a friendly talk with Adolphine, to advise her to separate the different elements a little at those evenings of hers, to make her invitations less heterogeneous and to tell Floortje not to wear a soiled ball-dress on an occasion like that! And then those three boys, with their dirty hands, rushing about the crammed drawing-rooms without any idea of manners, so badly brought up compared with her Addie, who perhaps had not been brought up at all, but who was such a nice little fellow of himself, so polite, stiff though he might be, and who talked properly and not with a splutter of low Hague slang! Oh, it was dreadful! And she was so afraid that Addie might catch some of it.... Poor Adolphine, what a struggle, especially with all Bertha's unattainable perfection before her eyes! For they all suffered from jealousy in their family: she had it herself; and Adolphine had always had it very strongly-developed from a child: jealous of her elder sisters and brothers.... Would she ever be able to give Adolphine a word of advice? Now that Floortje's wedding was near at hand, couldn't she be of use to Adolphine? She thought it such a pity that her sister— a Van Lowe, after all—was becoming so common; and, after last night, she was so afraid of that wedding; and it would be all the worse because Bertha's Emilie was to be married about the same time, in May, a couple of months hence. In any case, she would talk to Mamma about it, not for the sake of interfering, but because Adolphine was her sister, because she cared for her as a sister and because she had a feeling of pity for her, genuine, heart-rending pity....

"Mamma, what are you looking at?"

It was Addie's voice; and she saw that the boy had come to sit by her, because it was her turn now. He always divided his favours like that between his father and mother. For Van der Welcke at once took up the *Nieuwe Rotterdammer* and buried himself in its wide pages, in his corner.

"Oh, so you've come to sit by me at last!" she whispered.

"Mummy, don't be so jealous: do you want me to chop myself in two?"

He talked to her, amused her. She always admired the way in which he talked, prettily, sensibly and divertingly, with a sort of talent for small-talk. Very likely he had acquired it because, without him, his father and mother would have been silent, when they were not quarrelling. He talked of a couple of houses which they had seen yesterday; he talked of the landscape, said it made him feel a Dutch boy at once— wasn't it funny?—and kept his mother amused like a gallant little cavalier. And yet he had nothing of a dandy about him: a broad, short, firmly-built little man, in a coloured shirt, a blue great-coat and knickerbockers. He wore a soft felt hat, shaped like a Boer hat. She didn't like that hat, but he insisted on having one. But, even with that hat, how handsome he was! Oh, what a good-looking boy he was! His frank, blue eyes, a little hard and grave; his fresh-coloured, firm cheeks, with those refined, clear-cut features, Henri's features; his small mouth, which she loved; his square shoulders; his pretty, knickerbockered legs, with the square knees and the slender, rounded calves. Her child, her child: he was her all in all! He was the happiness, the grace of her life; because of him her life was worth the living!

He talked, but she saw a grave look in his eyes, a look graver than usual. Yes, she felt it: it was because of what was awaiting them, in an hour's time; the reception by the grandparents down there, at Driebergen.... Van der Welcke also was nervous, did not speak a word, folded his newspaper, this side and that.... Constance' heart beat in her throat, which was dry and parched with nervousness. And Addie's look became more fixed, more serious than ever. Yes, she felt it. There was a tenderness in the child's voice, as though he wanted to say:

"Mind you bear up, Mummy, presently...."

And, the nearer they approached, the quieter they became: Henri in his newspaper; she staring through the window; while Addie himself found nothing more to say and sat quite still, with his hands in the pockets of his little great-coat. No, she could never forget that those two old people had taken thirteen years, not to accept her as their daughter, but to look upon her child as their grandchild. During all that time, not a letter, not an attempt at reconciliation: a complete silence, an absolute death towards their only son, towards their only grandson. She was not thinking of herself; she asked for no affection from them, only for cold civility. She felt so much resentment, so much resentment that, when she thought of it, she almost choked. And, over and above, came the crushing consciousness that she had to be grateful because those parents had sacrificed their son to her, as they had once said; because they had insisted that Henri should marry her, even though it shattered his career. And that, that was what she could never forgive, because it had always wounded, because it still wounded her vanity.

She would have been grateful, for her son's sake, if they had decided that Henri, after a retirement of some years, relying on his influential connections, should resume his career, with her by his side. De Staffelaer had left the diplomatic service, was living at his country-place near Haarlem; and they could never have met him abroad except by some extraordinary coincidence.... No, that she never would and never could forgive them, because of her wounded vanity; it was that which caused the bitterness that almost choked her: the "sacrifice," Henri's career shattered through her. Had she not for five years been the wife of the Netherlands minister at Rome? Had she not filled her position with tact, with grace, even with consummate knowledge of the world, until the Dutch colony praised her *salons* above those of the other Netherlands legations abroad? Had she not taken pride in that reputation, taken pleasure in the fact that the Dutch colony and Dutch travellers found something in her dinners and receptions that reminded them of Holland and home? How often had she not been told, "Mevrouw, with you, in Rome, everything is most charming, especially when compared with this place and that;" her countrymen used often to complain to her of the dulness and stiffness and exclusiveness of so many of their legations. Would she not have been in her right place by Van der Welcke's side, even though people might talk and cavil at first, because, she, the divorced wife of a minister plenipotentiary, had afterwards married the youngest secretary in the service! But she would have shown tact, it would have been forgotten, it would have subsided into the past. She refused to believe but that all this would have been possible, not for any one else, perhaps, but certainly for her. And this was her grievance, that those two old people—and Henri with them—had never been able to see this as she did; that they had given her their son, with an allowance that meant poverty—two alms for which she was expected to be grateful!—but had left her and him and their child in Brussels, in a corner, like some unnamable disgrace! No, that was a thing which she could never forgive, never, never, never!

She was so deep in her thoughts that she did not notice that the train had stopped and that they had arrived at Zeist-Driebergen.

"Mamma!" said Addie, softly.

She started, turned pale. But she was resolved to control herself, to be dignified, to show those old people that she was not a worthless woman, even though she had committed a mistake, a false step in her life: very well, a sin, if they pleased, because she had loved. Addie helped her to alight; and her gloved fingers trembled in his firm little hand. But she was resolved not to give way: she must keep quite calm; yes, she would be calm and dignified above all....

"There's the carriage," said Henri, in a stifled voice.

He recognized the very old carriage of years ago. He even recognized the old coachman, who looked at him and touched his hat. The footman who opened the carriage-door was a youth, whom he did not know. And the coachman, as an old servant, bent over to him and, in a quavering voice, using the old title, said:

"Morning, jonker. Good-morning, mevrouw."

"How are you, Dirk?" said Henri, in a dull voice.

They settled themselves in the carriage. And Constance saw that Henri was setting his lips, gritting his teeth and clenching his jaws, as though with a violent effort to stop himself from crying like a child. Now and then he shivered, nervously, and stared out of the window. He recognized the villas on either side of the road, looking so melancholy in the middle of the bleak March gardens that stretched hazily in the damp mist; he noticed how much had been pulled down to make way for new houses. How changed it was! What a lot had been built lately! But yet there was something under those great cloudy skies, heavy with eternal rain, in that road, in the gardens of those villas: something of the old days, something of his childhood, something of the time when he was young. He felt like an old man coming home again: he, scarcely eight-and-thirty! It was as though he were ashamed in the presence of the familiar! And, very secretly, too weak to accuse himself, he accused her, the woman sitting beside him, the woman four years older than himself. He too was thinking of Rome now, of the rooms of the Netherlands Legation, of her, then Mrs. de Staffelaer, the wife of his chief, of their love-affair, first in jest, then in earnest, until that terrible moment in the room where they used to meet; De Staffelaer in the doorway; Constance fleeing through another door; and his interview with the injured old man, who had been good to him, in a fatherly fashion! And he blamed her for it: it was her fault! He was a young man then, with hardly any knowledge of the world; she, a woman of twenty-eight, married for over five years, had enticed him, had been the temptress! It was she, it was she: he blamed her for it! He had not loved her at first, during the first stages of the flirtation. There had been a chat, a waltz, a jest. Yes, then it had turned to passion; but what was passion? The flame of a moment, flaring up and then extinguished. And he knew it: from that day, when he stood as a culprit in the presence of that dignified old man, from that day the flame was extinguished. And from that day he began to see the life that lay before him: the scandal, which filled all Rome; the despair of his pious parents, far away at home, in Holland; Constance in Florence: their first interview there, himself yielding to his parents' wishes and asking her to be his wife, to marry him in England as soon as the divorce was granted. Since then, he had always seen his fate hanging before him; and it had crushed him, so weak, so small.... Amid the wretchedness, amid the ruin of his young life, beside that woman in whom he, who did not take blame to himself, never lost sight of the worldly-wise temptress four years older than he, beside that woman, the eternal obstacle, and amid that wretchedness, the only grace had been the child. That which might have increased the misery had been the mercy, from the first moment that he set eyes on it, little, red morsel that it was: the darling child; the child that was his, though the fruit of their misery; the child that, as it grew older, became his comfort; the child that felt with its little hands over his face and in his hair; the child that said "Daddy;" the child that he smothered in his arms! The child, her child, it was true, but his child also: his child, his son, growing up and soon becoming the little moderator between them and the reason, also, why they remained together; the child, growing up to boyhood and, without understanding or knowing, still feeling the eternal struggle, the eternal misery, until its eyes became more grave and it felt that it was the moderator and the comforter. The child, there it sat, opposite him: his handsome, sturdy boy, who looked like him, with the fixed, earnest, gentle eyes; and he was now going to show him to his parents: her child, it was true, the fruit of their misery, but his child and their grandson.

The boy glanced from his father to his mother. They both sat opposite him and both silently looked out of the window, half-turning their backs upon each other. The boy would so gladly have taken their hands, the hands of both of them, and said something: a word to unite them at this moment, which he felt to be very serious; but he did not know the word, cleverly though he knew how to talk as a rule. He glanced from his father to his mother, from his mother to his father; and they, they did not look, dared not look at him, feeling his glance and filled to overflowing with their own thoughts. Then the boy felt life sinking very heavily, like a weight, upon his small breast. He drew a very deep breath, under the heavy weight, and his breath was a deep sigh.

They both now looked up, looked at their child. Henri would have liked to throw out his arms, to feel his child at his heart; but the carriage now turned through a gate and drove along a front garden of rounded lawns, in which the rose-bushes, swathed in straw, stood waiting for the spring.

CHAPTER XI

They stepped from the carriage; the hall-door opened. The curtains of the front room shook slightly, as though with the trembling touch of an old hand; but there was no one in the hall to receive them except the butler who had opened the door.

Then Constance said:

"Henri, you go in first. I'll come presently, with Addie, when you call me...."

He looked at her, hesitating to say that he himself wished to go in with Addie. But she had laid her hand on the boy's shoulder and looked at Van der Welcke so steadily that he understood that she would not consent. And he went in, staggering like a drunken man, went into the room where the window-curtains had trembled.

The butler retired, not knowing what to do. And Constance sat down on the oak settle and drew Addie beside her. So she was meekly waiting in the hall, waiting the pleasure of her father- and mother-in-law; but it was of her own will that she waited now, after waiting nearly fourteen years for a word that would have called her to them. With a woman's delicacy, she had let Henri go in first to his parents; but she had set her mind upon taking her boy to his grand-parents herself. It was for her to do that; she insisted on her privilege, her right.... Henri's hesitation had not escaped her; but she had laid her hand upon her son's shoulder, as though taking possession of him.

She did not know how long she waited, but it seemed very long; and she had time to see every detail of the hall: the oak wainscoting; the three or four family-portraits; a couple of old engravings of city-views; the Delft jugs on an antique cabinet; the staircase leading to the floor above; the oak doors of the rooms, which remained silent and closed. She saw the pattern of the tiles in the passage and the colours of the wide strip of Deventer carpet.... Then, at last, the door of the front room opened and an old man appeared. Constance rose. The old man had Henri's features, but more deeply furrowed, and his clean-shaven upper lip fell in; his straight nose was more prominent and his ivory forehead arched high above a scanty fringe of iron-grey hair. His eyes looked out blue and hard, as Henri's eyes looked out. He was tall, Henri was short; his shoulders were broad and bent in the long, dark coat, Henri was square and straight. His hands were long, wrinkled and bony and they trembled; and Henri's hands were short and broad.... She made her comparison in two or three seconds, standing with her hand on her son's shoulder. Then the old man said:

"Come in, Constance...."

She went, gently pushing Addie before her, and they entered the room. She saw an old woman, with a large face that in no way reminded her of Henri. The grey hair, parted in the middle, was set severely in a silver-stiff frame; her complexion was yellow and waxen; her dark-grey eyes were full of tears, and peered painfully through that misty haze. Her figure was bent in the dark stuff dress; her legs seemed to move with difficulty; and her stooping body was almost deformed. She was holding Henri's hand....

"Constance," the old woman began; and her trembling hands were raised as though for an embrace.

"Here is your grandson," said Constance, stiffly.

She pushed Addie a little nearer. The boy looked out of his steady eyes, which were the eyes of Henri and of the old man, and said:

"How do you do, Grandpapa and Grandmamma?"

In the large, sombre room, his voice sounded dull and yet firm. The old woman and the old man looked at the boy; and there was an oppressive silence. They looked at the boy, and they were so struck with amazement that they could not find a word to say. The old woman had taken Henri's hand again; and the tears flowed from her eyes. Henri's jaws grated and he shuddered, nervously:

"That's my boy," he said.

"So that is Adriaan," said the old woman, trembling, and her embrace, which had not reached Constance, now closed upon the child. He kissed her in his turn; and then the old man also embraced him and the child kissed him back.

"Hendrik," said the old woman. "Hendrik, how like ... how like Henri, when he was that age!"

The old man nodded gently. The past was coming back to the old people; and it was as if they saw their own son when he was thirteen. They were so much surprised at this that they could only stare at the boy, as though they did not believe their eyes, as though it were some strange dream.

Constance stood stiffly and said nothing. But the old woman now said:

"It is a great pleasure to us to see you here, Constance."

Constance tried to smile:

"You are very kind," she said, pleasantly.

"But do sit down," said the old woman, trembling, and she pointed to the chairs.

They all sat down; and Henri made an effort to talk naturally, about Driebergen. The past that lay between them was so high-heaped that it seemed as though they were never to approach one another across this obstacle. So many words that should have been spoken had remained unspoken, for the sake of an harmonious silence, that silence itself became a torture; and so many years were piled between the parents and the children that it seemed impossible for them now to reach one another with words. The words fell strangely in the sombre room, which looked out upon the March garden and upon the road paling away in the vague mists; the words fell like things, strangely, like hard, round things, material things, and struck against one another like marbles clashing together....

It was the painful talking on indifferent topics that was almost impossible. For the words constantly struck against things of the past, things painful to the touch; and there were no indifferent topics. When Henri said that Driebergen was very much changed, he was referring to his many years of absence. When Constance made a remark about Brussels, she was referring to her long residence there, during which her husband's parents had refused to see her and looked upon her as a disgrace. When they spoke of Addie's life as a small child, it was as though they two, the father and the mother, were reproaching the grandparents. There were no indifferent topics; and a despairing gloom hung between the old people and the child, because they could not reach the child across their son and their daughter-in-law.... Outside, the wind rose, howling; the heavy grey clouds descended upon them like a damp mist; and the rain clattered down. Henri had thought of asking his father to take him into the garden, to see if he still recognized it, but the pelting rain prevented him; and he saw nothing but his mother's tears. In his heart, he laid these to his wife's charge. The past was piled up as a wall between each soul and its neighbour.

The boy felt it. He felt his breathing oppressed with all that gloom; and again and again he wanted to sigh, but he kept back his sighs. He did not know what to say; and he gave his grandparents the impression of a quiet, subdued child, who was not happy. They spoke to him too as old people do to a child, with condescending kindness, pointing out the little things in the room. The boy, who was accustomed to be a man standing between his two parents, answered nothing except in shy monosyllables.

Henri and Constance avoided looking at each other; and each of them, even in the same conversation, talked as it were separately to the old people. They were to stay to lunch—the old-fashioned Dutch "coffee-drinking"—and return at five o'clock to the Hague. The butler came to say that luncheon was served and pushed back the sliding doors. The dining-room lay on this side of the great, closed conservatory, a gloomy shadow in the pale daylight that streaked in through the rain; and the mahogany furniture gleamed with reflected lights, the table shone white and glassy. They sat down: difficult words fell now and again and sounded hard in the somewhat chilly room. The old woman with much ceremony offered a soft-boiled egg, or a tongue-sandwich which lay neatly arranged with its fellows on a tray. She herself filled the small china coffee-cups. It all lasted very long, was all very solemn and proper, with much formality about the egg and the sandwich. Addie felt as if he could easily swallow both the egg and sandwich in one gulp; and he had to restrain himself in order to eat the egg slowly and neatly in little spoonfuls and to chew the sandwich with little bites, so as not to finish too soon nor deprive the table of its excuse for being so elaborately laid. He was not sure whether he was still hungry or not when Grandmamma offered him a second sandwich; but he took it, because otherwise he would not have known what to do with his hands. He sat like a small, stiff little boy, shyly; and, when he looked up at his father, it seemed to him that he too was sitting as if he had eaten his sandwich too fast. Grandmamma herself buttered his bread for him and offered it to him, ready cut into strips. He ate the narrow fingers with a great effort at self-control.

It lasted endlessly long; and the table remained white, bare and neat, now that the sandwiches were finished; the empty coffee-cups gave the only touch of untidiness: the broken, yellowy egg-shells Grandmamma had put away on the sideboard. When they rose, Grandpapa asked Henri to come and smoke a cigar in his study; Grandmamma stayed in the sitting-room with Constance and Addie. On the road outside, the rain splashed in the puddles.

Constance felt a stranger in this house. Nevertheless, her mood became softer, because the old woman's eyes, in the stiff, silver-framed face, were still sad and constantly filled with tears. She was very sensitive to any emotion in another; and, though she fought against it, she herself felt moved. She wanted to talk to this grandmother about her grandson; and so she said how clever he was, how good to his parents. Mrs. van der Welcke nodded good-naturedly, but continued to look upon Addie as a child, while Constance was talking of him as man. The old woman did not fully grasp the meaning of Constance' words, but the sound of them increased her emotion. She called Addie to her side, said that he must come and stay with them in the summer: it was delightful in the country then, for games. The boy had it on his lips to say that his parents could not do without him; but he felt that his words would sound strange and elderly and priggish. And he only said, very prettily:

"I should like to, Grandmamma."

He played at being a little child, because Grandmamma happened to look upon him as one. Really he was thinking of something very different, thinking of the houses which he had seen yesterday with Papa and Mamma and which his parents could not agree upon, in any particular: the neighbourhood, the division of the rooms. Because he knew that the hotel was expensive and that both Papa and Mamma would become less fidgety once they had a house, he thought of cutting the Gordian knot and going by himself to the owner of a nice house near the Woods, not so very far from Granny van Lowe's. If he didn't interfere, it would be weeks and weeks before Papa and Mamma made up their minds. He knew that to take a house was a very serious matter, but he also knew that Papa and Mamma would never agree. He must needs, therefore, risk something and he would hope for the best, hope that all would turn out well.

"A couple of houses farther on, there are two very nice little boys: you shall see them when you come in the summer, Adriaan."

"Yes, Grandmamma."

His voice sounded very refined and soft; and Constance had to smile. But, while he sat there stiffly, with his shoulders squared and his legs close together, he was dividing the rooms of the house near the Woods. Mamma, meanwhile, was exchanging toilsome words with Grandmamma. He portioned out the rooms. Downstairs, the drawing-room and the dining-room, more or less as at Uncle Gerrit's: those two rooms always communicated in Holland, with folding-doors between them. And the little conservatory. And the little garden was quite nice. Upstairs, the large room for Mamma and the smaller one for Papa; and it was jolly that he himself could have that sort of turret-room, with a bow-window, in between their two bedrooms. So he would be between Papa and Mamma. Above that, there was still a sort of attic floor, but that did not concern him: Mamma must manage that. It was rather risky perhaps, to go to that fat man to-morrow—a contractor, Papa called him—and tell him that Papa had sent him to say that he would take the house.... Perhaps that house in the something van Nassaustraat was better, bigger. But it was dearer also.... Perhaps Papa would be angry, if he acted just like that, off his own bat; but, of course, there would be nothing settled in black and white. Only, if Papa and Mamma once knew that he had been to the fat man, well, they might be a little angry at first, might squabble a bit more; and then both of them would look at him and laugh and they would take the house and everything would be all right.... If they did not decide a bit quicker, if they went on squabbling, their Brussels furniture would suddenly be there, in front of their noses, and they without a house to put it in.... It was true, Granny van Lowe had said, "Be careful about taking a house:" that was all very well when people agreed; but that's what Papa and Mamma never did. They had come to Holland, because he had said:

"Why, I'm a Dutch boy, aren't I? Then let's go!"

Well, they would take the house after he had been to the fat man. There was nothing else to be done, though it was risky.

Papa came downstairs with Grandpapa, looking more cheerful: perhaps he had been talking to his father. They sat on a little longer and Papa took out his watch once or twice....

Then the carriage drove up; the old coachman, who had known Papa as a small boy, drove them to the station, where they arrived twenty minutes too soon.

Quietly, without speaking, they walked up and down, waiting for the train....

CHAPTER XII

Next morning, Addie went to play with Uncle Gerrit and Aunt Adeline's children and thought it very jolly to romp about like that with six or seven little boy- and girl-cousins, the oldest a girl of eight years and the youngest a baby ten months old. He amused himself in a fatherly fashion with all these youngsters, inventing new games and causing a certain sensation as a big, new, strong cousin of thirteen. The whole morning, however, he was thinking of the fat man, to whom he had been very early to say that Papa would probably take the house and would like him to call at the Hotel des Indes at seven o'clock that evening. He had gone on to Uncle Gerrit's from there, and in his heart thought it rather a bore, for, after all, he must prepare Papa and Mamma for the visit of the fat man, who was to bring a draft of the lease with him. So, after eating a sandwich at Aunt Adeline's, he played a little longer with the children, who were not going out, because it was raining, and, soon after, hurried to the Alexanderstraat, to Granny van Lowe's, where he knew that he would find Mamma. Constance was sitting with her mother and telling her about Papa and Mamma van der Welcke and how they had received her. Uncle Paul was there. Addie, a little nervous, asked where Papa was, where Papa had gone that afternoon.

"Papa went to look at a couple of houses in the Nassau-Dillenburgstraat.... Did you enjoy yourself at Uncle Gerrit's?"

"Oh, yes, they are nice little things. What are you doing this afternoon, Mamma?"

"I shall stay on a little with Granny and then we are both going to Uncle and Aunt Ruyvenaer's. Will you come too, Addie?"

"Well, I really want to talk to Papa."

She was jealous at once:

"You can never be a moment without your father. What does it mean? I haven't seen you the whole morning; and the first thing you do is to ask for Papa! I don't know where Papa is. Papa has an appointment, I believe, at the Witte Club, where he was to meet some old friends; but you can't go to the Witte!"

"Isn't Papa coming back to dinner at the hotel?"

"I believe Papa intended to stay and dine at the Witte. But I really don't know. I'm not in the habit of controlling Papa's movements."

He looked at her thoughtfully:

"I must absolutely see Papa before seven o'clock, Mamma."

"But why before seven o'clock? Is there anything you want? Won't I do? Don't I count at all?"

"Yes," he said, "when you're not so cross. The owner of the house in the Kerkhoflaan, near the Woods, is coming to call before seven."

"How do you know?"

"I went to him this morning, on my way to Uncle Gerrit's."

"Well?"

"And I told him Papa would probably take the house and asked him to come to the hotel, at seven o'clock, and bring a draft of the lease with him."

He suddenly became very uncomfortable, because his grandmother and his uncle sat staring at him.

"But, Addie," said Granny van Lowe, not quite understanding, "how did you come to do that? Did Papa tell you to go?"

"No, Granny, Papa said nothing about it, but it's a very nice house indeed; and, if Papa and Mamma could only agree, I wouldn't interfere; but, as it is, I really must. Otherwise the furniture will be here from Brussels and Papa and Mamma still looking for a house, each in a different part of the town."

He talked fluently, but he was very uncomfortable and his face was as red as fire, for it was plain that Granny did not yet understand; and Uncle Paul sat shaking with laughter and trying to pull him between his knees; and this was no moment for romping.

"Oh, don't, Uncle Paul, please!...."

But Paul laughed and shook him by the shoulders; and Grandmamma frowned; and yet it was really very simple; and Mamma thought so too, for she said, calmly:

"Oh, you went to that house, did you?... The one near the Woods.... How many rooms did we say there were?"

"There are the two rooms opening into each other on the ground-floor," said Addie, standing, with a serious face, between Paul's knees. "Upstairs, you can have the big bedroom and Papa the smaller one, with a little room next to it as a smoking-room; and then I should like that turret-room, with the bow-window, you know...."

"Yes; but, Addie, the house in the Emmastraat has bigger rooms."

"It is farther from Granny and two hundred guilders dearer; so put the house in the Emmastraat out of your mind...."

Granny van Lowe sat looking before her in dumb amazement; Paul listened attentively; and Constance and Addie continued to discuss the merits and demerits of the two houses:

"There's a big cellar in the house near the Woods ... and a nice little garden, do you remember?... And I think it jolly to be close to the Woods."

"Yes; but, Addie, it seems to me that, in the Emmastraat ..."

"Do put that house out of your mind, Mamma: it's damp...."

"And the contractor is coming, you say?"

"Yes, at seven o'clock."

Mamma van Lowe could only sit and stare at her daughter and her grandson by turns. Paul burst into a fresh roar of laughter at the sight of his mother's face.

"Yes, Mother, these are the times we live in! I never dared take a house for you; now did I?"

Constance for the first time appeared to realize that Addie must seem a little queer to her mother:

"Oh, he's always like that!" she said. "He helps us. He's a man. Aren't you, my man?..."

He now went up to her and kissed her, to please her:

"So you see, I must find Papa before seven o'clock, or he'll be angry," he said, keeping to the point.

"Well, shall we go round to the Witte together?" asked Paul.

"Oh, Uncle, that would be awfully good of you!"

"But I can't take you in, old chap!"

"No, Uncle, I'll wait outside, if you'll just look for Papa and tell him I want to speak to him."

"About a house you've taken for him!"

"No, don't be silly, Uncle."

"Good-bye, Constance; good-bye, Mamma: I'm going with my Nephew Addie ... to the Witte!"

And Paul stood up, choking with laughter, while Addie, afraid of missing his father, urged him to hurry.

"But, my dear," asked Mrs. van Lowe, "does your boy always take the law into his own hands like that?"

"Oh, Mamma, he is such a help to us!"

"But what a way to bring him up! That's not a boy of thirteen!"

"He is a very uncommon child. Where should we be if he didn't help us."

"So you think Van der Welcke will take the house near the Woods?"

"I'm sure of it!... And I'm quite sure too that, if Addie hadn't interfered, in another six months we should still be at the hotel!"

Next day, Van der Welcke, Constance and Addie went to have one more look at the house near the Woods.

And the house was taken, on a five years' lease.

CHAPTER XIII

While Constance went in and out of the shops, on her numberless errands, Paul never left her side:

"You see," he said, glad to have some one to listen to him for the first time in his life, "what I call human wretchedness is not confined to the social question, but exists everywhere, everywhere.... Look around you, in the street. It's raining; and people are walking under dripping umbrellas. Look at those women in front of us: wet skirts; muddy shoes, worn at heel, splashing through the puddles: that is human wretchedness.... Look at that man over there: fat stomach; squinting eyes; gouty fingers clutching a shabby umbrella-handle: that is human wretchedness.... Everything that is ugly, squalid, muddy, drab, abnormal from any one point of view is human wretchedness.... Look at all those shops, where you buy—or don't buy—trashy manufactured things that have blood clinging to them, things which you are now pretending that you need for your house: that is human wretchedness.... It's all ugly; and the trail of a morbid civilization shows through it all.... Look around you, at those big, lying letters, those gaudy posters: that is human wretchedness. One cheats the other; and the whole thing has become such a matter of system that nobody is really taken in. It's the same with politics and religion as with a pound of sugar or a box of throat-lozenges. It is all humbug and all human wretchedness. And it drags on, piecemeal, through any average human life. It is all squalid, vulgar, insincere, selfish, ugly and full of human wretchedness. You think me a pessimist? Far from it. I am an idealist: in my own mind, I see everything in a rosy light. My power of imagination is so strong that I see everything white and gold and blue, like the marble statues of ancient temples, with their blue sky and golden sun. But, when I take leave of my imagination, then I see that everything is human wretchedness: wars; politics; the fat stomach of our friend yonder; the rain; and those pots and pans which you're wanting for your kitchen. All life, high and low, general and individual, in the masses and in the classes, is squalid, ugly, insincere and full of human wretchedness. Look at that creature over there. What a miserable object: she is knock-kneed; her nose is a yard long; and the reason why she's in this filthy street is absurd! You think I don't know what I'm talking about, but I do. You never see anything beautiful except at the theatre, or in a book, or in a picture or an etching ... or in a great writer taking up his pen in defence of some outcast, as Zola did. But even then there is very little; and I at once see the human wretchedness through it all: the pose, the affectation—even that of soberness—the ambition to succeed, or to imitate some one or other. No one has a pure thought for purity's sake ... except a fellow like Zola. There's no beauty anywhere. Have you ever noticed, in a train, or in a tram-car, or at a theatre, all those stupid, ugly faces, those crooked bodies, either too fat or too thin, one with a blink—like this—another with a squint—like that—this one with little hairs in his ears and that one with hands that make you sick. I don't know if you understand me; but all of this, with politics and the social question and those swarms of fat stomachs like our friend's just now: all of this is what I call human wretchedness.... I may write a book about it some day; but perhaps my book itself would be merely human wretchedness...."

In the meantime, he had been following his sister into three shops, one after the other, and she had managed to make her purchases in between his philosophizings. Whenever he saw his chance, he went on speaking, walking aslant beside her and talking into her ear, constantly having to move off the narrow pavements of the Hoogstraat and Veenestraat, losing her for a moment, because they were separated by a couple of carriages going at a foot-pace, but soon catching her up again. And he never lost the thread of his thoughts:

"I see that you have never reflected much, just like most women. What I say is quite new to you. You have not even observed much. You should observe, you should note all the queer things and people about you. Not that you and I ourselves are not queer and behave queerly. We can't help it. We too stumble along in our human wretchedness. But in your boy—it was quite attractive—I saw something funny; and yet he was very serious, much too serious for a child. Your boy, your boy is certainly a man of the future. Sometimes you see a thing like that in a child: then you say to yourself, 'He'll be this, he'll be that, he'll be the other, later on, when he grows up.' Do you follow me? No, I see you don't follow me. It's just your motherly vanity that feels flattered! Oh, how small you are! That is your human wretchedness! Don't you see the sunniness in your boy? No, you don't see it. I saw it at once. It was most attractive. Not one of Bertha's or Gerrit's or Adolphine's children has it. I can't explain it to you, you know, if you don't understand.... Yes, Sissy, life is not gay. You are forty-two and I am only thirty-five, but I find it no gayer than you do. I see through everything too clearly. I should never be able, consciously, to join in anything that had to do with human wretchedness, to join in rushing after an unnecessary object. That is why I do nothing, except observe. I'm a dilettante, you see. My income is enough to live on; and I loathe myself for playing the capitalist with a bit of money like that, like the middle-classes; but I can't help it, you know. I ought to have been rich, very rich. I should have planted a castle on a mountain-top, amid the whiteness of the Alps, and I would have done a great deal to mend human wretchedness; but I would not have had it around me. I hate it so: I turn sick at the smell of a beggar; and meantime my heart breaks and I feel a physical compassion for the poor devil. It's the fault of my stomach or my nerves: they simply turn. It's very unfortunate when you're built that way.... How do you like my new overcoat, with the velvet turn-back cuffs? They're rather neat, aren't they? Pity they're getting wet. But it's good velvet, it doesn't spoil.... And yet, yesterday, I was really alarmed when I saw my back in two looking-glasses. I had no idea that I had such a rotten back, a back full of human wretchedness, in spite of my fine overcoat. The line went like that, with a sort of hump. It was terrible; it upset me for all the rest of the day. Then, in the evening, I sat down at my piano and played *Isolde's Liebestod*; and then it all passed.... You can't make your little brother out, eh? A mad chap, you think, what? Yes, I am—almost—the maddest of the bunch. Bertha is very well-balanced; only, her eyes are always blinking.... Karel: what he might have become, I don't know; but now he is a round nought, kept in equilibrium by the roundness of Cateau with her owl's eyes.... Then you have Gerrit: he looks well-balanced, but isn't; puts on a jovial and genial air; and is a melancholy dreamer all the time. You don't believe it? You'll see it for yourself, when you know him better.... Next come you: well, you yourself tell me you've had a strange life with your two husbands.... After that, they all go down-hill: Ernst behaves very oddly; Dorine too is sometimes queer, with that everlasting trotting about; and I look at all their queerness and have a tile loose myself.... So you think we are a very sensible family? My dear Constance, we have a great crack running right through us, slanting, like that! But we are nice people and we don't let the world know. You wait: you'll see. And now, Sissy, here's your tram and here I leave you..."

He helped her in; and she saw him walk away under his umbrella, carefully drying with his handkerchief the velvet turn-back cuffs of his new overcoat.

CHAPTER XIV

Those were busy days at the Van Naghels, full of all kinds of excitement. Emilie was to be married in three weeks; and in a fortnight Van Naghel and Bertha expected their son Otto back from India, with his young wife and their two children.

Otto had taken his degree early, married and gone to Java at twenty-four with a billet in the civil service. But he was unable to stay, because his wife had fallen ill on the day of their arrival at Batavia and she had been ill ever since. It annoyed Van Naghel to see his son's career interrupted, even though he was still young and Van Naghel could easily find him another appointment in Holland. But he had always been against this match: a delicate Dutch girl, with no money. They would have to take charge of the children, in Holland; and, though he was well off, though his wife had some money of her own, though he had his salary as a minister, it was, all told, scarcely enough for the very expensive establishment which they kept up: the eldest son on his way home from India with his wife and two children; two boys, Frans and Henri, who had been at Leiden for over two years and who were obviously in no hurry to take their degrees; three girls who were all out, the second of whom was now going to be married; another boy, of sixteen, and a girl of fourteen; their *salon*, to gratify Van Naghel's ambition, an official *salon*, a meeting-place for members of the higher government-circles, while the diplomatic set just passed through it; so expensive an establishment, from first to last, that Bertha had to work miracles of economy to keep things going on fifty thousand guilders, more or less, a year. And everything was growing dearer: the two boys, Frans and Henri, cost almost three times as much as Otto had cost; Emilie and Marianne, of whom the former had been out three years and the other just one, had much grander ideas, in every way, than Louise, who had been out six; the boys at Leiden were both to take part in the masque this year; Emilie was receiving a trousseau that cost three times as much as the one which Bertha had had in her day from Papa and Mamma van Lowe; Marianne must have her simplest dresses lined with silk; Karel, the schoolboy, a tall, thin, weakly lad, but nevertheless a member of all sorts of football-, cricket- and tennis-clubs, had an allowance for pocket-money that was positively ridiculous; and Bertha saw tendencies in her youngest girl that made her anxious for the future. And so, outwardly, it was a great house full of movement: Papa a minister, the girls presented at Court, the boys spending money lustily; and, inwardly, there was many a despondent conversation between Van Naghel and Bertha as to how they could possibly economize: of course, Otto must be helped first; the boys, of course, must take their degrees first; the girls, of course, were bound to go out; and Karel, of course, was obliged to keep up his football- and cricket-clubs. They might give one dinner less each winter, but that was really the only thing. And, if the boys, after taking their degrees, were to cost as much money as Otto was costing now; if Louise and Marianne also got married and had to have the same trousseau as Emilie: if it was to go on like that, always and always, with never a moment for taking breath and saving a little: then they did not know what they were to do; for, let Bertha calculate as much as she pleased, the thing was not to be done on fifty thousand guilders a year.

Then, if Van Naghel lost his temper, he reproached Bertha, saying that it was all her fault, that she was a Van Lowe, that the Van Lowes had never been able to calculate, that the Van Lowes' own housekeeping had been run on much too extravagant a scale, in the old days; but Bertha, blinking her eyes unmoved, reminded him that he owed his career to Papa van Lowe, to Papa's connections in the years, following upon his term as governor-general, when he still had a great deal of influence in Holland; and she showed him her housekeeping-accounts, in which she had carefully made the different entries, telling him that, if he absolutely insisted upon living on the scale they did, it could not be done for less, with the best will in the world.... And, seeing no way out of it, they made friends again and did not mention the subject of money for another month; and, outwardly, it was the regular household of a minister of state, full of solid Dutch comfort, with a tinge of modernity superadded: the children very much up-to-date, but the parents, nevertheless, sensible people of weight and distinction, quite aware how far they themselves could go and how far they could let the children go. The real position was not even suspected by a soul. Bertha never spoke to anybody, not even to her mother, of anything that had the faintest connection with money. To their relations and friends, the house in the Bezuidenhout spread its broad front with such an air of solid dignity, the staircases, the drawing-rooms and dining-room with their stately, handsome furniture, the children's rooms—more modern in style, but still with no flimsy affectation of tawdry elegance—all made so great an impression of imperishable prosperity that no one could ever have suspected that the two parents sometimes sat reckoning up for hours at a time to see whether they could reduce their expenses by as much as a thousand guilders that month. In this house of theirs, notwithstanding all the bustle, the dinners, the approaching wedding, the approaching home-coming of the eldest son, for whom a set of rooms was being prepared on the top floor, everything seemed to go so methodically, without any trouble—busily, it is true, but quite harmoniously—that no one would ever have suspected the least difficulty. Mamma van Lowe was constantly at Bertha's during these days and even neglected Constance a little; but she loved this bustle: the alterations on the top floor; the fuss about the trousseau; the rehearsals of the wedding-theatricals; the long tables to be laid, the flowers to be arranged, the visits to be discussed; dresses brought home; the undergraduates constantly at the Hague, noisy, merry and young: the old woman loved all this; it reminded her of her own house in the old days; it was like a repetition of her young life: only, she thought, she herself had often worried about money, even though Van Lowe had been able to save during his term as governor-general, and Bertha was so entirely without financial cares! How delightful that was! And she, as the grandmother, also interested herself in Emilie's trousseau; she gave her advice and never thought about money; she slowly climbed the stairs to the top floor, to see the nursery which had been got ready for her two great-grandchildren on the way home from India, proud of that fourth generation, delighting in that large family, that busy household, all that movement, which she missed so greatly in her own house, where her quiet life was interrupted only by those family-gatherings every Sunday evening. Yes, she loved being with Van Naghel and Bertha; she loved to see her son-in-law take a prominent place in society, as her husband had done in his time; she loved the solid, dignified, official house; and the modernity of the children, although now and again she would shake her head in disapproval, made her smile for all that, because she thought that people must go with the times and that Van Naghel and Bertha were very sensible not to hold the reins too tightly. It was true, there were manners which she did not like: that going out of young girls alone, letting themselves in at night with their latch-keys; but then it was only to a few personal friends, said Bertha, and it was impossible to make other arrangements. Yes, the old woman loved being here, in the house of her eldest daughter; and, though she cared for all her children, because they were her children, she felt more in her element at Bertha's than in the comfortable, middle-class, selfish house of Karel and Cateau, whom she blamed for having no children; and, though, she also liked Gerrit and Adeline's younger household, with the children ranging from eight years down to ten months, a troop of fair-haired mites, things were too simple and everyday for her there, did not remind her of her ancient splendours; she could not stand Gerrit sometimes, when he made fun of his old mother for mentioning, quite casually, that she had met the Russian envoy at Bertha's. And going to Adolphine and Van Saetzema's always vexed her: it was as though she did not recognize her child in Adolphine, with her badly-arranged, common house and Adolphine so bitter and so envious and jealous of Bertha, especially now that Floortje was engaged and her trousseau, of course, could not be as fine as Emilie's. Yes, she went to Adolphine's and discussed the trousseau there also, but she did not care about it: not because it was simple—a trousseau could be very nice in spite of that—but because Adolphine was always so spiteful, with her perpetual "Yes, that's good enough for us; but, of course, at Bertha's!..." She felt herself a mother to all her children—had she a favourite? She thought not—but she was very fond of going to Bertha's, because she found her own past there.

And what the old woman loved above all things in Bertha's house was the mutual sympathy, the family-affection which she had always fostered in her own house, which she still fostered, thanks to the institution of those Sunday evenings, to keep the children together at all costs. Yes, in Van Naghel and Bertha that sentiment, that constant thought for the children was very strong; and there was one thing which Mamma van Lowe had not done and which Bertha was doing, which was to receive the son again, after he had once left the house, now that he was returning with a sick wife and two little children. It touched her: oh, how good they were to their tribe; and what a thousand pities that that little doll-wife was so ill! And the children, too, had that same family-affection among themselves. Otto had always kept up a busy correspondence with his eldest sister, Louise, who was twenty-five and came next to him in age; the two Leiden boys were exceedingly nice to their three fashionable little sisters and Henri was even a little bit jealous because Emilie was engaged; only Karel was perhaps rather too much out of doors and away from the family-circle for so young a boy, with all his clubs and his importance; and, because of that, Marietje, the youngest girl, of fourteen, was left a good deal alone. And yet they all liked Marietje: her big brothers, the other girls.... Yes, that was the charming thing with all those children: the family-affection, the fondness for one another, the pride in the names of Van Lowe and Van Naghel, the refusal to suffer any outsider to say a word against a member of the family, even though criticism was not spared within the home itself. But that any acquaintance should dare to reflect upon a member of the family, that they would none of them permit. They had felt that fondness, that tenderness, even for Constance, because she was a sister. And the old lady remembered, in so far as concerned Constance, the philosophical reflexions of her youngest son, Paul; the trouble which Dorine had taken to assemble all the brothers and sisters on that first Sunday-evening; the ready compliance of all her children, for, out of respect to her, none of them had criticized that erring sister in front of her. She saw it in all of them: the family-affection for one another. They all felt themselves to be brothers and sisters; they stood up for one another, even though there were differences of opinion sometimes and even jealousy; they felt united within the family-circle.

That was the crowning glory of her old age, as a mother and grandmother. It represented to her a beautiful idea, a natural ideal, an illusion attained: a comfort for the peaceful declining years of the lonely woman in her big house. That she preferred to be lonely in her big house and would not have Dorine, nor Ernst, nor Paul to live with her was an eccentricity which in no way detracted from her cult of the beautiful idea, from her perfect happiness at seeing the ideal realized, the illusion attained. She had a happy old age. She had also had much sorrow in her big household, in spite of all her splendour, but not more than her natural share: money-troubles, because neither Van Lowe nor she was economical; two children lost, one after the other; while Constance' false step was certainly a very heavy blow, under which she suspected that Van Lowe had really succumbed, suffering silently and incessantly because of the grief which his favourite daughter had caused him.... But she, though she too had suffered, had shown greater elasticity, had not counted all that sorrow for more than her human lot, such as might befall any large household. And that she now, in her extreme old age, had all her children gathered about her in the same town, in a close family-circle, in an affectionate family-life: this she considered a great happiness; she thanked God for it. She had no more religion of the church-going kind than was held to be correct in her circle, which was very different from the orthodox Calvinistic circle of a few old Hague families; but she was grateful to God in her heart. She thanked God for her happiness, for her happy old age. All was well, now that she had Constance back also, back with the others at the Hague. Next to Buitenzorg, the Hague had always been to her the ideal place of residence. The Court was there; and her husband had taught her to love splendour. There was an atmosphere of official eminence in their circle in which she took pleasure as in an element that had become natural to her and in which Van Naghel and Bertha also had attained their distinction and their high position. Karel had returned to the Hague, after burgomastering elsewhere; and in him she had her son back again, although, in her secret heart, she did not like Cateau. Gerrit, who had been a subaltern at Deventer and Venlo, was now a captain at the Hague. And the other children had never left the Hague; she had always been able to keep them round her.

She was happy and she was not unthankful. She was even thankful that Otto was returning—although the reason, his wife's illness, was a sad one—because she would see her great-grandchildren. They were her first; she felt a new joy because of them, an unknown emotion. She had felt something like it when Otto himself was born, her first grandchild; but now that feeling was almost more intense, perhaps because it was a fourth generation, a continuation of the family, even though they were Van Naghels and not Van Lowes. She was a woman: she did not care so much about the name. Bertha was her daughter, Otto her grandson, his children her grandchildren. She traced them back in this way to herself and the sound of the name mattered less to her. They were her children, her grandchildren, her great-grandchildren; and she loved them all; with one great love, with a clannish love. That she lived alone in her big house was because she was old and could bear bustle only when it was expected, when she could prepare for it. The Sunday evenings were bustling, but they did not tire her. But to have Paul or Dorine living with her, to be for ever hearing them going in and out would have worked on her nerves. She wandered daily through all the rooms of the big house to see if everything was tidy and in its place. Dorine was slovenly; and Paul was anything but easy to get on with; and Ernst, with his collection of curiosities, she would never be able to have with her, because she was afraid of all the microbes that hang about those old things. But nevertheless she loved them all and she was glad that they lived at the Hague and that she saw them regularly. She was like that and no otherwise.

And she now came every day to Bertha's, waiting for Otto and his children, until Constance grew jealous and reproached her, saying that she never came to her new house near the Woods.

CHAPTER XV

The Van Naghels gave an evening-party at the Oude Doelen Hotel, two days subsequent to the signing of the marriage-contract between Emilie and Van Raven: a dinner, for relations and intimate friends, of nearly a hundred covers. After that, the young people were to do some theatricals; and, after that, there was a dance. Dinner was over; and Adolphine asked Uncle Ruyvenaer:

"Were you at their dinner-party two nights ago?"

"What dinner-party?"

"The day before yesterday, after the contract. They gave a dinner at their house. About sixty people. Only their smart friends and their Court set. We were not asked. Mamma went. But none of the brothers and sisters."

"I did not even know there was a dinner. We called in the afternoon to congratulate the bride and bridegroom."

"Well, that evening they gave their grand affair. To-night is only a small party for us and the rag-tag of their acquaintance. The other night, Bertha wore a low-necked dress and a train. To-night, she has a high frock."

Uncle laughed:

"Yes," he said, "these parties at hotels are always scratch affairs. The dinner was only so-so."

"Regular hotel-food."

"H'm. The champagne was good," said Uncle, who had drunk his fill.

"How badly Van Naghel spoke! Does he speak as badly as that when he introduces his Indian budget? And what a figure Van Raven's mother cuts! She looks like I don't know what!"

"Still, they're smart people."

"Yes, of course they're smart, or Bertha would never have seized upon him for her daughter! He's a fast creature, that future nephew of mine. And how Emilie hangs on to him! If Floortje hung on to Dijkerhof like that, I should give her a good talking-to when we got home. Emilie behaves just like a street-girl."

Uncle was in a good humour, because he had plenty to drink; he was puffing a bit and would have liked to undo a button of his waistcoat: that dress-waistcoat of his was getting rather tight for him.

"How pretty Floortje is looking, Adolphine. That white suits her."

She laughed happily; she felt flattered:

"Yes, doesn't it? It makes Emilie look so pale."

Mamma van Lowe passed on Otto van Naghel's arm:

"Is Frances better, my boy?"

"Yes, Granny, she's pretty well to-day. But she gets tired so soon."

He was tall and thin, with a scowl above his hard Van Lowe eyes, his grandfather's eyes. His two years in Java had made him so bitter that it was painful for his grandmother and his parents to listen to him.

"What a pity, Otto, that you had to leave India!"

"Oh, bah, Granny, what a country! It's all very well for you to talk: you know India as the wife of a resident and as the wife of the governor-general. But for young people, starting life...."

"Papa would have helped you, you know...."

"A lot of help Papa could have given!... A beastly country; a dirty, wretched country!"

"But, Otto, I thought it delightful."

"No doubt, in your palace at Buitenzorg. That goes without saying. But were you ever clerk to the magistrates at Rankas-Betoeng?"

"No."

"No, of course not. And that with a wife who topples over like a ninepin, twice a week, with the heat, flat on the floor!"

"Otto!"

"Oh, come, Grandmamma! It's the most confounded, beastly, filthy country I ever was in. We had much better sell those colonies to England; she'll only take them from us, one day, if we don't."

"Otto, really I'm not used to this language!"

"Oh, yes, Granny, I know all that official bombast about India! But we can't all be governor-general or colonial minister. If I ever become that, I shall begin to worship India at once."

"You're upset because Frances is ill."

"Ill? Ill? It takes a woman to be ill. She's not even that. She's a reed. If you blow upon her, she breaks."

"She was a delicate little thing as a girl, Otto."

"Well, but look here, Granny: I can't turn her into a robust little thing, can I?"

"For shame, Otto! Don't be so bitter. You've got two darling little children."

"Yes, children; I wish I hadn't. I'm sorry for the poor little devils.... Is the show beginning now? Tableaux-vivants, arranged by dear old Louise.... A play without words by Frans and Henri.... Stale things, these wedding-parties, always. I thought ours insufferable."

"My dear Otto, you're in an intolerable humour."

"I'm always like that now, Granny."

"Then I strongly advise you to exercise a little self-control, or you will never have any happiness in life, in your own or your wife's or your family's."

"The family doesn't affect my happiness."

"What do you mean, Otto?"

"Why, I don't live and move and have my being in my family, Granny!"

"Oh, really, my boy, you're too horrid! Take me back to my seat. I see your mother beckoning to me: she wants me to sit between her and Aunt Ruyvenaer. The performance is beginning...."

"Ye-e-es," Cateau was whining to Van Saetzema, Van der Welcke and Karel. "An evening-party of six-ty peo-ple. And the Rus-sian *Minister* was there, and the Mis-tress of the *Robes.*"

"Well, after all, if they have so many acquaintances," said Karel, under his breath, by way of excuse.

"Ye-e-es, but, Ka-rel, none of the fam-ily. Van der Wel-cke, were *you* invited, by chance?"

"No."

"Oh, not you ei-ther? Well, I should have *thought* that she would have asked Con-stance...."

"Why?" asked Van der Welcke, coldly.

"We-ell, because she used to go to *Court*, in the *old* days. And you *too*, didn't you, Van der Welcke?"

"Yes, I too," said Van der Welcke, drily.

"Van der Welcke," said Karel. "Did you get that card of mine?"

"What card?"

"Why, when you were expected in town, I called and left a card on you."

"So did I, you know, Van der Welcke," interrupted Van Saetzema.

"Oh, yes," said Van der Welcke. "It was very civil of you fellows. Well, I'll leave a card on you one of these days."

"Oh, I didn't mention it for that!" said Van Saetzema.

"I didn't mention it on that account!" echoed Karel, swelling with geniality. "Only I should have thought it a bore if it had been mislaid."

"Ye-es," whimpered Cateau. "Because then it would have looked as if we weren't friend-ly.... How red the *bride* looks, Saet-ze-ma! That white makes Em-ilie look so *very* red."

"Yellow, rather," said Van Saetzema.

"Ye-es," droned Cateau. "Now your Floortje, Saet-ze-ma, looks so *sweet* in white. And what a *nice* fellow Dij-kerhof is! Such a thorough *man*. But how pale Ber-tha looks!"

"Green, rather," said Van der Welcke, very seriously.

Cateau looked up, with her owl's eyes:

"Green?" she repeated, cautiously. "Do you re-ally think Ber-tha looks *green*, Van der Wel-cke? Yes, she is tired, no doubt."

"To-morrow," thought Van der Welcke, "all the Hague will know that I thought Bertha looked green...."

A tableau was discovered in the distance. The idea was Paul's and he explained it to Constance:

"You see, it represents Luxury. The great wheel crushing down upon Marietje and Carolientje is Industry; and Floortje is Luxury, standing in a dancing attitude on Industry and scattering gold and ropes of pearls at twopence a rope. It's not quite clear, perhaps, Luxury standing upon Industry and crushing Marianne and Carolientje. Floortje is fidgeting and giggling. Oh, I must tell you, Adolphine was delighted when she heard that Floortje, her Floortje, was to be Luxury and to crush Bertha's Marianne!"

Constance, surrounded by all her family, was in a gentle, happy mood:

"Oh, Paul, it's a very nice, motherly feeling on Adolphine's part, to like to see her child happy before another...."

Paul spluttered with laughter:

"So you think that Floortje is happy as Luxury, on the top of Marianne and that Marianne suffers badly underneath! Connie, how sentimental you are to-night and what silly things you say!... But you're looking very nice. Come, let's go and sit down here. Your hair is turning grey, but I have an idea that you leave it untouched for some coquettish reason, because it goes so well with your young features. It's a very pretty shade of grey. It's not old hair. But you're young still, you know. And you're looking nice, very nice...."

"I believe you're making fun of me...."

"I love good-looking people; and one sees so few of them. Just glance round the room: all ugly people; one walks crooked, another has a stoop, this one's bust sticks out for miles, that one has a fat stomach. I can't stand parts of the body that bulge: it makes me sick to look at them.... Yes, to be accurate, nearly everybody's ugly. Do you know, if you were to take all the heroines out of all the novels in the world, you'd just get one heap of pretty women. No novelist ever dares take an ugly, squinting, crooked or hump-backed heroine. If I were a rich man, I'd offer a prize for a hideous heroine.... Yes, look at Aunt Lot," and he imitated Mrs. Ruyvenaer's Indian accent, "glitter*ing* with dia*monds;* and her two hands patting her brown satin stomach. Another stomach; and I can't stand stomachs.... But good-natured, all the same, is Auntie! Look at Uncle: he's unbuttoned his waistcoat, the rude fellow!... Have you noticed my waistcoat, Connie? It's white drill, it's very smart.... I say, Connie, look at Mamma: what a grand old woman, the way she walks, laughs and talks! Now that's something like: you see at once that she's a great lady. Look at old Mrs. Friesesteijn beside her: common, noisy, spiteful; a figure like a charwoman's. Hideous, hideous!... Look at Ernst, Connie. Would you ever believe that was a brother of mine? Just like an old Jew; and what a dress-coat, what a dress-coat! Where on earth did the beggar get it cut? He spends all his money on jugs and vases!... Look at Gerrit, Connie. He's pretending to be gay again, the jolly hussar, with the broad chest all over lace frogs. Poor fellow, he's dying of melancholy! You don't believe me? It's true, I assure you.... Look at Adolphine, Connie. Just like a bird talking slander: pip, pip, pip! How

Bertha's ears must tingle! Great Heavens, those eyes of Bertha's, always blinking! She ought to have something done to them.... Look at Dorine, Connie. She always looks repulsive.... As a matter of fact, Connie, there are only two good-looking people in the room: Mamma and yourself...."

"And you, Paul...."

"Your husband has a good figure too: he has an attractive back. I have an eye for nice backs. I don't like my own back; and yet my coat sits well, doesn't it? A dress-coat is a very tricky thing. Nowadays, there is hardly a tailor who can cut a good dress-coat. Yes, my waistcoat is very smart: just look at it. The buttons are smart, aren't they? They are uncut sapphires. Yes, you have a smart little brother.... Come, take my arm and let's walk round the room. Have you heard: they're all furious, the Ruyvenaers, the Saetzemas, Karel and Cateau, because they were not asked to the first party? The idea was to give it before the signing of the contract, but Otto's arrival came and upset it. He's another failure, that Otto, with his little tissue-paper wife.... Look at those Van Ravens, Connie. They're hanging on for all they're worth to Van Naghel and Bertha, lest they should be degraded at being seen with the Saetzemas.... Tell me, Connie: are you glad to be back? Are you really fond of all these relations?... I don't believe I have that family-affection which you and Mamma have; and Bertha; and Dorine. Bertha has it in her own house; Dorine and Mamma go scattering kindnesses broadcast over all the children and grandchildren.... I say, Connie, this is what people call enjoying themselves, because two of them are going to get married. But look all round: there's not a soul really enjoying himself. And that's what Van Naghel and Bertha spend a couple of thousand guilders on: giving them some dinner and a dance and letting them gaze at my Luxury, with Floortje dancing on top of Marianne. Look at those faces. Not one is naturally cheerful. Nature, nature, Connie: there's no such thing as nature among people like ourselves! We have not a gesture, not a word, not even a thought that is natural. It's all pose and humbug with every one of us; and nobody is taken in by it. Really, it's a disgusting business, a society like ours, what one calls good society. Can't you understand an anarchist loving to fling a bomb into the midst of us: for instance, at Uncle Ruyvenaer's stomach? No anarchist likes a stomach: the stomach is the trademark of the bourgeois.... Now they're going to dance: look how hideously they're spinning round the room. Just like palsied sparrows. We human beings are much too solemn and heavy to dance with any grace. Look, it's almost ghastly. Through all that pretence at elegance and smartness and dancing and gaiety, you can see that one has a stomach-ache and another a head-ache, that Van Naghel is thinking of how they went for him in the Chamber yesterday and Adolphine wondering how she shall make her wedding-parties seem only half as grand as Bertha's. . .."

She let him talk and he never ended: he could go on prattling for ever. His mother, sisters and nieces often told him to stop, moved away and left him in the midst of his outpourings; but Constance liked him, saw, indeed, a good deal of truth in what he said, in spite of all his humbug. He saw through the people around him with an insight which surprised her and which she was startled to find was not wholly inaccurate. It was certainly true that these people were not simply natural and merry.

They had come there from politeness to Bertha and Van Naghel; but, in reality, one was tired, the other envious....

"Auntie," said Emilie, who was walking round the room on Van Raven's arm, "if Paul once gets hold of you, he'll never let you go...."

She called her youngest uncle by his Christian name. She was really a pretty girl, though Paul did not see any good-looking people there, and, by the side of her, her future husband was such a pale, insignificant person that people wondered why she had accepted him. She was rather thin, but there was something dainty, uncommon and original about her in her cloudy white frock; she had a pair of charming eyes of a strangely-twinkling gold-grey, like an unknown jewel; her hair was reddish, with a glint of gold in it; and there were a few tiny freckles on the clear-white complexion which often goes with that hair. She had a pretty laugh, a soft voice, a coaxing way of being nice and saying pleasant things; and, above all, she possessed an innate distinction and, as she passed, white and gleaming, she had something, one would almost have said, of a very beautiful alabaster ornament, or of a snowy azalea in the sunlight: a luminous fairness, dainty and transparently veined with palest blue. Constance knew that Emilie had a talent, something more than the usual girlish accomplishment, for painting, but that, in her busy life as a young society-girl, she had never had the opportunity to develop it. And Constance wondered at Van Raven, pale, thin, stuttering, stammering, spruce and yet awkward, with one shoulder higher than the other and his three hairs of a moustache twisted up towards his eyes. He was at the Foreign Office and he belonged to a family whose rigid Dutch orthodoxy was shocked by much in the Van Lowes, in the Van Naghels and especially in the Indian element of the Ruyvenaers: nevertheless, in view of the general reputation for wealth enjoyed by the colonial secretary, they had considered his daughter a suitable match for their son. Van Naghel and Bertha were making her a handsome allowance.

When Emilie and Van Raven passed on, exchanging civilities with the guests, Constance expressed her surprise to Paul:

"Can she really be fond of him?"

"She? Not a bit of it! Then why is she marrying him, you ask? That's just the mystery. Van Naghel and Bertha are not husband-hunters, like Adolphine. Louise has had three proposals and refused them all. And why Emilietje—that delicate, white little thing, who really has something nice about her: something artistic, something dainty, something exquisite and, I should say, almost something natural—why she accepted that weedy ass, who puts on German ways on the strength of a fortnight in Berlin, with his moustache twisted *À la Kaiser* and his stiff military bows, I really cannot tell you. Bertha, who was very glad when Otto got married, cried when Emilietje accepted this chap. The fellow's as stupid as my foot.... Those are neat socks of mine, aren't they?... Yes, Connie, why do some people get married? Adolphine and Saetzema: why? I ask you, in Heaven's name, why? Otto and Frances: why?"

She felt that he had it on his lips to say:

"And you and Van der Welcke: why?"

But he did not; and he ran on:

"Marriage is a terrible thing, I think. To pick out one among hundreds and say, 'I'll marry you, I'll live with you, I'll sleep with you, I'll eat with you, I'll have children by you, I'll grow old with you, I'll die with you: are you willing?' Great God, Connie, how is it possible that people ever get married? It's a toss-up always: I shudder when I think of it!"

"Paul, tell me: who are all these people?"

She knew hardly one of the acquaintances: some sixty people lost among the forty members of the family. This was the first time that she had "gone out" again at the Hague; and, although many of the guests had asked to be introduced to her, she had not talked much, had forgotten the names at once. Paul, greatly in his element, explained to her where the people had come from, to what set they belonged: people who did not know or never saw one another, or else did not bow although they knew one another, brought together at this wedding-party because one family knew the Van Naghels and the other the Van Ravens. It was doubtless because of these foreign elements that the party was so stiff, that the conversation was constantly flagging, that the people who did not dance wandered aimlessly around, watching the dancers with a look of resigned martyrdom. Emilietje moved about among them, white, diaphanous and very charming: with Van Raven at her heels, she exchanged a word with every one. Van Naghel and Bertha also were quietly busy as host and hostess, as society-people who are used to that sort of thing and who go through it mechanically, really thinking of what they will have to do next day. The members of the family kept on popping up among the mere acquaintances. And, in the midst of them all, the most fidgety was Dorine: she was very fussy, as usual, worked herself into a fever collecting things for the cotillion, did not dance, but just trotted about: Paul christened her the camel.

It was strange, perhaps, but Constance felt happy and contented at Paul's side. She had seen nothing of the sort for years; and she felt a certain peace and satisfaction at being in the midst of her own relations. Tears were constantly coming to her eyes: she did not know why. At the first Sunday-evenings at Mamma's, she had not felt this family-affection so intensely, perhaps because she was still too timid. Oh, how had she ever managed to live through those fourteen lonely years at Brussels! For years she had felt the delight of love, sympathy and friendship only for her child; and now she felt it for all of them. Through her there passed once more that feeling which was so strong in Mamma: an inward glow which she had not known for years, a good, comfortable feeling that she could now grow old, that henceforth she could devote herself to her child, in the familiar atmosphere of home and domesticity. And she did not notice, did not suspect that the family and the acquaintances were stealthily examining her, judging her and condemning her.

"She's a fast woman," said Mrs. Van Raven, Emilie's future mother-in-law, to Mrs. Friesesteijn. "It's a great trial for the Van Naghels to have this sister turning up from Brussels."

"After fourteen years," said the old lady, sharply, eager for news, for scandal, "after fourteen years, to give occasion for rooting up all those old memories!"

And Mrs. Friesesteijn was delighted that Constance had done so.

"She killed her father."

"I knew De Staffelaer. No one ever had a word to say against him."

"During all those years, her husband's people refused to know her."

"I hear that she is intriguing like anything to go down to them now."

"The child is not Van der Welcke's."

"No, his father was an Italian."

"She's really a most improper person."

"Marie's her mother, after all: one can't blame *her*."

"But the family...."

"Ought to have stopped her...."

"From coming to the Hague."

"That's what I think, mevrouw."

"Yes, so do I."

"She's living on her husband's people."

"Well, the Van Lowes all got something from the father, you know."

"It wasn't much."

"No, not much."

"It's a very unhappy marriage."

"Yes; and the boy is shockingly brought up."

"They let him do as he likes."

"Just think, mevrouw: *the boy took the house for them!*"

"You don't mean it!"

"Yes, really!"

"What a state of affairs: it's all so immoral!"

"What did she come to the Hague for?"

"She was bored in Brussels. And she wants to thrust herself forward here, at Court."

"So I heard."

"Yes, that's so. Old connections, you see: the Van Naghels and so on. She wants to go to Court."

"Oh, but the Van Naghels will take good care that she doesn't."

"At least, they will if they're wise."

"What an example for the girls, that aunt of theirs!"

"You know, De Staffelaer found her in Van der Welcke's arms."

The two old ladies whispered:

"No!"

"Yes, really!..."

"He's a low fellow, too."

"Yes, there's a woman in Brussels."

"If they had only stayed there!"

"How very select Aunt Constance is to-night," said Floortje to Dijkerhof.

"She's been sitting with Paul the whole evening," he answered.

"Of course, no one is good enough for her!"

"No. When you've been the wife of a diplomatist...."

"And afterwards Baroness van der Welcke...."

"What did they come to the Hague for, exactly?"

"Mamma thinks, because she is afraid that, when Grandmamma, who doesn't look far ahead, dies...."

"Well, what then?"

"Well, that she won't get her full rights."

"Oh, nonsense!"

"I tell you, she doesn't trust us."

"But, surely there's a will; and, in any case, the law ..."

"Yes, but she doesn't know that, by Dutch law, all the children share and share alike. And, to make sure of what she's to get, she wants to be on the spot when Grandmamma dies. They owe a heap of money."

"And does he do nothing for a living?"

"No. He used to sell wine at Brussels."

"Nice people, those relations of yours, though they are barons and diplomatists!"

"Oh, we don't look upon them as relations! Mamma said so distinctly."

"And so," said Mr. Van Raven to Van Naghel and Van Saetzema, "you think they came to live here merely ..."

"Because they were feeling very lonely in Brussels."

"But the family...?"

"Were against it. I myself discussed with Mamma van Lowe whether if wouldn't be better to advise them not to ..."

"And?..."

"Well, Mamma is the mother, you see. When all is said, Constance is her daughter. We all of us gave way. And then it is so very long ago that...."

"I must say," said Mr. Van Raven, emphasizing his words, "that it was very _generous_ of you all."

"Yes, Van Naghel took a very generous view of the case," said Van Saetzema, who looked up greatly to his brother-in-law—a minister, an excellency—flattering him, keeping on friendly terms with him.

"And we all did, all of us, as Van Naghel thought right."

"Still, one never knows," said Mr. Van Raven, thoughtfully. "But, forgive me: she is your sister-in-law; and it is *very* generous, *most* generous of you...."

Two aunts of Adeline's stopped the fair-haired little mother:

"Adelientje!"

"Yes, Auntie?"

"That new sister of yours: do you like her?"

"Is she nice?"

"Yes, Auntie, really very nice."

"But she's been an improper woman."

"Oh, Auntie!"

"Yes, yes, yes, my girl, we know all about it; you be careful."

"And don't become hand-in-glove too quickly."

"You're so thoughtless, Adelientje."

"And Gerrit is so good-natured."

"Take care, both of you!"

"A woman like that can do him harm in his career."

"Oh, come, Auntie! If the Van Naghels receive them!"

"Yes, but the Van Naghels disapprove of them strongly."

"Still, she's their sister."

"Everybody's talking about them. People say...."

"What?"

"That Constance is not ... well, that she's not her father's child!"

"But Auntie, that's a frightful thing to say!"

"Because the Van Lowes were always so respectable, she can't...."

"No, she can't be a daughter of...."

"Of old Van Lowe's."

"I say, Auntie, this is scurrilous!"

"Adelientje!"

"Auntie, I won't listen to another word!"

Cousins of the Van Saetzemas', talking with the IJkstras, relations of Cateau's:

"Poor dear Adolphine!"

"She's furious!"

"What at?"

"Oh, all sorts of things! First, because the Van Naghels gave a party at which the whole family were ignored."

"Oh, well, that certainly was rather...."

"Then, because Adolphine has no room in her house to give a party at which she would ignore the family in her turn."

"And because of the seat which she was given at dinner this evening."

"And because of Emilietje's two witnesses: her Uncle Van Naghel, the Queen's Commissary in Overijssel, and Karel van Lowe, whereas she says that Van Saetzema is older than Karel and therefore...."

"And also because of Emilietje's frock, because that flimsy white thing came from Brussels and cost three hundred francs."

"What a heap Van Naghel must be spending on the wedding!"

"No, it's Bertha: it's the Van Lowes who always throw money about."

"Exactly, that's what I say: Adolphine does the same thing, just as though she could afford it."

"That's because all of those Van Lowes are eaten up with pride and conceit."

"Yes, since the father became governor-general, they have always acted like megalomaniacs."

"The old lady is a regular peacock."

"And Bertha, with her smart acquaintances!"

"And then that Mrs. van der Welcke: she's got a nice past to look back upon! And she behaves as though she were the Queen!"

"They're quite an ordinary family, the Van Lowes."

"Yes, they're nobodies: the grandfather was a grocer."

"No!"

"Yes, I assure you!"

"And that mad Ernst, who's always studying the family-papers to discover if they are not of noble descent!"

"Oh, he's mad, if you like!"

"In fact, they're all a little bit mad."

"Yes, there's a strain of it in all of them."

"A strain? Something more than a strain *I* call it. And it's continued in the Van Naghels."

"Adolphine's the best of the lot."

"She's a megalomaniac, though, for all that."

"I say, this Mrs. van der Welcke: what has she come here for?"

"Well, she thinks the whole thing has blown over. It was fifteen years ago, you see. And she's married to Van der Welcke."

"Not according to Dutch law."

"No, but she can get married again."

"Yes, but they are not, they are *not* married according to Dutch law."

"Well, in that case, *I* don't look upon them as married at all!"

"Not according to Dutch...."

"No, but...."

"Yes...."

"No...."

"Yes...."

The party ended and the guests departed.

CHAPTER XVI

Next day, Emilie and Marianne van Naghel were hard at work in their boudoir. They shared a sitting-room between them; Louise, the eldest sister, had one to herself. Emilie was taking down water-colours from the wall:

"The room was so bright and cheerful!" she said, softly, and put the drawings together.

Marianne suddenly burst into sobs. The room was all topsy-turvy, because Emilie was collecting her belongings, and the wall-paper now showed in fresh, unfaded rectangular patches.

"What on earth do you want to marry that horrid man for!" cried Marianne, sobbing. "We were so happy, the two of us; we were always together. With you married, I shall have no one; and I hate the idea of arranging my room all over again."

Emilie seemed to be staring blankly into a blank future:

"Oh, come, Marianne: I shall still be at the Hague!"

"No, I've lost you!" sobbed Marianne, passionately. "What did you see in that man, what *did* you see in him?" She embraced her sister violently and insisted. "Tell me, tell me: what did you see in that man?"

"In Eduard? I love him."

"Oh?" said Marianne. "Is that all it means, loving a man? Is that love?"

A maid entered:

"Freule, there's a box come from Brussels, with your dresses. Mevrouw wants to know if it can be brought up at once, so as not to make a litter downstairs."

"Yes, they can bring it up."

Overwrought, Marianne had sunk into a chair and closed her eyes. She was in a state of nervous excitement, while Emilie, with strange calmness, was collecting boxes, portraits, ornaments.

"Emilie," said Marianne, resignedly, "what a mess you're making!"

"Never mind, I'm taking it all away."

"Yes, that's just it: everything's going away, everything's going away!"

"Marianne, do control yourself."

Two maids came dragging along a packing-case.

"Where shall we put it, freule?"

"Leave it there, in the passage."

Bertha came upstairs:

"Unpack it at once, Emilie, or the things will crease."

"Do you think it's my wedding-dress?"

"I expect so."

"Then it can go on the bed."

"No, it had better be hung in the wardrobe."

The servants opened the packing-case and produced cardboard boxes. A third maid entered:

"A bill from Van der Laan's, mevrouw."

"Marianne, here's my key-basket; just pay it, will you? It's sixty-six guilders."

The two Leiden boys came upstairs:

"Jolly beastly, I call it," said Frans. "You never find any one in the drawing-room, when you come home. Either it's a party, or else everything's upside down."

"Bless my soul, girls," said Henri, "look at the state your room's in!"

"I say, shall I help you unpack?"

"Mevrouw, I can't understand what the young mevrouw's *baboe*[10] says...."

"*Mau apa,*[11] Alima?"

"*Njonja moeda*[12] asks if *njonja besar*[13] would mind coming upstairs," said the *baboe*, in Malay.

"Yes, I'll come at once."

"What are you all doing here?" asked Marietje, at the door. "Mamma, has Emilie's dress come? May I see?"

"If you please, mevrouw, the old mevrouw and Mrs. van der Welcke are downstairs.... Shall I ask them to wait in the drawing-room?"

"Granny!" shouted Frans over the balusters.

"Half a moment!" said Henri, rushing down the stairs. "I'll fetch Granny and Auntie."

Marianne began sobbing again:

"My dear child, what's the matter now?" exclaimed Bertha.

"I'm going mad!" cried Marianne.

Emilie kissed her.

Old Mrs. van Lowe came slowly up the stairs, gallantly escorted by her grandson, and was met on the landing by her other grandson.

"Granny, Emilie's wedding-dress has come and she's going to try it on!" cried Marietje, excitedly.

"Am I in the way?" asked Constance.

"No, of course not, Constance," said Bertha.

"Come in."

---

[10] Maid, nurse.

[11] What is it?

[12] The young mistress, as who should say, the young mem-sahib.

[13] The great mistress, or great mem-sahib, used of the wives of residents and other high officials.

All the doors of the boudoir and bedroom were open. Louise came in—she usually kept out of the way at busy times—and, together with Bertha and the lady's maid, shook out the white dress, which straightway filled the whole room with a snowy whiteness....

"What is it, *baboe*?" asked Mrs. van Lowe. "*Njonja moeda* asks if *njonja besar* would come upstairs," repeated the *baboe*. "But perhaps if the *kandjeng njonja besar*[14] could come...." she added, piling on the titles out of respect for the old lady, who had once been the *njonja besar Bogor.*[15]

"Then I'll go up," said the old lady. "Constance, will you come too?..."

Very slowly, a little tired after the stairs, the old lady climbed up, with her hand on the baluster-rail. Constance followed her. On the top floor, there was a sudden draught; doors slammed.

"*Baboe*.... Is there a window open?"

The *baboe* ran about stupidly, unfamiliar as yet with Dutch doors and windows.

In a sitting-room, they found Frances, Otto's wife, with the two children.

"But, Frances, you've got a window open!"

"Oh, Grandmamma, I was suffocating!"

"*Baboe*, shut the window at once! Frances, how could you!"

"I can't, *kandjeng*!" sighed the *baboe*, pressing with the strength of a gnat on the bars of the solid Dutch window.

Constance helped her, pushed down the window.

"This is Aunt Constance, who has come to make your acquaintance, Frances. But Frances, you're still in your *sarong* and *kabaai*!"[16]

"Isn't that allowed, Granny? How d'ye do, Aunt?"

"Child, how Indian you've become in these few years!" cried the old lady, angrier than Constance remembered ever seeing her. "How is it possible, how is it possible! Have you forgotten Holland? In March, with the window open, in a tearing draught, with both the children, you in *sarong* and *kabaai* and Huig in a little shirt! Do you want to kill yourself and the children? *Baboe*, put a *baadje* on *sinjo*![17] Frances, Frances, I spent years and years in India, but even in India I was nearly always dressed; and, when I came back to Holland, I had not forgotten Holland in the way in which you, a purely Dutch girl, have forgotten it in these few years!"

---

[14] The old great mem-sahib.

[15] The governor-general's mem-sahib. Bogor is the native name of Buitenzorg, in Java, which contains the governor-general's palace.

[16] The native skirt, or garment wound tightly round the loins, and sleeved jacket, forming a costume which is worn pretty generally as an indoor dress by European ladies in Java.

[17] The young gentleman.

The old woman had taken the child on her own lap and was dressing it more warmly.

"Grandmamma, how you're grumbling.... It'd be better if you told cook to make Ottelientje's *boeboer*[18] properly: the child can't eat that starch they give her. And she told *baboe* that she had no time to cook it differently. The whole house has gone mad because Emilie is getting married. We really can't stay here, on the top floor at Papa and Mamma's."

"Frances, dress yourself first, or I shall get really angry."

"*Allah*, Grandmamma!" cried Frances, irritably; but, when Constance gave her the same advice, she flung a wrapper over her *sarong* and *kabaai* and remained like that, with her bare feet in slippers.

"No wonder you're always ill!" grumbled Grandmamma, still busying herself with the child.

"Oh, Aunt Constance, I wonder if you would run down to the kitchen and tell cook that Ottelientje can't have her *boeboer* made like that?"

"My dear Frances," laughed Constance, "the cook has never seen me, nor I her: and, if I went to her kitchen and talked about the *boeboer*, she would only turn me out."

"What a country to live in, Holland!" cried Frances. "My child is starving for food!"

"I'll go down to Mamma, if you like...."

"Yes, do, would you?"

Constance went downstairs. In the boudoir, Emilie, in her wedding-dress, was standing in front of a long glass. The heavy white satin crushed her, looked hard and cruel upon her, now that her hair was not done and she tired and pale.

"The bodice doesn't fit. It will simply have to go back to Brussels," said Bertha.

"It's sickening!" said Emilie; and the word sounded almost like a curse between her lips.

"Marianne, will you write the letter? I'll pin the dress up. Or no, I had better write myself. Constance, do look!"

"There's a crease here," said Constance, "but it's not very bad. Daren't you have it altered here?"

"Upon my word, I'm paying...." Bertha began, but she checked herself and did not say how much. "And to have it fit badly into the bargain!"

"Bertha, Frances asked me to come and see you."

"What about?"

"There's some trouble about Ottelientje's *boeboer*."

"I'll go up," said Bertha, worn-out though she was.

---

[18] Broth, pap.

The maid, holding up Emilie's train, followed her into the bedroom; Marianne and Constance remained behind alone. Constance saw that Marianne was crying.

"What is it, dear?"

"Oh, Auntie!"

"What is it?"

"Is life worth all this bother and fuss? Getting married, moving your things, dancing, giving dinners and parties, ordering dresses that don't fit and cost hundreds, being ill, having babies, eating *boeboer.* Auntie, is it really all worth while?"

"Why, Marianne, I might be listening to Paul!"

"Oh, no, I'm not so eloquent as Paul! But I'm suffocating with it all, I'm stifling and I'm terribly, terribly, terribly unhappy!"

"Marianne!"

The young girl suddenly burst into nervous sobs and threw herself into Constance' arms. Around her, the room was one scene of confusion; the doors were all open.

"Marianne, let me shut the doors."

"No, Auntie, don't mind about that, but stay with me, do! It's more than I can stand, more than I can stand! I'm so tired of this rush, of this unnecessary excitement, of the party yesterday, of those tableaux-vivants, of Floortje's jealousy, of Aunt Adolphine's spitefulness, I am tired, tired, tired of everything. I can't stand it, Auntie. I'm so fond of Emilie, we've always been together, it was so nice, so jolly; and now, all at once, she's getting married to that hateful man; and she's taking away her sketches; and it's all over; and now everything's gone, everything's gone! And Henri too is so upset about it: he dotes on Emilie, just as I do, and he can't understand either what she's doing it for. She's very happy here; Papa and Mamma and all the rest are fond of her; we had such a nice life, even if it was a bit overdone and I don't care for that everlasting going out; but now it's all over, all over! I sat crying with Henri yesterday; and at the party we had to be gay; and every one thought that he was gay, the gay undergraduate; and the poor boy was miserable; and yesterday I had to appear in that tableau; and Floortje was so horrid and spiteful; and Henri and Frans had a dialogue to do; and the poor boy couldn't speak his words; and I ask you, Auntie, why all this unhappiness, when we were so happy together?"

She clenched her fists and, through her sobs, suddenly began to laugh aloud:

"Oh, Auntie!... Ha, ha!... Oh, Auntie!... Don't mind what I say! I am mad, I am mad, but it's they who are driving me mad: Mamma, the boys, the servants, the *baboe,* Frances and the children! It's one great merry-go-round! Ha, ha!... Did you ever see such an everlasting rush as we have in this house?"

She was now sobbing and laughing together; and suddenly she remembered that she had let herself go too much with a strange aunt and that Mamma did not like these spontaneous confidences to strangers; and, because she wanted to recover herself, she suddenly became rather dignified and asked:

"Did you enjoy yourself fairly yesterday, Aunt Constance?"

"Yes, Marianne, I thought it very nice to be back among you all."

"Don't you like Brussels better than the Hague?"

"It was so quiet for us, lately, in Brussels."

"Rome, I should like to see Rome."

"Yes, Rome is beautiful."

They were now silent and they both felt that things of the past parted them, the new, strange aunt, who had come back from the past, and the young girl, who was suddenly afraid of it.

And, without understanding why, Marianne sighed, in the midst of this shrinking fear:

"Oh, for a joy, a real joy that would fill me entirely! No more dinners and dresses and excitement about nothing, but a real joy, a great joy!"

She felt so strange, so giddy, but she still found strength to say:

"It's a pity that you were away from us so long. We should always have liked you and Uncle very much, but now you are both so strange still, to all of us."

"Yes," replied Constance, very wearily.

And she did not understand why she suddenly felt very sad, as though, after all, for manifold reasons, she had not done well to come back, though there had been that hunger for her own people, her own kith and kin....

"A joy, a great joy!" Marianne again sighed, softly.

And she pressed her hands to her breast, as though distressed by her strange longing....

CHAPTER XVII

The furniture arrived from Brussels; and Constance found it delightful to arrange her house near the Woods. She had never expected to be so happy, just because she was back in her own country and among her family-circle. It was April, but it was still winter: a chill, damp winter, which seemed never to have done raining; above the Woods and the Kerkhoflaan, the heavy clouds were for ever gathering, sailing up as though from a mysterious cloud-realm, spreading the sorrowful tints of the lowland skies over the atmosphere, hanging everlastingly like a beautiful, leaden-hued melancholy of lilac grey, sometimes with the coppery glow of a light that always gleamed very faintly and never conquered, but just shone like copper in between the grey; and the endless rain clattered down, the endless wind howled through the bare trees, the endless clouds pushed and drove along, borne on the stormy squalls, as though there were an endless combat overhead, a cloud-life of which men below knew nothing. It was a melancholy of day after day; and yet, strangely enough, it stirred Constance gratefully: she smiled at the clouds, the clouds of lilac streaked with glowing copper as though a distant conflagration were shining through a watery mist; and very soon her house grew dear to her and she was glad that she lived in it. Addie was not going to school yet, but was working hard to pass his examination in July for the second class in the grammar-school. He was having a few private lessons and, for the rest, studied zealously in his room, which, built out, with a bow-window and a little leaden, peaked roof, he grandiloquently called his turret-room. He had helped Constance to get settled: he had helped Van der Welcke with his room; and now he worked and slept between the rooms of his parents and separated them and, whenever it became necessary, united them.... Strange, this family-life in the little house, where the parents, through grudges and grievances heaped up for years, could hardly exchange the least word, could hardly even be silent, without a tension in both their faces and in both their souls; where every detail of domestic life—a piece of furniture displaced, a door opened or shut—at once led to a discord which turned the tension into an offence. The very least thing provoked a bitter word; a reproach flashed out on the instant; resentment was constantly boiling over. And amid it all was the boy, adored by both with a mutual jealousy that made their adoration almost morbid, each hoping simultaneously that the boy would now speak to him or her and award his caress to her or him; and, if this hope were disappointed, at once an averted glance, uncontrolled envy, a nervous discomfort that was almost a physical illness.... And, by a miracle that had become a forbearing and compassionate grace, the boy, who was still the child of their love, was only a little older, for all this everlasting discord, than his actual years; had only grown a little more serious, feeling himself, at a very early age, to be the mediator; and, now that he was a couple of years older, now that he was thirteen, accepted this mediation, almost unconsciously, as an appointed task and a bounden duty, with only very deep in his childish heart the ache of it all, that things were so, because he loved both his parents. At table, at both meals, the child talked and the two parents smiled, though they avoided each other's glances, though, to each other, their words were cruel and pitilessly cold. After lunch, it was always:

"Addie, what are you doing this afternoon?"

"I have to work, Mamma."

"Aren't you going out with me?"

"Well, then, at three o'clock, Mamma."

After dinner it was:

"Addie, my boy, what are you doing this evening?"

"I have to work, Papa."

"Aren't you coming for a cycle-ride with me first?"

"For an hour, Papa, that's all."

And it was always as though the parents, almost stupidly, kept the child from working, happy as long as he sat with him or her, walked with her or cycled with him. It was so many favours that he granted; and he granted them not as a spoilt child, but as a man: he divided his precious time systematically between his work and his father and mother, conscientiously allotting what was due to each. And Constance would have a moment of faint, smiling pride, as though in a victory gained, when the boy went out with her in the afternoon.

"Addie, must you always wear that hat?"

Then, to please her, he did not wear his Boer hat, but a bowler, so as to look nice when walking with Mamma. And she relaxed, talked to him; and he laughed back; and she could just take his arm and walked with evident pride on the arm of her little son. Paul always said that she flirted with him.... Then Van der Welcke, having nothing to keep him indoors, went out, went to the Witte, looked up his old friends: young fellows of the old days, but now, for the most part, portly gentlemen, filling important posts; he no longer felt at home with them, even when they talked of the days long past: Leiden, their youthful escapades, their young years. He felt, when with these men who filled important posts, that his life was spoilt, thanks to an irrevocable fault. And disconsolately he came home, from the Witte or from the Plaats, and was a little gloomy at dinner, until Addie succeeded in cheering him up. Then, looking more brightly out of his frank, young, blue eyes, Van der Welcke asked:

"Addie, my boy, what are you doing this evening?"

He asked it as one asks a grown-up person, who makes an appointment or has an engagement; and the lad answered:

"I have to work, Papa."

"Aren't you going for a ride with me first?"

"For an hour, Papa, that's all."

Then Van der Welcke's face lighted up; and Constance reflected that she would be alone, all alone, sitting drearily at home, while the evening drew in. But the bicycles were brought out; and, like two schoolfellows, they spurted way: Van der Welcke suddenly brighter-looking, younger-looking; both, father and son, not tall, but well-built, sturdy and yet refined; their two faces, under the same sort of cap, resembling each other in that slightly heavy cast of feature: the short nose, the well-cut mouth, the square chin, the short, curly hair and the eyes of a happy blue, looking steadily along those roads in the Woods which sped under their devouring pedals; and they were like two brothers, they talked like two friends; and, just as Constance had done, that afternoon, Van der Welcke now let himself go in the evening, feeling, oh, so young and happy with his son-companion! On returning home, Addie would look in for a cup of tea with Mamma and afterwards go to his turret-room to work. And then Van der Welcke always had a pretext, just like a schoolboy, to go and sit with his son, instead of staying in his little smoking-room:

"Addie, my fire's gone out. Shall I be disturbing you if I come and sit in here?"

"No, Papa."

Or else:

"Addie, that wretched wind is blowing right against my window and there's a frightful draught in my room."

"Then come and sit in here, Papa."

The boy was never taken in, but remained very serious and went on working. And Van der Welcke settled himself quietly in the easy-chair, the only one in the room, with a book and a cigarette, and smoked and looked at his son. The boy, one-ideaed and persevering, worked on....

"He's an industrious little beggar," thought Van der Welcke; and he hardly dared move for fear of disturbing Addie. "He'll get through, this summer, though he was a bit behindhand.... One couldn't go on as we were doing at Brussels, with that outside tutor. It's just as well the boy came to Holland. He'll get through, he'll get through.... Four years at the grammar-school and then Leiden. And then he must enter the service. It's lucky that Constance doesn't object. But will he himself consent? I should like to see my son make his way in the career which I ... Oh, it was a damned business, a damned business!... However, without Constance I should not have had Addie, my boy. And Papa too would like to see him go in for diplomacy. Papa was pleased with him too: I could see that. He will have money later; Papa and Mamma are still hale and hearty, but he will have money one of these days.... Just look at the boy working! And he is so serious, poor little beggar, owing to this confounded life at home.... Still, he's fond of us.... Look at him working. I never worked like that. He gets it from his grandfather; that seriousness also. He makes straight for his object. I was always more superficial, younger too. The poor kid doesn't know what it means to be young. He will never be young, never go off his head. Perhaps, though—who knows?—later, at Leiden, perhaps he will be really lively, really go off his head. I wish it him with all my heart, my boy, my little chap.... I wonder what he thinks of his parents? He knows that his mother married before she married his father; but what does he know besides? What does he think? Does he judge us yet, that boy of mine? Will he condemn us later on? Oh, my boy, my boy, never throw up your life for a woman!... But it was a matter of honour, my father wished it.... Oh, Addie, may it never happen to you! But it shan't happen to you, my boy. There is something about him which makes me see that that sort of thing can never happen to him. He will go far: wait and see if he doesn't!... What does he get from me and what from Constance? Difficult, this question of heredity. I always think of it when I look at him like this. He takes after me, physically. That seriousness is his grandfather's. Now what does he get from the Van Lowes? Perhaps that tinge of melancholy he sometimes has. But he's a Van der Welcke, he's a regular Van der Welcke.... He's singularly well-balanced, that boy: what is harsh and rugged in Papa is ever so much softened in him. Perhaps that's from the Van Lowes.... It's enough for me to sit and look at him working. Constance doesn't know I'm here. She thinks we are sitting apart, each in his own room.... How can the boy stick it, working so long on end? What is he working at? Greek? Yes, Greek: I can see the letters. I always used to get up a hundred times: a fly was enough to put me off; and I never really studied: I just crammed, prepared for my examination in a fortnight, helped by Max Brauws.... Brauws! What's become of that chap, I wonder? Oh, one's old friends!... I simply could not study. Without Max Brauws, I should never have got there.... Yes, what's become of him?... But this beggar studies so peacefully, so industriously. He's a dear boy.... Oh, if he only had more young people about him, bright, cheerful youngsters! If only it doesn't do him harm later: this gloomy boyhood between parents who are always squabbling.... I restrain myself sometimes, for his sake. But it's no use, no use.... Heavens, how the fellow's working! I think I'll just ask him something. Or no, perhaps I'd better not: he always puckers up his forehead so solemnly, as though I were the child, disturbing him, and he the father.... Well, I'd better have another cigarette...."

And Van der Welcke, through the clouds of his fourth cigarette, watched his son's back. In the light of the lamp on the table, the boy's curly young head bent over his books and exercises as fervently as though the Greek verbs were the world's salvation; and Van der Welcke, a little irritated by all this industry, all this peace, all this quietness for two hours on end, became jealous of the Greek verbs and, rising at last, unable to restrain himself, said suddenly, with his hand on Addie's shoulder and something parental in his voice, though it was not very firm:

"Don't work too long at a time, my boy."

CHAPTER XVIII

Or else Constance would say, after dinner:

"I'm going to Granny's: will you take me, Addie?"

But he was very just; it was Papa's turn:

"Mummy, I was out with you this afternoon."

"Well, what of that?"

"I'm going for a ride with Papa."

Then she turned pale with jealousy:

"Oh, so you dole out your favours?"

He gave her a kiss, but she pouted, said she would go alone, in the Scheveningen tram, which would take her to Granny's door. But he drew her down upon his little knees:

"Let's play at sweethearts first, then."

"No, let me go."

But he held her tight and kissed her with very short, quick kisses.

"Let me go, Addie, I insist."

But he kissed her with a rain of quick little kisses, which tickled her, till she smiled.

"Look pleasant now!"

"No, I won't!"

"Come, look pleasant!"

"No, I won't look pleasant!"

But she was laughing, saw that her jealousy was really too silly....

And Van der Welcke, after dinner, was glad that it was his turn. He had come back very gloomy from the Plaats; and Addie had cheered him up during dinner.... Sometimes, even, Addie went quite mad. Then he wanted to romp with his father; and Van der Welcke did not object, until Addie discovered a little spot between Papa's brace-buttons where he was very sensitive and tickled him, furiously, just on that little spot.

"Addie, that's enough!" Van der Welcke shouted, playing the father, trying to inspire respect.

But Addie, quite mad, caught Papa round the waist, tickled him on that sensitive spot.

"Addie, I'll give you a thrashing!"

And Van der Welcke squirmed, nervously, ran madly round the room, ran out of the room, followed by his tormentor.

"Addie, if you don't leave off, you'll get such a thrashing that you...!"

But there was no holding the boy; and Van der Welcke, because of that sensitive spot, lost all his self-respect, cringed, entreated, laughed like a madman when Addie so much as pointed at it.

"Addie, don't be so silly!" cried Constance from the drawing-room.

Then he rushed to his mother.

"Hullo, are you jealous again? Do you want to play at sweethearts?"

But his father called to him, reproachfully:

"Come, Addie, let us start."

And Addie ran from one to the other like a little dog and at last landed on his bicycle with a ridiculous jump; and Constance stealthily watched him spurting past Van der Welcke, leaning forward over his handle-bar, pedalling like mad.

Then she felt happy, because he was merry, like a child....

Emilie had been married a day or two, when Addie said, at dinner:

"I went for a walk with Henri van Naghel and his friend Kees Hijdrecht."

"But, Addie," said Constance, who was very irritable that day, "why are you always with those boys? Do they really care for going out with you? Why not go to Aunt Adolphine's boys instead? They are your own age."

"Well, I can understand that Addie prefers Henri," Van der Welcke let fall, unfortunately.

"Why?" she asked, immediately up in arms.

He wished to avoid a dispute—he was sometimes more reasonable than she—and he merely said:

"Well, they're rather rough."

"It would be a miracle," she at once began to cavil, "if you ever saw anything good in the Van Saetzemas' house."

He looked at her with wide eyes, his fine, young, blue eyes:

"But, Constance...."

"Yes, you're always crabbing Adolphine, her husband, her house, her children...."

"But, Constance, I never mention them...."

"That's not true!"

"I assure you!"

"That is not true, I tell you! Only the other day, you said the house was vulgar; two days ago, you said Van Saetzema looked like a farm-labourer."

"But you yourself said, at Emilie's wedding...."

"It's not true: I said nothing. I tell you, once and for all, I won't have you always crabbing one of my sisters and her household. This time, it is the boys who are rather rough...."

"Oh, perhaps you want to see Addie like them?"

"I think it ridiculous for Addie to be always going about with undergraduates. The Van Saetzema boys are very nice and of his own age."

"And I think them three unmannerly young black-guards."

"Henri, I forbid you from this time forward to comment on my family in my presence!"

"Look here, you give your orders to your servants, not to me!"

"I won't have it, I tell you...."

But he flung down his napkin, rose from his seat, left the room suddenly, in a passion. Addie sat quietly looking before him, playing with his fork.

"Papa has very bad manners! To go throwing down his napkin, slamming the door, like a schoolboy!" she said, fretfully, involuntarily, as though to annoy Addie. But he frowned and said nothing; and she went on, "At least, in my father's house I was never accustomed to such rudeness!"

Suddenly, he clenched his little fist and banged it on the table till the glasses rang again:

"And now you keep quiet about Papa!"

He looked at her severely, with his blue eyes suddenly grown hard and a frown on his forehead.

She started and upset her glass. Then she began to weep, softly.

He let her be, for a few minutes. She cried, sobbed, bit her handkerchief. Then he rose, walked round the table, kissed her very gently.

"You have ... a nice way ... of talking ... to your mother!" she said, between her sobs.

He made no reply.

"A pretty tone to use to your mother!" she went on.

He took her by the chin and lifted up her face:

"For shame! To lose your temper like that!" he scolded. "And to grumble! And mope! And squabble! And upset yourself! And kick up a hullabaloo! Do you call that a pleasant way of dining?"

She buried her face on his breast, in his arms. He stroked her hair:

"Come, Mummy, be sensible, now. It's nothing."

"Yes, but Papa mustn't crab Aunt Adolphine."

"And you mustn't crab Papa. What did Papa say, after all?"

"That Aunt Adolphine's boys...."

"Were rough. Do you think they're girls, then?"

"No."

"Well, then ... What else?"

"I don't approve of your going out with boys so much older than yourself."

"Then you can tell me so, quietly; but it's no reason to go quarrelling like that. I can't eat any more now."

"Oh, Addie, just when I've ordered...."

"What?"

"Apple-pudding and wine-sauce."

"Well, it'll keep till to-morrow."

"Do have a little. You know you like it."

"Yes, but I can't eat when I see you so cross. It chokes me, here."

And he pointed to his throat.

"Have just a little bit," she said, coaxingly.

"If you're very good."

"Give me a kiss."

"But mind you're very good."

They laughed together; he gently wiped away her tears:

"You ought to see yourself in the glass," he added, "with those red eyes of yours!"

He sat down. She rang the bell. The servant brought in the pudding, displayed no particular surprise at finding that meneer had gone.

"Is there any cheese, for Papa?" he asked.

The servant brought the cheese; Addie cut a piece of gruyere, put it on a plate with some butter and biscuits, poured out a glass of wine.

"Addie...."

"Wait a minute," he said.

And he went upstairs with the cheese and the wine. Van der Welcke was sitting glowering in the smoking-room.

"Here's your cheese and biscuits, Father. You don't like apple-pudding, do you?"

"Oh, I don't want anything!"

"Now, don't be disagreeable. Eat up your cheese."

"I can't eat, when Mamma...."

"She's sorry already; she's all nerves to-day. So don't talk about it any more."

"I? I'm not talking!"

"No, but *soeda*,[19] now, as Aunt Ruyvenaer says. Will you eat your cheese now? Presently, we'll go for a ride."

He went away.

"Here I sit, just like a naughty child," thought Van der Welcke, "with my little plate of cheese and biscuits. That silly boy!"

And he ate up his bit of cheese and laughed....

---

[19] Quiet, that'll do.

Downstairs, Constance had put a piece of pudding on Addie's plate. He ate slowly. She looked at him contentedly, because he was enjoying it.

"If you hadn't fired up like that," he said, "I'd have told you something, about Henri."

"What about him?"

"That chap's going to be ill."

"Why?"

"He's so upset at Emilie's marriage that it's made him quite unwell. Kees Hijdrecht got angry and said, 'Are you in love with your sister?' And then Henri almost began to cry, Leiden man though he is. No, he wasn't in love, he said, but he had always been with Emilie, with Emilie and Marianne; and now she was married and would be a stranger. He was so bad that we took him home; and then he locked himself in his room and wouldn't even see Marianne."

"But, Addie, that's morbid."

"I dare say; but it's true."

"I must go round to Aunt Bertha's. Will you take me?"

"No, let me go cycling with Papa. He's sitting upstairs, eating his cheese for all he's worth. You'd better tell Truitje to take him up his coffee."

"But, Addie, what will the girl think when she sees Papa finishing his dinner upstairs?"

"She can think what she likes. It's your fault. Shall I come and fetch you at Aunt Bertha's at a quarter to ten?"

She looked at him radiantly, delighted, surprised. And she kissed him passionately:

"My boy, my darling!" she cried, pressing him to her heart.

CHAPTER XIX

In the same nervous mood in which she had been all day, Constance hurried, after dinner, to the Bezuidenhout, taking the tram along the Scheveningsche Weg and another to the Plein. When she rang at the Van Naghels', she thought it strange that there was no light in the hall, as she knew, from Addie, that they were at home that evening. The butler, who opened the door, said that he did not know whether mevrouw could see her, as mevrouw was not feeling well.

She waited in the drawing-room, where the butler hurriedly turned on the light before going to say that she was there. All round the big room were the faded and withered flower-baskets and bouquets of Emilie's wedding, the frail flowers shrivelled and brown and decayed, while the broad white ribbons still hung in silvery folds around them. The room had evidently not been touched since the wedding-breakfast: the dust lay thick on the furniture; and the chairs still stood as though the room had just been left by a multitude of guests.... Constance waited some time; then she heard footsteps. Marianne came in, looking pale and untidy:

"We are so sorry, Auntie, to have kept you waiting. Mamma is very tired and has an awful headache and is lying down in her room."

"Then I won't disturb her."

"But Mamma asked if you would come upstairs."

She followed Constance to Bertha's bedroom. Constance was astonished at the almost deathly stillness in that great house, which, on the three or four occasions that she had entered it, she had never seen other than full of movement, life, all sorts of little interests which together made up a bustling existence. There was no draught on the top floor, where Frances had her apartments; there were no doors slamming; she saw no maids, no *baboe*, no children: everything was quiet, deadly quiet. And, when she entered Bertha's room, it looked to her, in the subdued light, like a sick-room.

"I have come to see how you are."

Bertha put out her hand, silently. Then she said:

"That is nice of you. I am very tired and I have a head-ache."

"I shall not stay long."

"Yes, do stay. I don't mind you."

Bertha and Constance were now alone. And it struck Constance that a disconsolate sadness distorted Bertha's features and that she looked very old, now that her hair, with its grey patches, was down.

"All this rush has been too much for you."

"Oh, I don't know," said Bertha, vaguely. "There's always plenty of rush here."

"Still, it's just as well that you're taking a rest."

"Yes."

They were silent and there was no sound save the ticking of the clock. Then Constance stooped and kissed Bertha on the forehead:

"I wanted badly to see you this evening," she said. "Addie was out with Henri and he told me that Henri was so depressed. And so I came round."

"Henri?" said Bertha, vaguely. "I don't think so; he seemed all right."

"But Addie said...."

"What?"

"That he was so depressed."

"Really? I didn't notice it."

"Well, perhaps Addie was mistaken," said Constance, gently. "Come, I've seen you now, Bertha, and perhaps it's better that I should go and let you rest."

And she stooped again to kiss Bertha good-bye. But Bertha caught her by the hand:

"Do stay with me!" she said, hesitatingly.

"I am really afraid of disturbing you."

"No, please stay!" said Bertha. "I think it's nice of you to have come. You mustn't think me indifferent; but what's the use of talking? If one doesn't talk, everything is so much simpler. Words always mean so much.... Don't think me cold, Constance. I'm like that, you see: I never talk, to anybody. I prefer to withdraw into myself, when there's anything the matter with me. But there's nothing wrong now, I'm only a little tired.... Of course, I feel rather sad at Emilie's going. But we must hope that she will be happy. Eduard is not a bad fellow; and why should Emilie have accepted him, if she didn't care for him?... Do stay and talk to me. Tell me about yourself. It is the first time that we have had a real talk...."

"For years."

"Yes, for years. And much has happened, Constance; but it all belongs to the past now."

"Yes, but the past remains so long. Properly speaking, it never goes, it is always the past."

"Constance, it is twenty years since we saw each other."

"Twenty years. Papa has been dead fourteen years. It was my fault that he died."

"No, Constance."

"Yes, it was. You needn't mind: it was my fault. I know you all think so and I feel it myself. It was my fault. I can never forget that. I can never forgive myself that."

"Hush, Constance. Really, it's such a long time, such a very long time ago."

"But it will always remain ... a murder."

"You have the future before you now. There's your son...."

"Yes, there's my son. But it has come to this, that I am not living for him, but he for me."

"That is wrong."

"Yes, it's wrong. And my whole life is wrong, everything has gone wrong in my life. Oh, Bertha, I can't tell you how I yearned for Holland and for you all, how I yearned to be no longer alone, alone with my boy! Now, perhaps it will be different: among all of you, I feel at home once more. At home: do you know what that means? If I had remained away, things would never have come right. Now perhaps I can still hope: I really don't know...."

"Alone with your boy? Why don't you speak of your husband?"

"No, not my husband."

"Why not?"

"No, no. We only endure each other, for Addie's sake."

"Constance, don't forget...."

"What?..."

"What he did for you, what his people did."

"Oh, if only I had never accepted that sacrifice! If only I had gone right away, alone, somewhere far away! And then never come back to you all.... For, as it is, it was possible, after fifteen years; but then it would have been impossible.... To be grateful, to be grateful all the time, while all the time I am full of bitterness: I can't do it. I can't be grateful when I feel so bitter."

"But, Constance, you're back now and we are all glad to have you back."

"Bertha, I don't know if you mean what you say. I do know that I am happy to be back, in Holland, among you all. But I also know that, in twenty years, people drift far apart; and perhaps I, who had become a stranger, was not wise to come back to all of you, to want to be a sister to you again."

"Perhaps we shall have to get used to one another, Constance, as sisters; but you always remained a daughter to Mamma; and I am very glad for Mamma's sake."

"Yes, I feel that, that you all tolerate me for Mamma's sake. It is nice of you, but it is not quite what I should have wished."

"But, Constance, all that will come later. I am convinced that soon you will feel no longer a stranger. But don't be impatient; and let us get used to one another again.... And there is this too, that every one has his own interests in life; and it is a pity, but there is not always time to feel for another and to think of another. That is very strange, but it's true. Just think, it is two months since you came back to Holland; and this is the first time that we have had a chance of talking to each other. I have only once been to see you at your house. And all this is not from heartlessness, but because one has no time."

"Yes, Bertha, I know; and I am not reproaching you; and you've been very busy with the wedding...."

"And, when it's not a wedding, it's something else. It is always like that, Constance. And sometimes I ask myself, why: why do we do it? Why have all this fuss, all this bustle, all this excitement?... There is a reason for it all: our children's happiness lies in that direction. We do everything for our children, that's what it comes to. Van Naghel's being in the Cabinet, my giving dinners: the reason is always, though one doesn't always realize it, for the children, for their happiness. But, then,

Constance, then we ought to have our reward and see our children happy. In return for all our trouble and worry, for all this rushing about and weariness, for all the money we spend, we do want to see our children just a little happy. And then, oh, when I"—her eyes filled with tears—"when I see Otto and Frances: Otto discontented and Frances ill; Louise sad because of Otto, whom she is so fond of; Emilie married now—but how married, poor thing, and why?—and Marianne all nerves and not knowing what she wants; and Henri too so melancholy: then I say to myself, 'Why have we all these children, for whom we live and think and contrive? And wouldn't it be better not to have them? And isn't it better to have as little as possible in one's life and to make that life as small and simple and quiet as possible, once we have to live? Oh, Constance, all this aimlessness and uselessness amid which people like ourselves, women in our position, our environment, our set, turn and turn like humming-tops or fools: isn't it enough sometimes to tempt one to run away from it all and to go and sit on a mountain somewhere and look out over the sea? Women like ourselves marry as young girls, knowing nothing and having only a vague presentiment of our lives, that they will be like the lives of our mothers before us; and all that futility seems most important, until, one fine day, we find that we have grown old and tired and have lived for nothing at all: for visits, dresses, dinners, things which we thought were necessary, all sorts of interests among which we were born and brought up and grew old and which we cannot escape and which are worth nothing, nothing, nothing! And then, when we think that we have lived for our children and slaved and schemed and contrived for them, then it all comes to nothing, nothing, nothing; and not one of them is happy....' You see, Constance, I have talked to you now; but what's the good of it? Why say all that I have said? You'll go away presently and think, 'What a fit of depression Bertha had!' And that is all it was: a fit of depression. For, when I have had a couple of days' rest, why, then life will go on as before: I shall have two charwomen in at once; the whole house has to be done, after the wedding and because of the spring-cleaning. Well, then, was it really worth while to speak out? Oh, no, talking leads to so little; and it's best simply to do all the little duties that fall to one's share."

"I am very glad though, Bertha, that you have let yourself go. I did not know you thought like that; I myself have sometimes thought so, even though my life was not so busy as yours. But, in Brussels, I too sometimes thought, 'Well, yes, I am living for Addie: but, if he were not here, he would not have his own troubles in the future; and I should not need to go on living!'"

"And perhaps there are hundreds who think like that, in our class."

"Isn't it the same in every class?"

"Perhaps life is hopeless for everybody. And yet, when I am rested, to-morrow or the day after, and when my head-ache is gone, I shall start all this work over again."

They were silent, hand in hand; for a moment they had found each other again, were like two sisters. Then Bertha went on:

"When I lie here like this, with my head-aches, I always think of my children.... Yes, it was nice of you to come, Connie. Was Addie out with Henri, did you say? Isn't it morbid of Henri to be so melancholy? But my children are so dependent on one another, almost more than on their parents. Otto and Louise are always together; and then Frances is jealous. The two boys at Leiden are always together; and Henri was always with his sisters too; and Marianne misses Emilie. And still, notwithstanding that feeling for one another, notwithstanding that we do everything for them, notwithstanding that all our thoughts are for them, notwithstanding all we spend on them and for them, my children are not happy. Not one of them has received—what shall I say?—the gift of happiness. It is strange; it is as if life lay heavy upon all of them and as if they were too small, too weak to bear the burden of it. Tell me, Constance, what is your boy like?"

"I don't think he is like that."

"But then he is old for his years, isn't he?"

"Yes, but he is very sensible."

"Yes, he is a little man."

"He is strong, in mind as well as in body. I was going to say that he is just as though he were not little. He works entirely to please himself. And he is a comfort, to both of us. He is a strange child. He is not a child."

"And what is he going to be?"

"He will probably go into the diplomatic service."

She spoke the words and saw, in a flash, before her eyes, Rome, De Staffelaer, all her vain past. And, in that half-darkened room, in that hour of absolute sincerity, she asked herself whether that career would spell happiness for her son.

"Will Van der Welcke like that?..."

"Yes, but Addie must decide for himself. We shall not force him."

There was a knock at the door; and Henri put his head into the room:

"May I come in, Mamma?"

"Yes, what is it? Here's Aunt Constance."

"How are you, Aunt? I came to see how you are, Mamma."

The undergraduate was a tall boy of just twenty, with a pale, gentle face and dressed with the ultra-smartness of a youth who is "in the swim" at Leiden.

"Pretty well, my boy."

"I shall go back to Leiden to-morrow, Mamma."

"Oh?"

"Yes; and I shall probably not be home for some time. I mean to work hard...."

"That's right."

"There's really nothing else to do but work. It's so slow here, Auntie, now that Emilie's gone. Otto's all right, with Louise. She missed him badly, while he was in India. Funny brothers and sisters, aren't we? So exaggerated.... Well, Mamma, I'll say good-bye: I shall start the first thing in the morning."

He said good-bye and went away pulling himself together, putting a good face on his grief. Bertha began to weep softly.

A maid knocked at the door:

"Master van der Welcke, mevrouw."

"Addie's come to fetch me."

"Ask Master van der Welcke to come upstairs," said Bertha.

The boy came in. He remained near the door; in the half-dark room, he stood small but erect, like a little man:

"I have come to fetch you, Mamma."

The two sisters looked at him, smiling. Bertha had it on her lips to say that it was not right for Addie to go about the streets alone, but she said nothing when the boy went up to his mother. He looked capable of protecting her and himself against anything, though he was only thirteen: against the dark night and against life that bore down so heavily upon their small souls.

And a melancholy jealousy welled up in Bertha, while Constance was kissing her good-bye:

"Don't be too bitter, Constance," she whispered, "and cherish, cherish that boy of yours...."

CHAPTER XX

Constance, after this talk with Bertha, for days felt easier in her mind, as though filled with an indefinable contentment that bid fair to soothe and heal. Yes, she hoped that, gradually, she would win them all back like that, all her near ones, whom she had lost for years. She saw Mamma daily; and in these regular meetings between mother and child there was the sweetness of finding each other after long years of almost uninterrupted separation, a sweetness touched with a melancholy that held no bitterness, a mingling of glad tears and smiles over the happiness of it all. Also, Constance had now found Bertha again; and, though they did not see each other until Mamma's Sunday-evening, still there was more sisterly confidence between them, while Marianne grew to like running in at the Kerkhoflaan and would stay to dinner or go cycling with Van der Welcke and Addie. In this way, light bonds were established. As for Karel and Cateau, Constance was sorry, for in Karel she still remembered the brother with whom she used to play on the boulders in the river at Buitenzorg; but she had felt at once that she must not expect much from Karel, now that he and his wife had become mutual images of placid egotism, wrapped in their well-fed, middle-class life, in the sheltered comfort of their warm, shut house. No, Karel, she felt, she had lost, though they were conventionally civil to each other. With Gerrit it was pleasanter. Gerrit and Adeline would come now and then to take tea in the evening, after the children had gone to bed. Only it was a pity that Gerrit always insisted on crabbing and poking fun at the Van Naghels and their friends. This, Constance thought, was not very tactful towards Van der Welcke, because, though he and she did not go into society, it so happened that Van der Welcke had a good many old friends, at the club, who belonged to the aristocratic set. Gerrit was a boisterous, lively fellow, fair-haired, handsome, broad-shouldered and vigorous in his hussar's uniform; but his boisterousness was sometimes, she thought, rather overdone; and she suspected that Van der Welcke did not like Gerrit, thought him a little vulgar. And so she was always on the alert to take up the cudgels for Gerrit against her husband; and Van der Welcke said nothing about Gerrit and was even amiable and talkative when Gerrit and Adeline were there. Adeline was a dear little woman, a fair-haired, little doll-mother, with her seven children, like a family of flaxen-haired dolls: the oldest a girl turned eight, the youngest a baby of a year or so; and Gerrit was always making jokes about not leaving off yet; and indeed Adeline was expecting another in the autumn. So Constance got on well with Gerrit and Adeline, but still she felt out of touch with this brother too, even though Gerrit had such a charming way of bringing back the memory of their early days, when they used to play in the river at Buitenzorg. Yes, she was an interesting child then, Gerrit always said: there was something so nice about her; she was full of imagination; and it was curious to hear this great, heavy hussar going into ecstasies over that little sister of the old days: a frail, fair-haired little girl, in her white *baadje;* she used to walk on her pretty little bare feet over the boulders and invent all sorts of fables and fairy-tales, which her elder brothers were not quite capable of understanding and yet had to play at, good-humouredly, for the two brothers were very fond of their little sister. Yes, Gerrit always said, he had not understood until afterwards how much poetry there was in Constance in the days when she dreamed those stories, those fables, in which she often played a fairy, or a *poetri* out of the Javanese legends: at such times, she would wreathe her hair with a garland of broad leaves; she would look like Ophelia, in the water, decked with tropical blossoms; and the brothers must needs follow the tiny bare feet and the fancies of their little sister, who looked marvellously charming as she ran over the great rocks, ran through the foaming water, ran in crystal green shadows, which quivered over the river, under the heavy awning of the foliage. Yes, that had left a great impression on Gerrit; and he often talked about it:

"Constance, do you remember? What a nice little girl you were then, though you were a little queer!..."

Until Constance would laugh and ask if she was no longer nice now that she no longer ran about barefoot in a white *baadje* with purple *kembang-spatoe*[20] on her temples. Then Gerrit shook his head and said, yes, she was very nice still, but ... but.... And, diving back into his recollections, he said that, two years later, she suddenly changed, became grown-up and a prig and would dance with no one but the secretary-general.... And then Constance cried with laughter, because Gerrit could never forget that secretary-general. Yes, she would only dance with the biggest big-wigs: she was a mass of vanity, a real daughter of the *Toean Besar.*[21] And it was as though Gerrit were bent upon getting back that little younger sister who used to make up fairy-tales in the river behind the Palace at Buitenzorg, notwithstanding that he was now a big, heavy, powerful fellow and a captain of hussars. Then Constance would look at him, handsome, broad, fair-haired, vigorous, enjoying his drink or his good cigar, and she reflected that she did not know Gerrit and did not understand Gerrit: very vaguely she felt something in him escape her, felt it so vaguely that it was hardly a thought, but merely a haze passing over her bewilderment. Adeline sat very quietly in the midst of it, smiling pleasantly at those reminiscences, at those games of the old days:

"Yes, it's extraordinary, the way children play by themselves!" she said, simply; and then she would tell prettily of the games of her own fair-haired brood.

But Gerrit would shake his head: no, that was romping, what his boys did, but the other thing was playing, real playing. Until Constance laughingly asked him to talk of something else than her bare feet. And then the conversation took a more ordinary turn; and it was as if both Gerrit and Constance felt that, although they liked each other, they had not yet found each other. And in this there was a very gentle melancholy that could hardly be formulated.

Constance did not see much of Ernst. She and Van der Welcke and Addie had once lunched with him at his rooms and he had been a most amiable host: he showed her the old family-papers, which, after Papa's death, he had asked leave to keep,

---

[20] Tropical flowers.

[21] The great house, *i.e.*, the Viceregal Palace at Buitenzorg.

because he took most interest in them and they would be in good hands. He would leave them to Gerrit's eldest son: Gerrit was the only one of the four brothers who, so far, had provided heirs. He showed her his old china and called her attention to the different marks that were signs of its value. Next, he spread out an old piece of brocade, embroidered with seed-pearls, and said very seriously that it was a stomacher from a dress of Queen Elizabeth's. When Constance laughed and ventured to express a doubt, he became rather grave and almost angry, but graciously changed the conversation, as one does, a little condescendingly, with people who have said something stupid, who have not the same culture as ourselves.

When they sat down to lunch in his room with its beautiful old colouring, the table was so carefully laid, the flowers so tastefully arranged, with all the grace of a woman's hand, and the lunch was so exquisite and dainty that Constance, amazed, had paid him a compliment. He half-filled an antique glass with champagne and drank to welcome her to Holland. There was about him, about his surroundings, about his manner, something refined and something timid, something feminine and something shy, something lovable and yet something reserved, as though he were afraid of wounding himself or another. He had obviously devised this reception in order to give pleasure to Constance. The conversation flagged: Ernst never completed his sentences; and his eyes were always wandering round the room.... After lunch, he was a little more communicative and he then asked her if she had ever thought on the grace and symbolism of a vase. She listened with interest, while she saw something in Van der Welcke's glance as though he thought that Ernst was mad; and Addie listened very seriously, full of tense and silent astonishment. A vase, Ernst said, was like a soul— and he took in his hand a slender Satsuma vase of ivory-tinted porcelain, with the elegant arabesques waving delicately as a woman's hair—it was like a soul. For Ernst there were sad and merry vases, proud and humble vases; there were lovelorn vases and vases of passion; there were vases of desire; and there were dead vases, which only came to life again when he put a flower in them. He said all this very seriously, without a smile and also without the rhapsody of an artist or a poet: he talked almost laconically about his vases, as though any other view would have been quite impossible.... Constance had not seen him since that day, because he was the only one who did not come regularly to Mamma's Sunday-evenings. And she retained an impression of that afternoon spent with her brother Ernst as of something exotic and strangely symbolical, something, it was true, which she had liked and found pleasant and refined, but which, all the same, lacked the familiar cordiality of a brother and sister meeting again after a separation of years.

As regards Adolphine and her children, Constance, after a first sense of recoil, had, almost unconsciously, laid down rules for her feelings, though perhaps she did not see those rules so very clearly outlined in her mind. But, unconsciously, she positively refused to dislike Adolphine and, on the contrary, was positively determined to think everything about Adolphine pleasant and attractive: her husband, her house, her children and her ideas. If any one, even Mamma, said the least thing about Adolphine, she at once espoused her cause, violently. Through circumstances, such as the arranging of her own house and Emilie's wedding, she had not, as yet, been often to the Van Saetzemas'; but she promised herself not to neglect this in future and, with the greatest tact, to advise Adolphine in all sorts of matters. It operated strangely in Constance: the feeling of recoil, which, after all, was there; an absolute determination to act against this feeling of recoil; and, combined with these two, a silent wish, a gentle resolve to improve Adolphine in one way and another. She insisted that Addie should ask Adolphine's boys to lunch one Sunday; and, though her nerves were racked and she driven almost mad by their rude manners and coarse voices, she had controlled herself and deliberately played the kind auntie. Addie, sacrificing himself for Mamma's sake, had gone out walking with his cousins, but had taken the first opportunity of giving the young louts the slip. Knowing his mother's idiosyncrasies, he did not say much when he returned and even declared that they were not half bad fellows. When his father, however, asked him if he understood why Mamma encouraged those unmannerly cubs, Addie stoically replied, because they were cousins: one of Mamma's ideas; family-affection. Constance, meanwhile, was so tired of the three young Van Saetzemas that she did not venture to repeat the experiment.

Constance thought Dorine uncertain. Dorine was very pleasant, sometimes, to go shopping with, or would go shopping herself for Constance—it was she who asked, not Constance—and then, at other times, Dorine would be cold and nervously irritable. This was because Dorine had a positive mania for doing all sorts of things for other people, but, at the same time, was always craving for appreciation and never thought that she was sufficiently appreciated by any member of the family for whose benefit she ran about. But the mania was too strong for her; and she went on running about, for Mamma, for Bertha, for Constance, for Adolphine, and was always grumbling to herself that she was not appreciated. Yes, she would like to see their faces if she, Dorine, said, one day, that she was tired! What would they say, she wondered, if she ventured to suggest that one sometimes gets wet in the rain? Thus she always grumbled to herself, fitful, dissatisfied, discontented and yet never able to make a comfortable corner for herself, in the boarding-house where she lived, always tearing along the streets from one sister to the other. It was as though she had a mania that drove her ever onwards. She was miserable if a day came when she had no errands to run; and she would go to Adolphine and say:

"Look here, if you'd like me to go to Iserief's and ask about those pillow cases for Floortje, you've only got to say so; I'm going that way anyhow."

And then, when she went that way, she muttered to herself:

"At it again! Of course, there's only Dorine to inquire about Floortje's pillow-cases! Why can't the girl go herself? Or why don't they send the maid?"

Paul was the one whom Constance saw most often of all the brothers and sisters. He had begun by finding in her a fairly sympathetic listener for his endless unbosomings and philosophizings; then Van der Welcke liked him best and they sometimes had a cigarette together in the smoking-room; he was the most of a brother to them of the four: just an ordinary brother. He would arrive in the morning and run straight up to Constance' room, while she was still dressing, and declare that of course he could come in, though she was in her petticoat. When not too long-winded, he had an interesting way of talking which Van der Welcke appreciated. He always looked at Addie with the eye of a philosopher; and Addie liked him, found him great fun, with his exquisite trousers and wonderful neckties. Constance was fond of him; and it was in Paul that she had really for the first time met a brother again: in Paul, who had come least within her ken in the old days, when she was a girl of twenty and he a child of thirteen.

CHAPTER XXI

"So you're thinking of being presented at Court next winter?" said Van Vreeswijck, who had been a chum of Henri's at Leiden and who was now a chamberlain-extraordinary to the Queen Regent, as he and Van der Welcke were leaving the Plaats together.

Van der Welcke looked up:

"I wasn't thinking of it for a second."

"Really? I heard that you meant to, or rather that it was your wife's intention."

"I haven't exchanged a single word on the subject with my wife."

Van Vreeswijck took Van der Welcke's arm: "Really? Well, to tell you the truth, I could not quite understand it."

"Why not?" asked Van der Welcke, promptly taking offence.

"Look here, old fellow: I can speak to you frankly, can't I, as an old friend? But, if you're touchy ... then we'll avoid intimate matters."

"Not at all: what were you going to say?"

"Nothing that you won't see for yourself, if you think for a moment. But, if the whole question of getting presented at Court doesn't exist with you and your wife, then don't let me bring it up at all."

"No, no!" said Van der Welcke, becoming interested. "Don't beat about the bush; say what you meant to say."

"I couldn't understand your having the idea, or how the idea could ever have occurred to your wife: I tell you so, honestly. De Staffelaer is a relation of the Eilenburgs and of the Van Heuvel Steyns; and it would surely be painful for you and your wife to meet those people, wouldn't it?... That's all."

"Short and sweet," said Van der Welcke, still feeling put out.

"But that's the whole point of it."

"You're right," muttered Van der Welcke, gloomily. "Perhaps we ought never to have come to the Hague."

"Nonsense!" said Van Vreeswijck, rather feebly. "Your old friends are glad to see you back again. The question of the Court is non-existent with you both. Well, then there's nothing to fret about.... As for myself, I am more than glad to see you at the Hague again," he continued, more cheerfully, almost in a tone of relief. "I have the pleasantest memories of the occasions when I had the privilege of meeting your wife in Brussels. When would it suit you both for me to come and call?"

"Will you look round one evening? Or, if you really want to be friendly, come and dine."

"I should like to, above all things. When shall I come?"

"Day after to-morrow, at seven."

"Delighted. Just yourselves? And I'll call and leave a card to-morrow."

"By the way," said Van der Welcke. "You mentioned De Staffelaer: where is he now?"

"At his country-place, near Haarlem. He's still flourishing. He's well over eighty."

"He must be."

They parted. Van der Welcke went gloomily home. It was curious, but, every afternoon, when he went home from the Witte or the Plaats, he had that gloomy, unsettled feeling. The moment he set eyes on Addie, however, his face at once lighted up; but, this time, when the boy wanted to romp, before dinner, Van der Welcke began to think whether Constance would approve of his having asked Van Vreeswijck to dinner two days later....

They sat down to table:

"By the way," said Van der Welcke, hesitatingly, "I met Van Vreeswijck; and he wanted to call on you and asked when it would suit you."

"He might have done so long ago," said Constance, who had entertained Van Vreeswijck once or twice in Brussels.

"He apologized," said Van der Welcke, in defence of his friend. "He did not know whether you were quite settled. I told him he must come and dine one night and—if it's not too much trouble for you—I asked him to come the day after to-morrow."

"I think he might have paid a visit first."

"He said something about leaving a card to-morrow. But, if you don't care about it, I'll put him off."

"No, it's all right," said Constance.

It was an instinct with her to be hospitable, to have her house always open to her friends. But, until now, she had dreaded asking any one to meals, except Gerrit and Adeline, quite quietly, and, just once, Paul.

Paul happened to call that evening.

"Do you mind if I ask Paul too?" she said to her husband.

"No, of course not; Paul is delightful."

Paul accepted with pleasure. On the evening of the little dinner, he was the first to arrive.

"Addie is dining with Gerrit and Adeline," she said. "It will be nicer for him."

"How charming you've made your place look!" said Paul, enthusiastically.

She had a pretty little drawing-room, cosy and comfortable and gay with many flowers in vases. And she looked most charming, young, with the attractive pallor of her rounded face, the face of a woman in her prime, and a smile in the dimples about her lips, because the graciousness of a hostess was natural to her. Paul thought her the best-looking of all his sisters, as she stood before him in her black dress: a film of black *mousseline-de-soie* and black lace, falling in a diaphanous cloud over white taffeta. There reigned, in her rooms, in herself, the easy grace of a woman of the world, a quality which Paul had not yet observed in her, because until now he had seen her either quite intimately, in her bedroom, or at those crowded family-evenings. It was as though she had come into her own again.

Yes, as she now welcomed Van Vreeswijck, with a soft, playful word or two, Paul thought her simply adorable. He suddenly understood that, ten years ago, his sister might well have been irresistible. Even now, she had something about her so young, charming, engaging, pretty and distinguished that she was a revelation to him. She was an exquisite woman.

She had not hired a man-servant: the parlour-maid would wait. She herself drew back the hangings from the dining-room door-way and, without taking Van Vreeswijck's arm, asked the men to come in to dinner. A pink light of shaded candles slumbered over the table, with its bunch of grapes and its pink roses and maiden-hair fern, in between the crystal and the silver.

"But this is most charming!" said Paul, to himself, for he could not tell his sister so yet, as she and Van der Welcke were talking to Van Vreeswijck. "This is most charming! A party of four, like this, in this pretty room. That's just what I like. Compare all that formality of Bertha's. Bertha never gives these intimate little dinners. This is just what I like at my age"—Paul was thirty-five—"no formality, but everything elegant and nicely-served and good.... Excellent *hors d'oeuvres!* Constance knows how to do things! Compare the friendly, but homely rumpsteak which I sometimes get at Gerrit and Adeline's; or Adolphine's harum-scarum dinners.... No, this is as it should be: a quiet, friendly little dinner and yet everything just right.... Van Vreeswijck's dinner-jacket looks very well on him; only I don't like the cut of his waistcoat: too high, I think, his waistcoat. Those are nice buttons of his. But he's wearing a ready-made black tie! How is it possible! Strange how you suddenly perceive an aberration like that in a man: a ready-made tie! Who on earth wears a ready-made tie nowadays! Still, he looks very well otherwise.... Nice soup, this *veloute*.... What a duck Constance looks! Would you ever think that she was a woman of two-and-forty! She's like Mamma: Mamma also has that softness, that distinction, that same smile; Mamma even has those dimples still, in the corners of her mouth.... No, none of my other sisters could have done that, pulled back the hangings herself with that pretty gesture and asked us so naturally to come in to dinner.... You'll see, Constance will make her house very cosy, even though they are not rich and though they won't go into society officially. These friendly little dinners are just the thing...."

He had to join in the conversation now, with Van Vreeswijck; and Van der Welcke, who was in a pleasant mood, let himself go in a burst of irrepressible frankness:

"Tell me, Vreeswijck, who is it that's been saying we wanted to be presented at Court?..."

Van Vreeswijck hesitated, thought it a dangerous subject of conversation. But Constance laughed gently:

"Yes," she said, seconding her husband, "there seems to be a rumour that we have that intention; and the intention never existed for a moment."

Van Vreeswijck breathed again, relieved:

"Oh, mevrouw, how do people ever get hold of their notions? One will suggest, 'I wonder if they mean to be presented?' The other catches only the last words and says, 'They mean to be presented!' And so the story gets about."

"I shouldn't care for it in the least," said Constance. "I have become so used, of late, to a quiet life that I should think it tiresome to be paying and receiving a lot of visits. I am glad to be at the Hague, because I am back among my family...."

"And the family is very glad too!" said Paul, with brotherly gallantry, and raised his glass.

She thanked him with her little laugh:

"But I want nothing more than that. And I don't think Henri cares for anything else either."

"No, not at all!" said Van der Welcke. "Only, I can't understand why people at once start talking about others and, without a moment's hesitation, pretend to know more about a fellow's plans than he himself does. I never talk about anybody!"

"I must admit," Constance laughed, "that I often differ from my husband, but in this we are absolutely at one: I too never talk about anybody!"

"But that people should talk about us is only natural, I suppose!" said Van der Welcke and threw up his young, blue eyes, almost ingenuously. "They had forgotten us for years and now they see us again."

"He oughtn't to have said that," thought Paul. "Sometimes, he is just like a young colt...."

And he could understand that Constance occasionally felt peevish. These allusions, however slight, must necessarily vex her, he thought. Van der Welcke, when he let himself go, was capable of saying very tactless things. He generally restrained himself, but, when he did not, he became too spontaneous for anything. And Paul said something to Van Vreeswijck to change the conversation.

Yes, Paul felt for his sister. After all, that sort of past always remained, always clung about one. They were sitting here so cosily; Van Vreeswijck was a charming talker; and yet, at every moment, there were little rocks against which the conversation ran. Constance was behaving well, thought Paul: he had seen her quite different, flying out at the least word. But she was a woman of the world: she did not fly out before a stranger.... Here they were again, though: the conversation was turning on old Mr. and Mrs. van der Welcke. There they were again: he felt that Van Vreeswijck hesitated even before asking after the old people; and not until Constance herself said that she thought them both looking so well did Van Vreeswijck venture to go on talking about that father- and mother-in-law, who had sacrificed their son, who had refused for years to see their daughter-in-law and even their grandchild.... Surely it was better to talk about indifferent things....

But this was not only one of Constance' handsome, but also one of her amiable evenings. As a hostess, in however small a way, she came into her own and was like another woman, much more gentle, without any bitterness and ready to accept the fact that a rock had to be doubled now and again. Her smile gave to her cheeks a roundness that made her look younger. What a pity, thought Paul, that she was not always just like that, so full of tact, always the hostess in her own house, hostess to her husband too:

"How strange women are," he thought. "If I were dining here alone with them, in the ordinary course of things, and if these same rocks had occurred in the conversation, Constance would have lost her temper three times by now and Van der Welcke would have caught it finely. And now that there's a guest, now that we are in our dinner-jackets and Constance in an evening-frock, now that there are grapes and flowers on the table and a more elaborate *menu* than usual, now she does not lose her temper and won't lose her temper, however many rocks we may have to steer past. I believe that, even if we began to talk about infidelity and divorce, about marriages with old men and love-affairs with young ones, she would remain quite calm, smiling prettily with those little dimples at the corners of her mouth, as though nothing could apply to her... What strange creatures women are, full of little reserves of force that make them very powerful in life!... And, presently, when Van Vreeswijck is gone, she will rave at Van der Welcke if he so much as blows his nose; and all her little reserve-forces will have vanished; and she will be left without the smallest self-control.... Still, in any case, she is most charming; and I have had a capital dinner and am feeling very pleasant...."

The bell rang and, through the open door leading to the hall, Constance and Paul heard voices at the front-door:

"That's Adolphine's voice!" said Constance.

"And Carolientje's," said Paul....

"Oh, then I won't stay!" they heard Adolphine say, loudly, shrilly.

Constance rose from her chair. She thought it a bore that Adolphine should call just in this evening, but she was bent upon never allowing Adolphine to see that she was unwelcome:

"Excuse me, Mr. van Vreeswijck, for a moment. I hear my sister...."

She went out into the passage:

"How are you, Adolphine?"

"How are you, Constance?" said Adolphine.

She knew that Constance was giving a little dinner that evening and she had come prying on purpose, though she pretended to know nothing:

"I just looked in," she said, "as I was passing with Carolientje; I saw a light in your windows and thought you must be at home. But your servant says that you're having a dinner-party!" said Adolphine, tartly and reproachfully, as though Constance had no right to give a dinner.

"Not a dinner-party. Van Vreeswijck and Paul are dining with us."

"Van Vreeswijck? Oh!" said Adolphine.

"The one at Court?"

"He's a chamberlain of the Regent's," said Constance, simply.

"Oh!"

"He's an old friend of Van der Welcke's," said Constance, almost in self-excuse.

"Oh! Well, then I won't disturb you...."

The dining-room door was open. Adolphine peeped in and saw the three men talking over their dessert. She saw the candles, the flowers, the dinner-jackets of the men; she noticed Constance' dress....

"Do come in, Adolphine," said Constance, mastering herself and in her gentlest voice.

"No, thanks. If you're having a dinner-party, I won't come in, at dessert.... Oof! How hot it is in here, Constance: do you still keep on fires? It's suffocating in your house; and so dark, with those candles. How pale you look! Aren't you feeling well?"

"Pale? No, I'm feeling very well indeed."

"Oh, I thought you must be tired or ill, you look so awfully pale! You're not looking well. Perhaps you've put on too much powder. Or is it your dress that makes you look pale? Is that one of your Brussels dresses? I don't think it improves you! Your grey cashmere suits you much better."

"Yes, Adolphine, but that's a walking-dress."

"Oh, of course, you can't wear that at a dinner, at a dinner-party. Still, I prefer that walking-dress."

"Won't you come in for a moment?"

"No, I'm only in walking-dress, you see, Constance dear. And Carolientje too. And then I don't want to disturb you, at your men's dinner-party."

"I'm sorry, Adolphine, that you should have called just this night, if you won't come in. Come in to tea some other evening soon, will you?"

"Well, you see, I don't often come this way: you live so far from everywhere, in this depressing Kerkhoflaan. At least, I always think it depressing. What induced you to come and live here, tell me, between two graveyards? It's not healthy to live in, you know, because of the miasma...."

"Oh, we never notice anything!"

"Ah, that's because you always keep your windows shut! You want more ventilation, really, in Holland. I assure you, I should stifle in this atmosphere."

"Come, Adolphine, do come in...."

"No, really not. I'm going; make my apologies to your husband. Good-bye, Constance. Come, Carolientje."

And, as though she were really suffocating, she hurried to the front-door with her daughter, first glancing through the open door of the dining-room, noticing the hot-house grapes, the pink roses, screwing up her eyes to read the label on the champagne-bottle from which Paul was filling up the glasses. Then she pushed Carolientje before her and departed, slamming the front-door after her....

Constance went back to the dining-room. Her nerves were shaken, but she kept a good countenance.

"It was Adolphine, wasn't it?" asked Paul.

"Yes, but she wouldn't come in," said Constance. "It's such a pity, she's such good company...."

She did not mean it, but she wished to mean it. That she said so was not hypocrisy on her part. Any other evening, after Adolphine's comments, all in five minutes, on her house, her street, her candles, her fires, her dress and her complexion, she would probably have flung herself at full length on her sofa, to recover from the annoyance of it. But now she was the hostess; and she showed no discomposure and asked the men not to mind her and to stay and smoke their cigars with her, at the dinner-table. She herself poured out the coffee, from her dainty little silver-gilt service, and the liqueurs; and, when Paul asked her if she would not smoke a cigarette, she answered, with her pretty expression and the little laugh at the bend of her lips which made her so young that night and caused her to look so very charming:

"No, I used to smoke, in my flighty days; but I gave it up long ago."

CHAPTER XXII

Marietje van Saetzema stood at the window and looked out into the street. She looked down the whole street, because the house, a corner-house, stood not in the length of it, but in the width, half-closing the street, making it a sort of courtyard of big houses. The street stretched to some distance; and another house part-closed the farther end, turning it actually into a courtyard, occupied by well-to-do people. The two rows of gables ran along with a fine independence of chimney-stacks, of little cast-iron pinnacles and pointed zinc roofs, little copper weathercocks and little balconies and bow-windows, as though the architects and builders had conspired to produce something artistic and refused to design one long monotonous gable-line. But the new street—it was about twenty years old—had nevertheless retained the Dutch trimness that characterizes the dwellings of the better classes: the well-scrubbed pavements ran into the distance, growing ever narrower to the eye, with their grey hem of kerb-stone, their regularly-recurring lamp-posts; in the middle of the street was a plantation: oval grass-plots surrounded by low railings, in which were chestnut-trees, neatly pruned, and, beneath them, a neat shrubbery of dwarf firs. The fronts of the houses glistened with cleanliness after the spring cleaning; the tidily-laid bricks displayed their rectangular outlines clearly, even at a distance; the window-frames were bright with fresh paint, dazzling cream-colour or pale brown; the blinds, neatly lowered in front of the shining plate-glass windows, were let down in each house precisely the same depth, as though mathematically measured; and the houses concealed their inner lives very quietly behind the straight, nicely-balanced lace curtains. And this was very characteristic, that above each gable there jutted a flagstaff, held aslant with iron pins, the staff painted a bright red, white and blue—the national colours—as though wound about with ribbons, with a freshly-gilded knob at the top. All those flagstaffs—a forest of staffs, with their iron pins, for ever aslant on the gables—waited patiently to hoist their colours, to wave their bunting, twice a year, for the Queen and her mother, the Regent.

Marietje looked out. It was May; and the chestnuts in the grass-plots tried to outstretch and unfurl their soft, pale-green fans, now folded and bent back against their stalks. But a mad wind whirled through the street, which was like a courtyard of opulence, and the wind scourged the still furled chestnut-fans. The girl looked at them compassionately as they were whipped to and fro by the wind, the eager young leaves which, full of vernal life and pride of youth, were trying hard to unfold. The tender leaves were full of hope, because yesterday the sun had shone, after the rain, out of a flood-swept sky; and they thought that their leafy days were beginning, their life of leaves budding out from stalk and twig. They did not know that the wind was always at work, lashing, as with angry scourges, with stinging whips; they did not know that their leafy parents had been lashed last year, even as they were now; and, though they loved the wind, upon which they dreamt of floating and waving and being merry and happy, they never expected to be lashed with whips even before they had unfurled all the young bravery of their green.

The wind was pitiless. The wind lashed through the air like one possessed, like a madman that had no feeling: strong in his might and blind in his heartlessness. And the girl's pity went out to the eager leaves, the young, hoping leaves, which she saw shaken and pulled and scourged and driven withered across the street. The blind, all-powerful north-east wind filled the street: the weathercocks spun madly; the iron pins of the flagstaff creaked goutily and painfully; the flagstaffs themselves bent as though they were the masts of a fleet of houses moored in a roadstead of bricks.

The girl looked out into the street. It was a May morning. Standing in front of one house and looking for all the world like sailors on a ship were men dressed in white sailors'-jackets, busy fixing ladders and climbing up them to clean the plate-glass windows. They swarmed up the ladders, carrying pails of water; and, in the midst of the forest of masts, of the red-white-and-blue flagstaffs, they looked like seamen gaily rigging a ship.

Along the street went the brightly-painted carts of a laundry, a pastrycook, a butter-factory. Hard behind came loud-voiced hawkers pushing barrows with oranges and the very first purple-stained strawberries. And the whole economy of eating and drinking of those tidy houses, whose life lay hidden behind their lace curtains, filled the morning street. Butcher-boys prevailed. Each house had a different butcher. Broad and sturdy, the boys walked along in their clean, white smocks, carrying their wicker baskets of quivering meat held, with a fist at the handle, firmly on shoulder or hip, bending their bodies a little because of the weight; and they rang at all the doors. Sometimes, a couple bicycled swiftly down the street. At all the houses they delivered loads of meat: beefsteaks and rumpsteaks and fillet-steaks and ribs and sirloins of beef and balls of forced-meat; the maid-servants took the meat in at the front-doors, with an exchange of chaff, and then closed the door again with a bang. The butcher-boys largely prevailed; but the greengrocers, with their barrows arranged with fresh vegetables, were also many in number. The dairy, with its cart filled with polished copper cans, rang at every door; and notable for its ostentatious neatness was a van conveying beer in cans: the driver, who was constantly getting down and ringing, wore a sort of brown shooting-suit, with top-boots and a motor-cap; the cart was painted with earthenware cans swelling out in relief from the panels. A barrel-organ quavered on, playing a very doleful tune: the organ-man ground out a bit of dolefulness, stopped and then pushed on again; his old woman rang at every door, put the coppers she received in her pocket, as if she were collecting so many debts. Each time, the maids, in their lilac-print dresses, appeared at the doors, or leant out and looked from the open windows of the bedrooms, or called out and flung down the rich man's dole of coppers. Domestic economy filled the street, while the wind, the blundering, mighty wind, blew on. A gentleman passed on his way to his office, hugging a portfolio. Two girls flew by on bicycles; a lady hurried along on some urgent errand. But, for the rest, there was nothing but the economy of eating and drinking. It filled the street, it rang and rang and rang until all the houses chimed with the ringing. And the houses took in their supplies, the street grew quiet: only the wind blew the young chestnut-leaves to pieces and the flagstaffs groaned on their creaking, gouty pins....

Marietje turned away. She was a pale, fair-haired little thing of sixteen, with pale-blue eyes and a white, bloodless skin. Her hair, brushed off her forehead, was already done up behind into a knob. She wore a little pinafore to protect her frock. And now she sat down at the piano and began to tap out her scales.

The room in which Marietje was practising was the drawing-room. It was a fairly large room on the first floor, but it was so terribly crammed with furniture, arranged in studied confusion, with an affectation of elegance, that there was hardly space to move about or sit. On the backs of all the chairs hung fancy antimacassars, flattened by the pressure of reclining forms, with faded and crumpled ribbons. On all sorts of little tables stood nameless ornaments: little earthenware dogs and china smelling-bottles, set out as in a tenpenny bazaar. The wall-paper displayed big flowers, the carpet more big flowers, of a different species, while on the curtains blossomed a third kind of flower; and the colours of all these flowers yelled at one another like so many screeching parrots. In the corners of the room rose dusty Makart bouquets, which decorated those same corners year in, year out.

Marietje played her scales in the drawing-room, while the wind howled down the chimney, which smelt of soot after the winter fires. Conscientiously Marietje played her scales with her stubborn little fingers, constantly making the same mistake, which she did not hear and therefore did not correct, thinking that it was right as it was. Now and then, she looked up through the window: "Poor trees!" thought Marietje. "Poor leaves! See how the wind's killing them; and they're hardly open yet!..."

She played on, conscientiously, but she dearly wished that she could make the wind stop, to save the leaves, the young chestnut-leaves. She remembered, it was just the same thing last spring. The spring before that, it was the same too. And then, when the chestnut-leaves were at last able to unfurl themselves, in a quiet, windless moment, then they were scorched and shrivelled for the whole summer, for their whole leafy lives. Poor trees! Poor leaves!...

The stubborn fingers went on conscientiously, tapping out the scales and constantly playing that same wrong note with almost comical persistency: ting! The front-door bell was constantly going ting-a-ling, ting-a-ling! All those noises—the wind: whew, boo! The scales: ta-ta, ta-ta, ta-ta, ta-ta; ta-ta, ta-ta, ta-ta, ta-ta. The front-door bell: ting-a-ling, ting-a-ling! The barrel-organs in the street, two going at the same time. The colours indoors: the colours of the wall-paper and curtains and carpet, screeching like parrots. The cries of the costermongers outside: "Strawberrees!... Fine strawberrees!" The rattle of the greengrocers' carts, clattering over the noisy cobble-stones—all these noises rang out together and it was as though the wind defined and accentuated each individual sound, blowing away a mist from each sound, leaving only the rough, resonant kernel of each sound to ring out against the glittering plate-glass windows, along the goutily-creaking flagstaffs, into this room, where the parrot-colours jabbered aloud....

It blew and rang and screeched and jabbered; and the girl with her continual false note—ting!—heard none of it, but thought only, "Oh, those poor trees! Oh, those poor leaves!" in her gentle little, hypersensitive soul. Used as she was to the wind, the noises and the colours, she saw nothing but the trees, heard nothing but the rustling of the leaves, nor heard her own persistent little false note: ting!

Ting-a-ling, ting-a-ling went the bell; and the wind must have rushed through the front-door and up the stairs, for the drawing-room door blew open as lightly as though the great door had been no more than a sheet of note-paper; the maid came pounding up the stairs, the stairs creaked, another door slammed; the maid, at the door, screamed out something loud through the house, loud through the wind, loud through all the sounds and colours; another voice sounded sharply in reply; the maid went pounding down again, the stairs creaked and bang went the door:

"Will you please go upstairs, mevrouw?"

"Come upstairs, Cateau!"

"But am I re-ally not disturb-ing you, Adolph-ine?"

"No, come up."

"What a *wind*, eh, Phi-i-ine? Eh? How it's blow-ing!"

Ta-ta, ta-ta, ta-ta, ta-ta; ta-ta, ta-ta, ta-ta, ta-ta, went Marietje's scales, as Mamma entered with Aunt Cateau. Whew, boo! blew the wind. C-r-rack, cr-r-rack! went the flagstaff outside the window....

"Good-morn-ing, Marie-tje. And *tell* me, Phi-i-ine, was it a reg-ular din-ner?"

"Yes, it was a formal dinner."

"Oh, so they *do* see peo-ple? And I *thought* they lived so qui-etly. We are nev-er asked there; are *you*, Adolph-ine?"

"No, never."

"I do think she might al-so some-times show a little polite-ness to her brothers and sis-ters. We nev-er see peo-ple, as you know, *don't* you, Adolph-ine? Ka-rel doesn't *care* for it; he only cares for qui-et. *I* should rather *like* it. But it's Ka-rel, you see, who doesn't *care* for it. And who were there, Adolph-ine?"

"Oh, well, they know nobody, so it looked to me rather like a failure. Nobody except that Vreeswijck. No doubt, they'd had one or two refusals, for they'd asked Paul to make up the party."

"Oh, *Paul*? No doubt, one or two *must* have refused!"

"Yes, of course."

"Well, re-ally, Con-stance is ... But then *I* don't call a din-ner like that a *success*. Do *you*, Adolph-ine?"

"No, I thought it ridiculous. A dinner-party of four!"

"Were the men *dressed*?"

"Yes, dressed."

"And Con-stance? Low-necked?"

"No, not low-necked, but smart as paint. And champagne!"

"Re-ally! Cham-pagne as we-ell?"

"Yes, a cheap brand. And the rooms so dark: I didn't think it respectable. Such a dim light, you know. Quite disreputable, I thought, with those three men," said Adolphine, whispering because of Marietje.

"She can't hear, she's play-ing. Oh, re-ally! And what next?"

"Well, I think, if Constance wants to see people in that sort of way, she could have done so just as well in Brussels. She's supposed to have come here for the family."

"But she doesn't *ask* the fam-ily. Oh, you mustn't count *us*, Phi-i-ine. We al-ways live ve-ry qui-etly. It's Ka-rel, you see."

"But I feel sure now that she means to get presented at Court."

"Yes, by Vrees-wijck, no doubt. Will he present her to the *Queen?*' asked Cateau, rounding her owl's eyes.

"Oh, no!" said Adolphine, irritably. "But they mean to push themselves with his assistance."

"Oh, is *that* the way it's done? You see, *we* know no-thing about the *Court*. You wouldn't get Ka-rel to go to *Court* for any-thing! Not if you *paid* him! But *now* it's *quite* cert-ain."

"Yes, I'm convinced of it now."

"About the *Court?*'

"Yes."

"Oh! Well, I al-ways thought that Con-stance would have too much *tact* for *that*. And may I have a look at Floortje's trous-seau now, Adolph-ine? She'll be mar-ried *quite* soon now, *won't* she? In a week? Ah! And I al-ways think it so *nice* to be mar-ried in *May*, don't *you*, Adolph-ine?"

The two sisters' voices whined and snarled, the stairs creaked, the doors slammed. Ta-ta, ta-ta, ta-ta, ta-ta, went the scales. Whew, boo, whew! went the wind, roaring down the sooty chimney. Cr-r-rack! Cr-r-rack! went the gouty flagstaff. "Strawberrees!... Fine strawberrees!" shouted the costermonger outside. Ting! went Marietje's obstinate false note.

The girl looked up through the window.

"Those poor trees!" thought Marietje. "Oh, those poor leaves!..."

CHAPTER XXIII

Adolphine enjoyed showing Cateau Floortje's trousseau, with its stacks of linen. Adolphine attached more importance to her own house, her own children, her own furniture, her own affairs, matters and things than to anything else in the world. She was never tired of displaying, for the extorted admiration of the sister or friend who came to visit her, the thickness of her carpets, the heaviness of her curtains, the taste with which she had arranged the ornaments in her drawing-room; and she praised all that belonged to her, cried it up as though for a sale, inviting the appreciation of her sister or friend. In her heart of hearts, she was always afraid of being eclipsed and, in order to conceal her fear from the other's eyes, she bragged and boasted of all her belongings. The fact that she was a Van Lowe appeared in this, that she included her husband and children and puffed them up also in her general self-glorification. And in all her bragging one could easily detect a shade of reproach against her family, her acquaintances, the Hague, because nothing about her was properly valued: not she, nor her husband, nor her house, nor her furniture, nor her ideas, nor the street she lived in. And she explained at great length to the friend or sister her way of thinking, of managing, of calculating, of bringing up children, of furnishing, of giving dinners, of ordering a dress, as though all of this was of such immense interest to the friend or sister that nothing more immense could be imagined. If, thereupon, the friend or sister, for the sake of conversation, in her turn described her own thoughts, or arrangements, or methods of entertaining, Adolphine was unable to listen to a word and showed plainly that the affairs of the sister or friend did not interest her in the least and that, for instance, the quality of the covering of her, Adolphine's, chairs, or the fresh air of the street in which she, Adolphine, lived, or the velvet of the collar of the great-coat of Van Saetzema, Adolphine's husband, was of much greater importance. For she wanted the sister or friend to realize, above anything else, that in her, Adolphine's, life everything was of the best and finest kind: things animate and inanimate, things movable and immovable alike. Adolphine's cook, the sister or friend was assured, cooked better than any other cook, especially than Bertha's cook; Adolphine's dog, a pug, was the sweetest pug of all the pugs in the world. And, while she bragged like this, she was filled with a deep-seated dread, asked herself, almost unconsciously:

"Can my cook really cook? And isn't my pug, if the truth were told, an ill-tempered little brute?"

But these were deeply-hidden doubts; and, to her family and friends, Adolphine boasted loudly of all and everything that belonged to her and insisted upon an admiring appreciation of her children and furniture. It was part of her nature to want to be high-placed—she was her father's child—to be rich, to have everything fine and imposing and distinguished about her; and it was as though fate had compelled her, from a child, to have everything a little, a trifle less good than her family and friends. In reality, she was never satisfied, for all her boasting. In reality, she reproached life with its horrible injustice. As a child, she was a plain, unattractive girl, whereas Bertha was at least passable and Constance was decidedly pretty. That Dorine was not pretty either did not console her; she did not even notice it. Both Bertha and Constance had been presented at Court, one as a young woman, the other as a mere girl. After Constance' marriage, however, her father and mother had conceived a sort of weariness of society; and, whenever Mamma did suggest that it was perhaps time for Adolphine to be presented too, Papa used to say:

"Oh, what good has it done the others?"

And, for one reason or another, Adolphine had never been presented. She never forgave her parents, nor, for that matter, her sisters; but she always said that she did not care in the least for all that fuss about the Court. She was married early, at twenty; she accepted Van Saetzema almost for fear lest life should show itself unjust once more if she refused him. And Van Saetzema had proposed to her, even as hundreds of men propose to hundreds of women, for one or other of those very small reasons of small people which work like tiny wheels in small souls and which others are not able to understand, so that they ask themselves in amazement:

"Why on earth did So-and-so do this or that; why did this or that happen to So-and-so; why did So-and-so marry So-and-so?..."

Van Saetzema had a fine-sounding name, was a doctor of laws, had a little money: Adolphine had risked it. But, while Van Naghel, after practising at the bar in India, was making his way through interest, through his political tact, through the influence of Papa van Lowe, who liked him, while Van Naghel was placed on all sorts of committees, each of which raised him one rung higher in the official world of the Hague, until he was elected a member of the Second Chamber and at last entered the Cabinet as colonial secretary, Van Saetzema remained quietly jogging on at the Ministry of Justice, with out ever obtaining any special promotion, without ever receiving any special opportunity, without being pushed on much by Papa van Lowe, just as though Papa, with a sort of step-fatherly disdain, had thought this as little worth while as having Adolphine presented at Court. Van Saetzema was now chief clerk, was a respected public servant, performing his work accurately and well and even valued by the secretary-general; but there it ended. And this was the despair of Adolphine, who, ever since Van Naghel had become a minister, wanted to see her husband a minister too, a hope which there was not the least prospect of ever realizing. And so Adolphine had to look on at all Van Naghel and Bertha's distinction with envious eyes; and, however much she might boast of everything that belonged to her, that distinction, which she would never achieve, remained a torture to her vanity. It had come of itself, in the course of Van Naghel and Bertha's life—through Papa's patronage, through Van Naghel's own connections and his Overijssel family, which had always played a part in the political history of the country—it had come of itself that not only had Van Naghel attained a high level in his career, but his house had become a political and also an aristocratic *salon* at the Hague, as though, through their respective connections, Van Naghel and Bertha, after Papa van Lowe's death, had continued the tradition which, after the viceregal period, had prevailed in the

Alexanderstraat, where Mamma was now left peacefully leading her after-life as an old woman and a widow. On the other hand, Adolphine's house, in spite of all her wishes and endeavours, had never been anything more than an omnium-gatherum, a rubbish heap. She lacked tact and the gift of discrimination. She thought that for her too to have a busy house would give her something of Bertha's importance and distinction; and so she paid visits right and left and had a multitude of incongruous acquaintances, all belonging to different sets: the orthodox set; the Indian set; the official set; the military set; but not, alas, the Court set nor the leaven of aristocracy which, after Papa's death, at first used to leave a card, once a year or so, but had gradually dropped her. And so it had come of itself, in the course of their, Van Saetzema and Adolphine's, life, that their house had become an ever-increasing omnium-gatherum: a busy house, it is true, where they "saw people," but a nondescript house, where one never knew whom one would meet nor what the hostess was really aiming at. There was something maddening about Adolphine's way of turning her house into a busy house, crammed with people. She would propose, for instance, to give a small dinner five days later; she would ask eight people, but remember, two days before the dinner, that she might as well ask a few more; then she would send round a few quite formal invitations, couched in terms which were out of keeping with the interval between the date of the invitation and the date of the dinner, with the result that, first of all, she utterly put out the hired chef; that sometimes there was a bottle of champagne short; and that her guests invariably appeared in every possible gradation of evening-dress. Or, else, she thought of giving a big dinner, received a number of refusals, did not know whom to invite instead, asked people informally, or even by word of mouth, and found herself entertaining half-a-dozen guests with a super-abundance of dishes and wine, while once again the men were dressed, one in a swallow-tail coat and white tie, the other in a morning-coat; the ladies, one in a low-necked bodice, the other in a blouse: a disparity that was constantly giving them fresh shocks of dismay.

It was always a medley; and, even as she lacked the tact to give a successful dinner, she was doomed to lack the tact to achieve the distinction for which she craved. Her very husband thwarted her: a simple man, a little boorish in his ways, who trudged daily to his office and back, conscientious about his work like a schoolboy finishing his exercises and devoid of any particular ability or political adroitness. He approved of what Adolphine did, but could not understand that craving, that vital need of hers for distinction. It was true that he had caught from his wife that exuberant satisfaction with *his* wife, *his* house, *his* children, *his* furniture and *his* friends. He too knew how to boast of *his* coat, *his* office, even *his* minister, *his* secretary-general. But Adolphine might have stood behind him with a whip and would still have urged him to the summits of earthly and Haguish greatness. He was ponderous, fog-brained, a man who worked by rote, who went his way like a draught-ox, year in, year out, with the same heavy tread of a Dutch steer under heavy Dutch skies: he bore within him the natural instinct to be an inferior, an underling, to remain in the background and there to go on working in an accurate, small-souled, worthy fashion, in the little groove in which he had first started.

They had three boys and three girls and they were not bad parents. They, both of them, loved their children and thought of their children's welfare. But they knew as little of a system of education as of a system of dinner-giving; and such education as existed in their house was as ramshackle as their friends, their rooms, their tables. It was especially where her children were concerned that Adolphine had that mania for having and doing everything in a very imposing fashion, a fashion at least as imposing as that in which Bertha had and did things for hers. As Adolphine, however, was the only one of the Van Lowes who was, by exception, thrifty, her thrift often waged a severe struggle with her yearning for what was imposing. And so, whereas everything relating to the Van Naghels' household and the education of their children was conducted, as a matter of course, on the most expensive lines, which they both recognized as expensive, but which their tastes and their manner of life made it impossible to alter, everything at Adolphine's was done cheaply. And so, whereas Louise and Emilie and Marianne had been to expensive boarding-schools near London and Paris—great country-houses, where the daughters of wealthy men received a fashionable education, with dancing-lessons in ball-dresses, drawing-, painting- and music-lessons given by well-known masters—Adolphine, though inwardly eaten up with jealousy, pronounced those boarding-schools simply absurd and quite beyond her means and discovered one near Cleves, to which she sent Floortje and Caroline: a very respectable establishment, but one where German shopkeepers' daughters were taken in and where a very different tone prevailed from that of the aristocratic schools near Paris and London. This, however, did not prevent Adolphine from extolling *her* boarding-school as far above those silly, frivolous institutions to which Bertha had sent her children. And, as regards the boys, Adolphine magnified *her* three boys, Piet, Chris and Jaap: the eldest was to enter the East-Indian civil service; the two others were intended for Breda and Willemsoord, which was better than those two spendthrift Leiden students, who were at it again, wanting some thousands of guilders for their approaching masques, and far better than that lazy lout of a Karel.

Also, Adolphine was always drawing comparisons between her Marietje, a gentle, fair, white-skinned little girl, a bit subdued amid the blatancy of the others, and Bertha's Marietje: comparisons invariably in her own child's favour; but now, after Emilie's wedding with Van Raven, she drew comparisons more particularly between Emilie's wedding-preparations and all that she, Adolphine, was doing for Floortje and Dijkerhof. And brag and boast as she might, she, the exception among the Van Lowes, the thrifty Adolphine, who counted every twopenny-bit—where *did* she get those economical ideas from? Mamma van Lowe would sometimes ask herself—was unable to come within hailing-distance of what Van Naghel and Bertha and the Van Ravens and their friends on both sides had done; she thought it absurd, she thought it flinging money away, she grumbled to herself that everything had gone up so terribly in price: a deep-rooted prudence—an atavistic quality, a mysterious throw-back—disapproved of that luxury of parties, trousseaus, presents, flowers with which Emilie's wedding-days had glittered; she thought it ridiculous, she wanted to do everything more economically and yet she did not like doing everything so economically; and so there was an incessant struggle, both with herself and with Floortje, who also did not wish to be second to Emilie and who gave no thought to money: it was only her parents' money! But still, with her peculiar gift of self-glorification, Adolphine was now able to praise Floortje's trousseau to Cateau above all those lace fripperies of Emilie's.

"Much ni-cer and more last-ing, *I* think, Adolph-ine!" whined Cateau.

"Yes; and just look at those chemises, look at those table-cloths and napkins: there's quality there, you can't beat it," said Adolphine, patting the stacks of linen in the cupboard. "And all those silly presents which Emilie had, all that silver, which she can't use: what do young people, who of course won't be seeing people for the first few years, want with so much silver? I'm very glad that *our* friends have been more practical in choosing their presents for Floortje: *I* shouldn't have been at all pleased if Floortje had been set up in her silver-cupboard by people whom you may call acquaintances, if you like, but who, after all, are strangers."

"Ye-e-es," whined Cateau. "At Emilie-tje's reception, it looked just like Van Kempen's shop. I thought it so vul-gar and com-mon, didn't *you*, Adolph-ine?"

The epithets were not exceptionally well-chosen as applied to Van Naghel and Bertha—even Adolphine could see that—but she admired her own purchases and *her* friends' presents too greatly to say so to Cateau.

CHAPTER XXIV

Constance made it a duty to go often to Adolphine's during Floortje's wedding-preliminaries. She went out of her way to be cordial; she sent a beautiful basket of flowers on the day of the contract; she gave a handsome present, much more expensive than the one which she had sent Emilie; and she showed great interest in the party and the dinner that were to be given at the Witte Brug. She examined attentively the open presses with the stacks of linen composing Floortje's trousseau—"Just look at those chemises; and those table-cloths and napkins: there's quality there, you can't beat it. Just feel them, only feel them! Whereas those fripperies of Emilie's...!"—and listened attentively to the endless paeans of self-glorification, spent herself in admiration, was determined to flatter Adolphine and to make a good impression on her sister. Because, during those days, she had conscientiously set herself the task of winning over Adolphine, she swallowed the criticism that was never wanting, little spiteful arrows shot off in between the paeans:

"How pale you're looking! Have you been using too much powder again, or aren't you well?... What a pity that your boy is such an old gentleman, Constance!... Tell me, Constance: your father- and mother-in-law were not very nice to you, were they?... Constance, are those rings of yours real?... Oh, really? Upon my word, I thought one of those stones was paste...."

She swallowed it all, accepted the affront with a gentle smile, a word of almost assenting reply: "Yes, Addie is rather old-fashioned.... Oh, it was very difficult for Papa and Mamma van der Welcke.... You are right, that stone is a little dull sometimes...."

She swallowed it, took it all so gently and so submissively that Addie, when he happened to be present, looked up at his mother in surprise, thinking her so different from the woman whom he knew, who blazed out for the least thing at Papa and who always behaved towards himself as the spoilt little mother who wanted to be petted and loved by her boy. And the lad, in his small, bright, earnest, doughty soul, felt a sort of amazement at that puzzle of a woman's soul that was his mother's:

"Are they all like that, so queer? Or is it only Mamma? And why is she so forbearing towards Aunt Adolphine, when she can't bear the least thing from Papa?"

This made him still more of a little man towards his mother, with something protecting and condescending, because she was so weak and irresolute and excitable, but also with very much that was affectionate, because that strange womanliness possessed a charm for his small male soul.

Adolphine, however, on the day when the contract was signed, at the big family-dinner at the Witte Brug and the subsequent evening-party for all the friends and relations, boasted aloud in her self-complacency. She bragged to Uncle Ruyvenaer, to Karel and Cateau, to Constance, to Gerrit and Adeline: *those* were fine rooms, the rooms of the Witte Brug, much finer than the rooms in the Doelen; that was a splendid dinner, the dinner which *she* had given: it cost a lot of money, though, and she told how much, but added a couple of hundred guilders to the cost; and did they remember that impossible dinner of Bertha's, at Emilie's wedding, and the queer dishes that had been set before them? Wasn't it a splendid dessert, with beautiful strawberries, which *she* had given? And so *many* and at this season, too: but you had to pay for them! And how gay they had been at table, *her* family—as though that same family were not also Bertha's family—and *her* friends: so very different from that pretentious set of Bertha's! There was such a gay, spontaneous tone in the speeches and the conversation; and did Gerrit remember that deathly stillness at table at Emilietje's dinner? Such nice people, Dijkerhof's parents, *her* girl's future father- and mother-in-law.... And how well Floortje looked, didn't she? And the other girls were prettily dressed too. She boasted so breathlessly of everything, of every detail, that neither Uncle nor Gerrit had a single opportunity of expressing their appreciation, of giving voice to their admiration; and it was not until she had passed on, boasting right and left to her acquaintances—"Well, what do you say to *my* dinner? Well, what do you say to *my* party? Well, what do you think of *my* dress?'—that Uncle Ruyvenaer said:

"Any one would think that Adolphine had built the Witte Brug herself!"

"*I* think," whined Cateau, "Adolph-ine oughtn't to say all those things her-self, don't *you*, Ger-rit?"

"Well," said Gerrit, "it's a delightful feeling to be so pleased with your own self and your own children and your own dinner. But, if you think as you do, Cateau, why didn't you compliment her yourself?"

"Be-cause I *think*," whined Cateau, whining worse than usual, "that that dress doesn't look at *all* smart on Adolph-ine. What do *you* think, A-deline?"

"Oh, I don't know," said Adeline, good-naturedly.

"Con-stance, *you* have such *very* good taste: do tell me, do *you* think that dress looks *smart*?"

"I think Adolphine looks exceedingly well to-night," said Constance, irritably.

"I say, Sissy, you can't mean that!" said Gerrit.

"And, even if you don't think so, Gerrit, it's not nice of you to speak like that of your sister!"

"Oh, well, a little criticism!..."

"Yes, but to be always criticizing one another is horrid, I think," said Constance, angrily.

"I'm bound to say, though, that I think it a ramshackle party," said Uncle Ruyvenaer. "Who on earth are all these people?" he continued, putting on dignity, disdainfully. "I say, Toetie, are you enjoying yourself?"

"Yes, Papa, awfully!" said Toetie, as she passed on her partner's arm.

The Ruyvenaer girls, though no longer young, always enjoyed themselves "awfully," not caring whether it was at Bertha's or Adolphine's. Good-natured, kindly, simply and pleasantly Indian in their ways, they loved dancing, they always enjoyed themselves "awfully."

"And, Dotje, what do you think of *my* party?"

"Oh, Adolphine, so jolly your party: I'm enjoying it awfully."

And Dot also shone with gratitude and perspiration after dancing.

"Are those the Dijkerhofs' friends?" asked Mamma van Lowe, in a whisper, of Bertha, glancing towards a gentleman and a lady who had been introduced to her, but whose name she had not caught. "What strange friends those Dijkerhofs have! Such obscure people: one never knows who they are or what they are! Very vulgar people, I think. It's such a pity, Bertha, isn't it? Dijkerhof himself is not bad; and, if Floortje is fond of him, well, I suppose it will be all right; but I must admit I am sorry that Adolphine is mixed up with this lot.... And those people over there, Bertha, the stout man and the tall woman with whom Adeline is talking so familiarly: are those intimate friends? What curious friends she has!... It must strike Constance too, now that she's come back to it all. At our house there was a certain harmony, a set, as there is in your house now, Bertha. But, at Adolphine's, it's always such a queer lot, such a queer lot! I can't call it anything else. Goodness gracious, what a number of curious people!"

"Mamma," said Paul, "what do you think of this menagerie of Adolphine's?"

"Oh, Paul," sighed the old lady, a little nervously, "I was just saying to Bertha ... But we mustn't let any one else notice what we think...."

"I say, Mamma," asked Gerrit, "do you know who those two are?"

"No, Gerrit. Van Naghel, do you know who those two people are: that stout gentleman and that tall lady?"

"Yes, Mamma: it's Bruys and his wife. He's the editor of the *Fonograaf:* very respectable people, Mamma...."

"My dear Van Naghel!..."

Utterly perplexed, the old lady passed on, leaning on Van Naghel's arm....

Constance had overheard the comments of the family upon Adolphine's friends. She herself, newcomer that she now was in Hague society, was not so greatly struck by the fact that Adolphine's guests consisted of all sorts of dissimilar elements: she had sometimes at Rome had to suffer incongruous elements at her big receptions and she had often found, abroad, that it was possible for witty, polished, cultured people to exist, even though they did not belong to her set. Then again she considered that, at a wedding-party, which was attended by relations' relations and friends' friends, it was almost inevitable that the guests were sometimes entirely unknown to one another: wasn't it the same at Bertha's party? Yes, Bertha had given two evening-parties, in order to separate the elements; but hadn't the family found fault with this? Was there nothing but fault-finding and criticizing in the family; and did none think right what another did? Gerrit and Paul were now sitting beside her; and she heard them talking, condemning, criticizing, ridiculing.

"Poor, dear Mother: she's quite bewildered!"

"I say, Paul, are you allowing yourself to be introduced to Dijkerhof's uncles and aunts?"

"I'm not going to be introduced to another soul," said Paul, wearily blinking his eyes. "I'm here to make studies. The only way to amuse yourself in a Noah's ark like this party of Adolphine's is to make studies of the animal side of mankind. Look at Mrs. Bruys eating her cake with an almost animal satisfaction. Look at that uncle of Dijkerhof's dancing with Van Saetzema's cousin: it's almost disgusting."

"Paul," said Constance, "I've known you wittier than you are to-night."

"My dear sister, I feel myself growing dull here. The figures and colours swarm before my eyes so hideously as really to cause me physical pain. My God, the charm of our modern life, the charm at an evening-party of Adolphine's: where is it, where is it?"

"It's gone, it's gone!" Gerrit noisily declaimed. "Adolphine's charm is gone!"

"I don't think either of you at all nice!" Constance broke in, irritably. "Tell me, my dear brothers, is this irony, this fault-finding tone, usual among us? Has it become a custom for the brothers and sisters to carp and cavil at one another—and even for Mamma to cavil at her children—as I have heard you all do to-night? Does each of us criticize the other in a general cross-fire of criticism? I heard something of the kind at Bertha's party; but is there really nothing good here to-night? I feel bound to tell you I think you very petty, provincial, narrow-minded and cliquey: even you, Paul, for all your philosophy! You, Gerrit, are afraid of demeaning yourself by allowing yourself to be introduced to a few of Dijkerhof's uncles and aunts, whom perhaps you won't see three times again as long as you live; and, as for you, Paul, why are you so spiteful in your comments on absolute strangers who don't eat a cake in the exact way which you approve of? I think Uncle Ruyvenaer ridiculous: he's not particularly well-bred himself and he sneers at the breeding of Van Saetzema's friends; I think Cateau ridiculous: she hasn't the faintest pretensions to smartness, though her clothes may be good and substantial, and she criticizes Adolphine's smartness...."

"O dear, gentle soul!" said Paul, affectedly, and took Constance' hand. "O proud and noble one! O heroine in a sacred cause! You are a revelation to me! How broad are the principles which you proclaim, how great your tolerance! It is terrible! Only you, you dear, gentle soul, are not so sparing of the criticism which you criticize in us."

"Very well, I criticized you, for once; but you're criticizing others everlastingly."

"No, not quite; but we're only very small people and we think it fun to pass remarks on others," said Gerrit.

"I am a very small person, like yourselves. I have never met big people, in our 'set,'" said Constance, with a sneer. "What is any one in our set *but* small?"

"Good!" said Paul. "Well done! You got that from me. But proceed, my fond disciple!"

"I am frightened!" said Constance, earnestly. "You think I am only just exciting myself a little, but I'm frightened, I'm simply frightened. I hear so much criticism from the mouths of my relations on every side, criticism on a dress, on an evening-party, on a couple of utter strangers who happen to be friends of my sister's, that I am frightened of the criticism of my relations concerning myself, myself in whom there is so much to criticize."

"Come, Sis!" said Gerrit, good-naturedly, restlessly stretching out his long legs.

"Mayn't I speak out my mind, to my brothers?" asked Constance. "Have I come back to the Hague and to all of you, after being away for years, to behave as though nothing had happened to separate me from all of you who are dear to me?"

"O tender one!" said Paul. "Hearken unto the words of wisdom of your younger brother! You're afraid of criticism, because you fear that, where so much criticism is passed, in such a hot-bed of criticism as our family, you yourself will not escape a severe judgment. But let me tell you now that you don't know humanity, the humanity of small people. Small people criticize—because they think it fun, as Gerrit says—criticize a dress, or an evening-party, but they never criticize life. To begin with, they're afraid to: small people are interested only in what is not serious, in what is really not worth while."

"I don't believe you," said Constance. "That's a clever phrase, Paul, and nothing more. I am becoming distrustful. When I hear so much criticizing—even from Mamma—on Adolphine, I ask myself, 'What will my mother, what will my brothers and sisters find to say of me?...' Oh, perhaps it can't be helped; perhaps everything is insincere, in our set!"

"But not in our family," said Gerrit.

"You say that, Gerrit, with a nice sound in your voice."

"The captain of hussars with the nice sound in his voice!" said Paul.

"You silly boy! Be serious for a moment, if you can! I am frightened, I am frightened. Honestly, it makes me nervous. Perhaps I did wrong, perhaps I ought not to have come back here, to the Hague, among all of you...."

"Are you so disappointed in your brothers and sisters?" asked Gerrit.

"I am not complaining on my own behalf now, I am complaining on behalf of Adolphine. I think you others are not tolerant enough of anything that does not appeal to your taste. That's all. I am not complaining as far as I'm concerned. You have all received me very nicely; only, I am frightened. I'm frightened, I'm frightened.... Tell me, is it possible that there should be a strong family-feeling, a mutual kindliness, when the daily criticism is so inexorable?"

"The daily criticism in the family: what a good title for an essay!"

"Paul, do be serious!"

"My dear Connie, you know I can't. Alas, I can only be serious when I am holding forth myself!"

"Well, then, I'll let you talk...."

"That's generous of you. My Connie, you must remember this—it's a cruel law in our social life—that parents care much for their children, but children less for their parents; that the family-bonds become still looser between brothers and sisters; and that those bonds gradually become wholly loosened between uncles and aunts and nephews and nieces and cousins. Family-life may have existed in the days of the old patriarchs, who went into the wilderness with sons and daughters and herds, but it has ceased to exist in our modern days. At Gerrit's, although he has no herds, a little bit of it may still exist, because his children are very many and very small. But, when children are a little bigger, they want to stretch their wings; and then the family-bonds get loosened. If children marry, then each child has his own family—for so long as it lasts—and his own interests; and the bonds that bound together the patriarchal family of the desert flap lightly in the wind. Now how can you expect criticism, the greatest and cheapest 'fun' that man can have at his fellow-man's expense, not to be directed at relations, when the word 'relation' is really only a synonym for 'stranger'? There is no such thing as the family in modern society. Each man is himself. But in natures such as yours and Mamma's there remains something nice and atavistic that belongs to the patriarchal family of the desert: you would like to see the family exist, with family-love, love of parents for children and children for parents, of brothers and sisters and even nephews and nieces and uncles and aunts and cousins. Mamma, who has a simple nature, has instituted, for the satisfying of that feeling, a weekly evening at which we, who are related by blood but not by interest, meet out of deference for an old woman whom we do not want to grieve, whom we wish to leave in her illusion. You, my noble, gentle one, with your more complex character, feel a more powerful yearning for the old patriarchal life of the desert, especially after the sorrow and loneliness which you have known in your life. And you come to the Hague, with your pastoral ideas, to find yourself in the midst of polished cannibals, who rend one another daily into tiny pieces and eat one another up with their family-criticism. That your gentle nature should be shocked at the spectacle was only to be expected."

"So we are all strangers to one another," said Constance; and a chilly feeling passed over her, a melancholy rose within her at the sound of those words of Paul's, half banter, half earnest. "We are strangers to one another. That feeling which I felt to be deep and true within myself, when I was abroad, and which drove me back to my family and my country is what you call atavistic and has no reason for existence, since we no longer live in Mosaic times. So we are strangers to one another, we who, for Mamma's sake, continue to greet one another as relations once a week, at her Sundays, because otherwise we should give her pain; and my longing for you all, whom I had not seen for twenty years, my yearning for you, which brought me back to my own country, was no more than an illusion, a phantom?..."

"Well, Connie, perhaps I was cruel; but, really, you are so pastoral! Country, native country! My dear child, what beautiful phrases: how well you remember your Dutch! I have forgotten the very words."

"Sis, dear," Gerrit interrupted, "don't listen to the fellow: he's talking nonsense. He denies everything because he loves to hear himself speak and because he is a humbug: to-morrow he will be defending the country and the family just as he is demolishing then to-night, No, Sis, believe me, there are such things as family and one's native country."

"Listen to the captain, the defender of his country, with the nice sound in his voice!"

"There is such a thing as family. Not only with me, because my children are still young, as Paul has been trying to explain, but everywhere, everywhere. I feel that you are my sister, even though I didn't see you for twenty years. I did not recognize you at once, perhaps; perhaps I have not quite got you back yet: when I think of Constance, I always think of my little sister who used to play in the river at Buitenzorg...."

"Oh, Gerrit, don't begin about my bare feet again!" said Constance, raising her finger.

"But I feel that you are not a stranger, that there is a bond between us, a relationship, something almost mystical...."

"Oh, I say, what a poetic captain of hussars!" cried Paul. "Once he lets himself go...!"

"And country, one's native country," Gerrit continued, impetuously, "there is such a thing as one's country: I feel it in me, Paul, you sceptic and philosopher, old before your time; I feel it in me, not as something poetical and mystical, my boy, like the family-feeling, but as something quite simple, when I ride at the head of my squadron; I feel it as something big and primitive and not at all complex, when I escort my Queen; I feel that there exists for me a land where I was born, out of which I have grown...."

"Adelientje!" Paul beckoned. "Do come here, Adelientje! Your husband is so poetic, you must really listen to him."

The fair-haired little mother came up.

"I feel that, if any one says anything about Holland, about my native land, criticizes it, speaks a disrespectful word of my sovereign, I feel something here, here, in my breast...."

"Adelientje, do listen! Your husband is not an orator, but still he feels that he feels something; in short, he feels! Loud cheers for the captain of hussars with the soft note in his voice and the mystic feelings!"

"Gerrit, they're teasing you!" said Adeline.

Gerrit shrugged his shoulders, a little angrily, a little uncomfortably, and stretched his long legs across the carpet.

"Gerrit," said Constance, "I'm glad you said what you did."

"It's all nonsense," growled Gerrit. "There is a tendency, not only in Paul,—he's a humbug—but in all sorts of people in our set, Constance, of which you were speaking so scornfully just now, to run Holland down, to think nothing Dutch good, to think our language ugly, to think everything French, English or German better than Dutch. Those are your smart Dutch people, Constance, your Hague people, whom you meet in Bertha's drawing-room, Constance. If they go abroad for a couple of months, they've forgotten their mother-tongue when they come back; but let them be three years without going to Paris, London or Berlin, they'll never, never, never forget their

French, their English or their German! Oh, they know their foreign languages so well!"

"Gerrit," said Paul, "what you say is true; but just try and say it in fine Dutch, Gerrit!"

"And, Sis," continued Gerrit, stammering a little, but full of mettle, "that is why I think it so nice that you, a woman like you, who have lived for years in Rome, in just that smart, cosmopolitan world where patriotism tends to disappear, that you, who have been away from your country for twenty years, that just you have felt awaken in yourself...."

"Bravo!" cried Paul. "His words are coming!"

"A feeling for your country, for your motherland, that made you long to see Holland again. I would never have suspected it in you; and that, Sissy, is why I should almost like to kiss you ... but we're at a party...."

"And a party of Adolphine's into the bargain. And Adelientje is jealous."

"No, I'm not!" said Adeline, good-naturedly.

"Well, then, Connie, here goes!"

And Gerrit gave his sister an offhand kiss.

"You're a couple of pastoral characters!" said Paul. "I can't compete with you."

"And now, Constance, a glass of champagne ... to drink to all the family and to our native land," said Gerrit; and, with Constance on his arm, he walked across the room to the buffet.

"Adelientje," said Paul, "was there ever such a madman as your husband?"

But Adolphine approached triumphant, trailing her satin train, which she thought magnificent, and, radiant with self-complacency, asked:

"Adeline, tell me now, what do you think of *my* party?"

"Oh, beautiful, Adolphine!" said Adeline.

"Adolphine," said Paul, "your party is simply dazzling. I have been to many parties in my life, but one like to-night's, never!"

"And a good dinner, wasn't it?"

"The dinner was so good, it couldn't have been better."

"How do you like my new dress, Adeline? Just see how it fits."

She passed her hands over her bosom.

"It's a very charming dress, Adolphine," said Adeline.

"Adolphine," said Paul, "that velvet on the collar of Saetzema's coat...."

"Yes?..."

"That's *good* velvet."

"Yes, they're his new dress-clothes, from Teunissen's."

"And that satin of Floortje's dress...."

"Yes?..."

"That's *good* satin."

"Oh, what do you know about satin?"

"Every one's saying so."

"Really?"

"Yes, I heard them saying so all over the room."

"Not really?"

"Yes, as I moved about among the people, I heard it whispered on every side, like a rumour: 'Have you noticed the satin of Floortje's dress?... I say, did you notice the satin of Floortje's dress?...'"

Adolphine looked vaguely in front of her, not knowing what to believe:

"Well, that frock cost ... a hundred and twenty guilders!" she said, lying to the extent of forty guilders; and, radiant, she went on and talked to Mrs. Bruys, the wife of the editor of the *Fonograaf:*

"And, mevrouw, what do you say to *my* party?"

"Paul," said Adeline, in gentle reproach, "I was really frightened that Adolphine would notice...."

CHAPTER XXV

Constance was happy. She began to realize more and more that she now had what she had missed for years: her family; she held it a privilege dearer every day that she was back in her own country, in Holland. It was as though she became more and more penetrated with the consciousness that she had found all her near ones again, that they had one and all forgiven her the past; and sometimes she imagined that it was not really twenty years since she went away: those twenty years seemed to shrink. In her brothers and sisters she recognized by degrees all the peculiarities of former days, just as though they had grown no older; and Mamma had remained exactly the same. Nor could she but admire secretly the almost childlike simplicity of Van der Welcke, who moved about calmly in the midst of her relations, though they were all utter strangers to him and though he; of course, could have no family-feeling for any of them. He was most intimate with Paul and oftenest in his company. Constance would have liked to see more of Bertha, but it was true, they lived at some distance from each other; and yet they found each other again, as sisters, in that conversation shortly after Emilie's marriage. Constance indeed was surprised that an open-hearted talk such as this was not more often renewed between Bertha and herself; but, in any case, they now felt as sisters. As for Karel and Cateau, no, they remained distant and strangers, were hardly more intimate with her than if they had been remote acquaintances; but Gerrit had conceived a sort of passion for Constance; and, inasmuch as she had shown so much tolerance towards Adolphine, the latter really seemed a little more gently disposed to her, for Adolphine remembering all Constance' admiration and praise of Floortje's trousseau, had been heard to say:

"She's not so bad, Constance; Constance can be rather nice when she pleases."

It was summer now; and Constance felt happy. Bertha and her children went to Switzerland, where Van Naghel was to join them in August, and Adolphine went for a month to the Rhine, but Mamma remained at the Hague; and Constance was delighted to see her mother every day. They often drove out together; and they would leave the carriage in the Scheveningen "Woods" or in the Hague "Wood" and walk along the paths. And Mamma always talked about the children, or the grandchildren, or the two great-grandchildren: the children of Otto and Frances, who had gone to Switzerland with the others. As Bertha was not at the Hague that summer, the old woman had transferred her partiality to Gerrit's children, thinking them nice because they were so young. And so she and Constance often went to Gerrit's and found him in the little morning-room, ready to go out, in uniform, rattling his sword, clinking his spurs; fair-haired and heavy and strong in his tight uniform and varnished riding-boots, while two small girls and two small boys, all fair-haired, flaxen-haired, with soft, pink cheeks, climbed over him where he sprawled in his big easy-chair: Gerdy and Adeletje and Alex and little Guy; while the eldest, Marietje, eight years old, lifted the little baby heavily in her arms, and a bigger baby crawled among the legs of the table and chairs in search of a broken doll. In the midst of this fair-haired medley—all the children delicately built like dolls, with their flaxen curls and their soft, pink blushes—

Gerrit was like a giant, looked still taller and stronger; his uniform filled the room as he moved; romping with his children, he seemed able, with one movement, to send them all—Guy and Alex and Adeletje and Gerdy, who hung on to his arms and hands—tumbling over the floor, to the terror of Grandmamma, who thought him too rough; but Adeline was always very calm, herself also fair, softly-smiling, she too, with her delicate little fair face, her figure already assuming the rather matronly proportions of a little wife who has many children and who, although young, has lost all coquetry in regard to slenderness. She was simple and gentle, just a small, fair little woman, for ever bearing children to her great, heavy husband, as a duty of which she did not think much, because Gerrit wished it: a nature of smiling resignation, always pleasant and calm, never excited or upset because of her turbulent little brood and always calmly performing her motherly little duties. She was expecting her eighth in November; and there seemed to be always room in the small house for more and more turbulent, fair-haired children. Then Mamma van Lowe, who had come with Constance after lunch, would ask:

"Well, who's coming for a drive with Granny?..."

And usually it was so arranged that, besides Adeline herself, some four fair-haired little ones were taken into the landau: three of the children were crowded inside and Alex went on the box, entrusted to the special care of the coachman. Then Mamma van Lowe's face beamed with joy, while a long drive was taken through Voorburg, Wassenaar or Voorschoten, and the children were regaled on milk, if the opportunity offered. Or else they merely drove to Scheveningen; and Mrs. van Lowe made quite a stir at Berenbak's, every one staring at the carriage out of which, besides the three ladies, came the three little children, while Alex scrambled down from the box. The waiter would put two tables together; and ices and pastry were ordered. And, whereas, at the Van Naghels' house, the old woman enjoyed above all the veneer of state which distinguished their life, the life that reminded her of her own great days, she enjoyed herself in a different way amid that little brood of Adeline's, enjoyed all that fair-haired, merry, natural youthfulness, where there were no pretensions whatever to state: she was no longer the worldly grandmamma, interested in official dinners and receptions and the Russian minister, but the radiant grandmamma, who rejoiced at having so many dear little grandchildren, all so young. It was pleasant, she would say to Constance, that Gerrit had married rather late—he was thirty-five when he married—because through that, she said, she had so many young grandchildren. And it was nice, she said, that they were Van Lowes, the only little Van Lowes, three little sons to keep the name alive, for Karel had no children; and Ernst and Paul were sure never to marry, she thought. And, though she did not care much for the name and reckoned all grandchildren as profit, as so much to the good, she nevertheless felt most for the little Van Lowes, for the three little boys especially, for the heirs of the name which she had married. And so, while winter was the time which she enjoyed at the Van Naghels', she devoted her summer at the Hague to Gerrit and Adeline. She helped Adeline, who had to be very careful with a moderate income and such a large troop of little ones, and regularly, in the summer, the old lady dressed the fair-haired little children, gave them all something, saw that they had pretty clothes to go about in.

And Constance also delighted in this simple household, especially since Gerrit had conceived a sort of passion for her. Gerrit and Paul were her brothers now; and Dorine sulked a bit. She did not get on with Constance, she could not tell why. Constance had spoken so very nicely to her that first evening; and Dorine had helped Mamma, with all her heart, to prepare a cordial welcome for Constance among the brothers and sisters. But their natures were not made to harmonize; and Dorine was now muttering that Constance must always have men about her, that she got on best with Gerrit and Paul, who both paid court to her after a fashion. Her brothers had never paid court to her, Dorine, after any fashion. Yes, pretty women were always at an advantage, even with their own brothers. All she, Dorine, was good for was to trot about and run errands for the brothers and sisters. And yet it was very strange, but, since Bertha and Adolphine had been out of town and Dorine went oftener to Adeline's, she would ask of her own accord, "Adelientje, I'm going into town this afternoon: is there anything I can do for you?" and, when Adeline answered, "It's very sweet of you, Dorine, but really, there's nothing I want," Dorine would reply, "Well, just think again: I have to go into town, you see;" and then, if Adeline said, "Well, Dorine, if you're going in any case, would you look in at Schroeder's for some pinafores for Adeletje and at Müller and Thijs' for shoes: they all want shoes," Dorine would go off at a trot and hurry, with her wide-legged, shuffling gait, to Schroeder's and to Müller and Thijs', muttering to herself:

"When it's not Bertha or Adolphine, it's Adeline who manages to make use of me!"

"I think Gerrit a most companionable brother," said Constance, one evening, while Paul sat taking tea with her.

"Yes, he's a good sort, but he's queer."

"But why queer, Paul? You're always saying that and I have never taken any notice of it. Why is Gerrit queerer than Ernst or yourself?"

"Well, Ernst isn't normal either and I ... only just."

"But Gerrit, surely, is normal!"

"Perhaps. Perhaps he is. But sometimes I fancy he's not."

"But what does he do, what is there about him that's strange?" asked Constance, indignantly, like a true Van Lowe, defending her brother as soon as that brother was attacked.

"Gerrit has been married nine years. Formerly, he was a very lugubrious gentleman."

"Gerrit lugubrious!" Constance laughed heartily. "My dear Paul, your knowledge of human nature is deserting you. Gerrit, a healthy fellow, strong as a horse, an excellent officer, a jolly brother, a first-rate father with all his fair-haired little children:

Gerrit lugubrious! Where do you get that idea from? Oh, Paul, sometimes, from sheer love of paradox, you say such very improbable things!"

"You did not know Gerrit as he was, Constance."

"I knew him as a boy of fourteen, when we used to play in the river at Buitenzorg. Gerrit is still always flying into ecstasies about that time and my little bare feet! Then I knew Gerrit as a cadet and as a young subaltern, twenty years ago; and he was always pleasant and gay."

"And I remember Gerrit, ten years ago, lugubrious and melancholy."

"Oh, every one has an occasional mood! Perhaps he had an unhappy love-affair: why not Gerrit as well as another?"

"I may be wrong, of course."

"When I see Gerrit, in his big chair, with all those children climbing over his legs and chest, he looks to me the very personification of happiness. Oh, Paul, and I too, I too feel happy: I can't tell you, Paul, how happy I am to be back here in the Hague! And now, now you do all care for me a little again: even Adolphine was very nice lately, before she went away; and I am happy, I am so happy!"

"You have a very gentle, noble, pastoral nature, with a strong atavistic tendency!" said Paul, teasing her. "Look, here are your husband and your boy back with their bicycles, just like two brothers, an elder and a younger brother. They make a good pair. Now, if you're so happy, don't be jealous and try and remain as pastoral all the evening as you are at this moment ... even if your husband should enter the room presently!..."

CHAPTER XXVI

The old woman walked with slow steps along the paths of the garden, carefully examining each separate rose with her grey eyes. Her legs seemed to move with difficulty along the narrow gravel-paths that wound through the front-garden; and her frame was bent, as though deformed. In a wicker-work chair on the verandah sat the tall, old figure of the husband, his ivory forehead bulging above the pages of the newspaper which he held in his large, shrivelled hands....

Evening fell. A nameless grey melancholy fell from the pale summer sky over the country-roads, along which the peaceful villas faded into the shadows of their gardens. The old woman looked up at the sky, looked out over the road, with her hand shading her eyes, walked on again, slowly and painfully, carefully examining each separate rose.... Then she went back to the house:

"It is getting cold, Hendrik; don't stay out too long."

"No."

But the old man remained sitting where he was. The old woman went in, wandered through the sitting-room and the dining-room. She passed her pocket-handkerchief lightly over the furniture, looking to see if there was any dust on it; and, as the parlour-maid had cleared the table, she pulled the cloth straight, put a chair into its proper place, smoothed away a crease in the curtain. She went into the conservatory, looked into the back-garden. Her sad grey eyes gazed out into the grey melancholy of the darkling night. The wind rose, moaned softly through the topmost twigs of the trees.

The old woman looked round at the old man, but he remained sitting in the wicker chair, lost in the great pages of his newspaper:

"Don't catch cold, Hendrik," she repeated, gently.

"I'm coming."

But the old man remained sitting where he was. Now the old woman wandered down the passage, listened at the door of the kitchen and of a small back-room: voices sounded, the voices of the maids and the butler. Then she went up the stairs, wandered through the bedrooms, wandered through the empty spare-rooms, with a sigh, because they never came. Everything was neatly kept, hushed and quiet, as in a house that lacks life....

The old woman, bent and tottering, sighed, was restless. She wandered again through all the bedrooms and wearily made her way downstairs again, crossed the passage, entered the living-room. The old man was seated there now; the windows into the garden were closed. He had folded up his paper and, seated by the window, was still gazing out to where the road of villas grew darker and darker in the chill dimness of the late-summer evening, now beginning to rustle with the rising wind. Then, stifling a sigh, the old woman sat down at the other window, wearily folded her hands, placed her tired feet side by side on a stool.

The room grew dark, the windows turned grey, just outlined by the curtains. The road was more and more blurred in the dimness of the windy night. A grey melancholy reigned without and a grey melancholy reigned within, with those two old people, each sitting silent at a window, lonely and forlorn, drearily sunk in their own thoughts. They sat thus for a long time, quietly, without a word. Then the old woman said:

"It is Henri's birthday to-morrow."

"Yes," said the old man. "He will be thirty-nine."

And they said nothing more and stared before them. Then the old woman grew, restless again and rose from her chair with difficulty, hobbled through the room, holding on by the chairs as she went, and rang the bell:

"Light the gas and bring in the tea, Piet."

The butler lit the gas, drew the curtains and brought the tea. The old man sat down at the table with a book; and the light fell harshly on his ivory forehead and his blue-shaven face; his gnarled, bony hands cast large shadows over the book, turned the pages at regular intervals.

"Here's your tea, Hendrik."

The old man drank his cup of tea.

Then the old woman also took her book and read....

Slowly, in the course of years, she had read her Bible less and less, because she was wicked after all and because she had never resigned herself to the sacrifice which she had made, which it was her duty to make, before God and man. Then she chanced on a wonderful book which described what happened to people after death. And this book she read every evening.

But she was unable to read, this evening. As a rule, the old pair read, over their cup of tea, till ten o'clock, in silence, and then got up and went to bed. But the old woman could not read this evening. Her aching feet fidgeted on the stool, her bent body moved in vague discomfort. And she asked, still casually, nervously:

"Will Henri be thirty-*nine* to-morrow, Hendrik?"

"Yes."

She knew quite well that he would be thirty-nine, but she wanted to say it again, wanted to talk of her son. For fifteen long years, she had not seen him; and his birthdays, the anniversaries of the day on which she had borne him, her only child, had passed while he was very far away, too far for her to reach him and take him in her arms. For many years, she had hoped:

"Now it will come, now it will come nearer."

But it had not come nearer. Until suddenly it was very near, until suddenly it was there. Now it was here, after long, long years; and yet it was not here, it was far away....

She could not read, got up, went out of the room, across the hall. The old man stared after her, went on reading. And it was as though her disquiet kept increasing, as though a voice—one of those voices of which she had read in that strange book—said to her:

"Go, go to-morrow!"

Never had a voice spoken so plainly to her, the old woman, and as it were ordered her to go, to go to-morrow. She was very old, in years, in movement and in feeling; and she never, never travelled. She lived quietly in her house beside the country-road, summer and winter alike; and sometimes she went for a little drive in the neighbourhood: Beyond that she no longer went, for she was gouty and full of aches and pains which bent her withered back. For years and years, she had not travelled, had not sat in the train which, for years, she had heard whistling at the station, sometimes even heard rumbling. And now the mysterious voice so plainly and insistently commanded:

"Go!"

Then she went back to the room, sat down and, this time, was unable to stifle her sigh. She sighed. The old man heard, but did not know how to ask her why she was sighing. For years, for long years, there had been so little said between them. Only now, this spring, when Henri's letter came, they had spoken, but not much. A couple of days after receiving the letter, the old man said:

"I will write to him."

And that was really the only thing that had been said. But they had not lived so many years in silence, side by side, without learning to hear each other speak though both were silent. They knew, without speaking, what either said, silently in his heart. Only now, though the old man himself was thinking of Henri that night, he did not know what his wife was saying to him, silently, without words, in that one sigh; and this was because he did not read that strange book and never heard the strange voices. Therefore he sought for a word to say and found it very difficult to find a word, but at last he did speak and said, simply:

"What is it?"

He did not look up, went on reading his book as he spoke.

Then the old woman's aching feet fidgeted still more nervously on their stool; the bent shoulders shivered more nervously under their little black shawl; and she began to cry, softly.

"Come, what is it?"

He pretended to go on reading his book, because talking and crying were so difficult, and because it was easier to pretend to go on reading.

The old woman said, because his old voice had spoken gently:

"I should like to go to Henri, to-morrow."

Now they were both silent; and the old man went on reading; and the old woman, waiting for his answer, ceased crying, ceased moving her feet, her shoulders. And, after a silence, the old man said:

"Take Piet with you, then, to help you."

She nodded her head; and the tears flowed from her eyes, while she drew her book to her, inwardly pleased that he had said so much and said it so kindly. She sighed once more, this time with relief, and read on. But her eyes did not see the words, because she was thinking that to-morrow she would be going with Piet, the butler, in the train—in which she had not been for years and years—to the Hague, to see Henri.

"Go!" the voice had said. "Go!" the voice had commanded.

And she was going. It had come at last, come so near that it would be there to-morrow: not that Henri was coming to her, but that she was going to Henri, to kiss him, to forgive him....

And she read on, did not see the strange words which told what happened to people after death, but wept softly, inaudibly, over her book, wept for still contentment and peace, because he had spoken to her and had said:

"Take Piet with you, then, to help you."

When it was ten o'clock, he closed his book, stood up. And she would so much have liked to ask him if he too would come with her to-morrow, in the train, to Henri, because it was not so difficult and Piet could take the tickets. But she did not ask him, because she knew that it was even more difficult for him than for her to travel and go by train, that train which he also for years had heard whistling and sometimes rumbling. So she did not ask him, because he would certainly refuse. And without a doubt he heard within himself what she hesitated to ask him, for he said, gently:

"I shall not go; but give him many good wishes, from his father."

Then, stiffly and with difficulty, he bent his tall figure and his ivory forehead, went to her and kissed her on the brow. And she took his gnarled hand and pressed it gently. Then he went upstairs and she rang the bell.

The butler entered.

"Piet," she said, hesitatingly and shyly, and she blushed before the butler. "I am going to-morrow to the Hague, to Mr. Henri. It's his birthday. And I should like you to take me there."

The man looked up in surprise, smiled:

"Very well, ma'am, as you please."

And, as she went up the stairs, she tried to hold herself more erect; she felt younger....

CHAPTER XXVII

And in her room she hardly slept for nervousness about the great event that was to happen on the morrow. All the night through, while the wind moaned against the panes, she lay in bed, with unclosed eyes, listening whether she could not hear in the voices of the wind yet other voices, strange voices, voices warning or commanding the living.

She had never spoken to her husband about the voices, though he was well aware that she read the strange book and disapproved of her reading it, because it could not be fit and proper reading for people who, from their childhood, had believed that the best of all books was the Bible and the best of all beliefs the belief in the Lord, from Whom every sorrow came and every blessing. And she had hidden the strange book also from the old minister, who came to see them every week, since they both, growing older each year and ailing, had ceased to go to church: she put the strange book out of the way when he was expected on a Sunday-afternoon; but she studied it without concealment from her old husband and yet in silence, as though guilty of a secret heresy. He had asked her once:

"What are you reading there?"

And she told him the strange title and said that she wanted to enquire into things, but nothing further had been uttered between the two old people, though she heard him silently express his disapproval. But, since the day when, years ago, she had yielded to her husband and consented to the superhuman sacrifice of surrendering her son to the woman whom that son had plunged into unhappiness—because this sacrifice was the duty which was required of her by divine and human equity—since that time she had had no peace, read as she might in her Bible, talk as she would with the minister, pray as she did for hours on end. She had had no peace: deep down in herself she had always borne a grudge because Heaven had laid so heavy a sacrifice upon her, the mother. Her husband had had the strength of a man who pursues the straight path, the path of duty, and he had surrendered his son and lost him without a superfluous word. But she, though she also spoke no word, had not resigned herself; and her soul had rebelled; and she had thought that she was lost for all eternity ... until a gentle ray had come, by accident, to comfort her out of the strange book which, by accident, she had taken up and opened. And, still a believer, though she no longer went to church and though, in her heart, she did not agree with the minister, did not agree with her old husband, she nevertheless endeavoured to unite, to reconcile, to blend what remained of the old faith, which had once stood firm as a rock, with the new faith; and, when she prayed, she prayed indeed to the same God of her old, former faith, but she listened also to the voices, to that part of the invisible world which hovers around us and saves us and guides us and warns and protects us and sets its soft-smiling compassion between us and the rigid immutability of the divine grace or displeasure, tempering the divine brow into a softer glance. That was her secret; and what she silently told her husband of the new faith still remained an unpenetrated secret to him in the dumb evenings when they sat together and read and he heard her, in silence, say that she believed differently from what she once did because she had found no peace in that divine immutability.

And now the day came which was Henri's birthday. She dressed very early, with difficulty and with shaking hands, and, when Piet told her that there was a train at nine o'clock, she blushed and remained quietly waiting for the carriage to be got ready and for Piet to come and tell her. She was her ordinary self at breakfast, but tried, without attracting attention, not to eat, because the bread stuck in her throat; and, when, at the breakfast-table, her husband asked if she had not telegraphed to Henri, she answered:

"No."

Almost inaudibly and silently, she thus conveyed to her husband that she wished to give Henri a surprise.

She remained sitting motionless; did not wash up the breakfast-cups that morning, as she was always wont to do; was a little uncomfortable in the presence of her husband and the parlour-maid and Piet at this omission of her usual habit. She heard the clock ticking, the seconds falling away; and she was afraid that, if Piet loitered so, she would be late, or that there would be an accident. Luckily, the morning-paper came; and the old man plunged into its pages while she remained waiting, in her cloak and her unfashionable, black, old lady's bonnet, for Piet to come and say that it was time to go. The parlour-maid washed up the breakfast-cups; and she was afraid the maid would break one, because she was not used to it. It made quite a change, throughout the house, that she was going this morning by train, to the Hague, to Henri, whose birthday it was. She was uncomfortable and she feared that the people along the road and at the station would stand looking and wondering why Mrs. van der Welcke was going on a journey. And, when, at last, Piet came to tell her, she could not get up at first, because her old legs shook so and her feet pricked her, as though they had been asleep. But she made a painful effort, stood up, gave Piet her purse; and the old man said:

"Piet, will you look after mevrouw, getting in and out of the train?"

Piet promised; and she took leave of her husband. The carriage was at the door; and she dared not look at Dirk, the coachman, because she was shy, while Piet held open the carriage-door and helped her to step in, with some little difficulty. In the carriage, she shrank back, because the woman with the vegetables was just passing and she was afraid that she might see her. Also she reflected that the people in the other villas would be sure to see the carriage drive out and wonder what was happening, so early in the morning. But, when, at the station, Piet helped her to alight and led her to the little waiting-room and went to take the tickets, she was very shy before a lady and gentleman who were also waiting and who no doubt thought it very strange that she, an old woman, should go travelling like that. Fortunately, Piet had calculated the time and she had not long to wait, at which she was very glad, because the whistling of the trains and the ringing of the bell made her very nervous, terrified lest she should miss the train, and she did not know to a minute at what time it started. But Piet came to tell her and fetched her; and she tried to walk straight and, assisted by Piet, to climb into the carriage not all too painfully and laboriously. Piet had taken a second-class ticket for himself; and she would rather have had him come into her compartment, but he had, of course, not dared, from respect for his mistress, and she had not dared ask him. But she resolved to sit very quiet until Piet came to fetch her. The lady and the gentleman were in the same compartment as herself, but they were very polite: the gentleman had bowed and the lady too; and fortunately they did not look at her again, but talked to each other in low voices. And, when the train moved off, the old woman sat quietly, with set lips, looking out of the window at the meadows speeding past.... Now she was beginning to wonder what Henri would say and she also thought of Constance and of her grandson, Adriaan. And she was a little frightened at what she had done. They might be out, or very busy with the Van Lowes, Constance' relations. She did not quite know in what way Henri and Constance lived, at the Hague. Henri, it was true, had been to Driebergen again, just once more, by himself, but she had received no distinct impression from his words, because she had hardly listened, had only sat gazing at him, her son, whom she had not seen for so many years, who had not been allowed to exist for her.... She trembled suddenly at what she had dared to do, but it was now too late. She was sitting in the train; and the train was carrying her along; and also she did not know how to tell Piet, when the train stopped, that she would rather just go back again. Then, from sheer inability to do otherwise, she at last found courage to sit still and let the train take her on until it slowed into the station at the Hague and Piet came to fetch her and helped her climb down the high steps of the railway-carriage. Piet now led her slowly and quietly through the busy crowd of people, which he allowed to flow ahead of them, and out of the station, chose a nice cab, helped her in, gave the address of Baron van der Welcke, Kerkhoflaan, and got up on the box, next to the driver. And now, seated in the cab, which rattled over the cobble-stones, she was glad, after all, that she had persevered and she thought that it was not so very difficult, after all, and believed that, after all, Henri would perhaps think it nice of her to have come without notice. It was a long drive; and she had not been to the Hague for years and had forgotten the streets and squares; but, at last, the cab stopped and she looked out while Piet climbed down from the box, rang the bell, opened the door of the cab, helped her out....

Yes, she was there now and she trembled violently when the maid opened the door and she entered the hall. She was there now. And she could find nothing to say when a door in the passage opened and Constance, amazed, came out to her. This was the second time that she had seen that woman....

"Mamma!"

"Yes, I thought I would come, because it was Henri's birthday...."

She knew—she had not failed to understand—that her son was not happy with that woman and she felt a certain disappointment that it was not Henri himself who came out to welcome her.

But the astonishment in Constance' face changed to a look of soft and glad surprise. She was very sensitive to kindness and she felt that it was kind of this old woman to come: this old lady who never went anywhere, who had come with her butler....

"How pleased Henri will be!" she said, gently, and her eyes grew moist. "How very pleased Henri will be! He is out now, on his bicycle, but he'll be back soon. Come in, take off your cloak inside: I'm afraid there's a draught out here. Good-morning, Piet: so you've brought mevrouw? Go into the kitchen, Piet, will you? Come in, Mamma. How delighted Henri will be! He is sure to be in very soon. And this is my mother, who has also come to see us this morning."

She led Mrs. van der Welcke into the morning-room; and there stood old Mrs. van Lowe. And, when Constance closed the door, the two old ladies looked at each other and were both very nervous; and Constance felt like that too, trembling in her limbs. The old ladies looked at each other; and it was as though the two mothers, with that long, long look, asked each other's forgiveness, after many long years, for their two children. Then Mrs. van Lowe approached and put out her two hands; and her words sounded very simple:

"I am so delighted to make your acquaintance, mevrouw...."

Yes, they asked, without saying so, they asked each other's forgiveness for the offence which their two children had committed, years and years ago, against each other and against themselves and against their lives. They asked each other's forgiveness with the unspeakable gentleness of two very old women who still looked upon their children, whatever their age might be, as children, as their children. They asked each other's forgiveness without words, with a glance and a pressure of the hands; and Constance understood so plainly what they were asking each other that she quietly left the room, feeling suddenly like a child, a tiny child that had behaved badly towards those two mothers.... Constance felt it so intensely that she went by herself, through the dining-room, into the conservatory and wept, very quietly, swallowing her tears behind her handkerchief. And the old ladies were left together, the two mothers, so different one from the other: one, Mrs. van Lowe, a woman who perhaps had seen much more of life and understood it better than the other, Mrs. van der Welcke, who had always lived quietly, always at Driebergen, with her Bible ... until the strange book had fallen into her hands....

They were left together and the very many things which they said to each other and asked of each other, in silence, were not audible in the simple words of Constance' mother:

"May I help you take off your hat and your cloak, mevrouw?"

And, as she assisted Mrs. van der Welcke, she apologized for Constance and said:

"I think your arrival must have agitated her; you must not mind her leaving you for a moment...."

Then the old ladies sat down side by side.

"They seem to be very comfortable," said Mrs. van der Welcke and looked around her nervously.

"I am so glad to have my child back with me," said Mrs. van Lowe.

There was very much to be said between them, but they spoke only simple words, doubtless feeling all the unuttered rest. Their thoughts went back, many years back: how hostile they had then felt towards each other's children, who had disgraced each other and their two families; if they had met each other then by chance, as now, they could not possibly have looked at each other gently, as now.... But the years had toned down the pain and the cruelty; and now it was possible and even agreeable for these two, mother and mother, to press each other's hands and to exchange glances that asked for forgiveness.

"I also came to wish Henri many happy returns. He is sure to be back with Addie for lunch," said Mrs. van Lowe.

But Constance returned; and now, in her own house, in her own drawing-room, she felt shy and quite different from what she felt when, offended and slighted, she had stood before Henri's parents, at Driebergen, on that first and only visit. It was as though the combined presence of those two mothers made her like to a child that had done wrong. She felt as she had never felt before, felt small and childlike; and, when, as was often her habit, she went to sit close by Mrs. van Lowe, she took her mother's hand and laid her head upon her mother's breast and no longer controlled herself, but wept.

And Mrs. van Lowe again looked at Henri's mother, as though she wished to say:

"If it can be, do not condemn my child too severely, even as I do not judge Henri too severely."

And, because there now flowed through her soul a gentle happiness that had its source in contentment, Constance felt the poignancy of that moment of Henri's home-coming when, tired after his ride, he walked in with Addie and found his mother there, his mother, who never left her house, sitting there in his house, between Constance and Mrs. van Lowe....

Had some bond really been established at last, after long years? Had those who could find no point of union that other morning, at Driebergen, at last come closer? Was there really some sort of tie? And was it just that it took a very long time—years and years and then months after that—for things to become more or less easy and pleasant?... In this mood, Constance' voice instinctively had a softer note; and she felt at the same time a child to those two mothers and very old to herself, very old in this lulling of passion and anger and nerves. Would it be like this with her now, would her life just go on in a succession of more and more placid years, would she just live for her son? She asked herself this, deep down in her soul, almost unconsciously; and a shadowy melancholy floated over her, because of those two old mothers, because of Henri, because of herself. Was that how old age approached, like this, with these gentler years? She was forty-two, she was not old, but, still, was old age approaching in this way, so softly? And, while she asked herself this, in a passive, melancholy mood, devoid of anger and passion, there hovered about her a vague feeling that she would now grow old and that she had never lived.... Never lived.... Never lived.... It hovered, that shadowy discontent, in the midst of her gentle content.... Never lived.... She did not know why, but she thought for just one moment—a ghost of a thought—of Gerrit, of Buitenzorg, how they two, the little brother and sister, used to play in the river.... It was as if it had not been she, that little girl with the red flowers, as if it had been another little girl.... Never lived.... But what ought she to have done to feel that she had lived, now that she was growing old? Vanity, balls, her marriage, Rome, her love-affair, the scandal: was that living? Or was it all a mistake, mistake upon mistake, fuss and excitement about nothing?... Now, now it was over. Existence was becoming placid, less bitter, more kindly; but, still, she felt it, she had never lived....

But she did not know what she ought to have done to make her now feel that she had lived; and she let the strange feeling be lulled to rest in the soft melancholy that filled her, because of this gentle kindliness that had come now, with the years, the grey haze of years. She sighed the strange thought away and she thought that it had to happen and that it could not have been otherwise and that even so she would never have known anything different.... Never lived.... But, then, had hundreds of men and women around her ever lived?... And she now shook herself free of this strange mood; and, laughing softly, happy in spite of her melancholy, she saw that the table was laid and asked the two mothers to come in to lunch.

Was it the grey haze of years then?... Was she growing old and were things becoming easier and more pleasant?... And had she never lived?...

"I do think it so very nice," she said, "to have both the Mammas together at my table...."

CHAPTER XXVIII

In a small town like the Hague, the sudden appearance of Constance and her husband, after many years, could not but be the occasion for an interchange of gossip that was not easily silenced. The Van Lowe family had connections in various sets— the aristocratic set, the upper official world, the military set, the Indian set—and, just because of these connections in more than one set, there arose a cross-fire of criticism and condemnation, neither of which had lost any of its sharpness, even though people had not given a thought to Constance for years. On the contrary, the gossip was a sort of raking up of all that could be remembered of former days, a repetition of all the criticism and all the condemnation which these very people, for the most part, fifteen years ago, had passed among themselves, from one to another, as so much current coin. If it had sometimes seemed to Constance as though the period of her absence contracted and was no longer twenty years, to all those people who knew her, or knew her relations, or knew relations of her relations, that interval had no existence whatever; and it was as though the scandal dated from yesterday, as though she had married her lover, Van der Welcke, yesterday. And, while she herself, in her gentle happiness and melancholy contentment at being back among her kinsfolk, in her country, for which she had longed so greatly abroad, while she noticed nothing of this cross-fire, through which she walked quietly—in the street, at the time of the two weddings, at Scheveningen and now—it continued among all those people— acquaintances, friends, relations—continued, never ceased fire. To all of them she had remained the Mrs. De Staffelaer of old, who had never returned to the Hague since her marriage and who was now back with Van der Welcke. At visits, at tea-parties, at evening-parties, at the Witte or the Plaats, at Scheveningen, everywhere, the rapid cross-fire began, as a pleasant sport for all of them:

"You know, Mrs. De Staffelaer...."

"Van Lowe that was...."

"Yes, the one who went off with Van der Welcke...."

"Yes, I remember: she married him...."

"Yes, she's back."

"Yes, so I hear."

"Yes, she was out driving yesterday with old Mrs. van Lowe."

"So she's back again?"

"Yes, she's back!"

In this way the cross-fire began, suavely and rapidly, as a conversational sport.

"And so she is received by her relations?"

"Yes. And even at Driebergen."

"Is it really twenty years ago?"

"No, it can't be as long as that."

"She has a child."

"Yes, a boy; but not by Van der Welcke."

"The father's an Italian, I hear."

"Yes, an Italian diplomatist."

In this way the fire continued, brisk, crackling, fiercer and fiercer, until it went off like a brilliant and acrid fire-work:

"Well, I don't think the family will like *that* so very much!"

"You need only look at Van Naghel's face...."

"Or at the Van Saetzemas'."

"Why don't they keep her in the background?"

"Yes. What did she want to come back for at all?"

"I call it an impertinence."

"She was always intriguing as a young girl."

"That marriage with old De Staffelaer...."

"And what is she ferreting round for now?"

"Yes, what on earth is she ferreting round for in the Hague?"

And they ferreted round for what she was ferreting round for in the Hague. They ferreted very deep, very far, after the brilliant cross-fire; they dug up, among themselves, all the sand of their suspicions and flung it about one another's ears:

"They had a very expensive establishment abroad and were unable to keep it going any longer."

"She wants to be near her mother because she's afraid that, when the mother dies, there will be trouble about the will."

"It was he who wanted to come back, for the sake of an old mistress of his."

"She wants to go to Court."

"No, it's he who wants to go to Court."

"Yes, they both want to go to Court."

"She wants to go to Court...."

"She wants to go to Court...."

"She wants to go to Court...."

"But what a piece of impudence!"

"Even if she was in that set once...."

"That is no reason...."

"Why she should dream...."

"Of being presented...."

"Now...."

"Well, you'll see: this winter...."

"She wants to go to Court...."

"To Court...."

"But that's not the only reason."

"No, he too is afraid that his parents will disinherit him, as far as they can...."

"And now he proposes...."

"To soften them, by means of the child...."

"Which isn't even his!"

"What difference does that make?"

"The old people don't know!..."

And they ferreted very industriously and dug up the sand and kept up their cross-fire as a sport for the tea-parties and evening-parties, at the Club and at Scheveningen.

"Look here," said others, "Van der Welcke behaved like a gentleman."

"What! To run away with another man's wife?"

"No, but to marry her afterwards."

"There aren't many who would have done it."

"She's older than he."

"Six years older."

"No, four years."

"No one else would have done it."

"No, no one."

"And he was a deucedly decent fellow."

"Always was."

"Always was."

"She was older than he, she knew the world...."

"And she seduced him; he was quite a youngster."

It all sounded as though the years, the many years, had never existed.

"Yes, but, you know, it's sometimes difficult, for a woman who's young and pretty...."

"Then why did she marry such an old man?"

"Out of vanity, nothing but vanity."

They judged, defended and condemned her as though the years, the many years, had never existed.

The acquaintances of the Van Lowes, or of their acquaintances, or the relations of their relations were no worse than other people. But they met one another at tea-parties and at evening-parties, at the Witte and at Scheveningen, and they must have food for conversation. Whatever important things might be happening in the world, the one interest, when all was said, was to discuss, over and over again, a case like that of Constance. They disliked neither her nor Van der Welcke; and her case even attracted their interest, if not their sympathies. Only, the Van der Welckes must not think that their memory was so poor that they did not remember the "case" jolly well.... Only, the Van der Welckes ought not to have come back to the Hague, bringing fresh scandal into the exalted morality of the different Hague sets.... Only, there must be no question that people who were so much talked about should dream of being presented to Court....

"And nevertheless they do intend to be presented...."

Constance, in her quiet happiness, noticed none of it; and Van der Welcke, who, at the club, was within nearer range of the cross-fire, did indeed sometimes observe a look and gesture, sometimes overheard a word, but thought it of no consequence, even when it caused him a moment's irritation.

CHAPTER XXIX

After the summer holidays, Addie, who was now in the third class at the Grammar School, sometimes went to his Van Saetzema cousins on a Sunday afternoon, rather against the grain, for there was not much love lost between them. But, as he had not failed to notice that the three boys tired his mother greatly when they came to the little house, however much she liked to keep up the relationship, he made it a sort of duty to go to them once a fortnight, or so, either for a walk or for a bicycle-ride. It was more natural to him to go about with boys who were his seniors; he had made a couple of older friends at the Grammar School; and even Frans and Henri van Naghel, who were young fellows of twenty-three and twenty-four, said that it might sound very funny, but they always thought it jolly when Addie looked in. But, to please his mother, who disapproved of this tendency to spend his time with his elders, he would go and walk or bicycle with the three Van Saetzemas, while despising them in his heart for unmannerly young louts, stupid as well as ill-bred and, in addition, having their mouths ever full of coarse talk and suggestive jokes. They were not fond of Addie, but they looked up to him a little, just because they knew that the older cousins, the Van Naghels, the undergraduates, thought Addie a nice boy, though he was as young as the Van Saetzemas, while looking upon the Van Saetzemas themselves as mere brats not worth noticing. But, for this very reason, they did not see how Addie could care to go to Uncle Gerrit's and play with all those babies there. They thought him a queer boy, they did not really like him; but his intimacy with Frans and Henri van Naghel gave Addie a sort of manly, grown-up air which they secretly envied. And so, in order, in their turn, to appear manly and grown-up before Addie, they could never, walking or bicycling, pass a woman without exchanging a coarse word or phrase or disapproval, like young men-about-town who know all about everything.

Then Addie chuckled inside himself, for he could never laugh outright, even though he wanted to:

"You fellows sometimes call me an old fogey," he said, "but, whenever you pass a woman, you talk like old fogeys of things you know nothing about."

"Oh, do you know more than we do?"

"I don't say that, but I haven't my mouth always full of it."

Then they were angry, because their assumption of rakishness made no impression, and they did not understand how Addie could flatly admit his innocence and ignorance. They, on the contrary, were ashamed of their innocence and ignorance, were burning to lose both as quickly as possible, had not the courage to do so yet, though they sometimes did go down the Spuistraat of an evening. And Addie thought to himself:

"Mamma ought just to hear them, or to see them lounging along the streets; then she wouldn't ask me every Sunday if I have been out with Jaap and Piet and Chris!"

And, though they did not like Addie, they were flattered when he came and asked:

"Are you fellows coming for a ride this afternoon?"

They did not like him and they gave him all sorts of nicknames among themselves: Old Fogey, the Baron, the Italian....

Then Marietje would ask, gently:

"Why do you always talk so unkindly of Addie?"

And then the three boys laughed and teased Marietje with being in love with "the Baron."

But Marietje, who was sixteen, shrugged her shoulders, feeling grown-up already: in a year's time, she was going to boarding-school, near Cleves. No, she, who was sixteen, was not in love with a little cousin of thirteen, with a child; but she thought him a nice boy all the same. The three brothers and their friends had never danced, or talked, or bicycled with her, or paid her any attention, whereas Addie behaved like a gallant young cavalier. In that noisy, fussy, bawling household, the girl had always been a little fragile, a little pale, a little quiet, like a small, gentle alien that could not cope with the hard voices of Mamma and the sisters and the rough horseplay of the brothers; and Addie talked so nicely, so pleasantly, so politely, so gallantly, so very differently from Chris and Piet and Jaap.

"The Italian wasn't here last Sunday."

"Then he's sure to come to-day."

"He always comes once a fortnight."

"That's the Italian fashion."

"Why do you boys always call Addie the Italian?" asked Marietje.

Now the three burst with laughing:

"That's nothing to do with you."

"Little girls shouldn't ask questions."

"I think it a silly nickname," said Marietje, "and it means nothing."

They burst out laughing again, full of importance and worldly wisdom.

"That's because you don't know."

"If you knew, you'd think it witty enough."

"It's a damned witty nickname."

"Chris, what language!"

"So you want to know why Addie is an Italian?"

She shrugged her shoulders, played the grown-up sister:

"I think you're silly, just like children. That nickname means nothing."

They burst with laughter once more:

"Don't you know what they do in Italy?"

"In Rome?"

She looked at them, her louts of brothers; she vaguely remembered incautiously-whispered remarks about Aunt Constance, about the time when she was still the wife of the Netherlands minister at Rome, of that old uncle De Staffelaer whom she had never known.

"Well, look here: what do you think the name means?..."

She grew uncomfortable, fearing that they were suggesting something improper which she did not understand:

"I don't know," she said, "and I don't care."

"Then you shouldn't call it a silly name."

But now Marietje was really interested and so she asked Caroline, a little later:

"Do you know why the boys call Addie the Italian?"

"Because they're silly," said Caroline.

"No, there must be some reason, but they wouldn't tell me."

Now Carolientje was puzzled in her turn and she asked her mother, later:

"Why are the boys always calling Addie the Italian, Mamma?"

"I don't know," said Adolphine, sharply.

But the girls, both curious, continued to talk about the nickname and they sounded Karel and also Marianne and Marietje van Naghel.

No, none of them, either, knew what the name meant. But Karel was determined to find out and did find out:

"I know," he said to his little sister, Marie.

"I know," Marie whispered to the Van Saetzema girls.

But Marietje van Saetzema did not yet quite understand, but she would not let this appear, because Caroline would have thought her such a baby. If Auntie had never married an Italian, how could she have a son who was an Italian?

The nickname came to the ears of Herman Ruyvenaer, the youngest son of Uncle and Aunt, a lean little brown *sinjo* of fifteen, who mentioned the nickname at home to his sisters Toetie, Dot and Pop.

"*Allah*, it's too bad!" said the girls. "It's a shame of those boys, Mamma; just listen...."

"Oh, no, I don't believe it," said Aunt Ruyvenaer, when she heard. "Gossip, I say; *kassian*, Constance!"

But Uncle Ruyvenaer told her that it was so.

"But how do you know?"

"Adolphine told me herself."

"Oh, nonsense, she wasn't there!... *Kassian*, that boy and his mother!"

And Aunt Lot and the girls refused to believe, were indignant; and Auntie called her husband an old gossip. But the nickname was often on the lips of the young boy- and girl-cousins and of their friends at home and at school. Once, Addie thought he heard a boy shout to him, by way of an abusive epithet:

"Italian!"

He did not understand, did not even apply the word to himself and walked on.

Another time, however, bicycling with the Van Saetzema boys, along the Wassenaar Road, he grew angry because Jaap was trying his hardest to run over a cat:

"Leave the animal alone," cried Addie, furiously, "or I'll punch your head!"

"Oh?" roared Jaap. "You would, would you, Italian?"

Addie did not yet understand. But he had a vague recollection of hearing the name before. He did not at once recall the incident of that other boy:

"Why do you call me an Italian?" he asked.

The others were frightened, pulled Jaap's sleeve.

"That's nothing to do with it," growled Jaap, taken aback. "You say you're going to punch my head."

But Addie, in a flash, remembered the boy and that shout in the street near the school:

"Out with it!" he cried. "Why do you call me an Italian?"

Chris and Piet tried to smooth things over:

"Come, don't bother; he's talking rot."

"But why an Italian?"

"Oh, nothing, nothing!"

"Yes, there's something. I mean to know!"

"Keep your hair on; it's nothing."

"Out with it!" cried Addie, scarlet with rage. And he flew at Jaap's throat.

"Oh, hang it! Shut up!" shouted the two others.

But Jaap and Addie were struggling. Their boyish hatred suddenly burst forth:

"Out with it! Why do you call me an Italian?"

Addie was very strong, stronger than Jaap, who was a year and a half older than he and taller. He got him down: his small, hard knuckles were at Jaap's throat; and he was nearly strangling him. The others pulled him off:

"That'll do, I say! Shut up!"

They pulled Addie away from Jaap; and now Jaap, furious because he had been beaten, purple in the face, half choking, unable to control his hate, cried out:

"Because you're not the son of your father!"

"Hold your jaw!" shouted Piet and Chris to Jaap.

But the word was spoken and Addie was like a madman:

"You hound! You hound!" he yelled.

And he tried to fling himself on Jaap again.

The two other boys held him back. And a sudden reasonableness came to soothe Addie's passion: he must not let himself go like that, against that cur of a Jaap. When that young bounder lost his temper, he didn't know what he shouted and raved, "Italian!" and "Not the son of your father!" Addie shrugged his shoulders:

"I've had enough of cycling with you chaps. I can spend my Sundays better than in tormenting cats and quarrelling and fighting."

And he sprang on his bicycle and rode away.

"Italian!" Jaap screamed after him once more, forgetting everything, except his hatred.

Addie looked round; and he saw that Chris and Piet, both furious, were thrashing the very life out of Jaap.

He rode away, mastering his nerves. No, he could never again, to please Mamma, spoil his Sunday holiday with those cads of boys. This was the last time, for good and all! Besides, he felt that they liked him as little as he them. And then, suddenly, his thoughts went back to the strange word, the word of abuse, and to the boy who, once before, had shouted it after him in the street. That time, he had not imagined that it was he whom the boy meant.

Try as he would to keep calm, he was too much excited to go straight home and perhaps meet Papa and Mamma. He therefore rode to the Bezuidenhout, hoping to find Frans van Naghel in: Henri was not at the Hague, was working hard at Leiden.

He found Frans at home, in the two elder boys' sitting-room, smoking with a couple of friends.

"Well, old man, what is it?"

And he took Addie outside.

"I've been fighting with that cad of a Jaap. He called me an Italian, Frans. What did he mean?"

Frans started; and Addie noticed it, became suspicious.

"Oh, nothing, old man: it's just that he's an ass!"

"No, Frans, there must be some reason why he called me that; and I mean to know the reason."

"Don't worry about it, old chap."

"And the other fellows licked Jaap because he said it. And then Jaap also said ..."

"Well, what else did Jaap say, old man?"

"That I ... that I was not the son of my father."

Suddenly, while he was unbosoming himself in the warmth of Frans' sympathy, a light flashed across him. He remembered the mysterious fits of sadness of Mamma's, scenes with Papa, during those early days at the Hague, when he had vaguely noticed in his mother something as though she were asking for forgiveness, humbling herself before Grandmamma, before the uncles and aunts. And all this, taken in connection with Papa and Mamma's former residence in Italy, in Rome, caused to flicker before him as it were a reflection of cruel truths. As he looked at Frans, these cruel truths flickered up before him again. He had read much for his years; his school, his school-friends had soon revealed some of the mysteries of life to him, though he was still a boy, though he was still a child, with a child's innocence in his soul and his eyes, with the soft bloom of that innocence on his child's skin and his child's mind, even though there was something of a little man about him. And, suddenly, he saw everything: the rage of the boys because Jaap had given himself away, their confusion and now Frans' confusion....

"Not the son of your father?" repeated Frans. "They're asses, those three louts.... Come, Addie, don't have anything more to do with those clod-hoppers. When they're coarse, they're very coarse and they don't know what they're saying."

"Yes," said Addie, with sudden reserve, "that's what it must be, that's what it is."

"Come, Addie, come for a walk, will you, with the two Hijdrechts? We were going to the Witte; but, if you'll come with us, old man, we'll go to Scheveningen instead."

The boy's senses suddenly became very acute and he heard a sort of pity in Frans' voice. He began to feel very unhappy, because of that pity, restrained himself spasmodically from sobbing, gulped it all down: all about Italy and that he was not the child of his father. And he hesitated whether he had better hide somewhere, all alone, or stay for sympathy, with Frans....

"Come along, old man, come with us," said Frans. "Then we'll go to Scheveningen."

And he went at once and told the other two students, the Hijdrechts, of the change of plan.

"Then I'll leave my bicycle here," said Addie.

He went with the three young men, who, for his sake, did not go to the Witte; and they walked to Scheveningen. And it was as though he heard that note of pity in the Hijdrechts' voices too. Then, suddenly, on the New Road, he saw the three Saetzemas cycling back to the Hague.

"There are our three nice gentlemen," said Frans.

The three boys nodded as they passed:

"Bejour!"

But Addie did not nod back.

Scheveningen was overcrowded, with its Sunday visitors; but the Hijdrechts were quite amusing and Frans was always pleasant.

It was late, close upon six, when he decided to go home.

"Well, good-bye, old man," said Frans.

Addie pressed Frans' hand, wanted to thank him for the walk, but was too proud, because of that pity, and could not:

"I'll come and fetch my bicycle to-morrow," was all he said, dully.

And he went home slowly, alone. He felt as though he could not go home; as though he would have liked to walk somewhere else, anything to escape going home. He felt as though, suddenly, he had to drag with him a heavy sorrow, too heavy for his years, and as though it lay on his chest, on his throat, on his lungs. But he reached home at last, about half-past six.

"How late you are, Addie," said Constance, a little annoyed. "We've been waiting for you for the last half hour. Have you been with the three boys?"

"Yes," said Addie.

"Oh, then, it's all right," she said. They sat down to dinner, but Addie was quiet, did not eat.

"What is it, my boy?" asked Van der Welcke.

"Nothing," said Addie.

But his parents were not used to seeing their child like that and insisted on knowing what was the matter.

"I've been fighting with Jaap," said Addie. Constance, already a little annoyed, flared up at once:

"Fighting? Fighting? What about, Addie? There's always something with the three boys."

"Oh, nothing!" said Addie, evasively.

"Come," said Van der Welcke, "all boys have a fight now and again."

But Addie did not speak, remained stiff and silent. He did not answer, would not say why he had fought with Jaap. And he was reasonable, tried to eat something, so as not to upset his mother; but the food stuck in his throat. They hurried through dinner. When Addie was gloomy, everything was gloomy, there was nothing left, life was not worth the dismal living, Constance' new and gentle happiness was gone, gone....

"Shall we go and bicycle a bit, my boy?" asked Van der Welcke. "Or are you tired?"

"Yes, I'm tired."

"Remember, Addie," said Constance, coldly, "that we are going to Grandmamma's and that you have to change."

"Yes."

He got up, went upstairs, to his boy's room, not knowing what to say next, what to do with himself, where to sit, what book to take up; he remained standing, aimlessly, in the middle of the room, with that bottled-up sorrow of a whole afternoon lying heavy on his chest and lungs: that sorrow which he had dragged with Frans and the Hijdrechts to Scheveningen, quietly, without sobbing, amid that bustling crowd of Sunday visitors.

He stood there, aimlessly, dejected, when the door opened and Van der Welcke entered:

"Come, Addie, my boy, tell your father. What is it?"

"Papa," he began, yearning now, burning to know....

But he could not go on. It was his first sorrow and it was so heavy, so oppressively heavy.

"Come, my lad, what's the matter?"

"Papa...."

"Tell me, come on, tell me."

"Papa, am I not...."

"What, Addie?"

"Papa, am I not your child?"

Van der Welcke looked at him in astonishment:

"What's that?" he asked and did not understand.

"No, I'm not, am I? Yes, I know now!"

"Look here, Addie, what's the matter with you?"

"I'm not your child, am I?"

"You're not my child? What do you mean?"

"I'm the child of an Italian, am I not?"

"Of an Italian?"

"And that's why they call me the Italian?"

Van der Welcke, in his amazement, did not know what to say. He stared at Addie; and his silence meant confession to Addie.

"I am Mamma's child, am I not, but not yours? I am the child of an Italian...."

"My boy, who told you that?"

"Jaap."

"But, Addie, it's not true!"

"Oh, you only say that it's not true, but it is true...."

But now Van der Welcke, after his first amazement, suddenly realized the boy's distress and caught him in his arms and took him on his knees, there, in the big chair:

"Addie, Addie, I swear to you, it's not true! My child, it's not true, you are my child, you are my boy, you are mine, you are mine, mine, mine!"

"Is it really true?"

"You're mine, you're mine, Addie! They lie, they lie! Good Lord! My boy, would I love you so madly, if you were not my boy?"

And he pressed his son to his breast, his two arms tightly round him.

"Papa, can I trust you?"

"Yes, yes, my boy! God! Those vile people! Who says it and why do they say it? And it's a lie, Addie; they lie, they lie. You're my child, mine, mine alone, my son and Mamma's son, my child, my darling! Would we, your two parents, your father and your mother, be so fond of you, so passionately fond of you, if it were not so?"

Now Addie believed and he burst into sobs. He sobbed freely, he could no longer restrain himself and he felt as if he were sobbing for the first time in his young life. It melted away, all his young, small, natural manliness melted away; and he became as weak as a child, because Papa assured him that he was the son of Papa and Mamma and because he believed Papa, now. He sobbed wildly on his father's chest, clutching Van der Welcke in his sturdy little arms, until both of them were nearly stifled:

"Daddy, my Daddy!" he said, in little jerks. "Am I really your child? Oh, tell me again: am I your child? The whole day long, Daddy, I believed I was not your child! The whole day long, I was walking with Frans and the Hijdrechts, thinking I was not your son. And I didn't want to come back home, because I thought I was not your son. I wanted just to go away somewhere, because I thought I was not your son. Daddy, tell me, am I your son? Oh, I should have thought it so terrible if I was not your son! I should have thought it so terrible, because I love you so and because everything would have been for nothing then, if you weren't my father. They said that my father was an Italian and that you, that you were not my father. Tell me again, Daddy: are you my father?"

"Yes, my boy, I am your father."

He said it now with such conviction that Addie believed him absolutely. But the child still clasped his father to him, as though he would never let him go.

"Addie, how could you, how could you believe it for a moment?"

"But then why do people say it?"

"Because they are spiteful."

"But why do people say it?"

There was still a lurking suspicion in him. If he was not the son of an Italian, why did people talk about his parents' past, years ago, at Rome. And, though he believed Papa now, there was still much suspicion in him and he kept on saying to himself:

"But then why do people say it?..."

It tossed about in his mind, that there must be something that Papa was keeping back. But he believed, he wanted to believe Papa: yes, yes, he was Papa's child. And that was his great content, after the sorrow which he had suffered a whole day long: that he had not loved Papa for nothing, that he was the child of the man whom he loved....

"Addie!"

It was Constance calling from downstairs.

"Hush!" said Van der Welcke. "Hush, my boy! Say nothing to Mamma, let Mamma see nothing, for it would cause her so much pain, unnecessarily; and you do believe me now, don't you? You do believe me now, when I assure you that I couldn't possibly, Addie, couldn't possibly be so fond of you else?"

Yes, he now believed his father's word, which he felt to be the truth; he believed, but still, still there was something. But he did not want to ask anything more now: Papa himself was too much upset; and they had to go out, to Grandmamma's, because it was Sunday evening.

"Addie!"

"Go down now, Addie: Mamma's calling you."

He went out on the landing:

"Yes, Mamma, what time is it?"

"It's time to dress."

"Yes, I'll get dressed at once, Mamma."

He became a little man again, while his eyes were still screwed up and red with crying.

He once more embraced his father very tightly:

"Daddy, Daddy, I believe you!"

"My boy, my boy, my boy! Go now, my own boy, go and wash and get dressed; and don't let Mamma notice anything, will you?"

No, he would not let her see; and he would have a good wash, in cold water, wash his throbbing temples and his smarting eyes.

"Those damned people! Those damned people!" said Van der Welcke, cursing and clenching his fists.

Constance, downstairs, ready dressed, was waiting for them, a little put out because Addie had come home so late, because he had fought with Jaap, because he had refused to eat.

"Here I am, Mamma."

There was nothing to show what he had been through: he looked fresh and serious in his new blue suit; his voice was soft and propitiatory. Her face lit up at once:

"Tell me now, Addie, why you fought with Jaap."

"Oh, a boys' quarrel, Mamma, about nothing, really, about nothing at all! Jaap was tormenting a cat; and I can't stand that. Give me a kiss, Mamma."

He kissed his mother very earnestly, embraced her in his clutching arms. He would have forgiven her everything, if it had been really so, if he had been the son of an Italian; but it would have been an everlasting grief to him if he had not been his father's son....

CHAPTER XXX

Van Der Welcke kept himself under control that Sunday evening for Mamma van Lowe's sake, but he was really shocked at Addie's concern and by the calumnies that appeared to be stealthily uttered against him in the Hague; and, next morning, he went to the Ministry of Justice, asked to see Van Saetzema and, without beating about the bush, requested him to punish his son Jaap for his spiteful slander. Van Saetzema, losing his head in the face of Van der Welcke's lofty and resolute tone, stammered and spluttered, spoke to Adolphine when he got home and delegated the business to his wife. Adolphine, it is true, scolded Jaap for being so stupid, but, in doing it, created an excitement that lasted for days and penetrated to the Van Naghels, the Ruyvenaers, Karel and Cateau, Gerrit and Adeline, Paul and Dorine, until everybody was talking about it and knew of the incident, excepting only Mamma van Lowe, whom they always spared, and Constance herself. A couple of days later, Van der Welcke saw Van Saetzema again and asked him if he had corrected Jaap; and, when he perceived in Van Saetzema's spluttering a certain vagueness, a certain inclination to avoid the point, Van der Welcke, who was naturally quick-tempered, flew into a rage and said he would speak to Jaap himself. And, that same evening, three days after the Sunday in question, Van der Welcke went to the Van Saetzemas', was very polite to Adolphine and her husband, but told Jaap, in his parents' presence, that, if he ever dared repeat his slanderous insinuations against Addie, he, his Uncle van der Welcke, would give him a thrashing which he would remember all the days of his life. Van Saetzema lost his head: unaccustomed to such plain speaking, he spluttered and stammered, blurting out conciliatory words; and Adolphine told Van der Welcke that she was quite capable of punishing her children herself, if she thought necessary. Van der Welcke, however, managed to keep cool and civil towards the father and mother, but again warned Jaap, so that he might know what to expect. And the whole family soon learnt that Van der Welcke had been to the Van Saetzemas' and threatened Jaap; and all the members of the family had their different opinions, all except Mamma van Lowe, who was not told, who was always spared the revelation of any unpleasantness, from a sort of reverence on her children's part, so that she really lived and reigned over them in a sort of illusion of harmony and close communion. And Constance also was not told, remained gently happy, gently contented, with that calm, sweet sadness in her face and soul which was the reflection of her moods. On the following Sunday, however, merely knowing that Addie was still angry with Jaap, she said, at lunch:

"Addie, won't you go to the three boys to-day and make it up with Jaap?"

But Addie gave a decided refusal:

"I'll do anything to please you, Mamma, but I'll never go back to those boys."

Constance lost her temper:

"So on account of what you yourself call a boys' quarrel—about a cat—you wish to remain on bad terms with the children of your mother's sister!"

Addie took fright: it was true, the cause seemed very unreasonable.

But Van der Welcke, himself irritable under the restraint which he had been imposing upon himself, said, trembling all over:

"I don't choose, Constance, that Addie should continue to go about with those boys."

His determined manner brought her temper seething up; and all her gentle calmness vanished:

"And I choose," she exclaimed, "that Addie should make friends with them!"

"Mamma, I can't, really!"

"Constance, it's impossible."

Though she was quivering in all her nerves, there was something in the manifest determination of them both that calmed her. But she grew suspicious:

"Tell me why you quarrelled. If you can't make it up, then it wasn't about a cat."

"Let us first have our lunch in peace, if possible," said Van der Welcke. "I'll tell you everything presently, at least if you can be calm."

He realized that he could no longer keep her in ignorance. She collected all her strength of mind to remain cool. After lunch, when she was alone with her husband, she said:

"Now tell me what it is all about."

"On one condition, that you keep calm. I want to avoid a scene if I possibly can, if only for the sake of our boy, who has been very unhappy."

"I am quite calm. Tell me what it is. Why has he been unhappy?"

He now told her. She kept calm. She first tried to gloss things over, in a spirit of contradiction; but she was overcome with a deep sense of depression when she thought of her boy and his trouble. For one torturing moment, she doubted whether she had not been very wrong to return to her native land, to her native town, in the midst of all her relations. But she merely said:

"Slander ... that appears to be people's occupation everywhere...."

Now that she seemed calm, he resolved to tell her everything and said that he had been to the Van Saetzemas and threatened Jaap.

Her temper was roused, for a moment, but subsided again in the profound depression that immediately left her numb and disheartened. The torturing pain followed again and the doubt whether she had not been quite wrong....

But she did not give utterance to the doubt and simply went to the "turret-room," where her boy was:

"Are you going out, Addie?" she asked, vaguely, calm amid her depression.

"Let's go out together, Mamma," he said.

She smiled, glad that he was giving her this Sunday afternoon with that justice with which he divided his favours. She stood in front of him, with blank eyes to which the tears now stole, but with the smile still playing about her mouth.

"Shall we, Mamma?"

She nodded yes. Then she knelt down beside her boy, where he sat with his book in his hands, and it was as though she were making herself very small, as though she were shrinking; and she laid her head on his little knees and put one arm round him. She wept very softly into his lap.

"Come, Mummy, what's the matter?"

She now knew what he had suffered, a sorrow almost too great for one of his years to bear. She almost wished to beg his pardon, but dared not. She only said:

"Addie, you did believe Papa, didn't you?"

"Yes."

"And you believe me too, when I say that it's not true what people say?..."

"Yes, I believe you."

He believed her; and yet a suspicion lingered in his mind. There was something, even though that particular thing was not true. There was something. But he did not ask what it was, out of respect for those past years, the years that were his parents' own.

"My child!" she sobbed, with her head still in his lap. "Tell me, has my boy been very unhappy?"

He just nodded, to say yes, and pressed her to him, lifted her up, took her close to him on his knees, with the caress of an embryo man. She closed her eyes on her son's breast. She felt so weary with her depression that she could have remained lying there. It was as though the illusion was beginning to crumble to pieces, like a dear house of sympathy from which sympathy had shown itself to be absent.

"Don't let Grandmamma notice anything," she said, softly.

He promised.

She wanted to leave the old woman her happiness in her illusion, the illusion of that dear house of sympathy. Her own illusion was crumbling. And yet she thought that she was exaggerating, making too much of it, because a wretched boy had given her child pain:

"That's no reason why they should all be like that," she thought.

And she once more summoned to her mind the illusion of that great, dear house of sympathy for which she had yearned in her lonely exile.

"Come, Mamma, let's go out."

She released him slowly, smiled through her tears, as she rose from his lap and went to change her things:

"How small we all are!" she thought. "What small creatures we are and what small souls we have Is that life? Or is there something different?"

CHAPTER XXXI

The boy had grown serious. For that little incident represented more to him than a quarrel with a cousin about a word of abuse: it had suddenly opened a window to him, who was already none too young for his years, given him a view into the people around him, the big, older, grown-up, serious people, the people to whom he would belong later, when he too was big and old and grown-up; and, at the same time, it had given him his first great sorrow. The boy had grown more serious, more serious than he already was, now that he had discussed it calmly with Frans van Naghel and told him that he had asked his father about it and that the nickname was a pure slander. And the delicate bloom on his child-soul, which was like the soul of a little man, was not only offended by that slander and soiled by it and profaned, but that fledgling man's soul, with its downy freshness, was startled and astonished and shocked and did not understand why the people around him uttered slanders, the people for whom Mamma had longed because she missed them so in her loneliness and because she was filled with that strange feeling, that passion for her family. Why, why did people slander? Why did they speak evil? For he now felt that they all knew that nickname and perhaps all believed that slander a little, inasmuch as they all slandered. What did it benefit them, what did they gain by it, what good did it do them to slander for slander's sake? And the suspicion lingered; for, if it was not true, what they said about his father and mother, what was it that was true? He felt that there was something in their past, something that had never entirely disappeared, something that still embittered the existence of both of them, something that was perhaps the cause of their irreconcilable discord.

And the boy felt this so deeply, in the seriousness that had come with his new-found knowledge, that once, when he was alone with his father, he climbed on his knees and simply asked him to tell him what it was. He was a child, for he still sat on his father's knee, and yet he was already a sturdy boy, though short for his years; and, however serious he might be, he still had the soft bloom of his childhood on his cheeks and on his soul. True, his father was beginning to ask:

"Aren't you too big, my boy, to sit on your father's knee?"

But he himself did not think that he was too big yet. Seriousness and extreme childishness, manhood and boyhood were mingled in him; and, though he was a little man, he was also still a boy; though he was serious, he still remained a child.

He sat on his father's knees and asked him, gravely, to tell him what was true, if the slanders which people spoke were not true; for he felt that there was something. And he read in his father's eyes that he must not ask; and his father answered that he was still too young for his father to discuss everything with him. Then he fell silent, did not insist; but the suspicion never left him and he now knew for certain that there was something, because his father had told him that he was too young to discuss things with him. And so the boy became serious; and, when Van der Welcke came home to dinner from the club, he no longer found his cheerful Addie, who could talk so brightly and fill up the gap between him and Constance with his pleasant, boyish talk. The boy sat in silence, ate in silence, with his young soul full of suspicion, full of silent questionings as to what it really was, if the slanders which people uttered were not true. He loved them so fondly, with that love of his; and it made him profoundly sad that he did not know that thing of the past, because, for want of that knowledge, he was no longer living their life. He now wished that he was older, so as to be able to live their life and have the right to know. And he weighed what he did know in his soul that longed for certainties: he knew that Mamma had been married before and was divorced from the husband whom she never mentioned. Had it been that first husband's fault? Or had she made him unhappy? Addie did not know and was craving to know. And his longing was no morbid curiosity, but the result of his unnatural upbringing: his longing had come about quite naturally, after his first great sorrow, because his father and mother had both always looked upon him as almost more than their child, as their comrade, as their consolation, as their passion, to whom all the current of both their hearts went out. That Constance should have sobbed in his lap, that Van der Welcke should worship him as his warmest friend—him, their boy, their little son—had made his serious soul still more serious and as deep as a small, clear lake; and it could not be but that, after the first shock and the first sorrow, questions and longings should arise in him that as yet made no appeal to other children. His nature was healthy, the nature of a healthy child's soul, well and peacefully balanced in its early, sturdy manliness; but his existence between his two parents—it could not be called an upbringing—had worked on his nerves to the extent of now making him quiver with the wish to know.

Those were gloomy meals; and Constance asked Van der Welcke why Addie was so gloomy, so different from what he had been. Now that the boy was gloomy, with that new, strange and serious gloominess, they both sought each other more than they had done, talked to each other, calmly, without angry scenes. Now that the child was still suffering, they both, together, sought for a solution, how to stop his suffering. And, helpless in the midst of this entirely new confidence, they looked at each other as though in despair, because they thought the solution too terrible. The child wanted to know; and they, both of them, would be compelled—to stop his suffering, or, perhaps, increase it and feel his growing contempt and blame pressing upon them—both of them would be compelled to speak of the years past, of the gigantic mistake of their lives, the mistake which had given him, their child, his life! Oh, how they felt it, both of them, that past which never died, sunk in a bottomless pit, but always haunted them, haunting them more seriously, more menacingly now that Addie was growing older and had been unhappy and wanted to know! Oh, how helpless they both felt, while they stared at each other in despair because they did not know how to spare their darling, how to spare him, even though they would spare him to-day, how—how indeed?—to spare him to-morrow! And, because their sorrow was the same, the same sorrow for their darling, for their comrade, their consolation, their passion, it was as though, for the first time, after years and years, they were nearing each other and for the first time bearing together a part of the heavy burden of life that pressed upon their small souls. How were they to spare him, how were they to spare him?

Finding no solution, they each went their own way again, their eyes still blank with helplessness, their hearts heavy with despair. What had become of the melancholy contentment that had brought Constance her gentle happiness? And, when they met again at meals and the boy, the sensible, merry little comrade of old, who had always enlivened those meal-times, sat in silence, ate in silence, with his serious boy's face, firm in outline already and yet with the soft bloom of the child upon it, and his steel-blue eyes full of thought, then they would timidly stare at each other again and the same discouragement would send its cry of despair from out of their timid glance. This was no longer to be endured, this made them both suffer overmuch, this would have cost them their lives and the grace of their lives, this they could no longer face, this made them feel more helpless from day to day.

Though they both of them, separately, took him in their arms, he no longer said a word, accepted the fact that he was too young to know what was really true, if the slander was not true; but neither his face nor his soul brightened and the deepening of his gloom was the measure of their despair.

"What are we to do?" thought Constance. "What are we to do?" she asked Van der Welcke.

And she wrung her hands, feeling that the past was now doomed to remain for ever and that to think anything else was to invite disillusion. Oh, the past, which not only remained, which not only would cling to them for ever, but which grew, grew with the child, as though the sorrow of that past would always blossom anew, again and again, with perennial grief and woe! Oh, the indestructible sorrow, which always came back to haunt them, even though it seemed to have died, sunk in a bottomless pit, the abyss of past years! Until, at last, as in a cry for help in the helplessness that pressed and bore upon her more fiercely from day to day, clutching at her throat, inexorably demanding a decision, she made that decision and wailed:

"Tell him! Tell him! Tell him!"

And, as she uttered that wail, he saw her so prostrate under the decision that would bring down upon her the scorn, the rage perhaps, of their child, of their son, the death—O Heaven!—of his love, if he once knew and, above all, realized the truth, that he, her husband, felt pity for the woman who had turned his life into a long and dreary futility; and he said:

"I will tell him, I will tell him. But have no fear: if he does understand and realize it, he will love you none the less for it, Constance!"

She looked at him, feeling that he no longer grudged her their child's love, that he was not as jealous as she. And, for a moment, she thought of throwing herself on his breast and sobbing out the anguish which she felt pressing more and more upon her, felt coming towards her like a monster looming out of the future. But the emotion tugging at her heart-strings was drawn back violently; and she went away and flung herself on the floor in her bedroom and hiccoughed her despair ... because her son was going to be told!

CHAPTER XXXII

But he did not tell him that day. He merely persuaded himself that it was not necessary, that it would even be wrong to tell his son, his child, who was still so young, the past of their lives, that which he would hear of himself and know and understand when he was a year or two older. And on the following days also, hesitating, Van der Welcke did not tell him. But the gloomy meals continued, Constance' fits of helplessness continued; and she once again exclaimed:

"Oh, tell him! Do tell him!"

And they both felt so unhappy, because they were losing their child more and more every day, that he determined to tell Addie. He hesitated until the last moment, wavering, struggling within himself, not knowing what would be right, what wrong, knowing only that he was suffering beyond endurance. Then, one evening, he looked up his child in the "turret-room:"

"Addie, shall I be in your way if I sit here?"

"No, Papa."

The boy was doing his home-work. Van der Welcke sat down. He reflected that he would rather tell him some other day, when Addie was not working. The child worked on, silently, gloomily, grimly. And Van der Welcke suddenly exclaimed:

"Addie!"

"Yes, Papa?"

"Come here for a minute."

The boy stood up and went to him.

"Tell me, why have you been so gloomy lately, my boy?"

"I'm not gloomy, Daddy."

"You hardly speak to me or your mother. And it's not like you, to sulk. Are you angry with us?"

"No, Daddy."

"Aren't you angry with us?"

"No, Daddy: what should I be angry for?"

"Then be as you used to be, Addie. When you're not cheerful, everything in the house is so sad."

The boy smiled.

"I'll try, Daddy."

"But why try? Just be it, be it!"

No, Van der Welcke would not, could not tell him.

"I'll try, Daddy."

And he moved to go back to his books.

"Addie!"

"What is it, Papa?"

"Come here, come to me."

"I have my work to do."

"Come along, I want you."

The boy came.

"Come to me, here, on my lap. Perhaps it is the last time, Addie, that I shall take you on my knee. You are my little boy still; and presently, presently perhaps you will be a big son to me, with whom I shall discuss things ... and who will no longer sit on my lap."

He sat down on his father's knee:

"What is it?" he asked, quietly, sensibly.

"I am going to tell you, Addie."

The child understood:

"No, don't tell me," he said. "I am not inquisitive. And I am too young, perhaps, to know. It doesn't matter. I dare say I shall know, later on. For the present, I'm just your little boy."

He nestled against his father, in his arm:

"It's so jolly, sitting with you like this. Uncle Paul always says, when he sees us bicycling, that we are just like chums, but he has never seen us like this."

Should he tell him? thought Van der Welcke. Should he not tell him? If he told him, this would be the last time that he would take his son on his knees.

"I had made up my mind to tell you, Addie."

"No, don't."

He did not tell him that evening. And the boy tried to be as he used to, especially at meals, but he was not very successful; his cheerfulness sounded forced. Then, two evenings later, Van der Welcke said:

"Come here, Addie. Come and sit on my lap."

And that was the last time.

"Listen, I want to tell you all about it. When you know, perhaps you will feel a little older than you do now; but, when you know, you will be my child again, my son, won't you? My son, yes, who is becoming a man, but still my son, my friend as always. I'll tell you now. It's better that I should tell you...."

Then he told him, very simply....

And it was very easy, very simple to tell Addie, in quiet words. He told his boy that he had fallen in love with Mamma when she was the wife of another and that he had stolen Mamma's love, stolen it from that other man. He told the story so humbly, so quietly and simply as though it meant nothing, making this confession to his child, and as though he were pouring out all his sufferings of the old days into the heart of a friend. They sat talking for a long time; and it did them both good. Then said Van der Welcke:

"Addie, go to Mamma now. She herself asked me to tell you everything. Go to her now and give her a kiss."

The boy kissed him first, embraced him with throttling arms, with the grip of a friend's embrace. Then he went out; and Van der Welcke, quietly smoking, listened to his footsteps on the stairs. But then Van der Welcke started, with a shock, reflected:

"What have I done? O my God, no, no, no I ought not to have told him...."

But the house remained very quiet. Constance was sitting alone, in her boudoir. Her head was bent under the light of the lamp, over her needle-work, and her hair, changing so gently to its cloudy grey, curled tenderly about the delicate oval of her still youthful face. There was a sort of gentle, resigned peace in her attitude, with much pensiveness and sadness. When Addie opened the door, he stood still and she did not look up, thinking that it was Van der Welcke. Then he went to his mother....

She looked up, startled:

"Is that you?"

"Yes, Mamma."

She looked up at him; and suddenly it flashed across her that he knew....

"Papa has been speaking to me, Mamma...."

She gave a violent start, as though she had had an electric shock; her eyes closed, her head fell back, her hands fell slackly in her lap:

"O God!" she thought. "No, oh, no, he ought not to have told him!..."

He knelt before his mother and passed his fingers softly over her face and gently opened her eyes. She looked at him, with a pale, terrified, shocked face and staring eyes and distorted mouth. She saw his own fresh, soft child's face, smiling friendly....

"I know the truth now, Mamma," he said, "and, if people slander me now, I can bear it...."

She threw her arms around him, dropped her head upon his breast. She felt him in that embrace grown older, bigger, stronger, now quite a man. She now felt a protector in him. But she was ashamed and again closed her eyes:

"My boy!" she murmured. "Do you love your mother?..."

"Yes, Mamma."

Her face grew calmer, but her eyes remained shut.

"My darling!" she whispered, almost inaudibly, with closed eyes. "Thank you. Thank you. But leave me to myself now...."

He kissed her, with his manly tenderness, and then went out and shut the door. She opened her eyes, looked round the room. But it was as though she was ashamed before everything, before the walls of the room and the furniture around her; for she now closed her eyes again and hid her face in her hands.

And she sat like that for long, as though lost in thanksgiving for the mercy vouchsafed her by life....

But, between the two of them, the boy now brightened, strong in the power of truth and certainty, even though window after window had opened before him, giving him a glimpse into the world. Between the two of them, he recovered his former self, his former voice, his childish tempers even, became once more the consolation and the aim of their two existences. She went for walks on his arm; he went bicycling with him for long distances, full of air and space. The house resounded with his young, serious, no longer treble voice. When she looked at him, however, she thought that he had grown, had become broader; that the shape of his head, the curve of his cheeks were losing the childish softness that still belonged to his years....

And, when Van der Welcke felt bored in his smoking-room and went and sat with Addie in the "turret," always first punctiliously asking his son if he was interrupting him in his work, he no longer took him on his knee....

CHAPTER XXXIII

It was one morning during the summer holidays that old Mr. van der Welcke said to his wife:

"Why not ask the little boy to come and stay with us?"

There was never much said between the old people, but each understood without words, or from a single word, the thought that was passing in the other's mind.

Not until the evening did the old lady ask:

"The little boy alone?"

"Yes, alone ... or with Henri."

Two days after that, she suggested:

"Oughtn't we to invite them, all three, in that case? Constance as well?"

The old man said nothing and went on reading, as though he had not heard; and his wife did not press for an answer. But, at nightfall, when they sat staring at the dark summer evening outside, old Mr. van der Welcke said:

"No, I don't like her. Let us ask Henri and Adriaan."

She said nothing. She was used to obeying her husband's wishes; and she had brought up Henri also, long ago, to obey his parents' wishes. And Henri had obediently given up his life, given up himself, at their command, to that woman. Which of the two was more to blame, whether he had been the tempter or she the temptress, they did not know, they did not wish to know, because all temptation sprang from the evil one; but Henri was a man; and so the responsibility fell upon him. He being responsible, they had commanded him to sacrifice himself and thus to atone for his sin, in the face of God and man. That was how they had seen it at the time, how they had commanded, how it had come to pass. But he, the father, had lost his son through that command; and the loss always rankled....

"Henri and Adriaan alone," the old man repeated.

Now that he was repeating his few words, she knew that his will was irrevocable. She was sorry for it: the voices which spoke to her now and then, on nights when the wind blew, had gradually brought her to a gentler mood, as though they had been soothing music to her listening soul. Those voices had told her to go to the Hague; and there she had for the second time seen that woman, the bane of their life as parents, and met that woman's mother; and it was as though that meeting between mother and mother had been a gentle balm, as gentle and healing as the magic music of the voices, a balm that brought about a softer mood, that caused more to be understood, that caused much to be forgiven, in a gradual approach towards reconciliation, after so many, many dismal years of silent rancour and antagonism. In her, the old woman, the rancour had as it were melted away, since she had read the strange book, since she had heard the voices on gusty nights, since she had seen that woman's mother and known her sadness. In the old woman it was a gentle wish not only for reconciliation, but for some measure of friendship with that woman, the wife of her son, the mother of her grandchild. But she felt that there was no trace of any such wish in her husband's heart; and, because she could only obey, she said nothing and merely told him wordlessly that she did not think as he thought.

He heard her saying it without words, but he did not give in.

And, when they went to bed, he said:

"I shall write to Henri to-morrow."

He wrote to ask if Henri and Adriaan would come and spend a week at Driebergen, before Adriaan's holidays were over. Van der Welcke felt in the laboured words of that old man who was not used to writing that his father was implacable towards Constance. Constance felt it and so did Addie. And, when Addie, offended on his mother's behalf, said, angrily, that she was being left behind alone, she replied:

"It's better that you should go with Papa, my boy."

She thought it advisable for him, the grandson, the heir, not to provoke his grandfather. But she had never spent a week without him before:

"What can I do?" she thought. "He is growing bigger, older; I shall see less of him still as time goes on."

Yes, he had grown bigger, older; he was now fourteen. He was broad; and his voice was so curiously deep sometimes, was changing; but he remained small for his age. The pink childishness of his skin was becoming downy with a sort of blond velvet bloom; and that blond velvet was more clearly defined above his upper lip. But he was still a child in the innocent freshness which, despite his seriousness, wafted from all his being like a perfume.

"I'm going to Driebergen for a week with Papa," he said to Paul, to Gerrit, to Adeline. "Will you take pity on Mamma, Uncle, while I'm away? Will you, Auntie?"

They promised, smiling. Constance remained calm and peaceful. After those gently happy moods there had come to her, since Addie's quarrel with Jaap about the nickname and what had happened after the quarrel, a nameless depression that silently gnawed at her heart. She did not speak about it, did not mention it to Addie, nor to Gerrit, nor to Paul. She entombed it in the depth of herself.

Father and son went away; and the grandparents thought that the little boy had grown. The grandmother feared that the children of the villa close by would be too childish, after all, for Adriaan to play with. She said this with an air of disappointment, but also of astonishment and admiration; and, although Henri said that Addie could play very nicely with his Uncle Gerrit's fair-haired little tribe, even if he was a little paternal with them, yet the old woman sent no message to the villa.

It was beautiful at Driebergen and Zeist; and Van der Welcke enjoyed being there. And, as they had brought their bicycles, they went on long expeditions....

When alone with his father, Van der Welcke spoke out more and more. He spoke of the past, humbly, as though once more asking forgiveness of that stern father who to him, the son, seemed almost supernatural in his absolute virtue and stainlessness. He spoke of Rome, he even spoke of De Staffelaer, who was still alive, at his country-place near Haarlem, a man as old as Van der Welcke's father; he spoke of those last dismal years at Brussels, of how they had both longed for Dutch air and Dutch people, especially for their own families. But he also said that, however glad he might be to see his parents again, he thought that to Constance this renewal of family-ties was often a disappointment. As he talked, he felt himself the boy, the student, the young man of former days, who also had talked much with his father, with his father alone, even as Addie now talked with him. He spoke of his boy and admitted that he worshipped him, that they both worshipped him. The old man, quietly smoking his pipe, listened, taking a new interest in those younger lives, the lives of his son and grandson. The old man felt as though he were rediscovering something of his son, but he also felt him to be very far away from him, without love or fear of God.

Van der Welcke spoke on.... And, almost unconsciously, in this confession and avowal of his life and thoughts and feelings, he told how Addie had quarrelled and fought with his cousin, told of the talk in their circle and of the distress of his son. He told on, almost unconsciously, of the wavering, the struggle, the helplessness of Constance and himself when they saw their child pining with that distress. And, almost unconsciously, Van der Welcke confessed, quite simply, that he had spoken to his son as to a man and told his son the truth about his parents' past.

The old man, quietly smoking, had heard him in silence, glad to listen to his son's voice. What his son had told him to start with was strange to him: thoughts, feelings, experiences of a very strange life, differing wholly from his own. But what his son told him now made him doubt whether he had heard aright:

"What do you say?" he asked, thinking that he must be hard of hearing.

Van der Welcke repeated what he had said.

"You told ... Adriaan ... your past?... Told him about Rome and De Staffelaer?..."

"Yes, without entering into unnecessary details and with due respect for his youth, I told him the truth, the whole truth. The boy was suffering pain, was distressed because he did not know; and now he is suffering no longer."

The old man shook his head, put down his pipe:

"I don't understand," he said. "Or else there's something wrong with my hearing. You told ... Adriaan...?"

Van der Welcke repeated it again, smiling a little at his father's astonishment.

The old man understood that he had heard quite clearly. But he was so much shocked that he could not speak.

And it was only next day that he asked:

"How were you able to tell Adriaan that?"

"Just plainly and simply," said Van der Welcke.

"Just plainly and simply?" the old man echoed.

And not until that evening did he find more words; then he said:

"No, I can't understand it. I can't understand you, Henri. I feel that there is a very, very deep gulf between us. I feel that there is neither love nor fear of God in you, that everything in your life, in your relations with your wife, with your child, lacks a religious tendency. It makes me very sad. I could never have pictured things like that. I at least thought that you would have asked God's forgiveness daily for the sin you once committed, the sin against yourself, your parents, that woman, her husband, against the world, against God. I never imagined you, Henri, so obdurate, so entirely without repentance, regretting merely your own ruined life and shattered career. I can only pray for you and I will pray for you, every day. Still, I can understand want of faith. But what I can't understand is that you should—plainly and simply—corrupt the soul of your son, a child of fourteen, by telling him of your sin—plainly and simply—so that he might no longer suffer: those were your words, were they not? Now, when I repeat those words to myself and repeat them again and think over them and reflect upon them, I fail to understand them. I do not understand them. I feel that you must be entirely lacking in moral sense, in any idea of duty towards your child, in any fear of God, to be able to act like that, to be able to speak like that to your son, just to spare him suffering—plainly and simply—and I ask myself, 'Am I dreaming? Where am I? Whom am I speaking to? Is the man opposite me my son, my child, brought up by myself, and is what he is telling me the truth or an illusion?' And, if that illusion is the truth, Henri, if you are so entirely lost to every sense of moral and parental duty, then I am very, very sorry to hear it and I sit staring into a horrible abyss; and I confess that I do not understand you and that I understand nothing of the world, the times and the people of to-day...."

The old man had spoken slowly, measuring every word.

"Father," said Henri, "you and I are different; and I can understand that you, an old man, in your great goodness and transcendental sense of duty, cannot understand how I feel and think and act. Still, I do not believe that I have corrupted Addie and I am convinced that it was a good impulse that suggested to Constance and me to tell our child about our past at once and not to wait until he was a year or two older. Tell me if you think that he looks like a child whose imagination has been defiled. Tell me if you do not think, on the contrary, that he is a strong-minded boy who suffered from those slanders, when they reached him, simply because he did not know the truth, and who now, knowing the truth, loves both his parents with his clear, candid soul and is no longer in doubt, but knows."

The old man slowly shook his head with the tall, ivory forehead, while his gnarled hands trembled:

"Henri, you can thank God if your child, whose purity you have put to so severe a test, emerges from that test unstained."

Van der Welcke was silent, out of respect. He felt himself, notwithstanding his love, so far removed from his father that his heart was wrung and he thought:

"Will Addie ever, ever be so far removed from me?..."

CHAPTER XXXIV

The old man often reverted to that conversation:

"Henri, can you imagine me, your father, speaking to you, when you were thirteen, about a sin, a crime I had committed?"

No, Van der Welcke could never have imagined it! He was sorry now that he had told his father so much, seeing how shocked the old man was. And, though he tried to find soothing words, in order to calm his father after that shock, still everything that he said sounded too cynical, too modern, too flippant almost; and he no longer answered, but preferred to avoid the subject, when the old man returned to it daily, shaking his head and making his comments. And Van der Welcke was obliged to smile when his father often closed those comments with the remark:

"Don't let your mother know anything about it."

No, he did not tell his mother, because his father ordered him to leave his mother out of all this cynical philosophy and atheistical lack of principle, because his father thought that it would hurt her, his wife, whom he had always kept secluded from all knowledge of the outside world, until the scandal in Rome had come as a shock to both of them. And even then, in the years that followed, he had always hidden as much as possible of the world from his wife, holding that a woman, whatever her age, need not know, need not read, need not discuss, need not reflect upon all those things which, far removed from the two of them, were sin: sin such as their son had committed....

Van der Welcke now for the first time fully realized how grievous the shock of the scandal must have been to both of them, years ago. He, young though he was and but lately emancipated from his parents, had at once lost so much of those strict principles in his life in Rome, in his contact with women of the world, in his polished drawing-room talk on soul-weariness with Constance; and he now for the first time fully understood why they had not wished to see the two of them and why years had to elapse before there could be any question of forgiveness. And, however much he had longed for his father, in Brussels, he now felt that this longing was an illusion; that his father was a stranger to him now and he a stranger to his father: two strangers to each other, whom only a remembrance of former days had brought together again. And, curiously, though, as a child, he had liked his father better than his mother, his love now seemed to turn more to his mother, who had never become a stranger, who had always remained the mother, silently reading her forbidden book, longing simply for her child, to whom the voices had sent her....

"But, just as my father would never have spoken out to me, no more would I ever have gone bicycling with my father?" thought Van der Welcke, as he darted with Addie along the smooth roads towards the Zeist Woods.

They were like two brothers, an elder and a younger brother, neither of them tall, but both fairly broad, both with something delicate and high-bred and yet something powerful in their build—Van der Welcke was young still and slender for his nine-and-thirty years—and both, under the same sort of cap, had the same face, the same steel-blue eyes, the same straight profile, with its short nose, well-formed mouth and broad chin, though one was a man and the other a boy. They pedalled and pedalled and devoured the roads on that scorching August morning, talking gaily like two friends.

"Let's stop here, Addie, and take a rest," said Van der Welcke, at length, out of breath.

They alighted, leant their machines against a couple of trees, flung themselves on the mound of needles under the fir-trees, which rose silently and peacefully, calm as cathedral-pillars.

"I say, I'm tired," said Van der Welcke, feeling a little older, for the moment, than his son. "Addie, how you take it out of your father!"

Addie laughed, pulled off his cap and wiped his forehead with his handkerchief. Van der Welcke rested his head on Addie's knee.

"Move higher up: you're not comfortable like that," said Addie.

And, catching his father under the arm-pits, he hoisted him up a bit:

"No, that won't do either," he said. "Look here, you're squashing my stomach!"

"Is this better?"

"Yes, if you keep still, old chap, and don't move, you can stay like that."

And he passed his fingers through his father's short, curly hair, while Van der Welcke lay silent, closed his eyes and thought:

"Fancy me, when I was fourteen, pulling up my father by his arms and saying to him, 'Look here, you're squashing my stomach!... If you keep still, old chap, you can stay like that!'"

And he suddenly began to splutter with laughter.

"I say, what's up? What are you laughing at?"

"Addie, I was thinking, I was thinking...."

"Well, what were you thinking?"

"I was thinking...."

And Van der Welcke began to wobble up and down with laughter.

"Oh, but I say! Woa! woa! Don't go jumping about on my stomach like that! Hi! Stop! Keep still! What's the joke?"

"I was thinking ... of your Grandpapa's face ... if ... when I was your age ... I had hauled him up like that by his arms and said to him, 'If you keep still ... if you keep still...!'"

Addie's sense of humour made him see the picture at once: Grandpapa, getting on for forty and very stately and dignified, and Papa, a boy like himself; and Papa saying:

"If you keep still, old chap, you can stay like that!"

And both of them burst with laughter, one on top of the other; and Addie, whom his father's weight prevented from laughing as he would have liked to, flung his legs madly in the air, almost stood on his head, until Van der Welcke tumbled backwards, with his head lower than his feet:

"Bother you! I was just so comfortable!"

Addie took pity on Papa, pulled him up again under his arms, dragged him about most disrespectfully, first shoved his head on his chest ... no, that hurt ... then a little lower down ... on his stomach.... There, he could stay like that....

But Van der Welcke kept on laughing like a lunatic. And Addie was the first to recover his seriousness:

"Father, stop it now! Stop shaking about like that!"

Van der Welcke closed his eyes blissfully. The scent of the steaming pines floated on the summery air; the needles glistened and gave off their fragrance. And Van der Welcke fell asleep, with his head in his son's lap.

"Dear old Father!" thought Addie; and he stroked his father's round, curly head.

He looked down at him and, so as not to disturb his father's sleep, sat motionless, with his back against a tree. He looked down at him: dear old Father!... But he was not old, his father: he was young.... And, all at once, it seemed to Addie that he saw it for the first time: his father was young. And he thought to himself how strange it was that, when you are young yourself, you call everybody old: Granny van Lowe and Grandpapa and Grandmamma van der Welcke were old; and Uncle Ruyvenaer and Auntie were old; and the two old aunts, Auntie Rine and Auntie Tine, were very old, regular old mummies. But Papa, Papa was young. Why, he was only a year or two older than Uncle Paul, who was always the young man, the dandy, with his exquisite coats and beautiful ties. And Papa looked younger than Uncle Paul, Papa certainly looked younger.... Addie bent over him, while he slept. He lay quietly sleeping, with his face three-quarters turned on Addie's lap. And Addie, seeing for the first time that Papa was young, studied his face. Oh, how young Papa was: he was younger than Mamma! He looked much younger; he looked almost like an elder brother of Addie's. His hair, thinning ever so little over the temples, was still quite brown: soft, short, curly brown hair, almost close-cropped, but curling just a little, like his own. His forehead was white, like that of a statue, without a wrinkle, had kept white under the peak of his cycling-cap; and his cheeks, a little blue from shaving, were healthily bronzed. His eyelids were young, his lids now closed in sleep; his straight nose was young and his mouth, with the short, thick, curly moustache above it. His frame was young; and on Addie's knees lay his young hands, small, broad and dainty, with carefully-tended nails: Addie looked at his own finger-nails, boy's nails, which were torn rather than cut.... How strange that Papa should be so young! He noticed it for the first time. And for the first time he felt himself to have grown older, no longer quite a child, a boy still, but grown into a young man, even though he was only fourteen.... Yes, when you were a child, a real child, you looked upon anybody older than yourself as just old. Now, he was astounded: how young Papa was; and how much older Mamma was! True, her face was young still, but she had grey hair, she was forty-three.... He could imagine Papa with a very young wife, a girl almost, like one of the cousins, Louise or Emilie, or Floortje: Papa and a wife like that would make a good pair.... How young he was, how young he was!... He was now sleeping like a child, on Addie's stomach, peacefully breathing.... Dear old Father!... No, not a bit old: as young as a brother, as a friend, as a chum. So jolly too and so mad sometimes.... And then suddenly he would try to be the stern parent! Dear Father!—Addie laughed—That didn't come off at all! He loved him like that: so young, such a friend, such a chum, such a brother.... Mamma was his mother, always, even though he did sometimes flirt with her; but Papa was not a Papa, Papa was his friend and his brother. But, young though Papa was, Addie nevertheless thought it strange that he had said to him so often:

"My life is shattered, my career is done for."

Why was that? Was it only because Papa had had to leave the diplomatic service when he was still quite young and had married Mamma? But Addie was a sensible and prematurely intelligent child; and his bright, young intelligence could not admit that; and, suddenly, Addie thought, if things really were as Papa declared—his life shattered, his career done for—then Addie thought it wrong, disapproved of it, thought it weak of Papa, weak, morbid almost, yes, morbid. How was it possible that Papa, since the day when he had sent in his resignation, had never done anything but complain of that ruined career, reproaching Mamma with it, silently or out loud, and only picking up a trifle at Brussels with commissions on wine and insurances, whereas there was so much else: life, the world, the whole world open before him! And to him, to the boy himself, it was as though wide prospects stretched out before him, which as yet he only divined as a dream of the future, which as yet he only felt to be there, to exist for any one who is young and strong and healthy and has brains. But, while he thus wondered and disapproved within himself—so weak: why so weak?—he felt a sort of fond and gentle pity amidst his wonder and disapproval, combined with a sort of need to grow still fonder of that father, who was so young, so strong and ... so weak. His boyish hand rested gently on his father's curly hair, stroked it gently while his father lay sleeping; and, with a sort of tenderness, the boy thought:

"Why are you like that? How can you be like that? Why have you never overcome that weakness, become manlier, firmer? Poor, poor Father!..."

And it was strange, but, while he disapproved, he felt his love increase, as the love of the stronger goes out to the weaker and lesser: the stronger the one feels, the weaker the other appears to him; and thus the instinct is developed to protect and care for that other. And now he remained stock-still, thinking that he had really tired his father out, for they had ridden like mad that morning, intoxicated with the smooth length of the roads, giddied with excessive speed.

He remained stock-still, as though he himself were a father who was letting his tired child sleep in his arms. And, while he sat gazing at that young face of his father's, that white forehead divided with a sharp stripe from the blue, bronzed cheeks, there fluttered through his vision those new thoughts, like birds that were learning to fly, those dreams of wide prospects stretching away to dim futures at which he only guessed as yet, because the world was so wide and life so big. And, though these fledgling thoughts were all ignorant of the world and of life, they fluttered to and fro, fluttered away and then back to the nest, where they, the new-born thoughts, settled upon that greatest and strongest and most conscious feeling, that of love for the father who was so young that he was like a brother and so weak that he was as a child....

CHAPTER XXXV

Constance was much alone during those days. She was even more lonely than she had ever been in Brussels—when Van der Welcke was away about his wines or his insurances—because this was the first time that she had been parted from Addie. She saw her mother almost every day, however; but, for the rest, she mostly stayed at home, just as she had very often stayed at home in Brussels. A gentle melancholy had come upon her, after her fits of depression, a melancholy that impelled her to be much at home and much by herself. She was a stay-at-home woman: her house had the well-tended and attractive and comfortable appearance of a house which is loved by its occupant with the unadventurous feeling that home is the safest place. She busied herself in the mornings in a quiet way, did her housekeeping, gave her orders quietly and methodically; and her house always had an atmosphere of cosy, restful well-being, which seemed to calm her and persuade her to stay in it. The two maids, with whom she was always the calm, pleasant mistress of the house, liked her, did their work quietly and soon learnt what was expected of them. During these days when she was alone, she went all over the house with them, made them give Van der Welcke's room and Addie's room a thorough cleaning, went through every corner of her cupboards with her gentle, mindful fingers, the fingers of a dainty woman who imparted something of her own daintiness to everything that she touched.

She was not a great reader, did not play the piano, was not even particularly cultured. As a child, she had been fond of fairy-tales; as a child, she had even invented fairy-tales; but, apart from that, she did not care much for literature; poetry she regarded as insincere; and she did not know much about music. But there was something soft and pretty and distinguished about her, something exquisite and feminine, especially now that her vanity was really dead. She had an innate taste for never doing or saying anything that was ugly or harsh or coarse; and it was only when her nerves got the better of her that she could lose her temper and fly into a passion. But, owing especially to her sadness and to the grey and dismal years which she had passed, she had developed a very sensitive, soft heart, almost hypersensitive and oversoft. A word of sympathy at once fell upon her like kindly dew and made her love whoever uttered it. She had become very fond of her mother, more so than formerly, appreciating in Mamma the mother who kept her children together. She also shared that family-affection, that strange fondness for all her kith and kin. But she often experienced what Mamma never felt: the disappointment and depression and discouragement of loving with a love that was deep and inclusive those whose changing, complex interests were for ever taking them farther and farther out of reach. At such times, she just remained at home, in her own house, wrapped herself in her gentle melancholy, went over the house with the maids, who liked her, in order that everything might be very nice and neat. She had nothing of the Dutch housewife about her; and the maids often told her that Mrs. So-and-so used to do things this way and Mrs. What's-her-name that way. But she had so much tact that they did as she wished and accepted her distribution of hours and duties; and her house was always in order, comfortable, fit to live in. She had the gentle little fads of a woman who has no great intellect and who takes pleasure in almost simple, childish little femininities. If she happened to have a headache or felt out of sorts, she thought it pleasant to lie on the sofa in her bedroom with a heap of fashion-plates around her and quietly to think out all sorts of costumes, which she did not require and did not order, but which she just thought out, created, with the graceful fancy of a dainty woman who loves pretty clothes. Or she could amuse herself with tidying up her cupboards, going through all her laces and ribbons, folding them up neatly, smoothing them out, laying them in the different compartments of exquisite little Empire chests-of-drawers and scenting them with orris-root. Or she could go through her trinkets—she had not many—polishing her jewels and trying the effect of them upon herself with a pleased laugh at those pretty things which sparkle so brightly and enhance a woman's beauty. She was not interested in the larger questions, did not understand feminism, was a little afraid of socialism, especially because the poor were so dirty and smelt so horribly. Still, she was charitable, though she was not at all well-off, and often gave money to the poor and dirty, hoping above all that they would wash themselves. And yet she had a fairly logical intelligence, even though she was not cultured, even though she did not ponder deeply on social questions or on art. Now that her vanity was dead, she was a woman of the world, who thought the world tedious and tiresome and felt just a need for sympathy and soft compassion. And only sometimes did the strings within her seem to become more tensely stretched and there sounded through her something like a vague sadness that suddenly made her think and say to herself:

"How small we are and how small everything that we do is! I am growing old now; and what has there been in my existence? Could there be anything else in life? Or is life just like that, for everybody?"

In point of fact, she herself did not know that her heart had never spoken. She had fallen in love with Van der Welcke, at Rome, because of his good looks, in that atmosphere of vanity and drawing-room comedy which had made her, after reading a couple of fashionable French novels, talk sadly about her soul-weariness, parrot-wise, neither knowing nor feeling aught of what she said. She never even thought that there was another sort of love than that which she had felt for Van der Welcke; and, if she happened to read about it somewhere in one of her occasional fits of reading, she would think:

"It's only a book; and the author is writing fine words."

But, at the same time, her gentle nature was too superlatively and exquisitely feminine and also too motherly to look upon physical love as the only needful thing. No, what she had felt as a duty in the case of her first husband and as passion in the case of Van der Welcke had soon turned to mother-love. Married, in her passion she had at once longed for a child. And she had worshipped her child from the very first day....

CHAPTER XXXVI

Constance was in her bedroom one morning, arranging all sorts of things, when the servant came and said:

"Mrs. van Saetzema is here, ma'am."

Constance' eyelashes trembled and her lips contracted. She would have liked to make an excuse, to say that she was not at home; but she refrained because of the maid:

"Very well, Truitje; ask her to come up."

Adolphine came upstairs noisily, with elaborate gaiety:

"Good-morning, Constance, how are you? We hardly ever see you now. I say, have you been ill?"

"No."

"You are not looking well. Why is it so dark in here?"

"Dark?"

"Yes, I should feel stifled in a light like this. Oh, of course, it's the trees opposite! They take away all the light. My goodness, this is a gloomy house of yours I Aren't your husband and boy back yet?"

"No."

"I say, why didn't you go with them?"

"For no special reason."

"They're a very particular old couple, aren't they, that father and mother of your husband's? Whatever are you doing?"

"I'm tidying up my cupboard."

"You'd do better to go for a walk: you're looking so pale."

"But I'm perfectly well."

"I've come to ask if you'll come to dinner at my house the day after to-morrow. But you must make yourself smart. We shall be fourteen. My first dinner-party. It's a summer dinner. But we know such an awful lot of people; and I always begin my dinners very early. You see, it's quite plain, at my place, but jolly. Bertha doesn't begin till January; but she works everything out so closely. I like doing things handsomely. So it's settled, isn't it: you'll come?"

"I'm sorry, Adolphine. It's very nice of you to ask me, but I can't come."

"Why not?"

"I don't know your friends. And I don't care about going out."

"Oh!" said Adolphine, nettled. "I suppose my friends are not smart enough for you? I can tell you, I have the Hijdrechts coming and the Erkenbouts and the...."

"I'm not saying anything about your friends, but I don't care for dinner-parties."

"And you give them yourself!"

"I?"

"Yes, as I saw for myself not so long ago."

"I don't give dinner-parties. I have Van Vreeswijck to dinner now and again."

"To dinner ... with pink candles on the table?"

"Yes, with pink candles."

"Well, if you don't want to come ... this is a free country...."

"Fortunately!"

"You're rather upset this morning, aren't you?"

"Not at all."

"Is it just because our boys had a fight? You've adopted quite a different tone to me since: I've noticed. *I* can't help it if boys choose to fight."

"Adolphine, don't let us talk of matters that can make us say things which we might regret."

But Adolphine was angry because Constance had refused to come to her dinner. Her invitations had all gone wrong and she wanted Constance; also, she thought that Constance did not value the invitation; also, she thought Constance a snob, with that everlasting Vreeswijck of hers, that Court man....

"Regret?" she said, coldly. "I never say anything that I have to regret. But I can't help it if people at the Hague are saying unpleasant things about us all just now!"

And, working herself into a state of nervous excitement, she tried to cry, in order to make Constance, who was so unkind, feel, once and for all, that not only she, Adolphine, but the whole family had to suffer no end of pain because of Constance. And she managed to get the tears into her eyes and squeezed them out.

But Constance remained indifferent:

"What sort of things?" she asked.

"What sort of things?" snapped Adolphine, furiously, crying with temper, offended at the refusal, forgetting all the nice things that Constance had said about Floortje's trousseau, hating her sister at the moment. "What sort of things? That you are not Papa's daughter!"

"That I...?"

"That you are not Papa's daughter!" shrieked the other, getting more excited at every word, deliberately screwing herself up into a frenzy of nerves. "They're slandering Mamma, they're slandering Mamma! Yes, they're saying that you're not Papa's daughter!"

Constance shrugged her shoulders.

"Well, what do you say to it?" demanded Adolphine.

"Nothing."

"Nothing? Nothing?" cried Adolphine, beside herself because Constance remained so cool at such a revelation. "Nothing? Oh, I expect you're accustomed to have people talking about you. Well, I'm not, d'you see? I have always been used to decency and respectability in my circle, among my friends. No one ever talked about us before. No one ever said that *I* wasn't Papa's daughter...."

"You can't tell. There's time yet!" said Constance.

"Yes, you don't care!" Adolphine blubbered, furiously. "You, with your stuck-up coolness, you're so eaten up with conceit that you don't take anything to heart. I'm not like that. I'm sensitive, I'm easily affected, it hurts me when people talk about us. But then I'm not used to it as you are!"

And Adolphine kept squeezing the tears out of her eyes, wishing to convey that she was misunderstood and misjudged and very sensitive; wishing also to make Constance feel that it was Constance' fault and that there was plenty more that was Constance' fault. Constance, however, remained cool.

Though a single unfortunate word from her husband was enough to set her nerves on edge and her temper seething, she kept calm and cold towards her sister, because, after the fight between their boys, she had settled accounts with Adolphine, written her off as it were; and this feeling had depressed her too much to allow her now to excite herself into a quarrel. She wondered if she was overdoing it; and, to settle the matter, she said:

"I confess that I have never had such an experience of backbiting as here, at the Hague; in Brussels, at any rate, no one ever doubted the legitimacy of my child. But here—and even in your house, Adolphine—people seem to think that he is not my husband's son."

"How can I help that?" Adolphine began to blubber.

"No, you can't help it; at least I'm prepared to believe you can't. But I did hope that, if any one in your house spoke unkindly of your sister, you would have stood up for her, against your children, who perhaps did not quite realize all the mischief which their words might cause.... Let me finish, Adolphine: I am quite calm and I want to tell you this calmly.... If Addie had dared to speak of you in my presence as your children must have spoken of me, I should have been very severe with him. I was under the illusion that I might expect as much from you. I thought that there was still a family-bond, a family-affection, a family-pride among all of us; I thought that there was a mutual sympathy among us great enough, even though there was an appearance of truth in people's slanders, for that sympathy and pride to excuse and protect and defend the one who was slandered. The things that can be said about me are no secret. They are a matter of general knowledge; and I carry the punishment for my sin about with me as a burden on my life. But I have nothing more to reproach myself with than what is known as a fact. Don't think that I am making light of it. I only say that that is all there is. I should have thought that you would have known this, that you would have believed this, even if I had never told you. Addie is Van der Welcke's son as surely as I am Papa's daughter. What people like to invent besides is no concern of mine. I can't even understand why they care to invent at all, when I have already given them so much that is true to discuss. But it was a great disappointment to me,

Adolphine, to find that those lies could be countenanced for a moment in your house."

Adolphine, seeing that her pumped-up tears were making no impression, had time to recover herself while Constance was speaking. Inwardly furious, but superficially calm, she now said, spitefully, in a tone of sisterly reproof:

"You must have expected some disappointment on returning to the Hague?"

"Perhaps, but not this disappointment ... if you had had any affection for me."

"Come, Constance, it's not as if I wasn't fond of you. But it might have been better if you had not come back."

"It's a little late to speak of that now, Adolphine: I'm here and I mean to stay. When I wrote to Mamma six months ago...."

"Mamma is a mother."

"I thought that you were a sister."

"I am not the only one."

"I hope that the others feel more affection for me and more indulgence than you do."

"Bertha was against your coming. So was Karel."

"I thank you for telling me; but, as I said, it is too late now."

"Gerrit and the others don't count, because they don't see people. Bertha and Karel and I have our family, our friends."

"And I compromise you in their eyes, do I?"

"Your coming here raked up a heap of things which had been long forgotten. And I know as a fact that your father- and mother-in-law were against it."

"You seem to know a great deal; and I am glad that you are so frank."

"I am always frank."

"And so irreproachable."

"I could never have done what you did, never."

"I am so glad that you came to see me this morning, Adolphine. And that we have had this quiet talk."

"If you had written to me at the time and asked my advice, instead of writing to Mamma only, I should have told you my opinion quietly," said Adolphine, with a touch of sadness in her voice. "I should have recommended you, as a sister, for your own sake, not to come back to the Hague. You have become quite unsuited for Holland, for the Hague and for living among your family. Everything in your ideas, in your home life, in your way of bringing up your son clashes with our Dutch notions of what is right and decent and proper. I'm not saying this angrily, you know, Constance: I'm saying it calmly, very calmly. I daresay that is best. You dress yourself as no Dutchwoman of your age would think of doing. The fact that you have no one to your house except a friend of your husband's causes comment. The way in which you bring up your son is considered exceptionally lax."

"Anything more?"

"Yes, there's something more: why did you ever leave Brussels? That's what we all ask ourselves. Bertha was saying, only the other day, that you would make things impossible for her, if you thought of pushing yourself and getting yourself presented. And she declared positively that she would never ask you to her official dinners."

"Anything more?"

"Anything more, anything more: what more do you want? I'm not saying it to offend you, Constance, but because I like you and want to save you from further disappointments. Do you think it pleasant for Bertha and me to have our friends talking about our family as they are doing? And that they do so is your fault entirely."

Constance' hands were shaking; and, in order to employ them, she began to fold the laces lying on the table.

"Is that real Brussels?" asked Adolphine, with apparent guilelessness.

"Yes."

"Where do you get the money, Constance, to spend on those expensive things?"

"I get it from my lovers," said Constance.

"Wha-at?" cried Adolphine, in a terrified voice.

Constance gave a nervous laugh:

"I tell you, from all my lovers."

"Oh, don't say things like that, even in fun! I thought it was imitation lace."

"Yes, but you don't know much about lace, do you?" said Constance, very calmly. "Or about diamonds? And you have not the least notion how to dress yourself, have you? I sometimes think you look very dowdy, Adolphine. It may be Dutch and substantial, but I consider it dowdy. And, on the other hand, you oughtn't to buy such rubbishy, shabby-genteel things as you do. And you haven't much notion of arranging your house, either, have you? If you were capable of understanding my taste, I wouldn't mind helping you to alter your drawing-room. But you would have to begin by getting rid of those horrible antimacassars and those china monkeys and dogs. Do; I wish you would. And choose a quieter carpet.... Don't you find those dinners very trying, Adolphine? I should say that Bertha is more at home in that sort of thing, isn't she?... And so the Erkenbouts go to your dinners, do they? I should have thought that Bruis, of the *Fonograaf,* was more in your set. But I was forgetting: you haven't a set, really; you have a bit of everything, an omnium gatherum.... Curious, isn't it, that none of our friends of the old days—our little Court set, let me call it—ever come to you nowadays? What's the reason?... Of course, you have to make your house attractive, if you want to keep your acquaintances.... I suppose you don't care really about seeing people. It's such hard work for you.... You're more the good mother of your children, though I consider your girls, at least Floortje and Caroline, rather loud; and, as for your boys, you seem quite unable to teach them any sort of manners.... Well, if I can be of any use to you, if you want to alter that drawing-room of yours, you have only to say so and we will fix a day...."

Adolphine had listened gasping, unable to believe her ears. Had Constance gone mad? She stood up, shaking all over, while Constance, with apparent composure, continued to fold her laces:

"You're a deceitful creature!" she hissed, furious, so deeply wounded in every detail of her vanity that she could no longer control herself.

"Why?" asked Constance, calmly. "Perhaps I was, for months, with a view to winning your affection; and that was why I spent myself in praises admiring Floortje's trousseau. But now that I know that you love me so well, now that we have had a good, sisterly talk, now that we have given each other our advice and our opinion, I see no further need for being deceitful and I too prefer to express my sisterly feelings with the frankest sincerity."

"Do you mean to say you didn't like Floortje's trousseau?" asked Adolphine, raging.

But Constance mastered her quivering nerves:

"Adolphine," she said, coldly, "please let us end this conversation. It can't matter to you in the least whether I, your despised sister, like or dislike anything in or about you. Spiteful, hateful words have been spoken between us; and we have seen into each other's souls. You never had any affection for me, nor any indulgence nor mercy, whereas I believed that you had and tried to find a sister in you. I failed; and that is all. There is nothing more. We will end this conversation, if you please; and, if you don't mind, when we meet at Mamma's or elsewhere, let us act as though there had been nothing said between us. That is all I ask of you."

She rang. The parlour-maid appeared. Adolphine stood staring at Constance; and her lips began to swell with the venom of the words which she felt rising to her lips.

"It's to let Mrs. van Saetzema out, Truitje," said Constance, quietly.

CHAPTER XXXVII

Constance, when she was alone, burst into a fit of nervous sobbing.... Oh, that past, that wretched past, which always clung to her, which there was no shaking off! She thought life unjust and the family and everybody. She was not a wicked woman: there was only one mistake to be charged against her, the mistake of her heedless youth; and were the consequences to last for ever?... After all, what she now wished was so little, so very little, that she could not understand why it remained so unattainable. She merely asked to live quietly at the Hague, in her own country, and to be loved a little by all her relations, for whom she felt that strange, powerful feeling, that family-affection. That was all; she asked for nothing more. She demanded nothing more of life than to be allowed to grow old like that, with a little forgiveness and forbearance around her, and then to see her boy grow up into a man, while she, for the boy's sake, would endure her life, as best she could, by the side of her husband. That was all, that was all. That was the only thing that she, with her small soul, asked of life; and she asked nothing more; and it was as though all sorts of secret enmities around her grudged it to her. Whereas she wished for nothing but peace and quietness, enmity seemed to eddy around her. Why did people hate her so? And why could they not make somebody else or something else the subject of their talk, of their spiteful, malevolent talk, if they really found it impossible to do without talking?

She continued greatly dispirited for days, went out very little, seeing only her mother, to whose house she went regularly. Paul was abroad; and Adeline was expecting her confinement. Mrs. van Lowe noticed nothing of what was troubling Constance; and, when, on Sunday, the members of the family all met again, the old woman was radiant in the illusion of their great attachment to one another. The children always kept her in ignorance of their disputes, kept her, out of love and respect, in her dear illusion. Adolphine never spoke cattishly of Bertha, in Mamma's presence; was amiable to Constance. The old lady knew nothing of the quarrel between Addie and Jaap, nothing of the explanation which Van der Welcke had demanded from the Van Saetzemas.

When her husband and Addie returned, Constance spoke casually of her conversation with Adolphine. But, for the rest, she remained very silent and solitary and only saw Mamma and, just once, Adeline, the quiet little mother, expecting her eighth child. And once she went with her mother to call on the old aunts in their little villa near Scheveningen; and then it was:

"How are you, Dorine?"

"What do you say?"

"Marie asks how you are, Rine. She *is* so deaf, Marie."

"Oh, I'm all right.... Who's that?"

And Aunt Dorine pointed to Constance, always failing to recognize her, with the stubbornness of second childhood.

"That's Constance," said Mrs. Van Lowe.

"That's Gertrude!" Auntie Tine would say next. "Isn't it, Marie? That's Gertrude!"

"No, Christine, Gertrude died as a child at Buitenzorg."

But Auntie Tine was yelling in Auntie Rine's ear:

"That's Marie's daughter!"

"Marie's daughter?"

"Yes, Gertrude, Gertru-u-ude!"

Constance smiled:

"Never mind, Mamma," she whispered.

And Mamma said good-bye:

"Well, good-bye, Dorine and Christine."

"What d'you say?"

"Good-bye, Dorine and Christine; we must go."

"They've got to go!" yelled Auntie Tine in Auntie Rine's ear.

"Oh, have they got to go? Where are they going?"

"Home!"

"Oh, home? Oh, don't they live here?... Well, good-bye, Marie; thanks for your visit. Good-bye, Gertrude! You are Gertrude, aren't you?"

"Ye-e-es!" Auntie Tine assured her, in a shrill, long-drawn-out yell. "She's Gertrude, Marie's daugh-ter."

"Well, then, good-bye, Gertrude."

"Never mind, Mamma, let them think I'm Gertrude," said Constance, softly, indulgently, while Mrs. van Lowe became a little irritable, not understanding how very old people could cling so stubbornly to an opinion and a little sad at the thought of Gertrude, who was dead.

And so the weeks passed and the months, very quietly, lonely and monotonously: the dreary months of the unseasonable cold, wet autumn, with heavy storms whipping the trees in the Kerkhoflaan, the wind incessantly howling round the house, the rain clattering down. Constance hardly ever went out, shut herself up indoors, as though her soul had received a hurt, as though she would rather henceforward remain safe in her dear rooms. She was very silent, she looked pale, she often sat thinking, pondering—she hardly knew what—sunk in her melancholy, staring at the fury of the storm outside. She did not often have scenes with Van der Welcke now, as though a brooding sadness had numbed her nerves. At half-past four, she would go to the window and watch longingly for her son, would cheer up a little when she saw him, when he talked nicely and pleasantly, her boy who was becoming more of a man daily. But she did not see very much of him now that he went to the grammar-school and had a lot of work to do in the evenings, which, studious by nature, he did conscientiously. Van Vreeswijck came to dinner once every two or three weeks, generally alone, or perhaps, as Paul was still abroad, she would ask Marianne van Naghel, of whom she was very fond. It would be one of those cosy, daintily-arranged little dinners which she knew so well how to give; and that was the extent of her social doings.

Thus she lived in herself and in her house. The rooms in which she sat always reflected herself, a woman of elegant and refined taste, even though she was not exactly artistic; and those rooms displayed in particular the inhabited, sociable, home-like appearance that comes from the presence of a woman who is much indoors and finds solace in her home. And round about her the lines and colours of her furniture and flowers, her knicknacks and fancy-work all made an atmosphere of soft fragrance peculiarly her own, with something very personal, something delicate and intimate: a soft dreaminess as of really very small, simple femininity, without one really artistic object anywhere, without a single water-colour or drawing or fashionable novel; and yet with nothing in colour or form or line that could offend the eye of an artist: on the contrary, everything blending into a perfect harmony of small material things with inner personal things that likewise had no greatness....

One day, when Truitje brought her some circulars, letters and bills from the letter-box, Constance' eye fell upon a newspaper in a wrapper; and she opened it. She read the title of the little sheet: the *Dwarskijker;*[22] and, as she seldom received much by post, she thought that it must have been sent as an advertisement. Suddenly, however, she remembered: the *Dwarskijker* was an odious little weekly paper edited by a disreputable individual who pried into all the secrets of the great Hague families; who had often been tried for blackmail, but always managed to escape; and who as constantly resumed his vile trade, because the families whom he attacked paid hush-money, whether his attacks were based on truth or calumny. Constance was about to tear up the paper indignantly, when her eye caught the name of Van Aghel, a parody obviously meant for Van Naghel, and she could not help reading on. She then read a nasty little article against her brother-in-law, the colonial secretary, an article crammed with personal attacks on Van Naghel, describing him as a great nonentity, who had made money at the bar in India by means of a shady Chinese practice and had been shoved on in his career by a still greater and more pompous nonentity, his father-in-law, the ex-Governor-general "Van Leeuwen." The article next attacked Van Naghel's brother, the Queen's Commissary in Overijssel, and, in conclusion, it promised, in a subsequent issue of the *Dwarskijker* to give a glimpse into the immorality of the other relations of this *bourgeois* who had battened on the Chinese and who had rendered no real service to India. And the writer aimed very pointedly at Mrs. van Naghel's sister, another woman moving in those exalted circles whose end would soon be nigh in the better order of things at hand: she was described as the "ex-ambassadress;" and he wound up with the alluring promise to give, next week, full details of those old stories, which were always interesting because they afforded the reader a peep into the depravity of aristocratic society.

---

[22] The *Inspector.*

Constance, as she read on, felt her heart beating, the blood rushing to her cheeks; her hands trembled, her knees shook, she felt as though she were about to faint. She was growing accustomed to oral slander; but these written, printed articles, which everybody could read, came as a shock to her; and, with eyes starting from their sockets, she read the thing over and over again. She was filled with helpless despair at the thought that such things were being published about her and hers, that next week more things would be printed about her in that libellous paper. She was at her wits' end what to do, when, vaguely rolling her terrified eyes, she caught sight, among the bills and circulars, of another paper, which said:

"NOTICE!!!

"Why not become a subscriber to the

"DWARSKIJKER?

"Terms of subscription:

"50 guilders quarterly, post-free."

The notice was printed in the cynical capitals of blackmail; and she at once understood; she understood what that subscription of two hundred guilders a year to a scurrilous rag meant! But she also understood that, even if she sent the fifty guilders or the two hundred guilders that moment, it would be no safeguard against further defamation or extortion; and she did not know what to do....

She at first thought of concealing the paper from Van der Welcke; but she was so upset all day that, after dinner, when Addie had gone upstairs, she showed it to her husband. He grew furious at once, giving way to his naturally irritable temper, which he usually kept under control so as not to have too violent scenes with his wife. He swore, clenched his fists, walked up and down the room in impotent rage, longing to break something or to go out and revile the Hague, its streets and its people. To him also the printed libel—especially because it was printed, for every one to read—was a terrible disgrace, which he felt that he would have done anything to avoid. It also occurred to him to go to the office of the *Dwarskijker* and horsewhip the editor. And, without really knowing why or how, he allowed himself to utter that unpremeditated, illogical phrase, the phrase of a naughty child which does not stop to think when its temper is roused:

"It's all your fault!"

"My fault!" she echoed, vehemently. "And why, in Heaven's name? Why is it my fault?"

"It's your fault! You would come and live here, with that morbid craving of yours for your family. In Brussels, nobody knew us and nobody talked about us; and our life if not happy, was at least quiet. Here there's always something, always something! It's no life at all, our life here!"

"And you, weren't you longing to come back? Was I the only one who longed?" she cried, hurt by his unreasonableness.

But he did not hear her; and all his pent-up bitterness burst forth:

"I walk about the streets here every day, feeling as if every one were looking at me and pointing at me! When I go to the Witte or the Plaats, among all the men I used to know, I feel out of place, I feel like an interloper whom they don't want to own. It's your fault, it's your fault!"

"Indeed!"

"Why were you absolutely bent on coming back to Holland?"

"And you?"

"I?"

"Yes, you, you! Didn't you sometimes long for your parents, for Holland! Didn't you yourself say that it would be good for our boy?"

"For our boy!" he shouted, refusing to listen, in his impotent, seething rage. "For our boy!"

And he laughed more bitterly, more scornfully than she had ever heard him before:

"For our boy! A lot I can do for him here! However hard he may work, whatever tact he may show, even though he enters the career which I had to abandon, he will always, always be reminded of the scandal of his parents! For our boy! Let him become a farmer, if he must be a Dutchman in Holland, hidden somewhere from all our family, our friends and our acquaintances! And it's all, all your fault!"

"You are unreasonable!" she cried, wincing under his insults. "If we have anything to reproach ourselves with, then it falls upon both of us; and you have not the right to let me, me, a woman, bear the burden of our misery alone!"

"That misery would at least not have been discussed, mocked at, criticized, ridiculed, traduced," he shouted, raging and stamping, "if you had not insisted on coming back to Holland!"

"Was I the only one to wish it?"

"Very well," he admitted, losing all his self-control, "I did too. But we were both fools, to return to this rotten country and these rotten people!"

"I don't need them. I only longed for my family."

"For your family! The Saetzemas, with whom we have quarrelled already, to whom we never speak except at Mamma's; the Van Naghels, who are no use to us: is that how you want to live, for your boy, in Holland, here, buried away in your Kerkhoflaan, in your house, in your rooms, with no one but Vreeswijck, who sometimes does us the honour to come and dine with us? Whom do we know? Who comes to see us? Who cares a jot about us?"

"I only wanted the affection of my family!"

"And for the sake of that affection, do you want to go on living here like this, buried away, when you want your boy to pursue his career later on? Ha, ha, he'll go far, like that! Do you imagine that he'll succeed simply through examinations? No, influence is what he wants: that's more important than any number of examinations. And you want him to enter the service under those conditions, while his father and mother sit cursing their luck here, in the Kerkhoflaan? Well then, let him become a farmer: the future is with the proletariat in any case. Very well, it's the fault of both of us, the silly, stupid fault of both of us. But, if it's my fault, it's your fault too. Have you ever done anything to get on? I, at least in my own mind, reckoned on the Van Naghels; I thought to myself: My brother-in-law has no end of connections, we shall go to his house; I don't care about it for my own sake, but it will be a good thing, later, for the boy...."

"Oh? And have you no connections? Have your parents no relations? All your old friends at the Plaats: which of them comes to see us? Which of them, except Vreeswijck, has had the ordinary civility to call on your wife? Not one of them, not one!" she almost screamed. "Not that I want them here, any more than you want to dine at Van Naghel's; but, if you attach so much importance to connections, for the sake of our son, you could have done something else than cycle all over the Hague and Scheveningen, you could have pointed out to your friends that, as they condescend to know you in the sacred mysteries of that Plaats of yours, the least they could do would be to look you up at home and not to go on ignoring your wife, as though she were still your mistress...!"

"It'll always, always be like that!" he cried, raging impotently, almost to the point of tears. "We can never alter it, if we live to be sixty, if we live to be eighty!"

"Very well," she said, as though with a sudden intuition to join issue with her husband's unreasonableness. "You wish it for your son's sake! I'll do it! I shall speak to Bertha and I shall be the first to speak. I shall tell her what I want of her, as a sister. But I shall also expect you to have your son's interests at heart among your own acquaintances; and I shall expect to be presented in the winter. I never thought of it myself; but people have done nothing but talk about it from the moment that we came here; and now I mean to do it. What is the objection? That we shall rub shoulders with De Staffelaer's family! I don't care whom I rub shoulders with. My intention was simply to live here, amid the affection of my family; but, if that is to be denied me, if such wretched libels as this are to be published, if you reproach me with not thinking of my son's future, then I shall alter my line of conduct and talk to Bertha. You, on your side, talk to your friends at the Plaats and, if you have any pride about you, refuse to have anything more to do with them unless they accept your wife and yourself as belonging to their set. I will stand it no longer! I wished for nothing more than peace and affection, than to grow old here beside my mother and my brothers and sisters; but, if there must be a scandal, notwithstanding those simple wishes, well then a scandal there shall be, so that people can say, with truth, 'Mrs. van der Welcke is pushing herself into the circles to which she always used to belong.'"

"I can't do it!" he said, weakly. "I can't possibly do what you want. After putting up with the tolerance and condescension of my former friends, I can't go to them now and explain that my wife and I want to call on them and their wives and expect them to call on us in return."

"Then I'll do without you!" she said. "I'm not on speaking terms with Adolphine; but I don't need that jumble-set of hers. I believe that Bertha still has some sisterly affection left for me; and I shall talk to her and she will have to help me. But you will never be able to reproach me again with not thinking of my child's future. And, if you're too weak to show your friends what you expect of them, then I, later, when our son meets with difficulties in his career, shall have the right to reproach you as you are reproaching me now...."

"Reproach! I'm not thinking of reproaches!" he broke in, angrily, illogically, unreasonably. "I'm only thinking of that rotten paper, that rotten paper...."

He looked at it in despairing irritation:

"I'll go to the fellow, I'll slash him across the face, I'll slash him across the face!"

She laughed, scornfully:

"Shall you do that for the sake of your son's future?"

He controlled himself, clenched his fists, rushed from the room with tears in his eyes, flung himself in his chair upstairs, smoked cigarette upon cigarette, walked up and down in impotent rage....

That evening, Gerrit and Paul came round. They also knew about the *Dwarskijker:* they said that a copy had been dropped into Van Naghel's letter-box too. And Gerrit, getting furious, because Van der Welcke was still furious, said:

"If you want to break the fellow's jaw, Van der Welcke, I'm your man!"

Paul wearily closed his eyes and expressed disapproval with every bored feature of his face:

"My dear Gerrit, don't come playing the bold swashbuckler, thinking you can chop the world to pieces with your silly old sword. And you, Van der Welcke, for Heaven's sake, keep calm, if you don't want to make things worse than they are!"

"But what are we to do?" asked Constance, impatiently.

"Nothing at all," said Paul, philosophically.

CHAPTER XXXVIII

It was the middle of November; and Constance remembered that Bertha's second at-home day was on the third Tuesday of the month. The next number of the *Dwarskijker* was due in a day or two; and this, although she did not mention it again, left her practically no peace throughout that week, in her terror of printed words of spite and malevolence. And, as if to redeem her promise to Van der Welcke, she said that afternoon, at lunch, that she was going to Bertha's, as it was Bertha's day. He at once grasped her intention and, to tell the truth, was surprised that she had not given up her plan of pushing herself. He had rather imagined that the idea came to her in the nervous excitement produced by their conversation, but that she would not take it seriously after the excitement was past. He remembered that the family always looked upon those receptions at the Van Naghels' as something very official: Mamma van Lowe went to them once in a way; and Uncle and Aunt Ruyvenaer, although quite out of their element, used to put in an appearance once every winter, because they had done so at first, by mistake, and now did not exactly know how to stay away; but none of the other relations ever went. In the eyes of the family, those reception-days always retained a certain official importance and aristocratic exclusiveness; and Cateau, for instance, would say, very solemnly, to Karel that this was Ber-tha's *day*, with a certain respect for that day on which the upper two and three of the Hague sometimes put in an appearance, while Gerrit always joked about the inaccessible grandeur of those reception-days of her excellency his sister, as he called her in chaff....

Van der Welcke had it on his lips to ask Constance if Bertha knew that she was coming, or if Constance had at least mentioned her intention to Mamma van Lowe. But he did not feel in the mood to provoke a discussion; and in any case Constance would do as she chose. It was raining; he heard her tell the maid to order a carriage; and, as he was staying at home, to bore himself in Addie's absence in his little smoking-room, smoking cigarette on cigarette, he saw his wife step into the brougham at four o'clock and was struck with the elegance of her dress. He shrugged his shoulders, in gloomy disapproval; he was in a bad temper these days; he too was permanently upset by that rotten libel, that confounded rag, against which he had been helpless. He threw himself on his sofa again and smoked and smoked, could not make up his mind to dress and go to the Plaats, was almost unconsciously avoiding his friends.

Constance felt very calm, but had retained a certain bitterness all this time. The thought just occurred to her how Bertha would take her visit; but, even though the family treated the question differently, she meant to show Bertha that she considered it an obvious thing to call on her at-home day.

When her brougham stopped, she saw a couple of carriages waiting; the door was opened by the parlour-maid, even before she had rung; the butler, recognizing her, bowed, preceded her up the stairs, opened the door wide and announced her:

"Mrs. van der Welcke...."

Constance entered the drawing-room, where a few people, mostly ladies, were moving in the semi-darkness. But it was not so dark that she did not at once notice that Marianne looked at her in surprise, with such spontaneous, unconcealed surprise that it gave her something of a shock. She shook hands with Marianne with an easy smile and went up to Bertha; and Bertha also, as she very plainly noticed, was surprised and blinked her eyes as she rose. And Bertha, woman of the world though she was and accustomed to treat all manner of difficult drawing-room situations, seemed uncomfortable as she welcomed her sister:

"Constance."

She said it almost inaudibly and hesitated a moment whether to introduce her to a lady sitting beside her. But it was only for a moment; and then Bertha said, with her usual voice of the rather tired hostess, who performed her social duties because she had to:

"Mrs. van Eilenburgh; my sister, Mrs. van der Welcke."

Constance bowed, calmly and indifferently, said a word or two. Bertha mentioned a couple of more names; and Constance made a casual remark here and there, coolly and calmly. But she was really dismayed, for the first lady to whom Bertha had introduced her was mistress of the robes to the Queen and a niece of De Staffelaer's. She had already been reflecting that it would be her duty to write to Mrs. van Eilenburgh, to send her word officially of her wish to be presented; and she had also reflected that the mistress of the robes was De Staffelaer's niece. But the fact that the first lady to whom Bertha introduced her should be a blood-relation of the husband from whom she was divorced made her shiver superstitiously. She did not show this, however, and, without taking any great trouble to make herself amiable or sociable, she remained sitting where she was, so that Marianne now came up to her:

"How nice of you, Auntie, to look in on Mamma's day."

"She doesn't mean a word of it," thought Constance.

But it was awkwardness and astonishment, rather than insincerity, that made Marianne speak as she did. She could never have imagined that Aunt Constance should call on those at-home days, any more than the other aunts and uncles did, because their respective acquaintances were so entirely different.

"We were so busy in the spring, getting settled," said Constance, very calmly. "You remember, the furniture had to come from Brussels. But this autumn I thought I would pay my respects to Mamma. After all, I can't go on ignoring Mamma and only seeing her when she is in her bedroom with a headache!"

Marianne's surprise increased. Aunt Constance said this so calmly, so very calmly, as though it were quite a matter of course that she should call on an at-home day. And Marianne could not refrain from saying:

"Yes, it's very nice of you to come. For, you see, the aunts never come: Aunt Adeline never and Aunt Cateau never and Aunt Ruyvenaer only very seldom."

"Oh, really?" asked Constance, innocently. "Don't they ever come?"

"Auntie Ruyvenaer just once in a way; but the other aunts never."

"Oh? Don't they?" asked Constance, putting on an air of great surprise and rather playing with Marianne's bewilderment.

"Didn't you know?"

"No, I didn't know. But I don't call that very civil of the aunts. It's different with the uncles: men are not expected to pay visits. But I'm surprised at the two aunts, Marianne."

Marianne did not know what to say. She was not accustomed to weigh her words or to think that another might say things which she did not really mean. Nervously constituted as she was, she had something candid about her, something honest and frank.

"Well, I shall tell them," said Constance, with a laugh, "that they owe the same politeness to a sister as to any one else."

"Oh, Auntie, I don't think Aunt Adeline or Aunt Cateau or Aunt Adolphine would care to come!" said Marianne, not doubting Constance' good faith for a moment.

"Oh, wouldn't they?" said Constance, coolly. "Yes, I suppose Aunt Adeline is always so busy with the children. And Aunt Cateau...."

She did not complete her sentence, for two men, knowing that she was Mrs. van Naghel's sister, were asking to be introduced to her.

She did not want to stay long; and, in a minute or two, she rose and moved towards Bertha to say good-bye. Mrs. van Eilenburgh, however, was taking leave at the same instant; and Constance waited for a couple of seconds. And, in those two seconds, she noticed, very plainly, that Mrs. van Eilenburgh deliberately turned her back on her, as if to avoid her, saying good-bye to Bertha and giving Constance no opportunity of bowing. It was no more than a hardly perceptible movement and, in any other case, might have been a natural oversight; but, at this moment, Constance felt that it was done deliberately, with the intention of wounding. She gave an ironical smile, with a laugh in her eyes and tightened lips, and thought:

"She is De Staffelaer's niece. I shall meet plenty more of his nephews and nieces...."

She was now able to take leave of Bertha.

"Good-bye, Bertha."

"Good-bye, Constance, so nice of you...."

Constance, for a moment, looked Bertha straight in the eyes. She said nothing, she did nothing but that: merely looked into Bertha's eyes while still holding her hand. And, for a moment, they looked into each other's souls.

There were no more callers; the rest of the room was talking busily; and Bertha just had the opportunity to say something that forced its way to her lips:

"Constance, that article...."

"Yes?...."

"Van Naghel is very much upset by it."

Constance shrugged her shoulders.

"Have you heard about it?"

"Yes, I found a copy of it in my letter-box. It's one of those libels...."

"It's terrible."

"It's beneath us to let ourselves be worried by a thing like that."

"Yes, but ... it's most unpleasant ... for Van Naghel...."

"It's not particularly pleasant for me either, but...."

And she shrugged her shoulders again, refusing to admit how she had suffered under it, trembling in all her nerves at those printed words of scandal. But she understood that Bertha also had been suffering all these days under that shower of mud, which clung to you, however lofty your attitude of contemptuous indifference might be. And Bertha found another moment in which to say:

"Constance...."

"Yes?...."

"Mrs. van Eilenburgh ... is a niece...."

"Yes, I know."

"I am sorry ... that you should just have happened to meet her."

Constance once more shrugged her shoulders:

"Why?"

And she looked Bertha full in the face:

"Why?" she repeated. "There are things, Bertha, which I intend to treat as the past. I don't know if others will always look upon them as the present. If you wish to be a sister for me, in deed as well as in name, help me. Do you understand what I mean? I am determined to treat what happened years ago as the past. I've made up my mind to it, in spite of the fact that our friends, I believe, take pleasure in still looking upon the past as the present. It's a great compliment to me, no doubt, but, alas, I can't accept it: I am fully fifteen years older now; and I am determined to make those fifteen years count. Do you understand me?"

"I think I understand you, Constance."

"And you don't approve. You also want me never to grow old and never to bring my fifteen years into account."

"Ssh, Constance! There's some one coming in at the door...."

"Don't be afraid: I've finished. Good-bye, Bertha; and help me, if you can...."

She pressed her hand. Bertha was on thorns.

As she went out, Constance heard the butler announcing:

"Mr. and Mrs. van den Heuvel Steyn."

She gave a start; she knew the name: friends of De Staffelaer's; Van den Heuvel Steyn had a post at Court. Suddenly, she saw herself, years ago, as a young girl, calling on those people with De Staffelaer. She had not seen them for years, had not heard of them for years.

She passed them and saw that they had become old, very old, those friends of De Staffelaer's, two very old people. They looked at her too; and there was fury in their eyes, as though they were both surprised—that old lady and that old gentleman—to find Mrs. van der Welcke in any drawing-room which they entered, even though she were a hundred times the sister of the colonial secretary's wife. Their eyes crossed like swords; and Constance passed them very haughtily, looking over their heads and pretending not to recognize them. She shivered in the hall. It was pouring with rain. The butler called her carriage.

"It will be difficult," she thought, tired out with this one quarter-of-an-hour's visit. "But it is for my son. I must go through with it...."

CHAPTER XXXIX

A few mornings later, when Constance woke, she remembered that it was Saturday; and, with the apprehension which had kept her nerves on the rack all the week long, she said to herself, as she rose:

"This is the day ... this is the day...."

She went to the letter-box again and again, almost hoping to find the last issue of the scurrilous paper there. She was afraid also lest Addie, before going to school or on coming home, should see it in the box and look at it, to see what it was. She knew that Van der Welcke was thinking of it too and that this was why he did not go out and also kept coming down the stairs, as though accidentally, and passing through the hall, with a glance at the glass pane of the letter-box. She went and sat in the drawing-room, looking out for the postman or for an errand-boy who might strike her as suspicious.... The morning passed, Addie came home and her nervous apprehension never left her. The afternoon passed and she remained indoors, wandering through the hall and always, always gazing at that letter-box. Nothing appeared through the little glass pane. And the whole day was one long apprehension, one incessant oppression.

The next morning, Sunday, Constance again looked out of the window, but she had now made up her mind that nothing would come and that there was nothing in the *Dwarskijker*. She stayed at home that day too, as it was raining hard, and she saw nobody. At half-past eight in the evening, she went to Mamma van Lowe's in a cab, with Van der Welcke and Addie. And Constance, the moment she entered, saw that there was a certain excitement among the members of the family, all of whom were present. Even Mamma seemed uneasy about something; and she at once said to Constance:

"You were at Bertha's on Tuesday, child...."

"Yes...."

"Why didn't you ask me first, Connie?"

"Is a visit to Bertha such a very important matter, Mamma?"

"No, no," said the old woman, deprecatingly, "not that...."

But the old aunts arrived:

"How are you, Marie?"

"How are you, Dorine and Christine? So nice of you to come."

"What d'you say?" asked Auntie Rine.

"Marie says ... it's so nice of you to co-o-ome!" screamed Auntie Tine.

"Oh, ah! Did she say so? Yes, yes.... And who's that?..."

"That's Constance," said the old lady.

"Who?"

"That's Marie's daughter!" screamed Auntie Tine. "Marie's daugh-ter!"

"Whose daughter?"

"Marie's?"

"Bertha?"

"No, not Bertha, Gertrude: Ger-tru-ude!" yelled Auntie Tine.

"Oh, Gertrude?" said Auntie Rine, nodding her head.

"Oh dear!" said Mrs. van Lowe, upset by the thought of the little daughter who had died at Buitenzorg.

"Never mind, Mamma," said Constance. "They'll never remember who I am."

"They're so obstinate!"

"But they're so old."

"It makes me so sad to hear them always taking you for Gertrude. Poor Gertrude!"

"Come, Mamma, you mustn't mind."

"No, child. But, oh, why did you go to Bertha's on Tuesday?"

"What harm did I do, Mamma?"

"No harm, child. But oh dear!... Good-evening, Herman; good-evening, Lotje."

It was Uncle and Aunt Ruyvenaer, with their girls following behind. And Constance saw a look of pity in their eyes.

"I say, Constance...." whispered Aunt Lot.

"Yes, Auntie?"

"Does Mamma know about that hor-r-rid article?"

Constance turned pale:

"I don't think so, Auntie."

"But your sister Dorine must know...."

Aunt Ruyvenaer beckoned to Dorine, who was very fidgety:

"I say, Dorine, does Mamma know about that hor-r-rid article?"

"No, Auntie," said Dorine, forgetting to say good-evening to Constance. "I kept coming in and looking at the letter-box...."

"To-day?" asked Constance.

"Yes."

"What do you mean, to-day? A week ago, you mean."

"No, Mamma didn't see that article last week, but I was afraid about to-day."

"To-day?"

"Yes, to-day's article."

Constance caught Dorine by the arm:

"Is there something in it, to-day?"

"Yes," Dorine whispered, coldly. "Didn't you know?"

"Don't you know, Constance?" asked Auntie Lot.

"No, I haven't had it...."

"So you haven't read it, Constance?"

"No."

"Well, it's just as well, child," said Auntie, as though relieved. "Better not read it, eh? Hor-r-rid article. Scandalous, child, about you.... Eh, *soedah*[23] all those people.... And it's so long ago, you and your husband; and he is your husband now!... Eh, what I say is, leave her alone. Forgive and forget, *soedah!* But I tell you, people always love to *korek* about *tempo doeloe.*[24] It makes me sick when I think what people are!"

"Dorine, have you that article?"

"Do you think I carry it about with me?" said Dorine, irritably.

"Why are you angry with me, Dorine?"

"I'm not angry; but, when you give occasion...."

"I?... Give occasion?... Fifteen years ago?..."

"No, on Tuesday last. What an idea of yours, to go to Bertha's!"

"I intend to do more than that, Dorine. And I can't help it if I don't share your awe for Bertha's days...."

"At which you may meet all sorts of people...."

"Dorine, one has so many unpleasant meetings in this world," said Constance, haughtily. "You, you don't know the world."

"Thank goodness for that!"

"Then don't condemn me. You don't know why I am acting as I am."

"If you only kept to yourself...."

"I wanted to keep to myself."

"You give people occasion...."

"Yes, now: I give them occasion now...."

"Oh, children," said Auntie, "don't quarrel.... There's *soesah*[25] enough, with that hor-r-rid article!"

Gerrit arrived:

"I thought I'd just look in, Mamma...."

"How's Adeline?"

"She's well. The doctor called this afternoon. She's very well indeed. Oh, she doesn't upset herself for a small affair like that!"

The big, fair man laughed nervously, boisterously filling the whole room with his loose-limbed strength. Then he went up to Constance:

"Connie," he whispered, "I'm so furious, so furious!"

"I haven't read it."

---

[23] Enough of, have done with.

[24] To rake up old times.

[25] Fuss, unpleasantness.

"Haven't you? Haven't you? Then don't!"

"But what do they say?"

"Nothing. Don't read it."

But she hardly listened to Gerrit, for she now saw Van der Welcke and Paul standing in a corner, in the back-drawing-room. She moved in their direction. She saw that Van der Welcke, with his back turned to the other room, was reading something, screened by a curtain, while Paul was warning him, anxiously:

"Come, give it me, quick ... Van der Welcke...."

Constance was behind them:

"Paul, tell me, that article...."

"The scoundrels, the scoundrels!" Van der Welcke was hissing.

"Henri, have you it? Give it to me."

"No, Constance!" Paul implored her. "Don't read it, don't read it."

"Give it to me, Henri!"

"I want to read it myself first!"

And he cursed as he read:

"The damned scoundrels! And it's not true; it didn't happen like that...."

"But what is it they say?" Constance demanded, furiously.

Paul took her by the arm and led her into the little boudoir, where their father's portrait hung:

"Be quiet, Constance. Please, please don't read it! What good will it do you; all that dirty language, all that vulgarity? It's filthy, it's filthy!"

"And is there nothing we can do?"

"No, no, for God's sake, no!" Paul begged, as though preferring to hush up, everything. "Every one will have forgotten it in ten days' time."

"Is there nothing we can do?"

"What do you want to do?" Paul asked, changing his tone, harshly. "Surely you wouldn't sue the cad for libel?"

"No, no!" she said, startled and terrified.

"Well, what then? Keep quiet, don't read it don't upset yourself about it...."

But Van der Welcke came up to them. He was purple, there was no restraining him:

"I'm going to the fellow...."

"For God's sake, Van der Welcke!"

Uncle Ruyvenaer joined them:

"What are you doing in here? Oh, yes, that rag! It's disgraceful, it's disgraceful!"

"I want to read it!" cried Constance.

"No!" they all three exclaimed. "Don't read it!"

"Don't let Mamma notice!" Uncle Ruyvenaer warned them.

And he went away, full of suppressed excitement.

But they remained in the boudoir. The portrait looked down upon them.

"Oh, my God!" Constance began sobbing; and she looked up at the portrait. "Papa, Papa! Oh, my God!"

"Hush, Constance!"

"Let me read it!"

"No."

Adolphine appeared in the doorway. She said nothing, but realized what they were talking about and turned away. And they heard Adolphine say aloud, in a hard voice, to Uncle Ruyvenaer:

"It's their own fault!"

Van der Welcke flared up, no longer able to master himself. He spun round to the door; Paul tried to hold him back, but it was too late; and, on the threshold, with his face close to Adolphine's, he roared:

"Why is it my own fault?"

"Why?" asked Adolphine, furiously, remembering the lofty tone which he had adopted to her after the quarrel of the two boys. "Why? You should have remained in Brussels!"

"Adolphine!" cried Van der Welcke, purple in the face, seething, roaring, with every nerve quivering. "You're a woman and an ill-mannered woman; and so you can allow yourself to say anything you please to a man. But, if your husband shares your opinion that I ought to have remained in Brussels, he's only got to tell me so, in your name or in his own! Then I'll send him my seconds!"

Van Saetzema came up at that moment.

"Then I'll send you my seconds!" Van der Welcke repeated, blazing.

"For God's sake, don't, my dear fellow!" cried Van Saetzema, frightened to death.

And Adolphine began to clasp her hands together; she too was frightened and took refuge in a feeble exhibition of wounded vanity:

"He says I'm ill-mannered! He says I'm ill-mannered! The hound! The cad! I have to swallow everything! Every one says just what he likes to *me*!"

She was now really crying into her handkerchief. Everything in the two drawing-rooms seemed in one great ferment of excitement. On all sides, there were quick, hushed conversations, whispered words, nervous glances among the brothers and sisters and their juniors, the nephews and nieces; not a single quiet group had been formed; the card-tables remained untouched; and there was no one at the table in the conservatory where the children's round games were played.

"Herman!" Mamma called out, almost querulously. "Aren't you going to start a rubber?"

"Yes, do come along!" said Auntie Lot to Ruyvenaer, "*Ajo*,[26] shall we have a game? Come on, who's going to play?... You, Saetzema? Come along ... Toetie? Come along. Cut for partners.... Come, Paul ... Do!"

"No, Aunt, I won't play, thanks."

"Oh, it's difficult this evening!" said Auntie. "Van Naghel and Bertha not yet here, eh? Come on.... *Ajo* now, let's play! Ah, there are Karel and Cateau! Why are you so late, eh?... *Ajo* then, cut for partners ... let's have a rubber!"

And Auntie at once enlisted Karel and Cateau, refused to let them go, forced matters, insisted on having a nice, quiet, friendly rubber, as at all the usual "family-groups." But Cateau at once noticed the excitement infecting everybody in both the big rooms with restlessness and, catching sight of Adolphine, she managed, before cutting, to escape Auntie Lot and ask:

"Why, Adolph-ine, what are you cry-ing for? Are you up-set about any-thing?"

"The hound! The cad! And he wants to challenge my husband in addition!"

"Chal-lenge him?" cried the terrified Cateau. "A reg-u-lar du-el! No! The bro-thers and sis-ters will nev-er consent to *that!* There's too much been talked and *writ-ten* about the family as it *is!*" she whispered. "Writ-ten and *print-ed!*"

And Cateau's whining words bore evidence to the tragic alarm that fluttered through her sleek, broad-bosomed respectability, while her owl's eyes opened rounder and wider than ever.

But Auntie Lot came to fetch Cateau and dragged her by the arm to the card-table. The rubber was made up: Auntie, Karel, Cateau and Toetie. But they none of them paid attention to their cards, which fell on the table, one after the other, without the least effort of intelligence on the part of the players, as though obeying the laws of some weird and fantastic game of bridge.... Auntie was constantly trying to ruff with spades though clubs were trumps:

"Oh, what *kassian!*"[27] said Auntie.

"Ka-rel," said Cateau, excitedly, "as the eld-est bro-ther, you *must* inter-fere and *stop* that du-el!"

"I? Thank you: not if I know it!"

"You must, Ka-rel: You are the eld-est bro-ther.... Of course, Van Na-ghel"—and she pronounced the name with a certain reverence—"is the hus-band of your eld-est sist-er; but if he, if Van"—reverentially—"Van Na-a-ghel refuses to inter-fere, then it's *your* duty, Ka-rel, as the eld-est bro-ther, to stop that du-el."

"It won't come off!" said Toetie, good-humouredly.

"*Massa*,[28] brothers-in-law don't fight!" said Auntie Lot. "But Adolphine shouldn't have behaved like that.... Very wrong of Adolphine."

---

[26] Hullo!

[27] Bad luck.

"But it's sa-ad, all the same, *very* sa-ad, for Adolph-ine, all those art-ides," whined Cateau. "They up-set her. She's cry-ing, And it's anything but plea-sant for Van Na-ghel, don't you *think*, Un-cle?"

This to Uncle Ruyvenaer, who was standing behind her.

"It's beastly, it's beastly!" said Uncle. "They ought never to have come and lived here. It was very wrong of Marie to encourage them."

"Oh, well, Herman," said Auntie, "you must remember she's the mother!"

"Just for that reason...."

"Oh, Papa!" said Toetie, wearily. "That old *perkara!*"[29]

"Nothing but *korek* in *tempo doeloe* in Holland," said Auntie, crossly.

"Well, Aunt-ie," said Cateau, taking offence, "they're not al-ways so mor-al in the Ea-east!"

"But there's not so much talk in Java as here," said Auntie, angrily.

"Oh, I daresay they do some talk-ing there too!"

"But not so spitefully!" said Auntie, very angrily and finding her Dutch words with great difficulty. "Not ... not so cruelly, so cruelly."

"They ought never to have come and lived here," Uncle Ruyvenaer repeated.

And he fussed off to Van Saetzema, whose eyes were still filled with terror at the possible duel.

"Look, Mamma," said Toetie, winking towards Auntie Tine and Auntie Rine, who were sitting side by side in a corner of the big drawing-room, each with her knitting in her lap. "Those two are quite happy! They don't bother about all these matters! They don't know anything."

"In Holland...." said Auntie, crossly.

"But in the Ea-east!" ... Cateau at once broke in, spitefully.

The rubber was spoilt, for Auntie, in her present state of irritation, could no longer see the cards in her hand. The old Indian lady felt that there was hostility to Constance among the relations; and, with the kindliness of a nature used to the little Indian scandals, she thought it exaggerated. Moreover, Cateau's Dutch arrogance in speaking of "the East" had put her quite out of temper; and she flung her cards on the table and said:

"*Soedah,* I won't play with you any more!"

And, without further explanation, she broke up the table and walked straight to Constance, who sat talking to Paul in a corner:

"I'm coming to sit with you a bit, Constance!"

"Do, Auntie."

---

[28] Oh, nonsense!

[29] Business.

"What I want to say to you is, don't mind about it! Shake it off your cold clothes!"[30] What does it matter? Hor-r-rible article! But I tell you: shake it off your cold clothes!"

And Auntie talked away, suddenly lighting on all sorts of queer Dutch words and expressions, told Constance of horrible articles in India which people out there had shaken off their cold clothes.

At this moment, Bertha, Van Naghel and Marianne arrived, very late. Mamma at once went up to them. The people in the two rooms now made some attempt to adopt an attitude; and their excitement cooled down. But it struck them all that Van Naghel looked exceedingly tired, Bertha pale and Marianne as though she had been crying; her eyes were specks under her swollen lids. They exchanged vague, almost doleful good-evenings, giving a hand here, a kiss there....

After all the agitation, a gloom descended upon the family. The voices sank into a whisper. And, through the whispering, suddenly, the voices of the two old aunts sounded piercingly, as they spoke to the Van Naghels:

"Yes, yes, I remember you, I know you. Good-evening, Van Naghel."

"Good-evening, Aunt."

"Good-evening, Toetie. Yes, yes, I know you: you're Toetie, Van Naghel's wife. And who's that?"

"That's my girl, Auntie: Marianne. And I'm Bertha...."

"Oh, yes, that's Emilietje!" Auntie Tine screamed in Auntie Rine's ear, in a moment of sudden and not yet perfect lucidity. "That's Toetie's daughter Emilie-etje!"

"No, Auntie, Emilie is married!"

"What d'you say? Is she dead?"

"No," screamed Auntie Tine, "Floortje, Floortje is married! This is Emilie-etje!"

"Oh, I see! Good-evening, Emilietje."

A smile lit up gloomy features here and there. The aunts never knew any one properly, were always a little muddled among all those nephews and nieces of a later generation. And, as a rule, nobody troubled for more than a moment to remind them of the real names. With the stubbornness of extremely old women, they continued to cling to their confusion of generations, persons and names.

Constance, sitting beside Paul, watched Bertha. In an importunate obsession to immerse herself in what she, at that moment, called her own disgrace—especially as that disgrace had been stamped in print—she had done nothing but ask Paul:

"Let me read it!"

And Paul had done nothing but say:

"No, Constance, don't read it!"

---

[30] Aunt Ruyvenaer here perpetrates the blunder, common among half-caste ladies, of mixing up two separate Dutch proverbs.

Constance now saw, by the faces of Van Naghel, Bertha and Marianne, that they knew about it and had read it. All three said how-do-you-do to her in a very cold tone.

Van Naghel was at once asked by Mamma to make up one of the tables. The old woman, like Constance, had read nothing, knew nothing certain; but a word seized here and there had alarmed her, had worried her; and she felt very unhappy, as if on the verge of tears. She noticed in her children, as it were for the first time, something strange and hard, in the nervous excitement of that evening, something, it is true, which at once hushed and calmed down when she approached, but which left a strained feeling behind it, a lack of harmony which she did not understand. Was it because of that scurrilous paper? Or did they disapprove of Constance' going to Bertha's on her day? The old woman did not know; but never had a Sunday evening passed with such difficulty; and yet what was it all about? An article, a visit.... An article, a visit.... She endeavoured, despairingly, to look upon these things as small, as meaningless, as nothing; but it was no use: the question of the visit was very important, an undoubted blunder on Constance' part; and the article—Heavens, the article!—was, though she herself had not read it, a disgrace, raking up the scandal of years ago which soiled and defiled all her children, all, all her nearest and dearest. No, these things were not insignificant: they were great and important things in their lives. What, what could be more important than what might happen through that visit to Bertha and—Heavens!—a scurrilous article?...

Bertha refused to play, declared that she hadn't the head for it. And, though she had at first deliberately avoided Constance, she now seemed constantly, almost fatally, to be moving nearer her, restlessly, unable to keep her seat, amid the excitement which once more slowly took hold of them all, after their first attempt at calmness from respect for their brother-in-law, the cabinet-minister. But Constance went on talking to Paul and, in her turn, avoided her sister's glances; until, at last, Bertha, as though unable to keep it in any longer, sat down on a chair beside her and said:

"Constance...."

"Well?"

"Van Naghel is...."

"Van Naghel is what?"

"Van Naghel is ... very much put out. I can't understand how he can play bridge."

"What is he put out about?"

"About you."

"About me?"

"Yes, about you."

"I'm sorry, Bertha!" said Constance, coolly. "What have I done wrong?"

"Of course, it's not your fault, about those articles. But the first was exceedingly unpleasant for Van Naghel...."

"And the second I haven't read," said Constance, coldly.

"No," Paul broke in, "I advised Constance not to read it."

"And I don't mean to read it: it has ceased to interest me. Is Van Naghel put out by that article about me?"

"He's put out by the visit...."

"The visit...?"

"The visit you paid me, on Tuesday."

"Is Van Naghel put out by a visit which I paid you on Tuesday?" asked Constance, very contemptuously, in surprise.

"You ought not to have come on my day."

"I ought not to have...?"

"Don't be angry, Constance: I have had such a scene with my husband as it is! Don't be angry, for Heaven's sake! Don't misunderstand me. I am full of sympathy for you: you are my sister and I am fond of you; but that doesn't alter the fact that you were wrong, that you ought not to have come on my day. Why did you do it? I am so glad to see you at any other time. But just on an at-home day, when you risked meeting, well, just the people whom you did meet: Mrs. van Eilenburgh, the Van den Heuvel Steyns! Why did you do it? What made you do it?"

"So I am not fit to appear at my sister's at-home day?"

"Please, Constance, don't take it like that. I am not unsympathetic. We even had a talk once...."

Constance laughed aloud:

"Once!" she said. "Once!"

"Life is very busy, Constance. But I am always glad to see you. Only, only...."

"Only not on your days."

"It's not my fault."

"No, it's mine."

"Mrs. van Eilenburgh is a niece of...."

"De Staffelaer."

It was the first time that his name had been mentioned between them.

"The Van den Heuvel Steyns are...."

"His friends."

"So, Constance, you understand for yourself...."

"I told you on Tuesday, Bertha, I am going to make my fifteen years count."

"Constance, don't attempt impossibilities."

"What's an impossibility?"

"Don't think only of yourself. Think of us. Think of Van Naghel, of his position. You make it impossible for him, if you insist on...."

"Coming to your at-home days....?"

"For goodness' sake, Constance, don't be angry. It is impossible."

"What is?"

"For you to...."

"What?"

"To force the position. When Mamma spoke to us, eight months ago, about you coming to the Hague, Van Naghel at once said that our house was open to you and your husband, but that you must not push and assert yourselves."

"So that was the condition?"

"It was not a condition, Constance: it was merely advice, given in your own interest...."

"And in yours."

"Very well, in ours too. People come to my days, just because of my husband's position and connections, people who are relations and friends of De Staffelaer's, people who have never forgiven you and never will. Can't you see that for yourself, Constance? Must I explain it to you?"

"Bertha, I never had any desire to push or assert myself."

"Then what makes you?"

"What makes me?" And it was as though Constance was searching for the answer. "What but you, all of you?"

"Don't be unreasonable, Constance."

"What else did I want but to come and live here quietly at the Hague and see all of you again—my brothers, my sisters, your children—without ever dreaming of pushing myself? Who first spoke of pushing? You, you and your husband, Bertha!"

"Constance!"

"Who first spoke about the Court, Bertha? Adolphine."

"Please, Constance, please...."

"I never thought, Bertha, of getting presented at Court; but now I shall, at the first occasion that offers."

"Constance!" And Bertha wrung her hands. "It's impossible!"

"Yes, it *is* possible; and I mean to do it."

"Constance, how can you wish to defy people's opinions like that!"

"Because of those very people!"

"I don't understand you, Constance. All my friends...."

"Exactly, because of your friends."

"All our family...."

"Because of our family."

"Wait a bit, Constance. I don't understand you. I don't know what you mean to say. But just consider, just consider. You are not only making yourself impossible, but you are making us impossible: my husband, my house, our position, our children...."

"Nonsense!"

"It's not nonsense, Constance. Do you want to make me regret that we yielded to Mamma's wish to have you here again, near her, among us all?"

"No, Bertha, but I can no longer remain—for the sake of people, for the sake of the family—in the same obscure corner in which I remained for years in Brussels, where I was disowned by all of you as a disgrace. I can't do it, Bertha, I can't do it. I could do it, as far as I am concerned; but I can't, because of my son."

"He is a child still."

"He is growing older every day. I see, Bertha, that I ought either to have stayed away from you all, without indulging my modest yearnings and simple wishes, or else to have rehabilitated myself at once, in the eyes of all the Hague."

"Constance...."

"But it's not too late. It's not too late to repair my mistake. I can still take steps towards my rehabilitation. And I ask, I demand that rehabilitation, of you, Bertha, in particular."

"Of me?"

"Yes, Bertha, of you in particular. Just because you are the sister whose husband not only occupies a high position, but also possesses more connections than any of us in the set that used to be our father's. Just for that reason, Bertha, I demand my rehabilitation of you. If I'm not to be allowed to live quietly, in a corner, at the Hague, surrounded by a little family-affection; if those simple wishes are to be discussed and criticized; if they are the cause that my unfortunate past—my fault, my sin, whatever you like to call it—is raked up, not only in dirty little scurrilous rags, but also at the gossipy tea-parties and clubs at the Hague, then I will come out of my corner, then I will be rehabilitated: not for my own sake alone, but mainly for my son's; and I demand my rehabilitation of you. It is possible that you don't care for my sisterly love; but, as a condition of that love, I now demand my rehabilitation."

"But, good Heavens, Constance, what can I, what *can* I do for you?"

"What can you do for me? Receive me on your at-home days. Make it clear to your husband that you must receive me, that you can't act otherwise towards a sister than receive her, now that she has once—in an evil hour—returned to the Hague. Not hesitate any longer to introduce me to whoever it may be, in your drawing-room," she exclaimed, with her dark eyes quivering, her every nerve trembling, as she sat between Bertha and Paul.

Her sister was almost panting with suppressed excitement and helplessness, while her brother listened in dismay to her demands, which appeared to him, the *blasé*, world-worn sage, to contain no philosophy whatever. And Constance went on:

"What can you do for me? Look upon it as only natural—and try to make your friends look upon it as natural—that you should receive me!"

"I should be very glad to do all that you ask of me, Constance, if there was not the objection that we see and always have seen relations and friends of De Staffelaer's."

"Isn't your sister worth a single effort to you?"

"I can't choose between my husband and my sister."

"Bertha!" said Constance, almost weeping with excitement and nervousness. "Bertha! Try! For Heaven's sake, try to do what I ask! It's for my child! It's not for me: it's for my son! He will have to take up a career which I, which I made impossible for Van der Welcke. Do it for my son's sake. God in His Heaven! Must I go on my knees to you? Do it, I beseech you, Bertha: try, try to do it; speak to Van Naghel...."

"Constance, I will speak to Van Naghel; but how can you ever hope not that we, but that other people will forgive, will forget: De Staffelaer's relations, De Staffelaer's old friends?"

"Yes, I do hope it! And, if you help me, Bertha, if you help me, it will not be so utterly impossible."

"How do I know that Mrs. van Eilenburgh or the Van den Heuvel Steyns will ever come to us again, after meeting you at my house?"

"So you decline?" cried Constance, flaring up. "So you refuse?"

"Constance, I should like to do what you ask; there is nothing I should like better. But people, but Van Naghel...."

"Then let me speak to Van Naghel!"

"Constance...."

"Let me speak to Van Naghel, I say!"

"Don't make a scene."

"I shan't make a scene; but let me speak to Van Naghel. I see your husband is getting up: he has finished playing. Tell him I want to speak to him. Let Van der Welcke be present at our conversation. Paul, you must be there too...."

"But, Constance, why, why speak to him? I am so afraid Mamma will notice...."

"No, Mamma will see nothing. I want to give her as little pain as possible. But I must speak to your husband, in your presence and Van der Welcke's. I must, Bertha, and I will. Call your husband. And we'll go into the boudoir."

She rose, trembling. She was shaking all over; and, as she almost fell where she stood, a sudden thought arose in her and paralyzed all her energies:

"Why am I talking like this, thinking like this, wishing this? How small I am, how small my conduct is! Really, what does it all matter: people; and what they think; and what they write and say? Is that life? Is that all? Is there nothing else?..."

But another thought gave her fresh zest, fresh courage. She remembered the conversation which she had had with her husband a little while ago, she remembered his reproach that she was not thinking of her son, that she was doing nothing for her son, that she would let herself take root in the shade, continue to vegetate, in her disgrace, in her corner, withdrawn into herself, in her own rooms, would continue to sit "cursing her luck" in her Kerkhoflaan. No, she felt fresh zest, fresh courage; and she almost pushed Bertha as she repeated:

"Call your husband.... Paul, will you please call Van der Welcke and ask him to come to the boudoir?...."

She could hardly walk, she was pale as a corpse; and her black eyes quivered. She went alone to the little boudoir. There was no one there. Decanters, glasses, cakes and sandwiches were put out, as usual. She looked up at her father's portrait: Oh, what an ugly daub it seemed to her: hard, with the hard, expressionless eyes and all that false glitter on the yellow-and-white stars of the decorations! It stared at her like an implacable spectre, grim and unforgiving. It stared at her almost as though it wished to speak:

"Go. Go away. Go out of my house of honour, of greatness and decency. Go. Go away. Go out of my town. Go away from me and mine. Go. It was you who murdered me. You caused my long illness, you caused my death, you, you! Go!"

The little room stifled her. She would have liked to run away, but Van der Welcke and Paul entered.

"What do you want to do, Constance?" asked Van der Welcke.

"To speak to Van Naghel."

"Not an explanation?"

"I don't know. He's annoyed at my visit of Tuesday last."

"Annoyed!" Van der Welcke seethed. "Annoyed at your visit!"

"For God's sake, Van der Welcke!" cried Paul, terrified. "Don't always fly out like that. Do remember...."

"Annoyed!" foamed Van der Welcke. "Annoyed!"

"Henri, *please!*" cried Constance. "I thank you for resenting the insult offered to your wife. But restrain yourself: he'll be here in a minute. Restrain yourself, for Addie's sake...."

"Restrain myself! Restrain myself!" shouted Van der Welcke, like a madman.

The door opened. Van Naghel and Bertha entered.

"Do you want to speak to me, Constance?" asked Van Naghel.

"I should very much like to speak to you for a moment, Van Naghel," said Constance, while Paul made signs to Van der Welcke as though begging him to control himself. "Bertha tells me that you are sorry that I called at your house on Tuesday, on her reception-day."

"Constance," Van Naghel began, cautiously, trying to be diplomatic, "I...."

"Forgive me for interrupting you, Van Naghel. I ask you kindly, let me finish and say what I have to say. It is simply this: I regret that I went to your house, on Bertha's at-home day, without first asking if I should be welcome. I admit, it was a mistake. I oughtn't to have done it. I ought first to have spoken to the two of you as I am glad to be speaking to you now, Van Naghel, to explain my position and my wishes, in the hope that you will show some indulgence to your wife's sister and consent to help her fulfil a natural desire. You see, Van Naghel, when I arrived here, eight months ago, I had no other thought than to live here quietly, in my corner, with a little affection around me, a little affection from my brothers and sisters, whom I had not seen for so long. It is true, I had no particular claim to that affection; but, when I felt within myself a wish, a longing, a yearning for Holland, for the Hague, for all of you, I cherished the illusion that there would be something—just a little—of that feeling in my brothers and sisters. I don't know how far I was mistaken; I won't go into that now. Bertha has just told me that she feels to me as to a sister; and I accept that gratefully. Van Naghel, I cannot expect that you, my brother-in-law, should have any sort of family feeling for me; but, as Bertha's husband, I ask you, I beg of you, try to be a brother to me. Help me. Don't resent that I paid you a visit without notice and, in so doing, shocked and surprised you. But allow me, allow me—I ask it as a favour, Van Naghel, for my son's sake—allow me, in your house first of all, to try and attain ... to attain a sort of rehabilitation, in the eyes of our acquaintances, in the eyes of all the Hague. I stand here entreating you, Van Naghel: grant me this and help me. Allow me to come on your wife's days, even though I do meet friends and relations of De Staffelaer's. Good Heavens, Van Naghel, what harm, what earthly harm can it do you to exercise your authority and protect me a little and defend me against mean and petty slanders? If you show some magnanimity and help me to make people ... to make people forget what I did fifteen, fifteen years ago, they will drop their slanders; and I shall be rehabilitated, in your house, Van Naghel, just because of your high position and the consideration which you enjoy and your many connections and your power to carry out what you set your mind on. Van Naghel, if only you would help me: if not for my own sake, for my son's! It's to help him, later, in his career, which he will take up at his father's wish and his grandparents': the same career as his father's, which I ruined. I am asking so little of you, Van Naghel; and because you are you, it means so little for you to consent to my request. Van Naghel, Papa helped you, in the old days: I ask you now to help me, his child and your wife's sister. Let me come to Bertha's receptions. You know Mrs. van Eilenburgh: help me to prepare people for my intention—which they were really the first to suggest—to be presented at Court; and ask us, this winter, once, just once, to one of your official dinners."

She stood before her brother-in-law, pale and trembling, almost like a supplicant; and, while she besought him, the thought flashed through her mind:

"What am I begging for? How base and small I am making myself: dear God, how terribly small! And is that, seriously, life? Is that the only life? Or is there something else?..."

She looked around her. While she stood in front of Van Naghel, Bertha had sunk into a chair, trembling with nervous excitement, while Van der Welcke and Paul, as though in expectation, listened breathlessly to Constance' words, which came in broken jerks from her throat. Then, at last, slowly, as though he were speaking in the Chamber, Van Naghel's voice made itself heard, softly, with its polite, rather affected and pompous intonation:

"Constance, I shall certainly do my best to satisfy all your wishes, all your requests. I will help you, as far as I can, if you really think that I can be of use to you. Certainly I owe a great deal to Papa; and, if, later, I can possibly do anything for your son, I assure you—and you, too, Van der Welcke—I shall not fail to do so. I give you my hand on it, my hand. I shall certainly, gladly, with all my heart, help Addie in the career which he selects: you may be sure of that. But, Constance, what you ask me so frankly, to ... to invite you and Van der Welcke to one of our dinners, at which you would meet people who really, really would have no attraction for you: oh, you wouldn't care for it, Constance, I assure you, you really wouldn't care for it! And, if you want my honest opinion, honestly, as between brother and sister, I should say to you, candidly, Constance, don't insist on coming to our official dinners: they're no amusement; they're an awful bore, sometimes: boring, aren't they, Bertha? Very tedious, very tedious, sometimes. And the receptions, at which you are always likely to meet people you wouldn't care for: well, if you take my advice...."

"Is that all, Van Naghel, that you have to say, when I lay bare my soul to you, here, between brothers and sisters, and, without any diplomatic varnish, ask you, as far as you can, to rehabilitate me in your house?"

"But, Constance, what a word! What a word to use!..."

"It's the right word, Van Naghel; there is no other word: I want my rehabilitation."

"Constance, really, I am prepared to help you in all you ask: and whatever is in my power...."

But Van der Welcke flared up:

"Van Naghel, please keep those non-committal expressions for the Chamber. My wife asked and I now ask you: will you receive us this winter in a way that will make your set, which was once ours, take us up, even though we rub shoulders with De Staffelaer's nephews and nieces and even though people talk about what happened fifteen years ago?"

"Van der Welcke," said Van Naghel, nettled, "the expressions I choose to employ in the Chamber are my own affair."

"Answer my question!"

"Henri!" Constance implored.

"Answer my question!" insisted Van der Welcke, full of suppressed rage, feeling ready to smash everything to pieces.

"Well then, no!" said Van Naghel, haughtily.

"No?..."

"It's impossible! I have too many attacks to endure as it is, in the Chamber, in the press, everywhere; and I can't do what you ask. You have made yourself impossible, to our Hague society, you and your wife, the wife of your former chief; and it's simply impossible that I should receive you in my house on the same footing as my friends, acquaintances and colleagues. That is no reason why we should not continue to be brothers and sisters."

"And do you think I would wish for or accept your brotherliness on those terms?"

"Then refuse it!" cried Van Naghel, himself losing his temper and forgetting to pick his words. "Refuse it; and all the better for me! I shall be only too glad to have nothing more to do with you. Your wife compromised me the other day by coming to Bertha's reception, as if it were a matter of course...."

Van der Welcke clenched his fists:

"My wife," he echoed, "compromised you? By coming to...?"

"Van der Welcke!" Paul entreated.

"Yes," said Van Naghel. "She did."

"Don't you dare," cried Van der Welcke, "don't you dare to criticize my wife's actions in any way!"

"Your wife compromised us," Van Naghel repeated.

But Van der Welcke let himself go, unable to restrain himself any longer. He made a rush for Van Naghel, raised his hand:

"Take that!" he shouted, crimson with rage, utterly beside himself.

But Paul flung himself between them and seized Van der Welcke's arm. Bertha burst into hysterics, uttered scream after scream. Constance almost fainted. The two men stood facing each other, no longer drawing-room people, blazing now with mutual hatred:

"I am at your disposal, whenever you please!" said Van der Welcke.

"Of course you are!" yelled Van Naghel, his eyes starting out of his head, his cheeks scarlet as though he had actually received the blow. "Of course you are! You have nothing to lose. You can afford to behave like a quarrelsome puppy, hitting people, fighting, duelling...."

And, turning on his heel, quivering with rage and shame, he disappeared from their eyes through the door that opened on the landing....

The door of the drawing-room opened. Dorine, Adolphine and Cateau had heard the angry words, had heard Bertha's sobs and screams. They went to Bertha's assistance, while Paul urged Constance, who was half fainting, to go into the drawing-room. She staggered to her feet:

"My God!" she cried. "Henri! Henri! What have you done!"

Mrs. van Lowe came up, with Aunt Ruyvenaer:

"My child, my child!"

Constance was clinging to Paul like a madwoman and kept on repeating:

"My God! Henri! Henri! What have you done!"

Addie came up.

"Mamma!"

"Addie! Addie! My boy! My God! My God! What has Papa done!"

Mamma van Lowe dropped into a chair, sobbing.

But, at that moment, the two old aunts, sitting all alone in the second drawing-room, looked up. On those evenings, they used generally to doze, hardly recognizing the various relations, and to wait until the cakes and lemonade were handed round, going home after they had had them. But, this evening, sitting quietly in their chairs, looking quietly, with eyes askance, at the people talking and playing their cards and uttering their harsh judgments, they felt the usual peaceful calmness to be absent from Marie's family-Sunday. There was something the matter. Something was happening, they did not know what. But it suddenly seemed as though Auntie Tine, when she saw her younger sister, Mrs. van Lowe, bursting into sobs, became very lucid, for, opening wide and clear her screwed-up eyes, she said to Auntie Rine, very loudly, with the sharp tone of a woman hard of hearing, to whom her own voice sounds soft and almost whispering:

"Rine, Rine, Marie's crying!"

"What? Is she crying, Tine?"

"Yes, she's crying."

"What is she crying for?"

"No doubt, Rine, because one of the children's dead."

"Dead?"

"Yes, Rine."

"Oh, how sad! Is she crying?"

"Yes, she's crying. She's crying, Rine, about Gertrude."

"About whom?"

"About Gertrude. About Ger-tru-ude!" Auntie Rine began to scream. "She's dead, Rine."

"Is she dead?"

"Yes, the poor little thing died at Buitenzorg."

"Oh, how sad! Is Marie still crying, Tine?"

"Yes, she's still crying, Rine."

"But then who's that one, Tine?"

"Who, Rine?"

"That one, the girl standing beside her? She's crying, she's crying too!"

"Beside her?"

"Yes, can't you see? She's crying too!"

"Yes, yes!" screamed Tine, quite lucid now. "I know her; Rine, I know her quite well, quite well."

"Then who is it? Is it Bertha?"

"No, Rine!" Auntie Tine screamed, gradually more and more shrilly, always thinking that she was whispering in her deaf sister's ear. "It's not Bertha. It's not Bertha. But I know her, I know her."

"Then who is she?" Auntie Rine screamed, in her turn.

"I'll tell you who she is. I'll tell you who she is. It's Constance!" yelled Auntie Rine.

"Who?"

"Constance!"

"Constance?"

"Yes, Constance!"

"Constance?"

"Yes, Constance!"

"The bad one!" screamed Auntie Rine.

"Yes, Rine, the bad one, Rine. She's a wicked woman, Rine, a wicked woman! She has a lover!..."

"A lover?"

"Yes, Rine. Can you understand her being here? Can you understand that she's not ashamed? Can you understand her showing herself? Yes, Rine, she's a wicked woman, she's ... she's...."

"What is she, Tine?"

"She's ... she's a trollop, Rine!" Auntie Tine yelled, shrilly. "A common trollop! A trollop!"

"Christine!" cried Mrs. van Lowe. "Christine! Dorine!"

And she stood up and tottered, with outstretched arms, towards the two old sisters. But there was a loud scream and a laugh that cut into everybody like a knife: Constance had fainted in Paul's arms....

The boy, Addie, looked round with a haughty glance. He had heard everything, as had Van der Welcke, who stood listening apprehensively at the door of the boudoir. The son saw his father's deathly-pale face staring like a mask. He saw the horror of his grandmother and of all his uncles and aunts. He now saw his mother prostrate in a chair, her head hanging back, like a corpse. And his boyish lips, with their faint shading of down, curved into a scornful smile as he said:

"It's all about nothing!..."

THE END

Lightning Source UK Ltd.
Milton Keynes UK
UKOW03f2315120514

231562UK00001B/297/P